FAG HAG

ROBERT RODI

FAG HAG

To Tim—
Good luck with
Books— Hope you
enjoy it—
Robert Rodi

A DUTTON BOOK

DUTTON

Published by the Penguin Group
Penguin Books USA Inc., 375 Hudson Street, New York, New York 10014, U.S.A.
Penguin Books Ltd, 27 Wrights Lane, London W8 5TZ, England
Penguin Books Australia Ltd, Ringwood, Victoria, Australia
Penguin Books Canada Ltd, 10 Alcorn Avenue, Toronto, Ontario, Canada M4V 3B2
Penguin Books (N.Z.) Ltd, 182–190 Wairau Road, Auckland 10, New Zealand

Penguin Books Ltd, Registered Offices:
Harmondsworth, Middlesex, England

First published by Dutton, an imprint of New American Library,
a division of Penguin Books USA Inc.
Distributed in Canada by McClelland & Stewart Inc.

First Printing, February, 1992
10 9 8 7 6 5 4 3 2 1

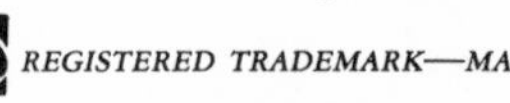

REGISTERED TRADEMARK—MARCA REGISTRADA

LIBRARY OF CONGRESS CATALOGING-IN-PUBLICATION DATA

Rodi, Robert.
Fag hag / Robert Rodi.
p. cm.
ISBN 0-525-93406-5
I. Title.
PS3568.034854F34 1992 *91-20293*
813'.54—dc20 *CIP*

Printed in the United States of America
Set in Garamond No. 3

DESIGNED BY STEVEN N. STATHAKIS

FOR JEFFREY,
OF COURSE

FAG HAG

PROLOGUE

Natalie Stathis moussed her hair until it stood straight up and resembled a henna-rinsed mushroom cloud. She applied more makeup than a vision-impaired Las Vegas showgirl, and put on the new smock-like Claude Montana frock that Peter said made her look like a hand puppet, forcing her to say "Fuck you" and hit him in the arm and pretend not to mind. Her wrists jangled with bracelets, all of them cheap and gaudy, although her ears were set with real diamonds—nine of them. And as she tagged along while Peter made his usual Saturday night rounds of Chicago's gay bars and discos, she beamed a smile that pleaded, "Notice me!" She pressed herself, all hundred and seventy-odd pounds, through crowds of taut, muscular young men and, through sheer flamboyance, attracted the attention of a few of them. And as she talked to them, using every ounce of feminine wile and wit at her disposal, they laughed in delight and flattered her and sometimes even kissed her, but never, never once, not even for a moment, did they stop looking over her shoulder for something better.

Now she sat with Peter—dear, loyal Peter—on the street

in front of one of the gay ghetto's many thrift shops, "airing herself out," as she liked to call it, shaking her hair, and flapping her clothes to get all the smoke out of them. She insisted on a five-minute airing after every night at the bars. And the reason she enjoyed it so much, kept insisting on it, was that Peter sat with her, and proved that he was hers. She would humor him; she would follow him to every gay watering hole in town and watch him search in vain for a man he could love, as long as they could sit on the street under the open sky, together, like a couple, for everyone to see. The pavement ran with spilled liquor and garbage, but Natalie felt like she was sitting on the throne of England.

She leaned back and shook her mushroom cloud. "Nice night," she said, luxuriating in the cool breeze.

"Mm-hmm," said Peter, staring at his shoes. He looked up at the moon, and as he craned his neck his Adam's apple was deliciously pronounced, the sexiest Adam's apple since Adam. His hair tumbled back over his shoulders—she had persuaded him not to cut it—and he sighed. He was Lord Byron, he was Saint Sebastian, he was Apollo—an object of worship, almost tubercular in the transcendent beauty of his suffering. Natalie was head-over-heels in love with him. Had she made him jealous tonight?

"That Brian guy's a doll," she said, watching him for a reaction. "You see me with him? Guy with the Rolex on?"

"Hmm? Oh. No." He ground some pebbles into the street with the heel of his Kenneth Coles.

"Invited me to his winter place in the Dominican Republic. Said I'd be a gas there, I could be his hostess. Think I should go?"

"If you want."

At times like this he nearly drove her mad. She sat up and wrapped her arms around her knees, something she was just barely able to do. "You're upset? I spend too much time talking to him?"

"No, no."

"What, then?" She reached out and curled a lock of his hair around her finger.

"I'm bored, I guess." He shook his head to get her fingers away from it, then looked her square in the eye. "I'm thirty years old, Natalie. I've been doing this bar thing since, Christ, twenty-two—one? Whatever. I'm bored with it. Every spring, first thaw, I'm out here looking, looking, looking, looking, then, bam!—it's winter and I hole up and feel sorry for myself again. I mean, is this any kind of life? Sitting here on a street with cocaine drying out my nose and liquor numbing my head and my ears all cottony from music that's too loud, and my head hurting from constantly wondering if *that's* the one or *that's* the one or—"

"*Jesus*," Natalie blurted, interrupting him; "of *course* it's any kind of life! Honey, I've *never* had as much fun as I've had with you. You're dazzling and sophisticated and brilliant, and—and—this is just your natural *environment*, that's all there is to it! The music and the lights and the—everything!"

He looked at her as though she had antlers growing out of her head. "Natalie, sometimes I think you don't know me at all."

"Sometimes I think you don't know yourself." She decided to try a different tactic; he was a hard case tonight. "Okay, say you *are* bored with it all. Maybe you *should* do something different for a while, then. Just to see. Take a few months off from all of this. You could read all the great books nobody ever gets a chance to read anymore. Like *Lolita* and *Moll Flanders* and *Remembrance of Things Past*." She was uncanny; she had memorized his bookshelf. "You could spend more time with your family. How old are your little niece and nephew now? You could get a pet. You could start a hobby—stamp collecting, or maybe something more active, like metalwork. You could be a sculptor. You could get into local history, travel around taking photographs of old tombstones or something. There are lots of things you could do. Just to see if it's more rewarding. If you're really feeling stifled, you kind of owe it to yourself." She sat back and sighed; a masterful performance, without a hint, even a trace, of sarcasm. And as she looked now at Peter's fogged eyes she could see the gears turning slowly behind them; she'd given him so much to think about that he couldn't possibly take it all in, not in his present state. He'd fall asleep with his mind a hazy jumble of hope, and wake up not remembering a thing. He was like a fine violin, and Natalie knew exactly which string to pluck to get the sound she desired from him.

"Vicki's seven," he said, slurring his words a little. "Alex is four." The niece and nephew.

"Do you have any recent pictures at home?" she asked.

He nodded and she smiled. They would go and see them later. Then it would be almost five in the morning; he would drop into bed for a dreamless sleep, and she would crawl in after him and hold him like she always did. And when he awakened a few hours later, he would turn and see her and say, "Natalie Stathis, you are a slut," and they would laugh as usual and then go out for breakfast at The Melrose to see who had hooked up with whom the night before, and Natalie would order French toast and a side of bacon in a state of perfect bliss because in the sunlight she and Peter could be seen together so much more clearly.

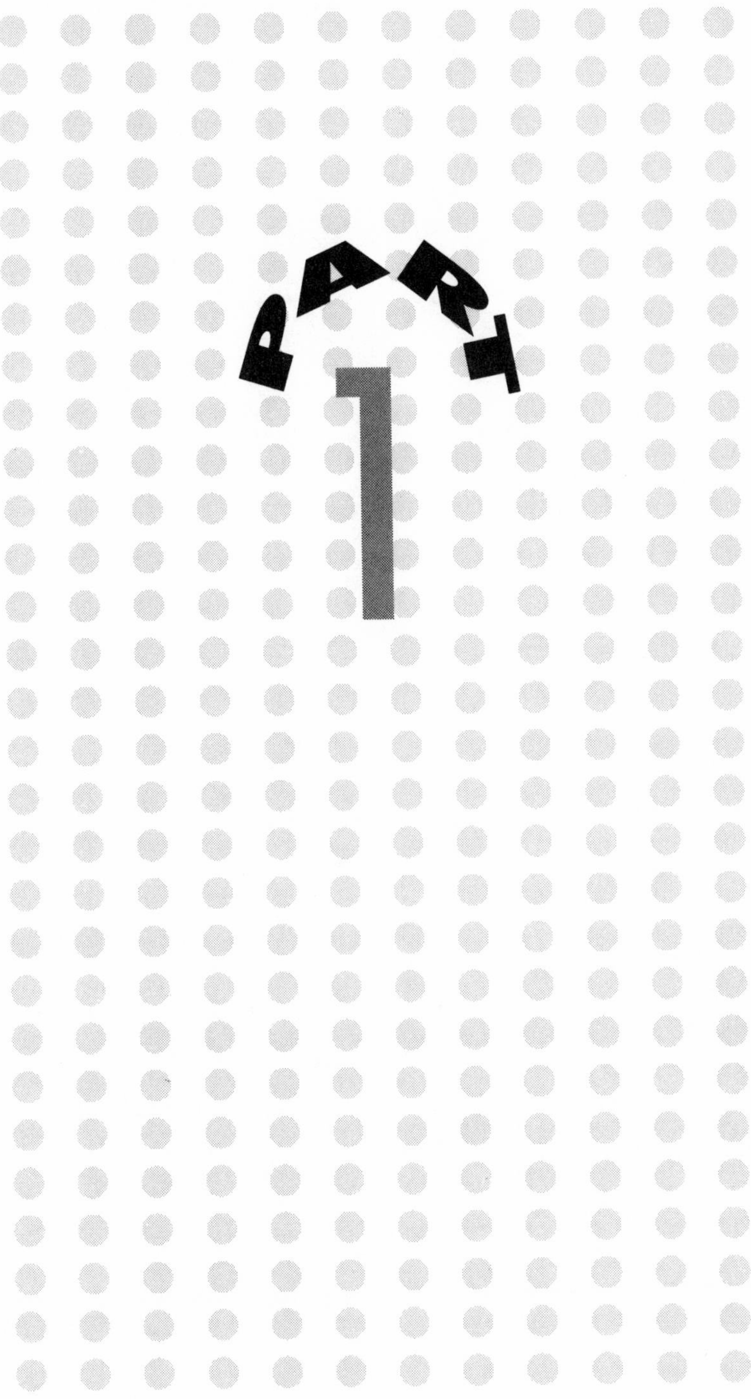

PART 1

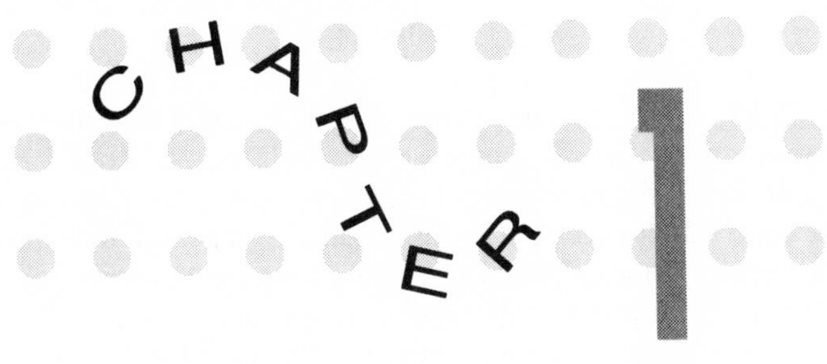

"Met someone *wonn*-derful," Peter sang into the phone, and at the other end Natalie made a grimace into the hallway mirror that might almost have cracked it.

"Great, honey," she said brilliantly, her face like death. "Where?"

"Hardware store this morning. We both wanted the last three-quarter-inch faucet aerator, and we got into a fight over it. By the time we were finished we were each insisting that the other one take it. He finally did, but I got his phone number instead, which, guess what, I'd rather have about a million times over."

Natalie steeled herself. It was about to begin anew: the siege of Cupid, the attack of Eros, the full-frontal assault of Romantic Love. She had fought this battle many times and won; when, she wondered in anguish, might she expect to win the war?

There was no time for self-pity. She had a strategy to implement. "Oh, honey, I'm so happy for you," she said. "Hope he's as wonderful as he sounds."

"What do you mean? Course he is!"

"Sorry, baby, I didn't mean to—well, you know how protective I am of you. And every time you meet someone I hope for you so much, I cross my fingers and just *pray*—but at the same time I dread seeing you hurt again, and maybe that makes me a little psychotic. Like, I can't help noticing that this guy got the faucet thing you wanted, and that it's up to *you* to call *him*, not vice versa—he's getting all the privileges so far. I know that doesn't mean anything, I'm just insane for worrying based on only that much information about him—"

"Yes, you are." He was irritated.

"Tell you what. I'm going to shut up now and you can tell me what a hunk he is." Peter started waxing eloquent about his new love, and Natalie took a letter opener from her coffee table, lowered herself onto her sofa, and held the portable phone to her ear while she repeatedly stabbed one of her throw pillows until it was disemboweled of its fiber-fill.

"His name is Maurice," Peter gushed. "Like the Forster book, isn't that a riot? He's got these incredible blue eyes and just shocks of blond hair. He was out jogging so he had on these shorts that left *nothing* to the imagination, my eyes were jumping out of their sockets. He's built like a fucking Greek sculpture or something. And he only lives about four blocks from me! And he takes the same bus every day, but I've never seen him on it—trust me, I'd remember. Our whole conversation was just a chain of coincidences. He works a couple of blocks from me, too—we can have lunch during the week!"

He went on and on in this manner, while Natalie listened with her teeth bared. Once the pillow was completely gutted, she sliced the pillow cover into threads, then flung the mess she'd made around the room, not caring. She rolled off the couch and onto the carpeting, kicked her heels madly, and arched her back; and yet all the time she writhed in jealousy, she still held the portable phone to her ear and occasionally interjected a "Terrific!" or a "Lovely!" to make Peter think she was euphoric for him.

After he finally hung up, she lay on the floor, utterly debilitated by frustration. She counted in her head the number of times she'd had similar phone calls from him. There'd been one for David, for Kyle, for Vince, Larry, Scott—too many to remember. And each time her reaction had gotten more quietly, frighteningly violent. She'd never thought she'd have to work this hard, never thought she'd have to ruin Peter's romances with so many men before winning him for herself. The faces of her victims all blended together now, their names, the details of their lives—in her delirium, she found she couldn't even remember the name of the new one. What was it? Something unusual beginning with M. Mortimer? Montgomery?

The phone rang again. She hit the "Talk" button and pulled it over to her ear. "Hello," she said emptily.

"Me again," said Peter. "Guess what? I was so excited I couldn't wait. I called him. Maurice, I mean." Maurice. That was it. "I asked him out for tonight. He said yes! Isn't that goddamn *great?* We're going to meet for drinks at Roscoe's. And from there, who knows . . . ?" His voice was merry with possibility.

"Honey, that's wonderful," Natalie enthused. "I'm so happy for y—" She turned off the phone in midsentence. It was a trick she'd learned, to get off undesirable calls without offending the caller. Who would ever dream that someone would hang up in the middle of one of her own sentences? Peter would simply assume he'd been disconnected. She hurriedly turned the phone back on and called the number for the correct time, then put it down and let the stilted voice at the other end continue to announce that at the tone it would be such-and-such and so-many-seconds. When Peter tried her number again, he'd get a busy signal.

Natalie hated Maurice without even having met him. She imagined that he was slim and superior and wore clothes with creases that could cut your fingers, which was how the men Peter fell for always looked. And what kind of fucking name was Maurice, anyway?

Peter couldn't wait for her to meet him, of course. Their first date went so well that Peter called her in the middle of it to tell her so, and to tell her that they'd already made plans to go to dinner the next night, at a French restaurant Natalie had been dying to go to for years. She winced at the mention of it. "Then we'll come to Roscoe's and meet you there, if you want," he said over the noise of the bar. She agreed, even though the idea of jackets and ties at Roscoe's seemed to her a disgusting affectation; she knew it must be the idea of that creature *Maurice*.

Saturday morning, she could find nothing to do but wonder "What are they doing now?," so she decided to bite the bullet and visit her mother. The messages Sandy Stathis had been leaving on her daughter's answering machine had been getting progressively more threatening, from "Please call" to "You'd better call soon" to "I'm changing my will" to "The dog gets everything, good-bye forever." It had been more than a month since Natalie had visited the ancestral homestead, so she hired a cab and took it to Oak Park; the driver was visibly gleeful at the idea of such a large fare.

Sandy Stathis lived in an old three-story colonial house that she couldn't keep up anymore because she'd spent almost all her money on causes. Her latest was Accessorizers Anonymous, which was for compulsive shoppers. "I can really relate to this one," she'd told Natalie over the phone a few weeks before. "You find a nice peach skirt and it only costs a hundred and fifty dollars so you think you can afford it, then all of a sudden you need a hundred-dollar belt to go with it, and a two-hundred-dollar scarf, and three-hundred-dollar shoes, and a four-hundred-dollar handbag, and then at the end of the month you spill marinara sauce on the skirt and it's ruined anyway. It's a compulsion; these women have got to learn to help themselves, the way I did!" The way Sandy Stathis had helped herself beat this habit was to spend all the money she needed to maintain it, which Natalie didn't think was the best approach. The only thing Sandy had left was the house, which was a significant asset; and the only thing that kept her from selling it was the idea that she would then have to move to Bellwood or Cicero or someplace equally inexpensive and horrible.

The driver turned down Sandy Stathis's street, which was exactly the kind of peaceful, tree-lined thoroughfare that had induced a desperately bored Hemingway to flee this very town decades earlier. Natalie forked over a stingy tip and bolted from the cab.

She let herself into the house with her key, and Carmen DeFleur, the family collie, raced up to greet her, a little wobbly in her old age. (Sandy always gave pets both a first and a last name; "They have their dignity, too," she insisted.) Natalie squatted to let the dog lick her face, which it did with an enthusiasm bordering on rapture.

"Who's there?" called Sandy from the corridor.

"Me, Mom," Natalie called back, lifting her head slightly so that the dog didn't accidentally French-kiss her.

Sandy Stathis appeared in a navy blue suit and bare feet, with an apron tied around her waist. She was drying her hands on a dish towel. Her hair was spectacularly coiffed.

"What gives, Mom?" said Natalie, astonished. "Never saw you in an apron before."

"I know, it's just humiliating. I actually had to go out and buy one. The dishwasher just refuses to work. I even tried kicking it." She threw the dish towel over her shoulder and kissed Natalie on the cheek. "Come on into the kitchen. I called a repairman, who was so rude on the phone that when he got here I wouldn't let him in. He was *very* angry. He must have told his office because now they won't send anyone else." They were in the kitchen now. "I keep thinking if I kick it hard enough"—here she gave the dishwasher a good, swift one with her naked foot—"it'll start up again. Filthy mechanical thing. How are you, dear? Where's that devastating young man of yours? Has he cut his hair yet?"

Natalie took a seat at the kitchen table and looked around her at the dizzying disarray; it was like a Williams-Sonoma store had exploded. The mess got worse with every visit. Sandy had married at seventeen, and gave birth to Natalie nine months later to the day, but even as a child Natalie had thought her mother an eccentric old lady. She was now in her midforties, still youthful; but the air of senile ineptitude about her had grown much more profound, especially since her second husband's death.

"Peter's busy," said Natalie. "This place is a pit, Mom."

"I haven't had time to clean," she apologized. She untied the apron and hung it up; the moment she turned her back, it slipped off the hook and fell to the floor. She joined Natalie at the table and continued. "Getting Accessorizers Anonymous off the ground has been an ordeal. We still don't have a meeting space; the church won't let us use their back room because they say the group is 'silly.' Father Litty's exact word for it. So you can see the kind of stigma we have to fight. It's an uphill battle. In the meantime, we've been meeting at each other's homes. I was the hostess last week. We had a hard case, then. We're supposed to be anonymous, but I'll tell you who if you'll keep it secret. Carolyn Bixby—do you remember her? Josie's mother. A sick woman! Do you know, she bought a cranberry cocktail dress that she liked so well, she actually bought a *car* to go with it? Nathan threatened to divorce her. I had to call him myself and assure him that she was getting help; he had the nerve to give us a deadline to cure her! How can people be so insensitive? Don't they know this is an illness? Am I boring you, dear? Why'd you just look at your watch? What on earth have you done to your hair? Is this why you haven't called?"

As usual, Sandy's steamroller stream of consciousness left Natalie totally unable to reply; she shook her head a little and said, "How's Carmen DeFleur?" The collie was under her chair now, panting happily at having Natalie home again.

"Fine. The vet says if she stays on the pills she'll be all right. But she keeps throwing them up. Honestly, I had no idea this dog was going to cost me a king's ransom in medical bills when I bought her. You kids both wanted one, though, so I fought Max tooth and nail and got one for you, and now you've moved away and I'm left alone with her, an overemotional dog with a thyroid problem who throws up on my Persian rugs twice a week. I'd get rid of her, but you and your brother would never speak to me again. It's so embarrassing. Greta Ledbetter came by last week and there was dog vomit in the dining room. I nearly swooned from mortification. Greta, of course, knows every household product manufactured since Jimmy Carter was president, so she spared me no detail on what to do, but finally she advised me to Scotchgard all the rugs. I said, 'Greta, this is a genuine, hundred-year-old Persian rug, not a fake from Marshall Field's. I am not going to laminate it like a driver's license.' She left in a snit and then two days later my auburn rinse was no longer a secret in town, and you can guess who was responsible for *that.* Now I can't decide if I should accept her invitation to her daughter Lisa's wedding—she's marrying some ill-mannered doctor from Jordan or Iraq or one of those horrible places where divorce is punishable by death. But I've already ordered a gift and I don't think I can return it. So you see all the trouble this dog has caused me."

Natalie put her hand to her cheek and stared at her mother in amazement. "You never change, Mom."

"Oh, for heaven's sake, what's that supposed to mean? You kids are so sarcastic. I can never tell if you're making fun of me or not. It's a sign of immaturity, I hope you know that. Sarcasm is the lowest of the arts, so naturally it's the first to be embraced by juveniles. I wish you'd outgrow it. I wish you'd—well, what *did* you do to your hair, anyway? And that outfit! Darling, you look like Pierrot! I wore something just like it one Halloween. Max went as Bluebeard. That should've told me something about Max, but I was naive. If I knew then what I know now! Could've spared myself a lot of Traceys and Staceys and Laceys over the years. Max did love his 'acey' girls. Honey, stop looking at your watch. If I'm boring you, just say so. It's a ridiculous color, anyway—who ever heard of a purple watch? Let me see the face. What on earth—are those monkeys?"

"They're just stylized people, Mom," said Natalie, feeling creepy with her mother's face practically pressed against her wrist. "They're by a famous artist, his name is Keith Haring."

"But they're just outlines," she said, astonished. "He got famous by doing just outlines?" She released Natalie's hand, and Natalie tucked it between her knees. "I suppose any generation that would call outlines of people art is the kind of generation that would put art on a watch face. You don't wear that to work, do you?"

"Not usually. I've got about twelve watches. I rotate them."

"Twelve watches!" Sandy crossed her arms. "I've had just two since I was a girl. We're very different, you and I. You're like your grandmother, flamboyant. I was always more commonsensical, more straightforward."

Natalie gave her a you've-got-to-be-kidding look.

She smiled and winked. "We have the same taste in men, though. Wouldn't have put up with all the 'acey' girls if Max hadn't been an Adonis. Where'd you say your young man was? Looks like a movie idol, that one."

Natalie shifted uncomfortably in her seat. "Mom, Peter and I aren't really together, you know. We're not a couple."

"Nonsense. You're inseparable."

"He's not in love with me, though."

She grimaced. "Well, you're in love with him, that's as plain as the nose on your face."

Natalie nodded. "So?"

She rubbed her forehead. "I'd give you a lecture on how demeaning it is to throw yourself at a man who's not in love with you, but it'd break my heart to do it. Do you mind if I don't?"

"Actually, I'd prefer it that way."

She leaned forward, yanked her daughter's hands from between her knees, and held them. "Listen. Carolyn Bixby has a son, Hank. He picked her up after the meeting last week and I saw him. Not an Adonis, but—well, kind of pleasant, in a solid sort of way. I asked her about him. He's twenty-seven, he's single, he's a real-estate agent, and he has his own two-story mock-Tudor house in Darien. He drives a Saab. I'll invite him to dinner, you can meet him. Say yes."

Natalie contemplated an eternity of middle-class paralysis with solid Hank Bixby and his big house and his Saab in a blighted suburb, no doubt with kids shitting and pissing on everything. She compared that to even a single night of lights and music and drugs and excitement with vital, beautiful, sexual Peter. "Forget it, Mom," she said. "I'll take my chances with the guy I've got."

Sandy sat back and sighed. "Very well." She raised an eyebrow. "Maybe he'd like you better, honey, if you just lost a little weight."

"*Mom*," snarled Natalie. It was a forbidden subject.

"Sorry, sorry, *mea culpa*," she wailed in mock abashment. She got up from the chair and headed into the dining room. "Will you help me move some furniture? The Landseer fell out of its frame, can you believe it, and it's stuck behind the couch. I tried getting it out with a coat hanger, but it's really jammed down there."

Natalie shook her head. Her mother wouldn't Scotchgard a hundred-year-old rug, but she'd go after a hundred-year-old painting with a wire prong. "Commonsensical and straightforward," was she? She'd have to tell her brother Calvin about that. He'd hoot.

After rescuing the Landseer from behind the couch, Natalie took Carmen DeFleur for a long walk around the block, and as the collie joyfully sniffed every tree and traffic sign and squatted about every three yards, Natalie's mind turned back to Peter. Had he and Maurice spent the day together? Were they even now walking down Halsted Street, looking in shop windows, and comparing notes on what they saw, laughing, making jokes, sharing their aspirations and hopes and reliving their pasts, forging bonds that would be, oh, so very hard to break? Or had they gone their separate ways this morning, each eager to call his friends and tell them about his wonderful new boyfriend? In which case, their bond would still be almost exclusively sexual. Their date last night—the dinner, the drinks afterward, all of it—could be counted as foreplay. They'd have been thinking ahead to the sex and not have their minds in the present. Now, however, that mystery was over, and everything depended on whether they'd spent the postcoital hours in each other's company, or apart. Natalie closed her eyes and prayed fervently for the latter.

Sandy begged her to stay for dinner, and, not for the first time, Natalie detected in her mother's tone an almost desperate longing. Although she felt for her, she refused; an entire meal's worth of her mother's inane prattle would drive her right out of her mind. She hugged her good-bye and walked to the train station, intent on a nice, leisurely ride back to the city. The numbing motion and noise of the train always pacified her, helped her to think without hysteria.

When she finally got home, it was nearly dark, and her little studio apartment was cloaked in shades of gray. In the far corner she could see the red light of her answering machine flashing, flashing. She rewound its tape, pressed PLAY, and went to the refrigerator for a Diet Coke as she listened.

Beep. "Natalie, it's Peter." (Rustling sounds, like sheets.) "Maurice just left, it's—Christ, it's ten-thirty in the morning. Last night was *incredible*. I can't wait to tell you all about it. Why aren't you home? Call me." Beep. "Hi, it's me again. What, did you go somewhere for the day without telling me? Not fair. I'm home alone and bursting with news. Call me! This is an order." Beep. "Me again. Uh-oh, it's starting. It's three, I was missing Maurice so I called his number, and no one's home. So I started getting crazy, thinking, he's out and I'm in, what does that mean? Why isn't he home worrying about what to wear tonight like I am? And why aren't *you* home? I need you to be there! Goddamn you, you harlot! *Call* me!" Beep. "Guess who? I hate the world. I took a nap and now it's five and I have crease marks in my face that no *way* are gonna come out by the time

Maurice comes by to pick me up. Hope he enjoys dating a disfigured man. I shall never forgive you for being away today. Good-bye. Have a nice life." Beep. "Me again. Seriously, remember to meet us at Roscoe's around eleven. 'Bye." A lengthy hiss followed. That had been his last message.

Natalie let her head fall back against a wall. Thank God, thank God, they hadn't spent the day together. Tonight would be an easy battle to win. Go ahead, Maurice, she thought; go to a French restaurant, enjoy Peter's company, even think about a future with him, if you like. Your hours of pleasure will be few enough. You are in my rifle sight, and I aim to kill.

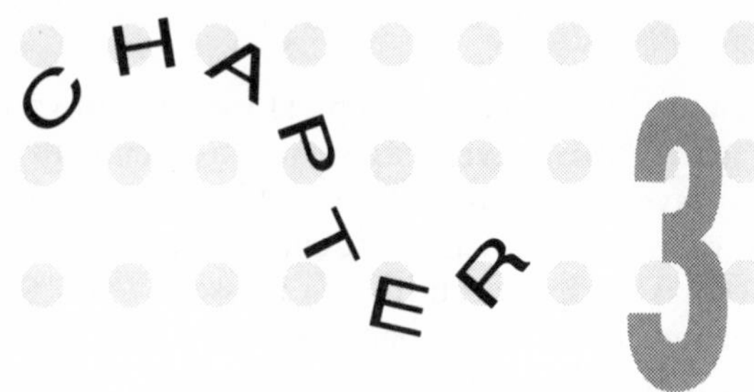

Maurice was everything she'd hoped he'd be: haughty, pretty, vacant—a typical Halsted Street cipher. She'd been waiting at Roscoe's for more than an hour, hiding her anger at Peter for being late by flirting with some of the beautiful boys in the bar, when all of a sudden he swept in, wearing his stunning Armani suit, with what could only be Maurice in tow; she was so glad to see Maurice's I'm-shallow-as-a-birdbath smirk that she instantly forgave Peter everything.

They were giddy; they'd had champagne. Peter giggled as he introduced her to Maurice, whose handshake was limp; Natalie smiled in triumph at the jellyfish grip and Peter beamed, thinking she was smiling because she liked Maurice.

"*Well*," said Maurice, with just the right degree of feminine lilt to his voice, "I've heard quite a lot about *you*, Natalie."

"I'm sure you have," she said in her most theatrical manner, "and I hate to disillusion you, but I'm not really a goddess. Appearances to the contrary." She lay her hand on his shoulder. "You, however, are one divine piece of work, Maurice."

He blushed crimson and tittered. "Oh—thank you."

She smiled. The first offensive was now successfully completed. Natalie, brilliant strategist that she was, knew that the quickest way to disarm a man was to tell him at once everything he was dying to hear. Now she'd feed him even more, and then, when he was thoroughly enjoying being flattered so outrageously, she'd suddenly stop. As a result, he'd hang on her every word, her every gesture, and try in an undoubtedly pathetic fashion to try to get her back on the subject of himself. In short, he'd be thoroughly co-opted; if he spoke five words to Peter the entire night, she'd be surprised.

"Yes," she said with a throaty purr, "*quelle* hunk!" She ran her fingers through his long, wavy hair; as she'd guessed, it was sprayed stiff. "I especially adore these lovely locks; so radiant! But so are your eyes. I can see why Peter's so bedazzled by you. And I can only imagine what's underneath that impeccably tailored suitcoat."

"Just a shirt," he said, his face nearly blood-colored now.

She elbowed him. "Oh, I think you know what I mean." She turned to Peter. "And he's a joker, too! What a prize, honey! He must be *gobs* of entertainment."

"Oh, I might have to agree with you there," said Peter suggestively. He turned and his eyes met Maurice's.

"Such a gallant, Old World sort of name, too," said Natalie, suddenly serious and reverent. "Are you really French, Maurice?"

"Oh, no," he said, still smiling stupidly, shaking his head. "Jewish, actually. My name's spelled M-O-R-R-I-S. I just like people to pronounce it with the accent on the last syllable. My way of being different, I guess."

Natalie noticed the surprise on Peter's face; he hadn't known this, then. "Why, how darling!" she said with a clap of her hands. But she was thinking, Maurice, you don't even need me—*you* could hang *yourself* if I gave you enough rope.

Now she turned herself off like a faucet, and her gush of compliments ceased. As if serenely unaware of any change in her behavior, she stared at the overhead TV monitor, on which was playing a music video of Guesch Patti singing "Étienne." Natalie studied it as though it were the most important piece of film the world had ever produced.

Peter turned to make romantic eye contact with Morris, but

found that Morris had his eyes glued firmly to Natalie; he was staring a hole right through her and had a perplexed look on his face. Every now and then he'd check the videoscreen, as if wondering what on earth could be so important up there.

Finally, Peter spoke up. "Yoshi's was wonderful, Natalie," he said. "Best restaurant I've ever been to. Food as good as sex."

"That's funny," she said, looking only at Peter, "I always think of it the other way around—that sex can sometimes be as good as food." They all laughed at this, Morris much harder than the others, and Natalie allowed her eyes to meet his eyes briefly and unmeaningfully before returning them to Guesch Patti.

It was well past midnight now, and the bar was getting crowded. Men were pushing their way into the throng of bodies, and Natalie allowed herself to get shoved between Peter and Morris, where she wedged herself tight. She held her Bacardi-on-the-rocks in front of her as if it were nitroglycerin.

"Haven't been here in ages," said Morris. "Been working too many weekends lately."

And what do you do, Morris? thought Natalie scornfully as she stared up at the monitor. Sorry, buster, I'm not going to ask it.

"Morris works at Amlings," Peter offered helpfully.

She smiled as if something delightful had occurred to her. She turned to Morris, then to Peter, and said, "Morris the florist!" She tittered. "Isn't that adorable?"

Morris went pale, and after an awkward silence Peter said, "Well, Natalie, it's only adorable if you pronounce his name incorrectly."

She gasped, then turned to Morris and clasped his arm again. "Oh, I'm so sorry, I forgot," she said. "Forgive me?"

"Of course," he said rather humbly.

Now he looks silly, she thought, with his ridiculous affectation about his name becoming an issue in the conversation. She decided to really lay it on: "Are you *sure* you forgive me? I want you to like me so much, honey—Peter's my oldest and dearest friend, I'd do anything for him!" That's it, make him feel like an outsider. She felt her powers of manipulation surge within her; this was a masterful performance.

Morris was completely flustered. He looked at Natalie's

half-empty glass. "Refill that for you?" he asked, and his voice actually cracked.

"No, thank you, darling."

He looked over her head at Peter. "Drink, babe?"

Babe! thought Natalie. Her stomach lurched.

"Light beer, thanks," said Peter.

Morris nodded and squeezed his way over to the bar.

Natalie immediately turned and grabbed Peter's arm. "I like him *sooo* much," she trilled. "I mean, first, he's drop-dead gorgeous, and he dresses to kill, and I cannot *wait* to hear how he fucks, but you can tell me that later. What I want to know now is, what is it about him that made you change your mind?"

"Change my mind? What do you mean?" His brow furrowed attractively.

"About dating a Jewish guy! You said never again, not after that guy Todd got all Hasidic on you, remember? You took him home for Christmas and he freaked out that your parents had a tree and a manger scene?"

"Oh, yeah," he said, laughing a little. "Well, I guess I shouldn't judge all Jewish guys by Todd. But as far as Morris goes, I didn't even know he *was* Jewish."

She looked at him as though he'd just admitted to some grave moral lapse. "No, really," she said.

"I'm not kidding. I found out when you did."

"I thought you were practically in love with this guy."

"Well, I am." He paused. "Practically."

"How can you be in love with someone when you don't even know something as profoundly basic as h—" She waved her hands and cut herself off. "No, no. I'm staying out of it. I suppose you have to go about this your own way, not mine. I just wish you oceans of happiness, and he does seem like an angel." She took a sip from her Bacardi, and when she looked over at him again his brow was still furrowed. She congratulated herself. Mission accomplished.

By the time the three of them left the bar, the dizzy drunkenness that Peter and Morris had brought from the restaurant had dulled into a kind of sullen soddenness. Morris wasn't keen on the airing-out ritual, but he and Peter insisted on Natalie sharing their cab, and after a chorus of no-I-only-live-four-blocks-away, she gave in. And by the way the ride passed in silence she knew that the reason they'd wanted to see her home was that they were no longer so eager to be alone with each other.

She sat back, satisfied, and planned the next move in the campaign.

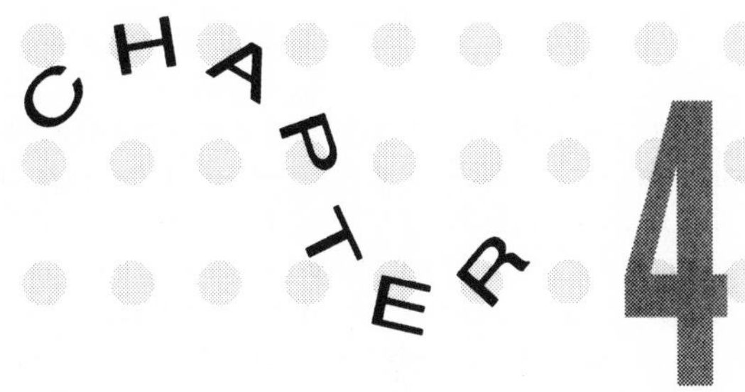

In the morning she suffered a setback.

It started with a call from her mother. "Well, thank God, Calvin's finally set a date," she said. Natalie was still in bed, and the sound of her mother's voice jarred her out of her pleasant Sunday-morning drowsiness.

"Mom, it's got to be seven-thirty," she said, knocking things off the night table in search of her alarm clock.

"Sorry, honey, I thought you'd want to know. He and Vera decided last night; it's going to be in two months. Saturday the twenty-third. At St. Edmond's here in town. I said, Why such short notice? Well, it turns out Calvin didn't have any trouble proposing, but when it came to actually setting a date he kept dragging his heels. I mean, he gave Vera that ring six months ago! So last night Vera made him promise, the first available date the church had, that would be it, and poor Calvin almost had a stroke because it turned out there'd been a cancellation for September! A couple was set to get married that day but the groom died of a brain hemorrhage, a strapping young thirty-year-old! Makes you wonder, doesn't it? We could go at any time. They say the good die young, but every time I hear that I think of your father. He died young, and if *he* can be called good then the rest of us have nothing to worry about."

She was starting on one of her endless digressions; Natalie jumped in to bring her back to the matter at hand. "Mom, this is ridiculous. I'm supposed to be a bridesmaid for Vera. Is she going to have dresses picked in time for a wedding in two months?" Secretly she was wondering, Can I lose any *weight* in two months?

"Honey, Vera is so ready for this wedding she could be walking down that aisle at an hour's notice. She's been straining at the leash for six months, remember, while your brother's played with his fingers. She's been up all night addressing invitations, whipping them out like a fiend. Calvin just sits in the background looking pallid. I wanted to call and tell you early, though, so you can get a date. You're not thinking of bringing Peter, are you?"

"Why not?"

"Oh, never mind. I really don't want to lecture you, dear. Bring him if you want. I have to go now, I have to call Vera's mother to see what color dress she's going to wear. I'm afraid I'm going to insist on peach for myself. Harriet always looked good in powder blue. Plus, she has all the accessories and doesn't have to buy any new ones that way, which is something one should always consider. I'll try talking her into that."

"You do that, Mom."

"Good-bye, dear." She hung up.

Immediately Natalie dialed Peter's number. It rang about twelve times before he answered dazedly. "Hello?"

"It's me, doll. Guess what? My brother's finally set a wedding date, end of September. Remember you promised to be my escort?"

He paused. "I did?"

She couldn't believe he was even questioning her on this. "Of course you did. You're not backing out, are you?"

"It's just that I don't remember it, that's all."

"I told you six months ago that my brother was getting married and said it'd be a blast if you went as my date, and you said that was a great idea."

"I said it was a great *idea*, Natalie. I didn't exactly *accept*."

The entire planet seemed suddenly very still. "What?" she said, her voice like ice.

"Six months ago, for Christ's sake! It was a good idea at the time, but times have changed. My weekends are—uh—kind of precious to me now."

"What do you mean? You're a free-lance artist. You don't work regular hours."

"I know, but—well, other people do."

She heard a giggle—the unmistakable, repulsive giggle of Morris.

"I really can't talk right now," he continued. "I'm not alone." He turned away from the phone and said, *sotto voce*, "Will you cut that out?"

She shook her head, wounded beyond belief. "Fuck you," she snarled, and she turned off the phone. It was an unsatisfactory gesture. That was the problem with portable phones; you couldn't slam them.

Almost instantly she regretted having cursed at him. It would drive him into the arms of Morris. That had been a tactical error. She mustn't let emotion taint her strategy now; she might lose everything. What could she do to make up for it? She rolled over and considered the problem rationally for a moment, then settled on a solution. She sat up, fluffed her pillows, pulled a notebook and pen from her nightstand, and composed the following note of apology:

Darling Peter,

I'm so sorry for having lost my temper this morning. Bad, selfish Natalie! You know how much I love you and the thought of that dreary wedding without you just fills me with trepidation and dread; it won't be any fun at all without you there to wink at and poke in the ribs and dish everyone with. But family occasions are meant to be a bore and a drudge, so I shall stiffen my spine and bear my lot with grace. Of course *your weekends are precious to you now, sweetheart, and no one in the world knows better than I how much you deserve them after the many disappointments life has handed you. Yet instead of paving your way to happiness, I've thrown up barbed wire in your path; you*

> *must feel utterly betrayed. Rest assured, I have now come to my senses. I beg your forgiveness. Why don't you and Morris come to dinner on Wednesday? Just some pizza and lots of wine. It's a school night, so it won't interfere with your delicious weekend debauches. I will entertain and enchant you both and prove to you my worth as a loyal friend and ally. I do so want to get to know and love gorgeous Morris as much as you do. Does he have a brother for me?*
>
> XOXO
> *Natalie*

She read it over and was satisfied. She decided to copy it onto her best stationery, and personally drop it in Peter's mailbox.

Convinced that she had salvaged her relationship with the man she loved, she lay back on her pillow and tried to think of a way to get rid of the man *he* loved by September. That wasn't far off—but, she thought, far enough. Now that she had a deadline looming before her, she might even rise to the occasion and have Morris banished from Peter's life by mid-August. If she used all her tried-and-true stratagems, she couldn't possibly fail.

And, she thought, what better place to begin than over pizza Wednesday night?

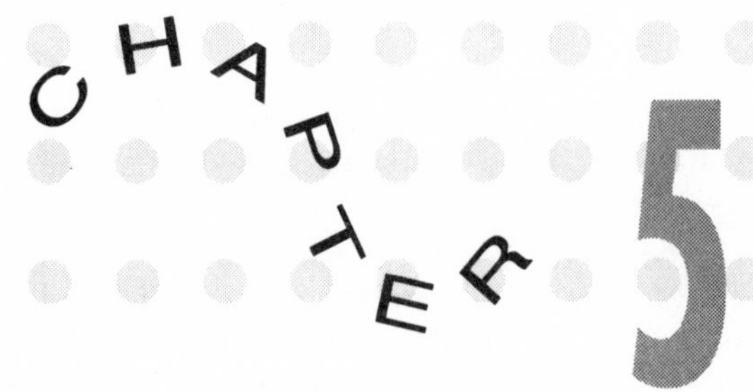

Peter accepted both her apology and her invitation, as she had known he would. Emboldened by her success, she set about her plan to divide and conquer.

On Wednesday morning, the temporary agency she worked for sent her to an office that needed a receptionist. Once the first flurry of morning calls had passed, she telephoned the floral shop where Morris was employed.

A young woman answered. "Amlings, Illinois Center."

"Good morning," said Natalie. "I'd like to order a bouquet from Morris Gross, please."

"Morris is busy with a customer at the moment. Can I have someone else help you?"

"Certainly not. I will wait for Morris Gross."

The woman sighed. "Okay." The sudden sound of music told Natalie that she'd been shifted to the limbo of the hold button. A full orchestra was playing an unspeakably syrupy version of 10,000 Maniacs' "Like the Weather." Will I ever be able to listen to that record again? she wondered as she shuddered in revulsion.

She was jolted to attention by Morris's voice. "Morris Gross speaking." He really did pronounce it Mor-REES. She rolled her eyes in irritation.

"Morris, hello, it's Natalie Stathis."

"Oh, hi, Natalie." She detected a touch of perplexity.

"I'm sure Peter has told you that you're dining *chez moi* tonight," she said, sounding as pleasantly authoritative as possible.

"That's right."

"And I thought, since I won't get home in time to serve anything fancier than pizza, wouldn't it be nice to have some special touch to mark the occasion, like flowers? And then I thought, if I'm to buy flowers, it must be from you!"

"Well—thanks. That's very sweet of you."

"So let's put together a big bouquet. Everything you like, all your favorites. Give yourself a nice, fat commission. Money is no object, now that my dearest friend has found his partner for life."

A long pause; that had taken him aback, as it was meant to. "Okay—sure," he said, his voice a little smaller now. "I won't spend too much, though. Don't want to break you." He laughed nervously.

"I'll stop by after five and pick it up. Thanks so much, Morris." Mor-REES; she'd said it perfectly, just like he did. "See you then. Oh, do you take American Express?"

"Yes—uh, actually, Natalie, now that I think about it, I feel I should bring something myself. You're going to all the trouble of feeding us; why don't I let the flowers be my treat?"

She was genuinely surprised; she might actually like Morris after all. Too bad he was doomed to become her newest victim. "What a sweet thought, Morris; no wonder Peter's crazy about you. I tell you what, do a *spectacular* arrangement and we'll split the cost. We'll knock Peter's eyes out. He'll be so pleased that we collaborated behind his back to pull it off; he wants us to be friends."

"So do I."

"I feel we are, already."

He paused. "Well—wonderful." Apparently he wasn't ready to say the same. "I'll see you after five, then."

" 'Bye, Morris." Mor-REES.

" 'Bye, Natalie."

She hung up and turned her attention to the three calls that had come in while she'd been busy with Morris. I'm not just a strategical genius, she thought; I'm a genius under fire!

After work, she hopped a cab and dashed across the Loop, then wove her way through the rabbit warren of shops and restaurants that connected the various buildings of Illinois Center until she found Amlings. Morris was waiting for her, with a pillar of green paper standing next to him.

"Oh, I don't get to see it first!" she said with a pout.

"Sorry, I had to wrap it during the slow part of the afternoon; business starts picking up now, and I don't get off till six." He was smiling; they were coconspirators—they'd forged a bond.

"What's it like?" she asked, lifting it in her pudgy arms.

"Tropical," he said, helping her; "lots of birds of paradise."

"Ooh," she said. "Thrilling!"

"Got to get back to work. You can pay me your half later. See you tonight."

"Okay, Morris." Mor-REES. "Thanks, doll. I'll call and let you know what time."

Success so uplifted her spirits that she decided to cab it all the way home. The thought of the pillar of flora on the 151 bus was too daunting, anyway.

She lived at Broadway and Aldine, in the heart of the city's gay ghetto. A fair number of its residents knew her by name, so that when she got out of the cab it was only natural that she ran into someone she knew.

"Nata-LEE," cried Curtis Driscoll from across the street. "Wha'choo be takin' into yo' house, main?" Curtis was black, but he only affected a jive dialect on the streets, as a kind of joke. In private conversations he always sounded like a statesman. He worked as a waiter at a downtown restaurant, and was just heading for the bus when Natalie passed him.

"Beautiful flowers, Curtis," she called back as she fumbled for her key. "Birds of paradise."

"Get outta town!" he yelled. "Got yussef a hot lay, Nata-LEE? You kin tell Curtis."

"Curtis can go fuck himself," she sang sweetly as she swung open the door and entered the vestibule.

Curtis laughed like a hyena, then saw his bus pull up at the corner and dashed away without a good-bye.

She climbed the stairs blindly, stumbling now and then, the paper rustling in her face. Thank God Peter's never been attracted to black guys, she thought; only way I'd ever get rid of Curtis would be to push him down a manhole.

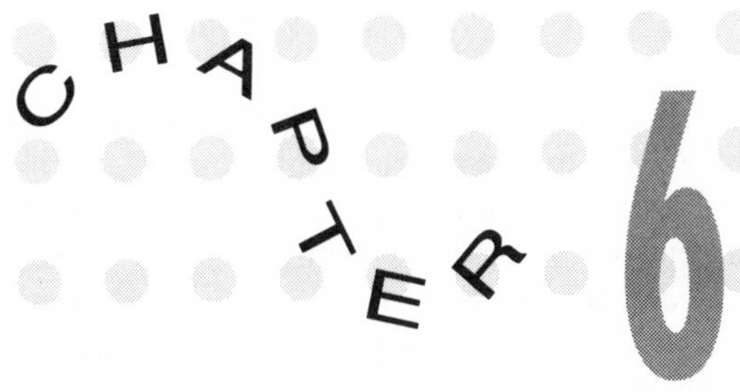

CHAPTER 6

As Natalie was fond of pointing out, "Only God and myself are perfect," so it followed that Peter must have at least one human failing, and his failing was lateness. It was, of course, an uncalculated lateness—he had no conscience of fashion, no desire to make a grand entrance. It was merely his inescapable fate to be persistently ten minutes behind the clock. But as this was his only failing, he was always gentleman enough to offer an apology on arrival.

So Natalie felt quite safe in calling Morris's number and telling his answering machine, "Morris, dear, it's Natalie; be at my place at seven-thirty for a delicious Pinot Grigio *avant de* pizza," and then calling Peter and leaving the message, "Honey, it's me; have your gorgeous ass here by eight." That would give her close to forty minutes alone with Morris, to fill his head with whatever she wished; and then would arrive trustworthy Peter, apologizing for being late. Morris would, of course, think that Peter was apologizing for being forty minutes late instead of ten, and they were unlikely to compare notes later and discover the discrepancy in their invitations. And if by some odd chance they did, she'd blush and say she merely wanted to be alone with Morris to get to know him better, as this was impossible with Peter around drawing all his attention.

Morris ended up being late himself, which irked her; he arrived at seven-fifty, his face red. "Sorry," he gasped as she let him in; "I barely had time to get home from work, wash my face, and rush over here." He was still wearing his work clothes.

She kissed him on the cheek and cooed over his exhaustion, then led him into the apartment.

"Peter here yet?" he asked.

"No," she said innocently. "I'm afraid we're all running a little late. Help me set the table?"

"Sure," he said, following her into the apartment's tiny kitchen. He looked around. "Nice place."

"Thank you," she said in her most gracious manner. She climbed atop a footstool and opened a cabinet. "I'm sure you like Peter's better, though." She winked at him.

He blushed. "Oh, well."

"Do you think it's big enough? I told him not to worry, but you know Peter." She handed him three blue Fiestaware plates and climbed down.

"Seems the right size for him," he said cautiously.

"No, I mean, for the two of you." She kicked the footstool back under the sink, then looked up and saw that he was astonished.

"Oh, how stupid of me," she said, waving a hand in dismissal; "forget I said that. Here." She opened the silverware drawer and started foraging through it, handing him knives and forks as she found them.

She'd deliberately delayed laying place settings because she wanted the things she was going to say to him to have a kind of casual, chitchat air about them, as though she weren't saying anything she thought remarkable. If they'd been sitting down, however, eye to eye, everything she was now saying would've had a certain weight to it; he might guess at her motives. But as she took dishes from the shelf and grabbed cutlery from a drawer, it seemed almost as if she were discussing the weather when she brought up the subject of Peter and Morris living together.

He helped her lay the places in silence, while she chattered on about how wonderful the flowers looked in the middle of the table. She noticed that the clock had now inched past eight. Time for Morris's second injection.

They went back to the kitchen and she took the bottle of Pinot Grigio from the refrigerator. "Would you be a dear and uncork it?" she said. "I'll get the glasses."

He reached for the bottle and she grabbed his wrist. "Morris," she said in a low voice; "I *hope* you've forgotten what I said earlier. If you haven't, at least promise me, *please*, that you won't tell Peter I've said anything. He'd be so angry. I just forget myself sometimes; I'm a very dizzy girl."

Her face was so close to his, he would have agreed to anything just to get her a respectable distance away. "Course I won't tell him," he said. "It's just—living together—I mean, that's nothing we've come close to discussing ourselves, that's all. It's very early."

She shook her head. "I don't dare say anything more. Don't tempt me." And she went to another cabinet, babbling about how Pier One Imports is such a good place to get inexpensive wineglasses, and who'd ever have guessed that?

For ten minutes more she prattled on about her favorite low-end stores and Morris responded with an occasional attempt at enthusiastic agreement, but she could tell that his mind was now a million miles away.

Then the doorbell rang, and it was Peter. She buzzed him in, and he loped up the stairs three at a time. He breezed into the apartment, kissed her, and said, "Sorry I'm late."

"Not at all," she said with fulsome forgiveness. "Morris and I have been getting to be great friends."

"Wonderful," he said. He went over to sweep Morris into a flamboyant lover's embrace, but Morris went stiff and it ended up being a peck on the lips. Peter, a little mystified, said, "You okay? Your day go all right?"

"Fine," said Morris, and Natalie, who was on the phone with her back turned, knew she'd scored a direct hit. The tone of that "fine" spoke volumes.

She ordered the pizza, then hung up and joined them. She could relax and enjoy herself now; her work was done. She'd dropped a pebble into still water, and tonight she could sit and watch it ripple outward, disfiguring Morris's reflection.

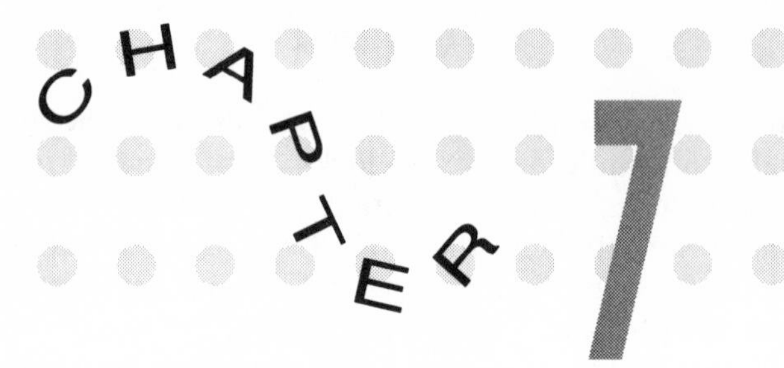

Chapter 7

By mid-August, the romance of Peter and Morris, which had begun in July with such fireworks, had diminished in intensity to the level of a household flashlight. Peter called Natalie almost daily with tales of Morris's peculiarities. "He freaks out every time we even get close to some kind of commitment," he complained one afternoon. "Last night he made dinner, and I told him I loved his chicken tarragon, and by the time I got the word 'love' out I could see he'd stiffened up and gone white. Like he was expecting me to end the sentence another way. What's he so afraid of? He never even talks to me anymore. In the beginning, it seemed like we'd never run out of things to say to each other."

Natalie clicked her tongue in sympathy and said, "Honey, maybe you should relax a little and let him make the first move." Or on another occasion she might advise him, "Honey, you've got to press the issue; he's obviously afraid of making a commitment, but that doesn't mean he doesn't *want* to, deep down." And Peter would take her advice, so that Morris would end up calling her, too, to say, "Natalie, what on earth is going on with Peter? One week he's ready to marry me and move in, the next he's at the other end of the couch with his arms folded. It's all up and down with him, like a roller coaster." And Natalie always said, "Peter is an artist, you have to respect the depths of his feeling for you, and the strange ways his love manifests itself," and Morris would say, "Oh," as if that were exactly what he didn't want to hear.

In spite of this, they were still inseparable, but Natalie thought that was due mainly to momentum; she had only to bring it to a halt. She found plenty of opportunities to do so, for more often than not she found herself invited to tag along with them on their outings together. And whenever the three of them were together, Peter spent more time talking to her than to Morris.

Typically, they'd go out to dinner and get roaring drunk, and Natalie would hold court. After dinner they'd somehow find their way to a bar, where the music was loud and the drinks flowed freely. There they'd hole up in a corner and Natalie and Peter would dish everyone in sight while Morris listened quietly.

Then, after they'd closed nearly every bar on the Halsted strip, Peter and Morris would depart for Morris's apartment (Morris having gotten so strangely averse to Peter's for some reason), and Natalie would lurch the few blocks to her own place, tanked.

But never so tanked as to miss any hint of an opportunity; all that she needed now was the killing blow, the one that would drive Peter and Morris apart forever.

Tonight, she believed she'd found it.

A few hours earlier, they'd dined at a Greek restaurant, where she almost got the three of them kicked out. After way too much Rhoditis, she'd picked up a forkful of her lamb-and-artichoke entrée and started to complain that it looked like "a fetal pig," at which Peter and Morris had almost hurt themselves laughing. Peter actually slid out of his chair!

Now they were at Berlin, a very loud bar with several video monitors, a dance floor, and lots of very young, Arrow-shirt-handsome men. Natalie and Peter were cutting up, true to form, picking especially on the barflies who had obviously put too much thought into their ensembles and now stood still as emperors of China, unable to move due to the weight of their sartorial majesty.

After an hour or so, Natalie noticed that Morris had been darting his eyes in a certain direction for the better part of the night. On the pretext of scratching an itch on her leg, she leaned forward and, following the path of Morris's gaze, saw a handsome blond against the far wall holding a bottle of beer and wearing a smoldering look. Then—oh, joy!—she saw him glance in Morris's direction.

They even looked alike. How could two such narcissists resist each other? Natalie resumed her running commentary with Peter, but in her head the gears were turning. When she and Peter left the bar tonight, they would have no Morris with them. She would see to that.

"Excuse me, honey," she said a few minutes later, and she heard herself slurring her words. Got to watch that, she admonished herself. Need to be alert now. She pushed herself away from the corner. "Gotta visit the ol' sandbox."

"Actually, so do I," said Peter. "Morris, keep our wall warm." He giggled at the joke.

She pretended to be a little wobbly on her feet, so that she listed several steps to the left on her journey to the john. This took her directly into the path of the man Morris had been eyeing. Peter disappeared into the men's room, so it was safe to act. She grabbed the strange man's hand and said, "Oh, stop with the wallflower act. Come on and shake it with me, handsome!" And she started to pull him into the crowd of dancers. He resisted like a mule.

Hers was the superior bulk, however, and soon they were on the dance floor. She turned and started to wriggle in time to the music; then, observing the naked anxiety on her partner's face, she stopped, peered at him, and said, "Oh, my God!" She put her hands over her face. "You're not Morris! I'm so fucking embarrassed!"

"S'okay," he said, and he started to edge away.

"You look exactly like a friend of mine," she said insistently. "I can't believe this! I must be totally trashed."

He smiled. "Never mind."

"No, you gotta see him now, so you know I'm not losing

my mind." She grabbed his shoulder and swung him in Morris's direction. "There he is," she said. "Guy in the khaki Girbaud pants—my friend, Mor-REES." She waved, and Morris blushed crimson. He waved back weakly, trying not to meet Natalie's companion's eyes.

"See the resemblance?" she asked. "Could be your double."

"Sort of."

"*Sort* of! Oh, come *on!* Well—I guess in a way, all gorgeous guys resemble each other—"

"Not at all," he protested at once, and she knew he meant, I'm not gorgeous at all (as if he could ever convince her he believed that).

"—but this is uncanny," she continued, not missing a beat. "You look alike, you smile alike, you even talk alike." She paused, then launched into the *Patty Duke Show* theme song: "You could lose your miiind," she trilled, and then she cracked up.

She grabbed his arm again and dragged him over to Morris. "You need a closer look, that's all." Morris noted her coming with a look of utter astonishment.

Soon she had the two men face to face. At this proximity she could see that she'd rather overstated their resemblance to one another, but never mind, it had served her purpose.

"This is my friend Morris," she said to her new acquaintance. "You might recognize him from your mirror. Morris, this lovely hunk of man I thought was *you.*" She turned to him. "Sorry, I don't even know your name."

"Nick," he said.

"Morris, this is Nick."

The two shook hands, and held each other's gaze for a telling moment. Natalie saw Peter returning from the men's room, and she called him over: "Honey, come and look, I've found Morris's evil twin!"

Peter approached them and was introduced, and then there was an awkward moment of silence. Natalie grinned like a circus clown.

Finally Peter said, "Well, there's some resemblance, Natalie, but not quite as much as you think. You'd agree if you were sober."

Ah, so he was irritated with her. That provided an opportunity. But she had to play this exactly right. She turned away and started to cry.

"Sorry," she said; "I didn't mean to embarrass everyone. Okay, they *don't* look that much alike. I'm a major moron. So sue me. So stick a fucking knife in my chest and put me out of my fucking misery." She darted away.

"Oh, for Christ's sake," said Peter in disgust. He turned to Morris. "Look, I have to go after her. Pain in the ass. Excuse me, okay?"

"I understand," said Morris.

She had staggered over to the public telephone and was leaning into its metal cradle now, sobbing very authentically. Two men stood a few feet away, necking obliviously.

Peter found her and put his hand on her back. "Come on, Natalie. I'm sorry."

"Fuck you," she bawled.

"No, really, I shouldn't have made you look bad in front of Morris and that other guy. I'm really serious. That was rude. You're just tough to handle when you get all weird like that. But that's no excuse, I know. I'm sorry. Really."

She turned and flung herself into his arms, and clutched him, sobbing, drenching a patch of his shirt in crocodile tears. She ran her fingers through his hair. "I love you so much," she wailed, and that, at least, she meant.

"I know, honey, I love you, too."

"I—I—I feel so bad sometimes," she gasped through her tears, "I feel like such an outsider sometimes, with you and Morris, like I don't fit in." And that was true, too. She was drunker than she'd thought. Genuine feeling was usurping her theatrics.

He pushed her away from his chest and looked into her eyes. "Of course you fit in. You're my best friend! I love having you around."

She sniffed and let a little burp of emotion escape her. "You mean it?"

"Shut up," he said. "Don't beg like a dog. Listen, I won't pretend that I don't sometimes think you'd be better off having a romance of your own instead of always getting so involved in mine, but as far as I'm concerned no one's come along who's anywhere near good enough for you, so fuck it, you can hang out with me and Morris till the day we die, if it comes to that. I know he feels the same way."

She hugged him. "Thank you so much, honey. I love you. You make me so happy. I'll try not to get so crazy anymore."

"Okay." He patted her ample bottom. "Okay. C'mon. Let's go back to our wall and get totally plowed."

They returned to their corner, but Morris wasn't there. Natalie said, "Don't worry, he'll find us if we stay where we are," and she went to buy two beers. The line at the bar was long, and when she got back Peter was still alone, and looking a little frantic.

"I don't see Morris anywhere in the crowd," he said nervously.

"It's pretty dense in here," she said, handing him his beer.

He took a swig, never taking his eyes off his surroundings. "Do me a favor and help me look for him, okay?"

"Okay," she said. "Anything for you, baby."

He started wading through the crowd to his left, and Natalie forged her way to the right. The crowd had gotten thick; dozens of perfectly tapered heads with perfect skin glanced her way, displaying rows of teeth like pearls on a string, glowing with health and happiness. So many beautiful men in the world, such an astonishing number. And then she met Peter in the middle again, and his eyes were like little galaxies, they brimmed with the raw stuff of existence; next to him, everyone else paled.

"Funny," he said. "Morris doesn't seem to be anywhere." He was practically shouting now; they were directly beneath a speaker.

She could tell that he'd reached the same conclusion she had, but he'd hate her if she gave voice to it first. Instead, she said, "Maybe he thought you took me home."

He raised an eyebrow, grateful for even so absurd an interpretation of Morris's absence. "Let's give him another ten minutes," he said.

Two hours later, she led him out of the bar. He could scarcely see; he was blinded by tears. There had been no sign of Morris.

No sign of Morris, and no sign of Nick.

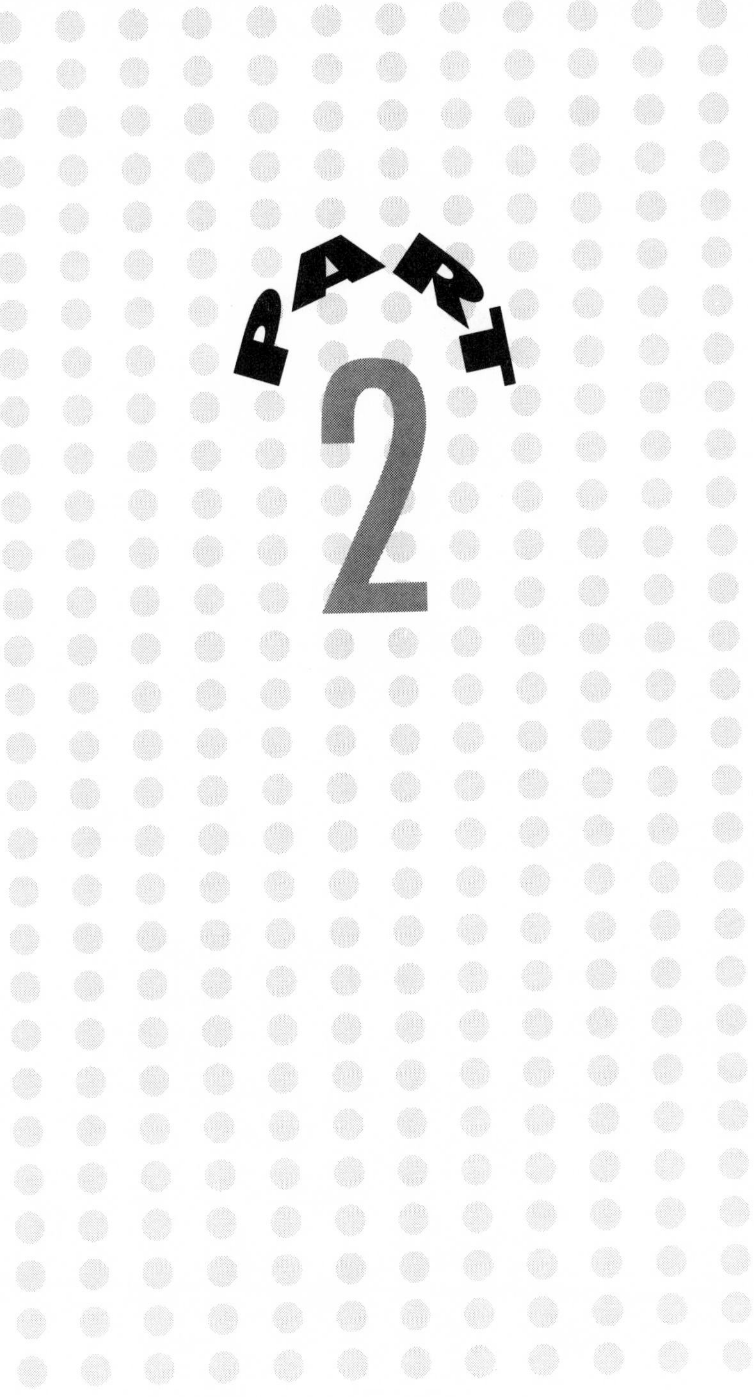

PART 2

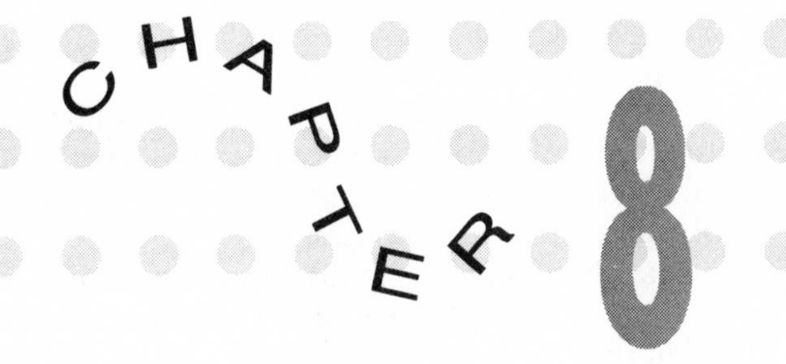

CHAPTER 8

Two days before Calvin and Vera's wedding, Sandy Stathis called her daughter. It was seven in the morning.

"Mom, why are you bothering me this early?" Natalie griped as she rolled out of bed and carried the portable phone to the kitchen. She got a tub of yogurt from the refrigerator and pried off its foil lid.

"I suppose you've already heard," said Sandy accusingly. "I suppose you've known all along and deliberately kept me in the dark."

"I wish you'd stop talking like a TV show and tell me what's on your mind," said Natalie, irritated. She spooned some yogurt into her mouth and immediately felt like throwing up. She was feeling groggy and stupid and ill. She'd been out celebrating with Peter the night before. He'd just gotten a full-time job rendering storyboards for television commercials. He was excited; he could give up the endless hustle of free-lance work and settle down to "getting paid for goofing off," as he put it. Accordingly, they'd drunk long and hard, and this morning, with a hangover grating on her brain, Natalie's social tolerance was nearly nil.

Sandy sounded hurt and betrayed. "Your brother and his fiancée just let it slip that they do not intend to have children." She paused. "Well?"

"Well, what? It's their business."

"It is not. It's mine, too. I'm the grandmother. Or I should be. I'm forty-seven years old and I don't have many years left."

"Oh, bullsh—"

"Language, Natalie. Now, I know I can't count on you for grandchildren, you keep chasing after Peter when he doesn't want you. But I thought I could count on Calvin, because he always does everything by the book; and now I've found out that he and Vera don't want to bring children into such a 'troubled' world. It's horrible, like something you'd hear hippies say in 1969. That's the worst part—losing your grandchildren to a cliché. I tell you, this wedding is ruined for me. I'll put on a good face, but I just want you and your brother to know that my heart will be breaking. Don't worry, I won't make a scene. I have a peach Christian Lacroix dress that looks so sensational everyone will think I'm on top of the world, and I intend to give that impression. And I have to be a good date, too. I don't want to spoil the wedding for my escort."

Natalie almost spit out a mouthful of yogurt. "Date, Mom? You have a *date?*"

"Of a sort. I asked Hank Bixby to take me. Carolyn's boy, remember? She and Nathan will be at the wedding, and they're on thin ice, you know—apparently the cranberry car incident was only one of many. Well, when Hank came to pick up Carolyn after the last Accessorizers Anonymous meeting, he took me aside and asked me to watch over her at the wedding, to make sure she and Nathan didn't cause a scene, and I said, oh, Hank, why don't you just come and watch over her yourself? So to allay their suspicions he's posing as my escort, as if he's doing me a favor, but he'll really be there to keep the peace between his parents. Also, I thought this would be the only possible way you'd ever meet him, with the both of you trapped at a party together."

"For Christ's sake, Mom."

"He's a decent man, Natalie. He's presentable and he's wealthy. And he fixed my dishwasher for me, God bless him.

He always dresses like he's on his way to a golf game, but that's his only fault as far as I can see. You could do worse."

"No, I couldn't—there is no worse."

"I don't want to argue with you. He'll be at the wedding with me, so the only way you can avoid meeting him is if you avoid me, which you'd better not dare because I'll never forgive you. I'll need all the support I can get, after watching my only son pledge to be faithful to a woman who's going to make him wear a latex sheath on his thingie for the rest of his life. Are you bringing Peter Pan?"

"Yes, of course I am."

"He's still not in love with you?"

"Not yet."

She sighed. "I don't understand it. You'd think a handsome boy like that would want to be in love."

"Oh, he does. He falls in love occasionally. But with all the wrong types."

"I'm surprised he hasn't got trapped into marriage by one of them. That can happen."

"Well—he has me to look out for him, and I won't let it."

"I wish I understood my own children. I wish I understood this strange relationship you have with that young man. I have to say, though, I am looking forward to seeing him in a suit and tie. In my day, all the young men wore suits and ties all the time. We always got to see them at their very best. I don't believe I've ever seen Peter wearing anything but baggy pants and shirts without collars."

"It's his look, Mom. He's an artist. He never really has to wear a suit."

"He does own one, doesn't he?"

"Oh, yeah, a gorgeous one. Armani. I helped him pick it out. Dark gray, double-breasted. You'll like it."

"Wonderful."

She'd finished the yogurt now, and tossed the empty tub into the wastebasket. "Got to run, Mom. I'll be late for work."

"Still temping, I suppose."

She shut her eyes in vexation. "Yes. So what?"

"So, when are you going to find yourself a career?"

"I have a career. It's called life."

"Now who's talking like a TV show? Very well, I'll let you go. I'm going to spend the day rethinking my plans for the spare room. Apparently there's no crying need to turn it into a playroom now. Unless I plan to get pregnant again myself."

"Don't you dare."

"Thank you for caring, dear. See you at the church."

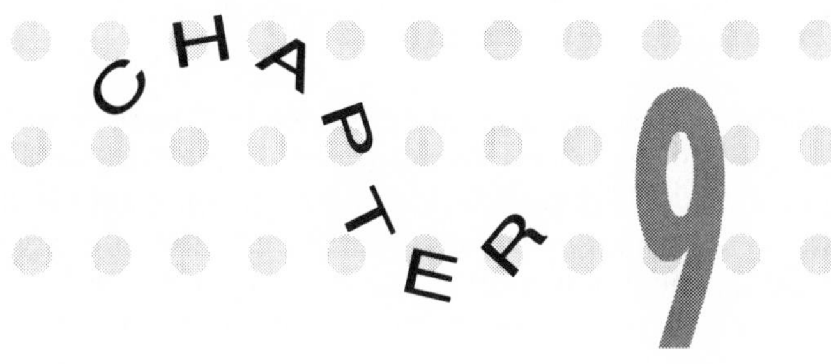

Chapter 9

The day of the wedding arrived with a dull, drizzly rain; Natalie knew, just by the looks of it, that it would keep falling all day. Her head began to ache. It was cold, so she'd have to cover her eggshell-blue bridesmaid's dress with the horrible old lamb's-wool coat she'd been meaning to replace for about a million years now. Her mother had already called her, hysterical about the rain—"The weatherman said clear skies! Why aren't these people held accountable for their blunders the way other professionals are?"—and she was beginning to dread the day. When Peter came over, looking less than his usual self because he was wet and hunched over (he didn't own a topcoat), she decided that desperate times called for desperate measures, and she fetched from the refrigerator a bottle of gold-label Veuve Clicquot she'd been saving for an undetermined special occasion.

So by the time they made their way downstairs and hailed a taxi, they were roaring drunk. They giggled and cracked jokes in pig Latin that were only funny because the Pakistani driver was so obviously befuddled by the stream of uck-fay ou-yays and ull-bay it-shays.

When at last they reached St. Edmond's, Natalie shoved a wad of bills into the driver's hand and made a smooching sound at him; then she and Peter leapt out into the rain and raced up the stairs. They were late, of course; the traffic from the city had been dense, and Sandy Stathis was standing at the back of the church with the vein in her forehead prominently proclaiming her anxiety.

"Where have you two been?" she asked hoarsely, taking them by their arms and nearly yanking them inside. "Natalie, you go right through that door, Vera's waiting in the vestry with the other girls and I hope to God she hasn't had a cardiac arrest by now because you'd be to blame. Peter, this is Vera's brother, David, he'll seat you." Peter winked at Natalie as the usher led him down the aisle.

The wedding went off without a hitch, of course; Calvin looked suitably nervous, Vera looked suitably radiant, the church was strewn with gorgeous floral arrangements, and the organist didn't miss a beat in either the processional (Clarke's "Trumpet Voluntary") or recessional (the hornpipe from Handel's "Water Music"). At one point during the ceremony, Natalie sought out Peter in the congregation, and when she found him, their eyes met and he made a grotesque face. Still drunk, she barked out a laugh, then quickly pretended it was the beginning of a cough.

All of Vera's bridesmaids were willowy and thin except for Natalie, and she was glad she'd had the champagne because it had emboldened her. Without it, she didn't know if she'd have been able to stand there, maintaining the pathetic fiction that Vera's bridesmaids were all a matched set in eggshell blue, when one of them was so clearly responsible for rather more of that color's appearance on the altar than the rest.

Still, she carried herself gracefully, and she'd been told before that she had a pretty face, and besides, all these suburban girls had hairstyles that were about six years out of date, so who cared about a few extra pounds? Certainly not Peter. Every time she looked his way, he winked, or yawned theatrically, or pretended to be asleep, or crossed his eyes to try to crack her up.

She looked over the rest of the congregation. They all blended together, the same sea of heads she'd seen at every such gathering: the weepy old women, the red-faced, uncomprehending old men, the young marrieds feeling odd at being on the other side of the fence now. She thought them all hopelessly mundane. Then, for the first time, she noticed her mother in the front pew, a look of regal composure on her face, and next to her a great sofa of a man with Mormon-cut hair, thick glasses, and a bad plaid suit. That must be Hank Bixby. He obviously hadn't picked up his mother's accessorizing habits. She regarded his dull, broad face with contempt, then swept her gaze across the church to rest again on angelic, ascetic-looking Peter, who, when he noticed that she was looking at him, pretended to pick his nose. There was no comparison at all.

After the ceremony, the wedding party returned to the altar for photographs, and Peter waited at the back of the church. He was clearly bored; he paced back and forth while the photographer, a flamboyant old queen, cajoled his subjects into a variety of poses, all of them "EX-quisite!" She felt such love for Peter now, for enduring this endless waiting on her behalf. Why had she ever doubted that he would be here with her, beside her for her brother's wedding? They were meant to be together! She remembered the anxiety she'd had over that dreadful Morris character; in the end, he hadn't been any harder to get rid of than the others before him. No one could really come between Peter and her. It was silly to consider it. In the end, he couldn't help but recognize this, couldn't help but love her, need her, even—eventually—want her.

She was posing now with the rest of the wedding party. A geeky groomsman stood behind her and put his hand on her shoulder. She rolled her eyes. Well, it was a small duty, and soon over. Then she and Peter would be free to have fun, fun, fun.

CHAPTER 10

Calvin and Vera's reception was held at the Pump Room, one of Chicago's oldest and most magnificent restaurants. Vera's parents had rented out the entire place, and now it was filled with bouquets of flowers, graced by the sweet sounds of a local string quartet, and overwhelmed by an astonishing seven-tiered wedding cake (carrot with white carob frosting, at Vera's insistence).

The moment after they arrived, Natalie hustled Peter into the ladies' room, hid him in one of the toilet stalls, and produced a vial of cocaine from her purse. It had been months since they'd indulged; Morris hadn't approved, and neither of them had the budget for regular use. But this was a special occasion, and if Natalie was going to stand in the receiving line next to those twiglike bridesmaids, she needed some chemical courage.

They each snorted two tiny spoonfuls, one up each nostril, and licked the spoon clean. Then they stood in the stall giggling at the clandestine nature of the act, and waited for the pleasant numbness in the nose and throat that told them they were on their way to a high. Natalie popped the vial back into her purse, opened the stall door to check for visitors, and discovered one of her great-aunts at the sink, applying rouge to her time-bleached cheeks.

She gently shut the door again and gestured to Peter that he should be quiet; but after a few more minutes with no sound of the great-aunt's departure, Natalie said aloud, "Oh, fuck it," grabbed Peter by the wrist, and dragged him out, just as another guest was coming in. They didn't stop to see what kind of reaction they'd caused, although they heard the great-aunt emit a little shriek; they just continued, laughing, into the restaurant, where Natalie helped Peter find his table.

"Here you are," she said, lifting his place card. " 'Mr. Peter Leland.' Let's see who's sitting next to you." She picked up the card to the left. " 'Miss Emily Verzatt.' Oh, my God, Peter—that's the great-aunt we just left in the john!" Peter blanched, and she laughed and said, "Just kidding. I don't know who this is. One of Vera's relatives, I suppose." She looked at the next few places. " 'Mr. Gregory Romano,' 'Mrs. Gregory Romano.' Oh, I've heard Calvin mention Greg—someone he works with at the bank." She moved on. " 'Mr. Lloyd Hood.' What a dreadful name. I don't know him." She reached the last place at the table. " 'Miss Patricia Kellogg.' Oh, Peter, hooray!"

"What is it?" he asked.

"Patsy Kellogg is Vera's friend from Hong Kong," she enthused. "My mom told me that she canceled at the very last minute—she's not coming! So you have an empty seat next to you, which means after the toasts I can leave the wedding party's table and come hang out with you during dinner!"

"Hooray!" he echoed.

"I'm going to drop my purse into the seat just to reserve it for me," she said. She wagged a finger at him. "Don't you *dare* go rooting around in there for more blow!"

"Would I do that?" he said innocently.

She rolled her eyes and traipsed across the restaurant, feeling incredibly light on her feet; it might have been the coke, but more likely it was Peter. She felt so sure of him right now, so certain of his undying devotion.

She took her place in the receiving line, between one of the eggshell-blue twigs and one of the groomsmen, who, by the way he said "How extra-OR-dinary" to all the guests, she presumed must be gay; she decided to ask Peter his opinion later. It would be safe to do so; the groomsman had a full beard, and Peter abhorred facial hair.

As the line of grinning faces, half of them unfamiliar, all of them uninteresting, passed by her and shook her hand and exchanged with her the awkward pleasantries that were required of these occasions, she made it a point to check on Peter's whereabouts every few seconds. He was at the bar now, ordering a drink; wait, he was laughing, sharing a joke with the bartender. Her antenna went up; the bartender was good-looking. Another face erupted into her sphere and blocked her view; she dispatched it with as much firm politeness as she could muster, and when it had moved on, Peter was no longer to be seen anywhere near bar or bartender; she heaved a sigh of relief.

All at once there was a new face, a broad, plain face burdened with thick glasses. Natalie recognized the Mormon haircut at once. "Hello, Natalie. Your mother pointed you out to me at the church. I'm Hank Bixby."

"Enchanted to meet you at last, Hank," she said, extending her hand. He shook it, and his touch was clammy.

The line was stalled. Goddamn it, thought Natalie, move, move, *move*! She continued to smile radiantly at Hank.

"Your mother is a lovely woman," he said at last.

"Yes, isn't she."

The line began to move again. She almost sighed in relief.

At long last, the receiving line had received all, and Natalie, her hand aching from having shaken so many others, made a beeline for Peter's table. Most of the guests had already taken their seats, and she was grateful to see that Peter's table was full except for her seat and that he looked desperately bored.

"Hello," she said, in the exact cadences of an Oak Park matron; only Peter got the joke. "I'm Natalie Stathis, Calvin's sister. I'm afraid I don't know any of you, but Peter, here, is my date for the evening, so I'll probably be joining you all later."

"Hi, I'm Emily Verzatt," said a suntanned teenage girl to Peter's left. "I'm Vera's cousin." Natalie said, "How nice to meet you," and instantly thought, She's been put at our table to make her feel like a grown-up.

The man next to her got to his feet and said, "Hi, Natalie, Greg Romano. I feel like I know you already—Cal's mentioned you a lot. We work at the bank together. My wife, Brandy." Natalie nodded, smiling graciously and thinking, Couple of suburban dweebs.

Then a rather attractive, although seriously balding, man stood up and said, "Pleasure to meet you, Natalie. I'm Lloyd Hood." He shook her hand and she noticed that his suit was a tad too big for him.

They all chatted amiably for about a nanosecond, then Natalie excused herself. "I'm due at the table of the wedding party. So delighted to meet you all. I'll see you soon." She winked at Peter, and he mouthed the words Don't go! as he bulged his eyes out in alarm. She smiled and turned away.

The toasts to the bride and groom were predictable in their frat-boy smuttiness, but Natalie laughed at them all the same. The best man went on interminably, Vera's father got embarrassingly emotional, and Calvin himself toasted his bride in a jokey manner that Natalie felt sure Vera would make him regret on the wedding night. Then the priest recited a blessing, and that was predictable, too. And then the Pump Room's efficient staff filed in, holding salads in the air.

Natalie looked at Peter's table and found him staring into thin air as the Romanos carried on an animated exchange with little Emily, no doubt about where she wanted to go to college and all the conversational banalities that that subject entailed. Lloyd Hood, too, was silent, one eyebrow cocked. He appeared to be half-listening to the Romanos.

Natalie noticed that Patsy Kellogg's place had been given a salad without regard to there being no one there to eat it, so once the entrée had been served—roast duck, God bless Calvin and Vera—she slipped away from the wedding party and took the empty place at Peter's table. "I'm joining you for dinner," she said. "And how are you all doing? Having fun?" She patted Peter's thigh beneath the table.

"Uh-huh," said Emily as she swept her long hair behind her neck. Natalie noticed the half-empty champagne glass at the girl's place. Well, no wonder she was happy.

The Romanos and Emily then resumed their conversation, which continued throughout the meal. By the time dessert was served, Peter looked so bored that Natalie decided it was her duty to bring the spark back into his eyes. She figured the best way to do that would be to have a little fun with Mr. Lloyd Hood. She turned to him and said, "Mr. Hood, how did you come to be here?"

He met her gaze. "Oh, I'm kind of a friend of Calvin's. I sold him his first gun."

Natalie's jaw dropped, and Peter muffled a guffaw. It was so seldom that *anyone* took Natalie by surprise.

"His—his—"

"First gun," Lloyd repeated. "A snub-nosed thirty-eight. I own a gun shop."

"I—I didn't even know Calvin had a gun."

He smiled at her, and it was an infuriatingly patronizing smile. "Well, Calvin and I tend to travel in circles where *not* owning a gun is a remarkable thing."

She stared at him, her lower lip just hanging there, like an awning. She was totally undone. She'd meant to tease this man, to amuse Peter, but now she had no idea how to proceed.

"Where is your gun shop located, Mr. Hood?" Peter asked, merriment evident in his voice.

"Call me Lloyd. It's at Armitage and Damen." Peter raised an eyebrow and he continued, "I know—not what you'd think. Everyone thinks gun shops are all buried on the South Side somewhere."

"Kind of a yuppie neighborhood, isn't it?" Peter asked.

"Most of my customers *are* yuppies."

Natalie sat back and straightened the folds in her dress.

"How'd you get into that line of work?" Peter asked.

Lloyd shifted in his seat, as if uncomfortable about going on, but he continued all the same. "Well, it was pretty much a reaction against the attacks that've been made in this country on our basic freedoms. Everyone's trying to curtail free speech, freedom to bear arms—I don't know, I guess I just thought it'd be a pretty indelible statement of my ideological support of the Bill of Rights if I went in the opposite direction and opened a gun shop. I've always owned guns, myself, since I was a teenager."

"What, you're some kind of hunter?" Natalie asked, disgusted.

"No, no; I don't hunt for sport. I don't have any strong

objection to it, but I don't do it myself. I mainly go in for a little target practice now and then. Keep myself sharp." He smiled. "Never know when you'll need it."

Peter was sitting with his elbows on the table and one of his hands covering his mouth; Natalie knew the set of his facial muscles well enough to know that there was a grin behind that hand. He was staring at Lloyd Hood.

"But, Mr. Hood," she continued, "don't you think it's been demonstrated so brutally in this country that guns are a plague?"

He shook his head. "No. The plague is organized crime, the plague is the welfare state. Guns are just the tools used by the spreaders of that plague."

"But if we took the guns away, w—"

"We'd still have the plague," he said, cutting her off.

My God, she thought, staring at him; how can I ever have found him attractive? He's a reactionary right-wing pig!

Suddenly Peter spoke up. "This country's a democracy," he said, "and it's up to the people to decide these things, and a lot of people, a lot of intelligent and caring people, have decided that guns are dangerous and should be outlawed. So you really can't place the selfishness of the gun lobby above the concern of the majority."

Lloyd was wearing an excited look now. "Peter, I don't even know where to begin to answer you. First of all, I certainly *do* put the NRA above the left-wing whiners, because the NRA is protecting a basic freedom of the American people, while the leftists are trying to curtail that freedom; maybe they really do believe that gun control, or even outlawing guns, is a worthy cause, but that's a subjective opinion, isn't it? And since they're the ones who are always insisting that morality is subjective, how dare they reverse that opinion on selected issues like this one? They're setting themselves up as moral oligarchs. Because, you see, despite what you think, the majority of people in America *still* believe in the right to bear arms, so democratic principle isn't an argument you can use against me. Aside from which, I'm not a great believer in democracy, anyway."

Peter was aghast. "What would you rather have? Communism?"

Lloyd gave him a you-know-better-than-that look. "I think

you can tell from everything I've said that I'm no Communist. I firmly believe that the state exists to serve the individual, rather than the other way around—which is why I find the liberal drift in this country so pernicious; they always place the individual at the service, and the mercy, of the state—this gun issue is just one example of that. But I also think that democracy in its purest form is mob rule, and democracy as it's practiced today is a virtually worthless method of making cosmetic changes in a governmental machine that is firmly entrenched in power and immune to the vagaries of the election booth—or the precepts of the Constitution, as we've seen illustrated repeatedly since Watergate."

Peter's face was reddening. "Well, what kind of government do you want instead?"

"No kind of government. I'd like to live in an anarchist state, where everyone is responsible for his own backyard."

"Oh, yeah? What the hell would keep the country going, then?"

"Trade." He said it with the fervor of a priest invoking the Savior.

"And who regulates trade?" Peter asked. By now the Romanos and Emily were watching and listening, a little alarmed at how heated the exchange had gotten.

"Trade regulates itself," Lloyd said, "or rather, we, as consumers, would regulate trade based on what we buy. Ideally, an educated and informed public would consume only quality goods and services, and trade would prosper because of that. I guess what I'm really talking about is a consumer-determined meritocracy."

At this point Sandy Stathis appeared at the table and tapped Natalie on the shoulder. "Honey, I'd like to have my picture taken with you and Calvin," she whispered. "Shouldn't take a moment."

Natalie excused herself and rose from her seat; Peter was so involved in his discussion with Lloyd that he barely noticed her go.

The photo session turned out to be a trap. After one picture with her children, Sandy told the photographer, "All right, now just one of me with the bride and groom," and she said to Natalie, "Go and stand over there by Hank."

Hank Bixby was off to one side, waiting like a puppy dog for Sandy. Natalie swallowed, approached him, and said, "Hello again, Hank."

"Long time, no see," he said, and he actually laughed at the joke. Natalie couldn't believe her ears.

"Perhaps you'd care to dance," he said, and for the first time she noticed that the dance floor had been cleared and a band of what looked like Rastafarians had set up their instruments and were preparing to play.

"Oh—well—thank you, Hank. Yes. Sure. Lovely." She peered over her shoulder at Peter, who was now leaning over the table, speaking with great intensity to Lloyd Hood. She decided it was safe to leave him. He obviously wasn't with anyone dangerous.

"Now," called Sandy, "Natalie, you and Hank come and join us for a picture," and Natalie felt like killing her. By the time that shot had been taken, the band had started up. Calvin and Vera were summoned to open the dancing with a quick whirl through "their song," the Barbra Streisand tune about evergreens. Then the band kicked in with an old Four Tops tune, and Hank dragged Natalie onto the dance floor.

The Four Tops number segued into an old Jackson 5 hit, and Hank, a truly terrible dancer, flapped his arms and twirled about, and showed no sign of tiring. Natalie felt the seams of her dress begin to strain and feared they might burst.

The band then segued into an old Temptations song, and Natalie thought, This is the end. Hank was leaping about like an acrobat; it was mortifying.

Suddenly Peter appeared and tapped Hank on the shoulder. "Mind if I cut in?" he asked. Hank, sweaty and bewildered, had no choice but to bow out. He left the dance floor mopping his brow with a handkerchief.

Peter took Natalie in his arms and gave her a spin. She shrieked with delight.

"Finally got rid of the right-wing reactionary pig?" she asked.

"Who, Lloyd?" he said as he bumped his hips against hers in time to the music. "Interesting guy."

"Oh, Christ, Peter! He's a Nazi!"

He laughed, grabbing her by the waist for another twirl. "That's a bit melodramatic."

The tempo slowed; the band slid into an old Smokey Robinson ballad. Peter took Natalie in his arms and glided romantically across the floor. She melted, and found her nirvana on his left shoulder pad. To think that, for a while, she'd been in danger of having to come here without him! But this was the payoff to all her efforts, this moment, now, in his arms; she'd won. He was hers, he was hers.

They shared every dance that night; they were inseparable. When their energies started to flag, they fled to the men's room for more cocaine, and that kept them going for the rest of the night. Soon the air was heavy with smoke, and empty glasses swarmed over the tabletops; there was an exhausted feeling in the air, as if the building itself were asking people to leave. The remaining guests were straying out the door. The band finally packed up and left. It was eight-thirty.

"Guess we should hit the road," said Peter.

Reluctant to let the evening end, Natalie nevertheless agreed.

She visited the ladies' room, he the men's, and they met outside a few minutes later. Peter hailed a cab.

They rode in silence for a time. The lights of the city drifted by Natalie's window; combined with the steady hum of the taxi's engine, the effect was hypnotic. She settled onto Peter's shoulder and then turned to look at him.

There was a twinkle in his eyes.

"What is it?" she asked.

"I hate to spoil the mood; I can practically hear you purring."

"What? What?"

"I've got the *best* story," he said eagerly.

She sat up. "Oh, tell me!"

"In the men's room a few minutes ago, I ran into Lloyd Hood."

"The right-wing reactionary pig?"

He nodded. "We stood next to each other at the urinals."

"Did you peek?"

He laughed and hit her arm. "No, listen. Even better. He got all nervous, you know, all mealymouthed, and then he asked me if maybe I'd like to continue our discussion over dinner sometime."

Natalie felt the floor fall away. "No way."

"I'm not joking. The right-wing reactionary pig is a queer." He grinned. "And I have a date with him!"

She threw back her head and emitted a howl of laughter.

PART 3

Peter started his full-time job on Monday and celebrated with Natalie on Monday night. They met at her apartment, finished off the rest of the cocaine, and went to Berlin, where they hopped up and down on the dance floor for two hours (it being too crowded to actually dance).

Later, as they sat on the curb airing out, Peter said, "Really, Natalie, these late nights have got to stop. I can't sleep if I'm wired like this, and I've got to get up early these days."

Her heart sank a little, but she'd known this day must come. Neither she nor Peter had put much thought or energy into their careers since they'd met two years before. He'd scraped by, doing cartoons for various local magazines and newspapers, but he never really applied himself to turning a profit at it; and she still worked as a temporary secretary, wanting to keep her freedom to take a day off whenever she wished. But they were getting a little long in the tooth for such frivolity, and Peter's new job obviously signaled the end of their weeknight revels.

She stretched her legs into the street and sighed. A gay couple passed behind them, mincing in the most embarrassing manner and chattering at each other like magpies, their lisps overlapping. After they'd gone, she looked at Peter and they both laughed.

"Well, God bless 'em," Peter said. "Not everybody can be butch."

They were silent for a time. Then Natalie said, "Well, it's been fun. And what a way to end an era, huh? That wedding, then tonight. Feel like my nerve endings are sticks of dynamite. With the fuses lit."

He smiled. "Guess we've got to grow up sometime."

"Funny, isn't it—just when you get to the point where you can afford stuff like blow, you can't use it 'cause then you can't do the job that lets you afford stuff like blow." The sentence rambled out of her, and they both laughed at its awkwardness. "We'll still have wild weekends, though," she said.

"Oh, sure."

"In fact, let's plan a big bash for Friday! We can have it at your place. It's your celebration, after all."

He shook his head. "Can't. Friday's my date with Lloyd Hood."

She rolled her eyes. "You're not really going through with that!"

"Why not?"

"He's a fascist!"

"He's not, Natalie. He's a libertarian. He has opinions you wouldn't expect. Like, on abortion, he's really strongly pro-choice. And he's one hundred percent against U.S. intervention in El Salvador and Nicaragua and all those places. And, of course, he's pro-gay rights. Well, kind of."

"What does that mean, 'kind of'?"

"Well, he says he's always hated going to gay rights rallies because it implies that he believes the government has the authority to decide who has civil rights and who doesn't. Whereas he believes that *everyone* has civil rights, just by being born, but the government selectively denies those rights to groups it doesn't like, like gays and women and the mentally ill. So when he goes to gay rights rallies, he feels like he's playing by the government's rules, y'know, treating them like it's up to them to grant or deny us our rights, when they have no moral authority to do any such thing."

Natalie stared at him in disbelief. "When did he tell you all of this?"

"Oh, we talked on the phone yesterday."

"I see." She was uncomfortable with this entire conversation. Here was Peter, sitting on the street with her like always, his gut full of beer and his nose full of blow, and he was talking politics and ideology like some kind of fanatic. What was happening here?

When he'd first told her that Lloyd had asked him out to dinner, she'd felt nothing but amusement at the ridiculousness of it. Just imagine beautiful, sensational Peter with that balding, badly dressed nut case! But now, here was Peter parroting him at one in the morning on Halsted Street, slurring words like "civil rights" and not even noticing.

She still couldn't believe that Lloyd was any kind of threat. And if he were, surely she could dispatch him with a flick of her wrist—he'd be no trouble at all. Not like the others.

And yet, there was this odd difference in Peter's manner tonight. Not at all headlong in lust or love, as he was at the beginning of every other affair; he was calmer, more rational. Perhaps that meant that Lloyd meant nothing to him; she just wished she could be sure.

"Well," she said, treading carefully, "where are you and Lloyd going on Friday?"

"I don't know yet. We haven't decided. It doesn't really matter."

It doesn't? she thought, surprised. It always has before.

Natalie wasn't working the next day, so she slept late; it helped to make up for having slept badly. Lloyd Hood's unfathomable presence had dogged her dreams.

She rolled out of bed at eleven and put herself on the bathroom scale, figuring that as long as she was depressed anyway, she might as well check her weight. To her stupefaction, she was down three pounds. Peter hadn't even noticed.

Angry, she decided she'd better consider an anti-Lloyd campaign. She knew next to nothing about him, and wondered where she could get some dirt. Suddenly she remembered her brother; it was Calvin who'd invited Lloyd to the wedding, because Lloyd had sold him his "first" gun. Maybe there was something damning there—maybe Lloyd was armed to the teeth, a raving paranoid.

She hadn't talked to her mother since the wedding, so she called her now.

"Honey, you couldn't have phoned at a worse time," Sandy Stathis said. "I'm just setting up for a luncheon meeting of Accessorizers Anonymous."

"This won't take long, Mom."

"Well, I like that! You scarcely speak to me at the wedding, then days go by and I don't hear from you, and when I finally do you tell me you don't want to talk long. Honey, don't you know what it means for a mother to see one of her children get married? Didn't you think to call me the next day to see how I was feeling, or at the very least to gossip about everyone's outfit?"

"I had a hangover! And if that's how you felt, why didn't you call *me*?"

"I was far too disgraced by your behavior to do that. Honey, you spent the entire reception making a fool of yourself over that male model of yours."

"Peter's not a fucking model, Mom."

"Language, Natalie."

"Well, what do you exp—"

"As I said, you scarcely spoke to me, you ignored your brother, you never welcomed Vera into the family, and you made poor Hank Bixby feel like an also-ran."

"He *is* an also-ran."

A brief pause. "You're a very proud young lady, Natalie. Life will bring you down a peg, and don't come crying to me when it does."

She sighed. "Can we please get back to the reason I called?"

"By all means. Let's do what Natalie wants. Natalie has decreed."

"Don't make me hang up, Mom."

" '*Make*' you!' Oh, of course. If you did something as rude as that, it'd be my fault, wouldn't it?"

"Mom," she said determinedly, "at Peter's table at the reception there was this guy, Lloyd Hood, who owns a gun store. That's why he was invited. He said he sold Calvin his first gun. Did you know that Calvin was into guns?"

"Well, if he is, it's his own business, and all I can say is thank God he's not having any children, then. A house with guns is no place for babies."

"So, you didn't know about this gun thing he's into?"

"Calvin's just like you, he never tells me anything."

"So he probably never mentioned this Lloyd guy, either."

"Not a word. You know your brother. What would you expect him to say? 'Mother, I just bought some wonderfully destructive firearms from my good friend, Lloyd the gun merchant'? Not likely! If Calvin had his arms and legs amputated, I'd be the last to know about it. I'd have to see him and say, 'Darling, what happened to your limbs?' And then he'd treat me like I was intruding."

Natalie sighed. "You don't happen to know his number in Hawaii, do you?"

"I'm afraid not. Why do you want to go bothering him on his honeymoon?"

"I just want to get the scoop on this Lloyd guy."

She brightened. "Why? Are you interested in him?"

"Oh, for Christ's sake, Mom. He's a lunatic. He sells guns!"

"So does Adnan Khashoggi. I wouldn't mind if you married him."

"Ick," said Natalie. "You're weird."

"I have to go, honey. At any moment I expect the girls and—oh, did I tell you? We have a male member now, too!"

"No way!"

"Frederick Kelsey, who works with Doris Kuntz at her real-estate office. Apparently he spends all his commissions on jackets and shoes. Very flighty fellow; I think he might be—well, you know."

"No, tell me."

"You know, a—a—"

"Gay, you mean?"

"Yes, that."

"So what?"

"Oh, nothing, nothing, nothing. It's just so hard for me to imagine. Men together, I mean. Doing *it*. But Frederick is obviously no John Wayne. You couldn't ever imagine calling him Fred. Terribly amusing, of course; keeps us all in stitches."

"How nice."

"Lives with his mother! Can you imagine?"

"*No*," said Natalie with too much oomph.

"Was that sarcasm again? It does you no credit. You'd think I'd reared you in New York or someplace awful. Do you get it from television? Everyone on television is so sarcastic these days. Oh, I really have to go, dear. And I'm so disappointed, I never got to scold you for ignoring the Bixbys."

"Why on earth should I have paid attention to the Bixbys? I don't even know them!"

"Well, it's just that Hank likes you so very much, and—"

"Oh, Mom. Get real!"

"Carolyn and Nathan are having difficulties right now, but if Hank started seeing you I'm sure they'd be united in their joy for th—"

"Mom, you have to go!"

"You're right. We'll discuss this later. Good-bye, dear."

"We will not. Good-bye, Mom."

She turned off the phone and simmered. A whole week before Calvin returned from Hawaii! She couldn't afford to wait till then.

CHAPTER 12

Peter's new office was downtown. On Friday, the temporary agency sent Natalie to the Loop for the day, to type Federal Express airbills at a public-relations office that was doing a massive press-kit mailing. The work was maddeningly dull, so she arranged to meet dazzling Peter for lunch.

They went to Marshall Field's all-you-can-eat Italian cafeteria. Natalie, feeling that losing three pounds had done her no good, threw her diet to the winds and had a heaping plate of pasta smothered in clam sauce.

Peter looked like hell. There were actually bags under his eyes, and his hair was limp. "Working nine to five is killing me," he said. "My body clock is still set on free-lance time—up at noon, start work at three, dinner at nine, party till one, bed at two. I'm all screwed up."

"You look it." She sprinkled dried peppers and grated cheese over her rotini.

He propped up his head with his hand. "I don't know if

I'm up to going out tonight," he said. "I actually feel nauseous. I'm not even hungry. I'm going to call Lloyd and cancel."

She felt a little flurry of joy. "Oh, that's too bad."

"You think so? I thought you didn't like him."

"I like him fine," she lied. "He's just not like anyone I've ever met before."

"I know what you mean," he said. "He's one of a kind."

She didn't like the admiring way he'd said that. "Well, he'll understand if you cancel." She dug into the pasta; delicious!

"Oh, I know he will; he's that way. It won't be a problem. We'll just go out tomorrow instead."

She raised an eyebrow. Maybe this cancellation wasn't the great boon she'd thought. All it amounted to was a postponement. Maybe there was a better way. . . .

She reflected on the times she and Peter had gone out when he'd been overtired; he'd been cranky, quick-tempered, even rude. Once, after he'd been up two days straight finishing a job and then gone out with Natalie to celebrate its completion, he'd gotten so fed up with her gossip and prattle that he'd told her to shut the fuck up and she'd slapped him. That had led to their longest break—an entire week of being angry with each other and not calling.

If she could convince him to go out with Lloyd tonight, despite his obviously exhausted condition, maybe the same thing would happen. Lloyd would go on and on about ethics and government, in his pushy, holier-than-thou manner, and Peter would get fed up and walk out on him. It was certainly worth a try.

She wiped her mouth with her napkin. "I'm so glad he's the understanding type," she said. "So many people these days just can't deal with disappointment. I mean, think of it; how many men do you know who, if they were looking forward to a date all week, psyching themselves up for it and planning for it and just getting all excited, only to have it canceled on them at the last minute—how many men do you know who would be understanding about that? Damn few, by my experience. Lloyd must be a prince."

Peter twirled his linguini with his fork and scowled. "Y'know, he probably *has* been looking forward to it all week."

"He'll get over it," she said, her mouth half full. "It's only a postponement till tomorrow. You need your sleep."

"We wouldn't have to stay out late," he said, ignoring her. "I don't know. Maybe I shouldn't let him down. I mean, I'm just tired, not dead."

She looked at him. "Peter Leland, you have no idea how to take care of yourself."

He shrugged. "Guess not. Well, hell. I'll just go. If I start to flag, I'll tell him we have to make it an early night, that's all."

She sighed. "Well, I suppose."

She finished her pasta and went back to the buffet for seconds. When she returned, Peter was staring into space.

"Honey? You there?" she said teasingly, resuming her seat.

He looked at her dully. "Huh? Oh, yeah. Just *really* tired, that's all."

"You do look like death warmed over," she said, digging into her food.

"*Okay*," he barked; "you don't have to keep harping on how bad I look!"

She was thrilled by his irritation; with any luck, he'd tear Lloyd to pieces this evening.

Natalie slept well that night; she dreamed giddy dreams about Lloyd offending the barely conscious Peter and of the tremendous bust-up that must follow. Lloyd didn't stand a chance. He wasn't beautiful enough, or stylish enough, or witty enough to have any hold over Peter after a scene like that. She woke up feeling silly that she'd ever considered him a threat.

By nine o'clock, Peter hadn't called, so she took an enormous risk and called him first. The phone rang eleven times and she debated hanging up, but then he answered. "Good morning," he said, his voice drowsy but unmistakably cheerful.

"Hi, honey, it's Natalie," she said, furiously trying to interpret his mood. "I was so worried about you being out late last night in that exhausted state. Just wanted to check on you, see if you're okay."

"I'm wonderful," he said, and offered nothing more.

"Oh," she said, momentarily stumped. "You stayed in, then, like a good lad?"

"Not really. When Lloyd got here, I explained that I was

really dragging my heels, and he understood. So we just went to Ann Sather for a quick dinner and then I came home and went to bed."

"I," not "we." Natalie grinned in triumph. "Doesn't sound like much of a date," she said. "Why did you send him home? Was he horrible to you?"

"Well, actually, I did invite him up. I mean, I was too tired for sex but I thought we might cuddle, at least. And then, in the morning, who knows? But he turned me down. I think he's really old-fashioned. He seemed kind of shocked that I'd suggest it on the first date."

Natalie was a little apprehensive now. "He's a prude, too?"

"I guess. I thought it was kind of cute, to tell the truth."

Lloyd Hood, the gun merchant—*cute*? She was having trouble with that one. "Well," she said, "I'm sorry it wasn't starry-eyed romance and skyrockets," she said desperately. "But they can't all be. Someone else will come along, never fear."

He laughed. "Don't be silly. I like Lloyd a lot. Over dinner, he really got my adrenaline flowing. We had this great discussion about corruption in big business. I asked him how he could support a free market when the corporations in this country are destroying it with their criminal greed, you know? And he starts in with this theory he has that that's all because companies are *allowed* to incorporate—that if he had his way, corporations would not exist. Like, a company is just what it says, a company of individuals running a business, and responsible for it. But a corporation is just what it says, too: a single entity, and, in the eyes of the law, the equivalent to an individual like you or me. Which it shouldn't be. Lloyd says corporations encourage corruption because, if you commit a crime on the job, it's really the corporation committing the crime, not you; you're hiding behind this legal identity that doesn't really exist, this monolithic corporation that takes the rap for you—and can afford to. Lloyd says that every man should be completely responsible for his own actions, and that corporations allow them not to be."

She knit her brow. "That's what you talked about? On a *date*?"

"I thought it was fascinating. I really perked up. Wasn't until we walked outside and the night air hit me that I felt tired again."

She sighed. "Peter, you amaze me. I think of a good first date, I think of dinner at Charlie Trotter's with a bottle of Dom Perignon and lots of thinly veiled sexual come-ons for conversation. You go to Ann Sather, for heaven's sake, and talk legalese with this guy, and then don't even go to bed with him. And you're all happy about it!" She laughed, wanting him to recognize the ridiculousness of it.

He didn't speak right away. Then, his voice low, he said, "I don't know, Natalie. There's something about him. When I'm with him—it was this way at the wedding, too—I feel like I'm in some kind of better world where things matter more than they normally do. Where everything's in this kind of terrific, stark relief. It's kind of an adventure. It's exciting. And as for sexual come-ons, let me tell you from firsthand experience, ideas are an aphrodisiac. Probably because Lloyd is so passionate about them, I started to get really turned on by talking to him. Sexually turned on, I mean. In spite of how tired I was, I was really bummed when we went our separate ways after it was all over. He's got me hot and bothered, kid. Really hot and bothered." He took a deep breath. "I mean, like no one before."

"That's wonderful," she said through gritted teeth. "I hope it's not some kind of weird phase you're going through, I hope this is the real thing at last." That ought to scare him, she thought.

"I don't even want to conjecture about that," he said flatly.

"Well, you've never hesitated to say you were in love before."

"I don't think I even knew what love was before."

Her heart almost exploded. "And you do now?"

"I didn't say that."

"But you jus—"

"I think I'm beginning to understand, that's all. There are deeper currents than I've tapped before. More levels. I feel like a novice at this. All the relationships I've had—and, boy, you know how many that is—and this is the first time I feel like I've really, y'know, *connected* with someone on that basic level, call it the soul, whatever. I'm just a little out of my depth right now."

"You certainly are," she said, anger and frustration stinging her forehead. "Honey, I want you to be careful. We're talking about a guy who's antigovernment and proguns. It sounds scary. Like you're dating a John Bircher or something."

"But it's not like that at all, I've told you. He believes in the same things I do—equality, justice, improving the lives of the poor, rights for gays and women and everybody, the right to privacy, all that stuff. You can't label this guy. Every opinion he's got surprises me, yet makes sense when you consider his context. It's a little magical being with him. He's like an intellectual wizard."

In spite of all this, Natalie still couldn't bring herself to accept that Lloyd was a real threat, the greatest ever; the bottom line was, Lloyd wasn't beautiful. She decided to bring that into play. "Well, the brain-power must make up for him not being so hot to look at, huh?"

There was a long pause. "Natalie, what are you talking about? He's adorable! Just because he's balding, that doesn't mean he's ugly."

She scratched her cheek; a nervous gesture. It was as if she'd forgotten how to speak. She had nothing to say.

"God, look at the time," he said. "I've been in bed eleven hours. Better get up or inertia'll keep me here all day. Care to join me for breakfast?"

"Sure," she said. She wasn't keen on it, but she thought if she declined he might call Lloyd.

"Melrose okay? Half an hour?"

"Fine. Meet you there."

"We can go to Unabridged Books afterward. I want to look up some stuff Lloyd recommended I read."

At breakfast, in a restaurant full of the most beautiful gay men in the city, Peter managed to keep his eyes focused on her; it was her dream come true, except that he kept talking about another man.

"Lloyd liked the wedding, but he hated the religious aspect. He says in Roman times marriage was a civil contract, and doesn't it make more sense to do it that way today?" "Lloyd says the Kennedy administration bears the brunt of the blame for perpetuating Vietnam, but Kennedy gets off light 'cause he was killed before the shit hit the fan." "Lloyd says modern art is a scam and modern artists are charlatans, and that the main reason it keeps barreling on is because it caters to 'a specialized market of dupes,' as he calls it." Lloyd says, Lloyd says, Lloyd says.

Incredibly, the entire breakfast passed without even a hint of gossip. On the way out they passed a gay couple who, three weeks before, had caused a sensation when they'd gotten into a slapping match at Sidetrack. Peter had relished the gory details, but now he merely waved hello, then turned back to Natalie without even making a comment about them!

She decided to remain completely oblivious to his newfound obsession with Lloyd and Lloyd's judgments on the world, so once they entered the bookstore she left him to his searching, determined not to show the slightest curiosity in anything he bought. She hovered by the magazine rack, reading a cryptic short story in *The New Yorker*, until he called her from the counter and said he was ready to go.

Lloyd *couldn't* be a threat, she kept telling herself. It wasn't *possible*. This was a phase that Peter was going through. Perhaps she had allowed him to be too frivolous with his life, too carefree and footloose, and as a result he'd fallen under the influence of the first serious man who came along.

And yet Lloyd was so *very* serious. That, surely, would be his downfall. How much of his insistent blather about ideology and philosophy and morality could someone of Peter's sublime and joyful nature take? It was only a matter of time.

She repeated this to herself over and over during the morning she and Peter spent together, repeated it in the face of every Lloyd-said-this and Lloyd-said-that, repeated it in defiance of the presence, invisible but inextinguishable, that hung over her day like a swollen rain cloud. And when Peter finally left her, laden with books and flushed from so much talking, he kissed her good-bye and told her he loved her and that he and Lloyd were seeing a Japanese film that night, he'd call her tomorrow. So she even got Lloyd wedged into the same sentence as Peter's declaration of love for her. That awful man was worming his way into the core of their relationship, and she hated it.

In a funk, she bought a pint of Ben & Jerry's chocolate-fudge ice cream and ate the whole thing on her way home. Then she sat in her dim apartment and watched videocassettes of old movies all afternoon, and when they ended she felt lethargic and depressed.

The last movie she'd watched was *An Officer and a Gentleman*, which ended with a full-dress-uniformed Richard Gere lifting a grimy Deborah Winger into his arms and carrying her away from her factory job and into the sunset. The television was dark now, but every time she looked at it she saw that scene replaying itself. It had given her a little shudder of ecstasy, and now she couldn't dislodge it from her mind. She tried to replay it with Peter and herself in the starring roles, but gave that up at once; it was silly and embarrassing. Such flourishing, grand passion would certainly never be part of their relationship.

Once she realized this, she asked herself why, then, she bothered pursuing him. Was it because a beautiful, exciting, funny gay man who doesn't want to sleep with you is better than a dull, plain, predictable straight guy who does?

As far as Natalie was concerned, that was more or less the case. Ever since her first encounter with them, she'd found gay men the liveliest, most fun-loving people she knew. They laughed the most, gossiped the most, danced the most; they were the most guilt-free people she'd ever met, the least inclined to depression, the least likely to be haunted. Of course, as she got to know them, she learned that this wasn't really the case—especially in the wake of Battleship AIDS—but they continued to put on one hell of a show. Whereas virtually all the slow, inconsiderate *heterosexual* men she ever met had paunches and bad table manners and loved to wear disfiguring clothing bearing the hideous logos of inane sports franchises. It was only in the gay community that you could find the kind of man who made a dashing, dazzling, heterosexual icon like Richard Gere look dime-a-dozen.

Peter, for one.

She first met him when he was dating a friend of hers, Will Hammond. Will was extremely theatrical—a stockbroker by day, he threw off the shackles of respectability at night and gloried in the kind of effeminate behavior her gay friends referred to as "nelly." He was devastatingly handsome, however, and Natalie loved being seen with him; and even though he ruined the ruggedness of his cigarette-ad looks whenever he opened his mouth, she put up with him because he was such a nonstop riot. He was like Oscar Wilde crossed with Margo Channing—his tongue should've been registered as a deadly weapon.

When he waltzed into Roscoe's one night, displaying Peter like a hunting trophy, she knew right away that it was a mismatch. Peter was boyish, quiet, and just the tiniest bit vulgar; Will was loud, jaded, and excessively refined. She watched as Peter recoiled from the sarcastic jibes Will tossed at his intimates, to their great delight. Feeling pity, she took him aside, leaving Will and his cronies to their bitchiness and *grande dame* mannerisms. Peter was transparently grateful; they retired to the alley to do a couple of lines of coke, and when Peter finally smiled—for the first time that night—the full glory of his beauty hit her, and hit her hard. As of that night, Will and Peter were history, and Natalie and Peter started a history of their own, one that had survived nearly a dozen of Peter's subsequent romances.

She knew Peter's family and he knew hers; she'd celebrated two successive birthdays with him, and two Christmases, and two New Year's Eves, and last year they'd taken a week-long holiday together in the Michigan resort town of Saugatuck. Once, when their respective finances were at their worst, they'd even considered moving in together; she was, unfortunately, unable to subvert the sudden flow of free-lance work that restored him to solvency and kept him firmly in his own digs.

Now, however, he seemed farther away than ever. Now he was involved with a man who had derailed him, put him on another philosophical track. He'd gone from being a practicing bacchant to a tireless Promethean; from an epicurean to a stoic; from a hedonist to a Platonist. He'd given up frivolity for discourse, and pleasure for learning. She couldn't reach him anymore. She'd tried gossiping, she'd tried flattery, she'd tried regaling him with jokes and stories, all to no avail. He had his head in the clouds, and lofty clouds they were.

Well, he'd soon come down to earth again. As she made herself a dinner of curried tofu—in atonement for the Ben & Jerry's—she made a vow to stop Lloyd as she had stopped all the other men who had presumed to take Peter from her. But she felt no anguish now, no violent anger at having to act; she still couldn't take that bald little fascist seriously enough. And until she found the well of anger inside her, she knew her actions would mean little.

CHAPTER 13

Peter surprised her with a phone call at nine in the morning. He was clearly distraught; his voice gave him away. She could barely hear him, he was so hushed—"quailed" was the word that came to mind.

"Well, this was the quickest on record," he said, and he attempted a laugh. "Guess I wasn't cut out to be on the ideological front lines."

"You mean it's over with Lloyd?" she asked, not even caring that delight colored her voice.

"It's over with Lloyd," he said. "We had a *huge* fight last night."

Her head dropped back into her pillow and her eyes fell shut; she'd been right all along. He'd never been a threat. Too different, too odd—too far from Peter's usual realm. She was inexpressibly relieved.

"What happened, honey?" she said, full of genuine pity.

"This movie we went to see last night—I picked it out, because I'd heard it was such a big hit in Japan. And, well, it was sort of a comedy about this lady tax collector who gets to the top of the department because she's so ruthless. Sort of a satire on the whole Japanese macho thing, y'know? With this little freckled lady outwitting all the guys. You really end up rooting for her. I really liked the movie and I said so afterward, and Lloyd—well, he just got visibly angry. He said that income tax was a crime that governments commit against their people, and that any film like this that glorified tax collecting and tax collectors was just statist propaganda and should be condemned as such. It just seemed like such a violent reaction against a—well, a kind of charming little film. I said, Oh, come on; y'know—relax, it's only a movie. Well, then he just exploded. Kept saying it's *not* only a movie, that art is important, and that immoral art does its part in maintaining an immoral social order—Christ, I can't even *remember* all the things he said. People on the street were looking at him. And Natalie, I don't know, I just felt he was being silly—I tell you, I liked that movie. I don't care if it was moral, I liked it."

"Of course you did," she said. She was leaping around the room, portable phone in hand.

"He wouldn't even share a taxi home with me. He just hailed his own cab and left me standing on the street corner. I kept calling after him, saying, y'know, Come on, don't act so silly, but he just kept going. I thought he might call during the night or something, or even first thing this morning, once he'd calmed down. But he didn't. And, y'know, I'm pissed off. I don't want to hear from him now. I just want to forget this whole weird episode. Natalie, let's go somewhere today, somewhere far away. Let's take a day trip, just get lost somewhere. Okay?"

"Okay," she said, radiantly happy. "I would absolutely love to."

A few hours later they were strolling down Oak Park Avenue eating ice cream cones. Peter couldn't get over the colors of the trees—"Autumn is such a wild season," he said—or the sheer number of them. He rarely got away from the city, and Oak Park's cleanliness, crispness, and strange homogeneity both attracted and repelled him. "Isn't this where the Stepford Wives live?" he asked Natalie.

The trip hadn't completely distracted him from his failed romance with Lloyd. Every once in a while he'd see something that would inspire him to begin, "Lloyd says," but he'd always catch himself. Natalie noticed the dullness in his eyes, and even though he gave every appearance of having a good time, she knew better.

They stopped at a precocious little tavern and had a beer. "I don't understand you," she told him. "You've been on exactly two dates with this Lloyd guy. You never even slept with him, for God's sake. How does he rate this kind of mourning?"

He shrugged and drew a line with his finger on the frosted beer mug. "I guess it just seemed like such a dirty way to end something that had seemed so clean before," he said. "I feel bad about that. It was a bad ending. Lloyd always went on and on about the primacy of reason in human affairs. But I don't think he was very rational about the way he ended things. It kind of spoils everything that went before."

He's play-acting, she thought, just going through the motions. He just needs a jolt to get him back to his old self. And she knew what kind of jolt would do the trick.

"After you finish your beer, we'll visit my mom," she said.

Sandy Stathis was delighted to see them and practically yanked them in from the front step. "Wonderful to see you both," she said. "Take off your jackets, come in, and get warm." They weren't cold, but they complied. Carmen DeFleur kept sniffing Peter's leg, as though his scent were unique and fascinating.

They followed Sandy into the house, and Natalie was amazed at the change in it. "Mom, everything looks *great*," she said. "You hire a maid or something?"

"Only for a day," she said, taking a chair in the sitting room and inviting her guests to follow suit. "She really did the place proud, didn't she? I had to have it look nice, since there was a social worker coming by to judge me."

"A social worker?" Natalie said. "Oh, my God! What for?"

"Well, you know how upset I've been about the grandchild issue," she said. Natalie rolled her eyes. Sandy turned to Peter and explained, "Calvin and Vera won't be getting pregnant. They're afraid a nuclear holocaust would make a mess of their baby's formative years." Then she turned back to Natalie and continued. "I guess I was feeling sorry for myself, and then I thought, by God, I'm moping when I should be coping! I decided to do something positive, but I didn't know what. Then later I read in the paper about one of the women's groups in town that's started a program where you, well, *adopt* an inner-city child on weekends, and show them that life isn't all gang wars and crack dealers."

"It's not?" muttered Peter, and Natalie surreptitiously punched him in the arm.

"So I joined the group and signed up for the program, and a social worker from some Chicago department of child welfare or something stopped by to okay me—you know, to make sure I wasn't going to be a bad influence. And I got approved. So starting next weekend I've going to have a little black granddaughter from the projects running around."

"Oh, for Christ's sake, Mom," Natalie said. "You don't know what you're getting into! How old is this girl?"

"Eight," she said, picking up a folder from the coffee table. She opened it and showed them a picture of a fairly adorable young girl with a reluctant smile and distrusting eyes, and about seven pigtails of varying lengths. "Her name is Darnita Reynolds. Her parents are both dead and she lives with her older sister, but the older sister is only seventeen herself and has a baby, and would love to get Darnita out of the house on weekends. Isn't it exciting?"

Natalie had grave misgivings about this plan. "Mom," she said, lowering her voice to show how serious she was, "I know you watch TV a lot and think you know what goes on in the inner city, but I can assure you, you don't. I mean, this kid could be an addict herself, or a thief, or a—God, I don't even know what! You can't tell what anyone brought up in that environment is capable of doing. At eight years old she could be a pretty big girl. She could overpower you and hurt you, did you ever think of that? She could get up in the middle of the night and sneak into your room and pl—"

"Oh, for heaven's sake, Natalie, you're being morbid!"

"Yes, for heaven's sake, Natalie," Peter echoed, teasing her.

"For your information," Sandy said, jabbing her finger in

the air for emphasis, "I'm perfectly prepared for her to be a drug addict or a thief or an abused child, or even to have mental problems. Why do you think I signed up for this program? I'm sitting here in my big Oak Park home with my entire life in order, and I think to myself, I'm a success; I've pretty much lived the life I wanted to live. Now my labors are over, with you and Calvin grown up and on your own—and certainly neither one of you ever calls me for advice—so isn't it time I taught somebody else how to achieve what she wants to achieve in life? Isn't it only right that some poor, underprivileged, and perhaps deeply troubled young girl should be pulled away from her poisonous environment and given the benefit of all I have to teach? I don't care if she deals heroin and carries a switch-blade, Natalie. I'm ready for her. I'll make a lady out of her if it kills me. But anyway, enough about me. How are you two doing? Peter, darling, we didn't get a chance to talk at the wedding. It's been months since we've had a chat, hasn't it? Probably since your last haircut. You look healthy and happy! You *are* staying to dinner, aren't you? I'm uncanning a ham."

Natalie opened her mouth to decline the invitation, but Peter spoke up: "I'd love to stay, Mrs. Stathis. We've got a lot of catching up to do."

Natalie felt like dying.

Sandy was unbearable during dinner. She was so happy to have Natalie at her table again that she broke out champagne, and that most magical of liquids succeeded in loosening a tongue already looser than it should be. Over mashed potatoes she turned to Peter and said, "Natalie tells me you've been unlucky in your romantic life. You've obviously never had the experience of loving a really good woman."

"I certainly haven't," said Peter merrily, and Natalie kicked him under the table.

"Oh, that's awful! But I want to caution you, don't fall in love just for the sake of it. One day you'll have a rude awakening, like I did. Natalie's father, Warren—God rest his soul—I married him because I fancied myself in love with him. What I was really in love with was the idea of being in love. Well, of course it was a disaster. It was like being in prison. Six months after the wedding I would've done anything to divorce him, but in those days divorce was a scandal—hard to imagine today, but it's true. So I had to grit my teeth and just endure it. Then, about a year later, Warren went out with his friends to shoot some deer, but the only thing that got shot was Warren. Suddenly I was free. I was a widow, with a baby in my arms and another one on the way, but I wasn't afraid, I was eager to move on. I resolved never to make the same mistake again. I vowed I'd marry for true love next time. And I did; I met Natalie's stepfather, Max, whom I adored, which was lucky for him because if I hadn't adored him I'd probably have killed him. He lied to me, he cheated on me, he stole money from me—but every now and then he'd bring me flowers and flash that roguish grin, and I'd melt. True love sails over a lot of inconsistencies, you know."

Peter looked strangely serious. "I believe it."

"We were an odd couple, but we lasted. Right up till the day he died, just a few years ago. Cancer of the pancreas." Her eyes started to mist, and Natalie turned scarlet with mortification. "You'd think I'd have wished the old dog dead, the way he treated me, but to this day I don't know how I get through a night without him. And you know what? At the end, he only wanted me in the room with him. Only me. Just knowing that gives me the courage to go on."

Peter, who'd had more than his share of the champagne, suddenly astonished everyone by bursting into hysterical sobs.

Both mother and daughter leapt from their chairs and ran to him. "Are you all right, honey?" Natalie cried, hugging his shoulders. "Mom, look—you've upset him! How could you?"

"Such a sensitive boy!" cooed Sandy, patting his head. "Oh, isn't he a darling?"

After a moment, Peter managed to compose himself. He dried his tears and apologized profusely. "*Jesus*, I'm sorry," he said. "I don't know what came over me. That was just such an incredibly sad story, Mrs. Stathis. I guess I just lost it."

She sat down again and beamed at him. "I know, dear. I know it's sad. And it's so wonderful to have someone recognize that. My own children don't see how sad it is. You've made me very happy, Peter. I feel a little less alone now."

Natalie sat and played with her food, wondering if there

was anywhere in the world she could take Peter that someone wouldn't try to steal him from her.

"What on earth happened to you in there?" Natalie asked him the moment they left the house.

"I just got upset by your mom's story," he said, looking embarrassed. "I couldn't help thinking how sad it was."

"You weren't thinking about anything else, then?"

"No, no."

The train ride back to the city passed in silence. Peter sat with his head resting against the window and stared at the landscape as it swept by. Natalie felt uneasy, as if there were something just beyond the range of her vision, something that darted away every time she tried to focus on it.

She accompanied Peter to his apartment; he didn't object. Her heart began to race. He'd had an emotional day, plus a catharsis at her mother's dinner table—complete with a shower of cleansing tears. Might he be open to the possibility of some gentle sex tonight? If it was ever going to happen between them it would happen tonight. After all, they'd slept together, platonically, many times; they were no strangers to each other's bodies. That barrier was already down. She had a feeling that if she pressed her advantage, she could easily lead him to the next plateau. He was like a child tonight, fragile and manipulable.

He unlocked his apartment door and let her in. The second before he turned on the lights, she saw his answering machine blinking. No, she thought; no, no, no.

He hadn't seen it, and the lights were on now, rendering it less obvious. She grabbed his arm and led him into the kitchen. "Got anything else to drink, baby?" she asked him. She opened the refrigerator, still hanging on to him with one hand.

He smiled. "Come on, Natalie. It's Sunday night. I have to be at work in the morning. You have what you want, but I'm not drinking anything else."

She shut the refrigerator and faced him. "Poor sweetheart," she said. "Bet you could use a nice back rub."

He raised his eyebrows. "I wouldn't say no to that."

She was thrilled by her success. "You just go and take off

your clothes, doll. I'll be right behind you." After I erase that message, she added to herself.

"Okay." He edged away from her and out of the kitchen; she only released his hand when their arms had stretched to their limit.

From the kitchen she watched him as he walked to the bedroom, scratching his nape. At the last second, however, he snapped his fingers, then backed up and peered at the answering machine.

Shit, thought Natalie. Christ almighty fucking *shit.*

He rewound the tape and played it.

"Peter, this is Lloyd," the tinny recording began.

Natalie lifted her hands to her face and erupted into tears.

"I've spent the whole day trying to tell myself that I was right to do what I did," Lloyd continued; "but I couldn't convince myself. And I'm a pretty convincing guy." A pause. "Then I tried being honest with myself, and I realized that that whole scene I created was just a way of dealing with my fear of becoming involved with you. Because I care about you such a—such a great deal." Another pause. "Well, the thing is, I'm sorry, and I expect you to forgive me." A moment of nervous laughter. "As a matter of fact, I'm going to insist on it. I can guarantee you, I won't behave in a psychotic manner again. I think you can believe that. For the record . . ." Another pause. "For the record, I think you're—I don't know how to put this." A longer pause, then his voice came back with a little crack in it, as though he were moved by emotion. "I think you're beyond ideology. I think you're beyond morality. I think—I think you're a miracle." Click. The hiss of blank tape.

Peter had his hand on his mouth now. He stood for what seemed a very long time, then heaved a long sigh; it wavered as it came out of his mouth.

He turned and approached the kitchen. Natalie turned her head to try to prevent him from seeing her tear-swollen eyes.

"Did you hear that?" he asked her, his voice barely audible.

"Yes."

He took a step forward, then stopped. "I'm going to go and see him now."

"Oh."

He backed up and grabbed his jacket. "Lock up before you leave, okay?"

"Yes."

He slipped out the door and was gone.

She stood in his kitchen, listening to the hiss of the tape and to the pounding of her own heart, and the world was very still in spite of that; terribly still, as if awaiting a storm that was only moments away.

Finally, Natalie believed it. She believed that Lloyd was a threat, the worst ever.

She didn't go home that night; she crawled into Peter's bed and lay there, empty of feeling. Still no anger. She wondered where it could be. Didn't she love him? Then why didn't she feel the violent rage she always felt when someone new came into his life?

She wondered about it for hours, her head on his pillow, her eyes wide. Eventually she determined a reason: She couldn't feel anger because, unlike Peter's other lovers, Lloyd hadn't taken Peter away—instead, he had changed him utterly. The Peter she loved wasn't involved with a new man; the Peter she loved did not exist at the moment. He'd been battered into a new shape by Lloyd's constant hammering.

She fell asleep wondering how she could bring him back again. It was so important that she bring him back again. She might have no clear idea of the life she wanted to lead with him, but life without him was inconceivable—a vast expanse of misery, stretching on until her death. And if a romance with Peter sometimes seemed just as inconceivable, well—tough. She was going for broke. It was either the peak, the summit, the acme —meaning Peter—or nothing. Whatever kind of love they could share—even the flimsiest, the least satisfying—even if she had to utterly debase and humiliate herself to get it, that's what she wanted. He was her highest value, the full realization of her image of perfect humanity, perfect masculinity.

Except for that one little area, of course. That one little, damnable, excruciating, unshakable area.

At the crack of dawn, she got up, dressed, and left Peter's apartment, not wanting to be there when he arrived to change for work.

A few hours later, he phoned her from his office. "Lloyd and I made love last night." That was how he put it. Not "Lloyd and I slept together" or "Lloyd and I had sex." It jolted her. She'd never heard him speak of "making love" to anyone.

"It was—it was—well, words fail me." Words had never failed him before. "It was like the fulfillment of something I didn't even know I'd been dreaming of." He'd never spoken of fulfillment before. He'd never spoken of dreams before. "Such incredible intimacy. Such a powerful sense of, I guess I'd call it rightness." He'd never spoken of those things before. "I'm in love with him." He'd said that before, but now his tone was that of a different man.

"Oh," she said, her voice dead of expression. "Congratulations."

"I told Lloyd that you were with me when I played his message. I told him that you were as moved by it as I was, that it actually made you cry. He was really touched by that; he hadn't realized how close we are. He wants to have you over. To his place, for dinner, just the three of us. He says he's a good cook. Guess we'll find out together. Friday okay?"

"Okay," she said.

"You sound funny. You all right?"

"Fine," she said. "You'd better get back to work."

"I know. Well—thanks for listening, doll. I love you."

"You're welcome."

She hung up.

Still no anger. She felt dead of all feeling. Where was it hiding?

She walked through her week like a zombie. She smiled at

no one. On Wednesday, the head of the office where she was working called her agency and asked them not to send her back; she'd given the other employees "the creeps."

She ate lightly all week. She hadn't any hunger. Nothing so strong as an appetite or a desire was in her. Her meals were joyless. Her sleep was dreamless. She watched television without laughing. She listened to music without pleasure.

On Thursday night, she found her anger.

She was at the Evergreen supermarket, picking up a few staples. Milk, bread, nothing colorful or exciting. She didn't check the prices; she didn't care. She would pay whatever the clerk told her she owed. Nothing mattered.

She heard someone call her name. "Natalie!" It was Peter's voice.

She turned. It had sounded as though he'd been directly behind her, but she didn't see him there.

"Hey! *Natalie!*"

Wait—*that* was him. The man she'd looked right past.

He came up to her and kissed her; she stared at him in horror. She thought she might be sick.

His hair was gone. He'd gotten a haircut. There was almost nothing left. Nothing to shake the water out of, nothing to let blow in the wind, nothing to tousle, nothing for her to run her fingers through. He'd gotten a haircut.

He noticed her shocked expression and self-consciously ran his hand over his scalp. "Oh, you noticed, huh? It was supposed to be a surprise when you came to dinner tomorrow night. I know, I know—it's a little more boot camp than I wanted, but it'll grow. Lloyd likes it this way."

"Th—that's—why you did it?" she said, her voice shrill. "For *Lloyd*?"

"Well, mostly. He didn't like the long-hair look. Tell you the truth, I was getting a little tired of it myself."

She was trembling. Tears popped out of her eyes. "My God—I'm really losing you, aren't I?" she said.

He grimaced. "Oh, come on. It's just a haircut."

She shook her head. "It's more than that. You're gone, totally gone. Everything I once—" Her voice was in danger of breaking; she forced herself to stop. "Peter, you have to excuse me. I can't talk right now. I'm too upset."

"I don't understand you," he said, annoyed. "Why does everything have to be so fucking dramatic?"

She felt like the earth was moving. "Excuse me," she said. She left her cartful of groceries and walked out of the store. She went directly home and crawled into her bed. A few minutes later, her doorbell sounded. Peter, no doubt. She ignored the insistent ringing and eventually it ceased.

She quaked with anger. Her bed shook. Her teeth gritted against each other. An hour passed. Two. Her telephone rang and she wouldn't answer it. Soon the sun disappeared and she lay in darkness, clutching her pillow. She looked balefully out her window at the starless sky. Her bed shook.

CHAPTER 15

When she awakened the next morning, the anger that had been so hot the night before had become a cold, deadly thing. Now she could set about subverting Peter's romance with Lloyd in earnest. But so much time had been lost, and they had gotten so far. And worst of all, she had no plan.

She knew what she had to do first. She called Peter at the office and said, "Honey, I'm so sorry about last night. Do me a favor and pretend it never happened."

"What never happened?" he said happily, glad to put it behind them.

"Thanks so much, sweetie. See you tonight. What's Lloyd's address?"

Lloyd, it turned out, owned his own house in a North Side neighborhood called Ravenswood Manor. Natalie had a second cousin who'd once lived there; it was the most domestic, and one of the most charming, city neighborhoods she'd ever seen. It seemed not to have changed since the forties.

The perfect place for two gay men to settle down, she thought. They could be urban pioneers without too great a risk to life and limb. Change the complexion of the neighborhood without making too many waves. Get a dog, maybe two—Peter had always wanted an Irish setter.

Well, she knew better than to try to spook Lloyd by implying that Peter wanted to move in with him. Maybe that worked with Morris and his ilk, but Lloyd would probably pick up the phone and call a moving van.

Her stomach fluttered all day; on the job, at lunch, on the way home. So much depended on her performance tonight. If only she had an idea of what to do!

Finally, her nerves were so bad she thought they might debilitate her.

Time to get plowed, she decided.

She got off the bus and went straight to Bulldog Road, where she ordered a Bacardi on the rocks. There were a few men in the bar already, the hard-core, after-work crowd that drank like there was no tomorrow.

She took a swallow of her drink and looked around, hoping to see no one she knew.

Oh, my God. There was someone. Will Hammond. The man she'd stolen Peter from, more than two years before. He'd never forgiven her for that.

He saw her, and a positively evil leer stretched across his face. He got up from his stool and made his way over to her.

"Natalie, you horrible thing, haven't seen you in *ages*," he said, kissing her on the cheek.

"Will, you pig, you're as handsome as ever," she said, smiling brilliantly. "How do you manage it, with all the naughty things I hear you've been doing? There must be a really scary portrait of you in your attic or something."

"Bitch," he said, and he took the stool next to hers. She wished she were anywhere on earth but here. An Indian leper colony, a Soviet gulag—*anywhere.*

"So," said Will, folding his hands over his knee. "Where's your playmate, Peter?"

She knew instinctively not to lie to him; he might already know the truth, and he'd leap on her like a lioness on a wounded gazelle. "Oh," she said, "Peter's got himself a new man."

"A serious man?"

"A *very* serious man."

"As in capital L?"

"As in capital L."

He raised an eyebrow. "That's what I've been hearing. But I haven't seen them out together."

"It's a relatively new thing. Just one week so far."

"One week and it's capital L?" he said, pretending shock. "Well, I confess myself appalled! The crisis of our age, Natalie, is that people have no moderation. They spend years avoiding commitment, then once they weary of that they get married over a handshake. It shows a want of sense."

"I know, I know."

"What's she like? The new Mrs. Leland, I mean."

Natalie flinched. Among the things she hated worst about Will was his insistent use of the feminine mode when discussing his gay brethren. "Well," she said, "he's a bit of an intellectual. Not like any intellectual you ever met before, though. Not a socialist or anything. Just the opposite. He's a—what do you call them?—a libertarian. It's pretty much all he talks about. Government and philosophy, stuff like that. Free enterprise."

He put his hand on her shoulder. "Thank *God* you've warned me!" he said. "What if I'd gotten curious and invited them to a dinner party? Can you *imagine*? My intimates gathered to frolic and play, and the new Mrs. Leland wanting to discuss the Consumer Price Index and the Joint Chiefs of Staff! I'll be sure to steer clear of *that* one. Tell me more!" He wriggled in his seat, enjoying this.

"Well—he's not much to look at. Balding. Doesn't know how to dress."

"Good heavens! What does Peter *see* in her?"

She twirled her glass, not wanting to meet his eyes. "Be honest with you, I don't know. I suspect he's flattered that Lloyd treats him as an equal. An equal mind, I mean. You know, almost everyone else has always treated him like a hunk of meat."

"But darling, that's the way we *all* treat each other—and Peter was never any different, I can tell you that from firsthand experience!"

She shrugged. "Well, then, I don't know what the appeal is."

Will sighed and raised an eyebrow. "And how is poor Natalie taking all of this?"

"It's a little sobering. Peter and I were just talking about it the other day. Growing older and becoming more responsible, you know. Settling down. He's got a full-time job now, too. We still love each other dearly, but I think our future's going to be less dazzling than our past."

"So, you don't feel left out in the cold at all?"

"What? Oh, no. Matter of fact, I'm having dinner with them tonight."

"How kind of them! I just hope they didn't invite you out of pity."

Her face flushed with anger. Don't get defensive, she warned herself; that's what he wants. "I don't *think* I'm an object of pity, Will," she said in carefully modulated tones. She finished her drink in one gulp.

"But my dear, of *course* you are! There's that old song, isn't there?"

She faked a smile. "Whatever you say. Must run. Love to all the boys."

She picked up her purse and started to leave, but from behind her she heard him begin to sing. She recognized it as an old Judy Garland tune, but he had changed the words:

Ever since this world began
There is nothing sadder than
A one-fag fag hag
Looking for the fag that got away

She stopped dead in her tracks. The world seemed to eddy about her head. She thought she might faint from fury.

Don't turn around! she warned herself. Just keep going! Keep walking out the door! He's dying for you to turn and fight! It's what he wants more than anything!

She wouldn't fight, then; but she couldn't just leave, she couldn't let him insult her with impunity.

She turned and faced him. She let the tears in her eyes flow freely.

"Well, you've done it," she said. "You wanted to hurt me, and you've done it."

He was taken aback by this response—it was the last thing he'd expected from her. He tried to cover his embarrassment with bravado. He clapped his hands and said, "Magnificent performance! Give that woman an Oscar!" Other patrons in the bar were watching them now.

Natalie sighed. "You're an intelligent man," she said. "You're good-looking, you're successful. Surely you can find something to make you happy besides humiliating people who have less than you. People who have nothing left." Tears were streaming down her cheeks now.

He seemed about to reply, but she'd taken the wind out of his sails. He turned away from her and ordered another drink. He looked positively sheepish.

She left the bar weeping.

Fag hag. *Fag hag!* It rang in her ears as she walked home; it was the only refrain she heard on the street—she imagined everybody whispering it as she passed.

Fag hag! She'd heard that label applied, derisively, to other women; not to her. Yet what else could she be? Her entire life was devoted to the company of gay men who didn't care a damn for her—who found her an amusing diversion, a sparkle of color in their monochromatic, all-male realm. Was she as pathetic as that? An anomaly? A figure of fun? A silly indulgence, of no importance—not beneath notice, but not much above it, either?

No, no—there was Peter. He had lifted her above that. Her love for him, and his for her, were not of that kind. Their love was real; it was genuine; it existed on a plane above the shallow revels of persons like Will and his hysterical "intimates."

Peter had been her salvation from that kind of life. She saw him as her salvation still. He was her bedrock; he was her religion. She must have him back, or be lost again—have him back, or be prey to the pity and contempt of the world. Will had shown her that.

She arrived home, at long last. It had been a doleful trek.

She changed her clothes for dinner. She would dress down; she would not sparkle tonight like some Roman candle; she would not be a "fag hag" for Peter and Lloyd. She would be herself. She would be who she was. And she would show Peter what Lloyd was, some way, somehow. No more subterfuge. No more tricks or stratagems. Now it was head to head, Lloyd versus Natalie, in the arena of combat, with Peter in the box, his thumb at the ready. Up?—Down?

CHAPTER 16

The cab left her standing on the sidewalk in front of Lloyd's domain. It was an old prewar row house with an Art Deco door but no other discernible emblem of style. It rose two stories, and the trees around it were tall and riotous with color. She thought it looked homey and peaceful. A nest for two birds, neither of which could lay eggs.

It was getting dark, and there were lights on in the house. She carried a paper sack with a chilled Chardonnay in it. She went up the walk to the house and rang the doorbell.

Now we meet as enemies, she said to herself.

But in fact, it was Peter who answered the door—shaven-scalped Peter. It was like a fresh wound to see him this way again.

"Hi!" he said brightly, opening the door wide to admit her. "Come on in! Good to see you, honey!" Everything he said sounded false.

The house was warm. She took off her jacket and handed it to him. She could smell something cooking.

"Lloyd's in the kitchen," Peter said, hanging up her jacket

in the vestibule closet. "We're having catfish; can you smell it? Lloyd says catfish is a better buy than chicken, 'cause it's richer in protein. Also some brown rice and broccoli. I've gotten Lloyd into low-fat eating. He says he never considered that there was no mind-body dichotomy until he met me."

I'll just bet he said that, thought Natalie. She handed him the Chardonnay. "Here."

He took it and peeked into the bag. "Oh, honey, *thanks*," he said, a bit fulsomely. "Wonderful of you!" He kissed her. "Come on, I'll open this. You can meet Lloyd again. You only met him the once, right?"

She nodded. He led her to the kitchen at the back of the house. "You know, I've never seen you in blue jeans before," he said as they walked. "Never even knew you owned a pair. You look kind of different tonight—jeans, your hair. Like a hippie or something."

You'll regret that, she thought, her anger clattering around in her brain like a wind-up toy gone berserk.

The house was sparsely furnished; the decorations were minimal. But everything was quality—an oak writing desk, a rosewood dinner table. Venetian blinds hung in every window, and a series of framed black-and-white photographs adorned the hallway—all portraits, some of children, some of wizened ancients, many in between. "Lloyd likes faces," Peter explained.

In the dining room there was a threadbare Oriental rug. For a homosexual's house, this was all surprisingly masculine. Not a tassel or a curtain in sight.

When she saw Lloyd in the kitchen, he was squatting down before the oven, checking the catfish. When he stood and faced her and smiled, she was astonished to find him attractive; he was kind of like a balding Charlie Sheen. Suddenly she remembered that she'd been attracted to him on first sight, at the wedding. Her subsequent hatred for him must have rendered him daily more ugly in her memory.

He and Peter were both wearing blue jeans and sweatshirts with the sleeves rolled up. They already looked like they'd been married a dozen years.

Lloyd stuck his hand out and said, "Hi, Natalie. Glad you could come." His smile was charming.

"Thanks," she said. They stood there, nothing else to say.

"Natalie brought wine," said Peter, making a deal of noise with the paper sack as he got it out. Natalie turned and looked around the kitchen; clean, bright, filled with implements.

"Thanks, Natalie," he said. Then he turned to Peter. "Why don't you open it up, hon? Keep us occupied till dinner's ready."

Peter opened the bottle and poured three glasses, keeping up a mindless stream of chatter just to fill the silence. He gave a glass to Lloyd and one to Natalie, then held up his own and said, "To friendship."

"To friendship," said Lloyd.

Natalie looked at them and said, "Can I have an ice cube in mine?"

His toast spoiled, Peter seemed lost and embarrassed for a moment, then went to the freezer and got Natalie an ice cube. He plunked it in her wine and said, "Come on, I'll give you the tour."

She'd already seen most of the ground floor, so they went upstairs. The bathroom was large and old-fashioned, with enormous faucet knobs and pastel-green tiling. The guest room was furnished with a futon and an old dresser. The master bedroom contained an antique wardrobe and a king-size platform bed. She stared at that bed as though, through force of will, she might set it on fire.

Downstairs again, she noticed all the books in the house. In every room, even the kitchen, they were present—on shelves and piled in corners and sitting on windowsills and resting on tables. She read some of the bindings: *Wealth of Nations*, Adam Smith. *Democracy in America*, Alexis de Tocqueville. *Two Treatises on Government*, John Locke. Not a movie-star biography to be seen.

"Lloyd likes his books," she said in the sarcastically understated way they always employed when discussing fanatics.

"Yeah," Peter agreed obliviously, "he's a constant reader. He reads everything and everywhere. He reads at breakfast, he reads in the john, he even reads in the car, at stoplights. Probably why he's so brilliant. Come on, I'll show you the basement next."

The basement was small, but for its space was the most remarkable part of the house. Half of it was taken up by an enormous gun rack with what Natalie was sure must be every conceivable kind of firearm; the other half was filled with shelves of bottled water, canned foods, medical kits, and the like.

"Lloyd's a survivalist," said Peter in the exact same tone he might have said, Lloyd's a Capricorn.

Natalie's roving, incoherent anger suddenly rallied and focused on this one point. This would be it; this would be Lloyd's undoing, or nothing would.

"A survivalist?" she said. "Peter—wait!" He had started up the stairs again. "Get down here. A *survivalist*?"

He turned on the stairs, and she looked up at him—it was just his silhouette, the light behind him half-blinding her.

"Yes," he said. "You know, someone who believes he's responsible for his own safety in a disaster."

"I've read about survivalists," she said. "They're nut cases, Peter! Haven't you heard? They're just waiting for the bomb to drop so they can take over!"

He laughed. She wished she could see his face. "Natalie, there are as many smear campaigns against survivalists as there are against homosexuals," he said. "Lloyd can explain it all better than I can. Come on upstairs."

She followed him, panting with excitement. I've got him, she exulted; this has *got* to be the thing that puts him under! A survivalist! Oh, thank you, God! Thank you, Jesus!

But over dinner, seated at the rosewood table with candles burning and the catfish giving off a light and appetizing scent, Lloyd launched into an eloquent defense that left Natalie baffled as to how to reply.

"There's no end to the variety of disasters that can befall a civilized society," he said. "A natural calamity, like a fire or a hurricane, could destroy half the city, disrupting trade and communications. A social upheaval, like a riot, could cut off entire communities from goods and services. An economic depression can suddenly skyrocket the price of food above the average man's budget. Even something as mundane as a heavy snowfall can isolate a neighborhood for days. Forget nuclear disaster, Natalie; that doesn't concern me. If the Soviets ever decide to launch their missiles at us, one of them's going to have Chicago's name on it—we'll all probably be disintegrated in the first flash. What concerns me is my survival in cases like the ones I've just mentioned—examples of which are already on the books. I'm prepared for them to happen again. Are you?"

She smiled, as though amused by his weirdness. "Kind of a gloomy way to go through life, isn't it?" she said. "Expecting the worst? Seems to me kind of paranoid."

"Not *expecting* the worst," he said; "*preparing* for it. There's a difference. It's just another kind of insurance, really. If I crack up my car and someone else's, I've got insurance to get me through that. Doesn't mean I'm expecting it to happen. If I become disabled with my mortgage unpaid, I've got insurance for that. Doesn't mean I'd like that to happen. If I get cancer and need to be hospitalized—well, you get the idea. Same principle here. If something—anything—happens that deprives me of the benefits of civilization, I'll be able to survive a few weeks until order is restored. I'll also be able to protect myself against bandits, thieves, killers, whatever, and if time passes and nothing changes, I can go out and hunt my own food. Now, I don't want to see this happen. I like civilization. I like popcorn and listening to the radio and getting pills to cure me when I'm sick. But the worst has happened before—history is full of examples. I think it's foolish not to prepare."

"That's what we've got a government for," Natalie said, desperate to pin him down. "They've got measures they can take when something bad happens. We're not a tribe of savages, you know. We've got a central authority to take care of these things."

He looked at her with benign condescension; it made her want to strike him. "You can trust the government if you want," he said. "But I look at it and I see a corrupt, top-heavy, inefficient dinosaur—a government that can't balance a budget or attract new business or even institute a waste-management program without screwing it up, that can't prevent gangs from ripping the city apart, or people from starving to death on the mayor's doorstep. Well, that's not a government I'm going to depend on for my safety in the event of a municipal or national emergency. I'm a man, Natalie; I'm capable, I'm intelligent, I'm strong, I've got my wits. There's no reason I should *want* to depend on anyone but myself."

Peter stared at Lloyd with unabashed adoration as he made this declaration.

"Well, what about the people who *can't* take care of themselves in a disaster?" she snarled. "What are *they* supposed to do? You're pretty heartless of their account, if you ask me."

"Natalie, I can't buy medical insurance for everyone in case they get cancer. I can't buy car insurance for everyone in case they get into a wreck. And I can't buy supplies and guns for the entire world in case there's a crisis situation someday. And what are you implying by that question—that I should make myself helpless and vulnerable, just because some people are always going to be? Are you implying that the right thing to do is suffer and starve with everyone else, if it comes to that?"

"No, I—I—" Goddamn him, he was slippery! "I just want to know—what *about* those people? If you ran the world, how would you save them?"

"I don't want to run the world, Natalie—precisely because I *don't* have an answer for that. Power doesn't interest me. But, to answer your question, I think, since government has proven itself so inept, it's up to private, philanthropic organizations to take care of society's disadvantaged and disenfranchised."

"And what are you doing to help them? The organizations, I mean."

He raised an eyebrow. "Well. *Touché*. I guess I don't do a lot." He turned to Peter. "Natalie's very incisive." He turned back to her. "I've always said we should all look out for our own backyards, Natalie, but by that I mean our extended backyards, our communities. It's in our own interest to do so. You're absolutely right, I should get more involved in community projects to help the down-and-out. Maybe I could set up a crisis shelter or something, so in the case of a disaster they'd have someplace to go, where there was food and water and medical supplies. A kind of survivalist refuge for the homeless. What do you think of that, Peter?"

"I think it sounds great!"

"How'd you get into all this stuff, anyway?" she asked him, her head aching. Find something! she told herself in a panic. Find something fast! You're losing! You're losing!

He sat back in his chair. "Same as everybody else, I guess.

I read Ayn Rand as a boy. That pretty much launched me into individualism and atheism and antistatism. From there, I discovered libertarian politics, which kind of used some of Rand's ideas as a springboard. And from libertarianism I got into survivalism. My life's been a chain of 'isms,' I guess, but I think they're good 'isms.' " He laughed at that. "But, yeah, it definitely goes back to reading Ayn Rand when I was fifteen or so."

She stared at him, utterly befuddled. "How did reading Ayn Rand ever get you into that political stuff?"

He knit his brow. "What do you mean?"

"I mean, what's she got to do with government and individualism? Isn't she just, y'know—a pornographer?" She was pretending moral outrage now. I've got him! she thought. It's not much, but it's a flaw in his I'm-so-above-it-all posturing! I've got the fatuous, pretentious pig!

There was a long pause. "I've heard Ayn Rand accused of being a lot of things," said Lloyd, "but never a pornographer."

She turned to Peter in triumph. "Remember when we flipped through one of her books in B. Dalton's that day? Just for kicks? And it was all this pie-in-the-sky language for fucking?"

"No," said Peter, bewildered.

"Oh, for *Christ's* sake, come *on*, we *did*," she said, panicking.

Lloyd said, "I haven't read her in years, but I don't recall th—"

"Wait!" Peter cried. "I know what she means! She's thinking of Anaïs Nin! She's getting Ayn Rand mixed up with Anaïs Nin!"

Lloyd smiled and put his hand to his mouth, and Peter tried to keep down a chuckle; but a moment later they both burst into simultaneous gales of laughter. Peter's eyes brimmed with tears, and Lloyd slid his chair back and dropped his head between his legs; his back quaked with the force of his laughter.

And Natalie, her literary greenery now the object of high hilarity, sat enveloped in her defeat, without a clue as to how to act; and there was only one thing on her mind. It was a new concept for her, something she had never before embraced, not in two years of reducing herself to petty manipulations to end Peter's romances. It was a concept of a much higher caste, and of deeper circumstance; and as she sat, mortified, buffeted by the laughter of the man she loved and the man he loved in turn, it swelled in size, growing from a concept to a motivation. And she was able, then, to give it a name, and to say that name to herself, and to relish that name:

Revenge.

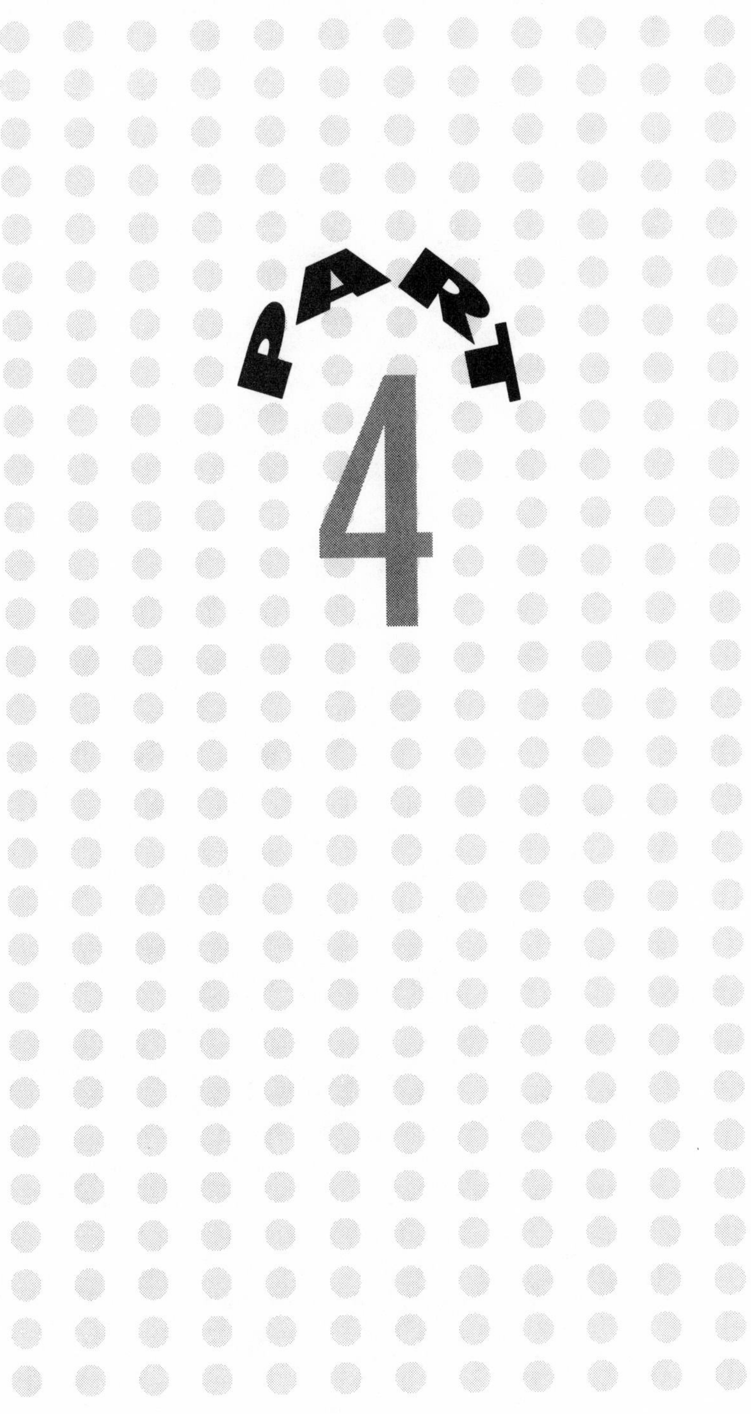

PART 4

Natalie's phone rang the next morning, but she was afraid it was Peter calling to get her impression of Lloyd the Wonderful, so she let her machine take it. When she got out of bed an hour later, she played the message.

"Natalie, it's your mother," it said. "Get over here as soon as possible. I need help with Darnita or I'll lose my mind."

She felt her heart lurch. Did this girl have her mother at gunpoint or something? She threw on some clothes, raced outside, and hopped a cab.

Twenty-five minutes later she was banging on Sandy Stathis's front door. In her haste to leave, she'd forgotten her key.

Sandy answered the door, looking like she was at her wits' end. "Oh, my God, Natalie—thank you for coming!" She hugged her.

"Mom, what is it? Where's the kid?" She stepped inside and removed her jacket.

"She's in the next room playing with Carmen DeFleur."

"What's wrong with her?"

Sandy put her hand to her forehead. "She's a little angel,

is what's wrong with her. Speaks when she's spoken to. Reads books. Looked at my crystal cabinet and recognized Waterford when she saw it. Wants to see my good china. Honey, this girl is from the projects! I thought she was going to be a disaster! I thought I could spend my autumn giving her 'tough love' like on TV! Then I could go on the Oprah show with her and everyone would think I was a saint. And what happens? They send me a tiny, black Tricia Nixon. I try to get her to tell me what it's like living in the midst of death and terror, and she just *stares* at me like I'm from Mars. Honey, I don't have the slightest idea what to do with her! I've been watching her play with the dog for an hour now, totally stumped. And I've invited Greta Ledbetter over for tea this afternoon to see how I'm playing Henry Higgins; I told her I had a girl from the projects come to me to learn to be a lady. I know I shouldn't have lied, but I told her I'd met Darnita already and that I had my work cut out for me. There's no way she's going to believe I've made this much progress already." She clutched Natalie's shoulder. "Honey, you have to help me teach this child some bad manners by teatime!"

Natalie chuckled. "Mom, you're a trip."

She went into the TV lounge and found the tiny girl, in a yellow *faux* chiffon dress and ankle socks, sitting on the floor with Carmen DeFleur. They were tugging a rawhide bone back and forth. "Hi, there," said Natalie.

"Hello," said the girl. "I'm Darnita."

"I'm Natalie." She squatted down. "Want to play Candyland?"

"What's that?" Her eyes were big and alert; she was beautiful and innocent. All of Natalie's fears about her evaporated.

"It's a game. I've got it in my old closet somewhere. I'll go get it, okay?"

"Okay."

She left the lounge and started for the stairs. Sandy was there waiting for her. "Well? Well?" she stage-whispered. "What's she doing now?"

"Smoking crack," said Natalie.

"Don't you make fun!" she scolded. "She isn't really, is she?"

"Mom—Christ!" Natalie said, laughing.

A few minutes later, Natalie had set up the Candyland board

and even persuaded her mother to play along. Darnita enjoyed it so much that she couldn't stop giggling, and the sound of her laughter was like an elfin machine gun.

"She's very cute," said Sandy later, after Darnita had gone down for a nap.

"Yes," said Natalie, "but a little too old for Candyland. She grasped it right away. What is she, eight? You can move her up to more challenging games. Also, she's the perfect age for a jigsaw puzzle. What books was she reading?"

"She found some of your old ones. All those etiquette books I used to give you in vain."

"Fine. Let her find her own level, Mom. That's really what she's here for. What you have to offer, more than anything, is your home and your example. Just relax and enjoy her and let her take everything in."

"She's really *very* cute," said Sandy. "If she'd say the *f* word in front of Greta Ledbetter, she'd be perfect."

Natalie shook her head and sighed in resignation.

"You're good with children, darling," Sandy continued. "You really ought to have some someday. You're not getting any younger. How are things progressing with Peter?"

Immediately, Natalie's face fell into a scowl. "You'll be glad to know I've finally given up on him."

"Oh, no! Say you haven't!"

"What do you mean? You've been after me to dump him ever since you heard he wasn't in love with me!"

"Yes, but that was before I made him cry. That was such a touching thing for him to do. I kept thinking, Look at that sensitive boy—what a nice son-in-law he'd make!"

"Well, don't count on it, Mom." She paused. "He's gay."

Sandy stared at her for a moment, uncomprehending. "Pardon?"

"He's a homosexual. I knew it from the day I met him."

She sighed and sat back in her chair. "Oh, Natalie."

"I know, I know."

"You know what?"

"I know what you're going to say."

"Well, that's more than I know. I'm speechless." She shook her head. "You've been chasing a homosexual for, what—two years now?"

"He was worth chasing."

She looked at her daughter with unbearable pity. "My poor baby."

"Oh, don't, Mom. I knew the risks."

"But you didn't believe them."

"No, I didn't believe them."

Sandy looked at her shoes, then up again. "Well, I'm glad you've put him behind you. But two years is a lot of lost time to make up for. Do you have any idea what you'll be doing now? For dates, I mean."

"Not quite yet. And if you bring up Hank Bixby, I'll break your knees. But before I get on with my life, I have a little bit of unfinished business with Peter."

"Say," said Sandy, brightening. "Maybe I can fix him up with Frederick Kelsey!"

"Who's that?"

"I told you—the man in our Accessorizers Anonymous group."

She rolled her eyes. "Mom, I guarantee you, Peter Leland would never go out with any man who lived with his mother in the suburbs. Besides which, he's already involved with someone. Seemingly for the long run." Accent on the seemingly, she said to herself.

"Oh, really? What's he like?"

"Well, if you must know, it's Lloyd Hood. Calvin's friend."

She was thunderstruck. "Lloyd Hood, the gun merchant? Is a fairy?"

"He's gay, yes."

"And he's Peter's boyfriend now?"

Natalie nodded.

"Well, this is a day for surprises!" She shook her head as if to clear it. "Does Calvin know?"

"Oh, no. I forgot to call him. He's home now, isn't he?"

"Yes, he's been home since yesterday! Haven't you called him?"

"No."

She grimaced. "All right, young lady. Now that this Peter nonsense is over, I want to see you straighten up a bit. You can start by respecting yourself a little, but you can continue by respecting your family. I don't want to chide you too harshly, because you were good enough to run over here for me this morning, no questions asked. But your brother and his new wife were both hurt by your snubbing of them at the wedding, and now, not even to call them after they've come back from their honeymoon—that's sheer hurtfulness. You call them today. I'm putting my foot down."

"I will, I promise."

She looked at the clock. "I should start getting tea ready. Would you like to stay? You've never met Greta Ledbetter, have you?"

"No thanks, Mom. I'd better get back home. Things to do."

She got her jacket, petted Carmen DeFleur good-bye, and headed for the door. Sandy opened it for her.

"Thank you for coming over, honey."

"Sure, Mom."

"And thank you for opening up to me. I love you for it."

Natalie blinked. What a surprising thing to say! "Well—I love you, too, Mom."

Suddenly Sandy reached out and hugged her, and she found herself hugging back.

A little cyclone of emotion whipped itself up from nowhere and threatened to grow larger; Natalie pushed herself away. "Well," she said, making an effort to seem unaffected, "you have fun with your 'granddaughter' today."

"I'll try. Maybe I can get her into some of your raggedy old clothes by the time Greta gets here."

Natalie laughed. " 'Bye, Mom."

" 'Bye, dear."

She shut the door, and Natalie walked to the train station.

CHAPTER 18

There were two messages from Peter waiting on Natalie's answering machine when she got home; each urged her to call him at once. She ignored them; he would just want to wax eloquent about Lloyd, and she couldn't stomach that. Instead, she dialed her brother.

"Hi, Tubs," he said merrily. It was his childhood nickname for her; she'd never been able to break him of it.

"How was paradise?" she asked. "Did it agree with the new Mr. and Mrs.?"

He laughed. "Thought I'd have to *drag* her back. What's up?"

She winced. Was it that obvious that she wanted something from him? Was it so impossible that she should ever phone him just to chat?

She resolved to change that. But for the moment, she had to give in. "I called to ask you about Lloyd Hood."

"How on earth do you know Lloyd Hood?"

"From your wedding, moron."

"Oh. Yeah." He paused. "It's kind of weird to think that everybody in my life now knows everybody else."

"Well, we do. Matter of fact, I had dinner at Lloyd's house last night."

"No way!"

"What do you mean, 'No way'?"

"You and Lloyd Hood? That's like Oliver North dating Bette Midler."

"Fuck you," she said. "I hope your sunburn hurts."

"It's deep, dark, and painless, Tubs." He laughed.

"For your information, Lloyd and I aren't dating. I'm not his type."

"I should say not!"

"My friend Peter, you remember him?"

"Your date at the wedding, sure. Guy Vera couldn't keep her eyes off of."

"Really?"

"Thought she'd change her mind about me at the altar. She was really smitten. Must've asked me a million questions about you and him. That guy almost ruined my honeymoon."

"Well, I have something you can tell her about him."

"What?"

"*He's* Lloyd's type."

"Come again?"

"They're fucking, Calvin."

A long silence. "This some kind of joke?"

"I wish it were."

"You're full of shit, Natalie."

"Look, Lloyd Hood is gay and he's fucking my friend Peter."

"Bullshit."

"Why would I lie?"

"That's what I'm trying to figure out."

She carried the phone to the kitchen and got a Diet Coke from the refrigerator. She was actually enjoying this.

"Cal? You still there?" She popped the can open.

"Yes." A pause. "You expect me to believe that Lloyd Hood is gay?"

"When was the last time you saw him with a woman?" She took a sip of soda.

"That's got nothing to do with it."

"That's got *everything* to do with it."

"We didn't exactly socialize."

"I bet you didn't!"

"I've shot target practice with that guy! We've shot traps at the gun club together!"

"Now, *that's* got nothing to do with it."

Calvin let out a sigh. "Well. This is something. I don't know what to say."

"Does it matter to you?"

The longest silence yet. "I guess not. I mean—hell, I don't know. No reason it should, really."

"Just when you think you know someone," she said, beginning to nudge him in the direction she wanted. She took another swig of Diet Coke.

"No kidding," he said. "He should've told me, you know."

"Bet he told you everything else." Nudge, nudge.

"Oh—I don't know about that. I mean, all he really ever goes on about is, y'know, government and taxes and all that political shit. I guess I thought he was a pretty decent guy because he was so smart and such a good shot."

"So he never told you anything else about his life?"

"No. And I never asked. Guess I thought there wasn't much to it, y'know? Someone talks night and day about free enterprise, you don't get the idea they're real live wires on the dance floor, you read me?"

"Yeah," she said, sighing. This was no good. Calvin could tell her nothing.

"What's his house like?" he asked.

"Spare, masculine, hundred percent quality," she said. "Like Thomas Jefferson lived there or something."

"Goddamn! That's what I thought! I can't believe that guy's a fag."

"He's a homosexual, Cal," she said. "But he's definitely *not* a fag. Trust me, there's a difference."

"You learn something every day."

"This is true."

"I *am* kind of pissed he didn't tell me, though. I mean, I invited the guy to my wedding!"

"So confront him. Bet you could wangle an invitation to dinner with him and his boyfriend."

"Man, is this weird!"

"Well, anyway, I just wanted to see what you thought about it. I'm having a little trouble with it myself."

"Oh, Christ! I forgot! Did you know about Peter?"

"More or less."

"Still, must be rough."

"Well, yeah."

"Sorry, Tubs. I was all wrapped up in my honeymoon and everything, when I should've been here for you to talk to."

Natalie was stunned. "Calvin! What a sweet thing to say!"

"Well, I *am* your brother. I want you to be as happy as me and Vera."

"Someday, I'm sure."

"You gonna be okay?"

"Oh, please! I'm not a shrinking violet!"

"Y'know, Mom told me about Hank Bixby, an—"

She screamed.

"What did I say?" he asked, alarmed.

"What do you think? Mom should jus—"

"Seems like a great guy, Natalie."

She screamed again.

He laughed. "Well, listen, Tubs, I gotta run. I'm picking up Vera at the tanning parlor in ten minutes. She's determined not to lose her color."

"Give her my love. Tell her I'm sorry I wasn't more—y'know—sisterly at the wedding."

"Like she would've noticed," he scoffed.

"What? You mean—she didn't?"

"Tubs, she had people pawing at her all night."

"But Mom said you were both offended that I didn—"

"*Mom* was the one offended," he said. "I can't believe she tried to put that in our mouths! No, you were fine. We didn't need you fawning all over us."

Natalie was steaming over her mother's duplicity. "I'm so glad we had this little chat, Calvin."

"Me, too. See you soon?"

"Sure. 'Bye."

As soon as she had hung up the receiver, the phone rang. She didn't have to guess too hard who *that* might be. Well, Mr. Leland could call till the cows came home. She had better things to do.

She tossed away her empty Diet Coke and left the apartment. It was still light outside and she strolled down Broadway, looking in shop windows without really seeing, rehearsing fights with her mother in which she skewered her with righteous sarcasm and reduced her to a heap of sobs.

"Well, if it isn't Miss Natalie Stathis," said someone to her left.

She turned and met Kirk Bergland's big, shining eyes. He was an old friend who had once had an unrequited crush on Peter. He wasn't very attractive, and far too eager to please, but he idolized Natalie and, at this point, she felt like taking advantage of that.

"Kirk, darling," she said, gripping him by the shoulders and air-kissing his cheeks. *"Quelle surprise!"*

"And how is the most beautiful woman in the world?" he asked, outrageously.

She was about to take offense until she saw in his face that he had meant it to please her. He wasn't enormously witty, that's all. "Oh, you evil thing," she said, patting her hair. "You'll turn my head, I declare you will."

"Out shopping?" he asked as they resumed walking.

"Just strolling," she said flirtatiously. "Hoping some nice young gentleman will come along and sweep me away for a drink."

"Done!"

An hour later, half tanked at Sidetrack, her ego was completely restored. Kirk had flattered her so ridiculously that she was all aglow, even though she knew he hadn't an ounce of sexual interest in her.

"So tell me about Peter," he said, sucking down a Manhattan. Kirk knew how to drink.

"What's to tell? Been domesticated."

"Doesn't surprise me. I'm just amazed he was on the market for so long." He looked a little sad.

She patted his arm. "You'll find your Prince Charming soon, I'm sure."

"What's his lover like? I mean, he must be magnificent!"

"He's out of the ordinary, that's for sure."

"It kind of helps, you know? When you're as lonely as I am, it helps to know that it's possible—that two people *can* find each other and love each other equally and li—" He stopped and turned away. Natalie thought he might cry. "Sorry. I should stop drinking now."

"So should I," she said, pushing away her half-finished Bacardi. "How many of these have we had?"

"I haven't been counting."

"That many!" She folded her arms on the bar and rested her head on them. "Thanks for cheering me up, Kirk. You're a doll deluxe."

He blushed. "You know I'd do anything for you."

"You would not! You old snake charmer."

"I would so!"

"You wouldn't kill a defenseless animal for me, would you?" She giggled. She knew he was an ardent animal-rights activist.

His head lolled a bit drunkenly as he considered this. "A spider, maybe."

"A spider's not an animal, it's a *bug*." She shrieked with hilarity.

"A bug is an animal," he insisted in the face of her laughter. "It's a *kind* of animal."

"Not necessarily," she said. "A bug could be a slur—a slurvay—" She cracked up.

"What are you saying?"

"A bug could be a survlay—" She cracked up again.

"I don't know what you're saying," he said, starting to laugh himself.

"A bug could be a sur-vlay-lance device," she said. The word had trundled out of her like a pull toy.

"A what?"

"You know—what you put in someone's home when you want to listen to them when you're not there—when—" She cracked up again.

"A surveillance device!" he said, interpreting her. "That's what you're saying!"

Suddenly she sobered. An idea had come to her, instantly

neutralizing the wobbly power of the alcohol. "Yes, Kirk. That kind of bug." She looked at him, her gaze suddenly intense. "Those must be hard to get."

He shrugged, and took a swig from her abandoned Bacardi.

"I mean, I don't imagine you can just buy them at Radio Shack. I wouldn't even know where to begin trying to get one."

He raised his eyebrows, as if all of this required no response, then turned and finished off her drink in one gulp.

"Kirk."

He faced her.

"Listen to me."

"I'm listening."

"Have you ever been bugged?"

"Buggered? You bet! Often as possible!" He barked a laugh.

"Seriously, Kirk." Her calm seemed to be unnerving him; he shifted on his stool. Suddenly the rest of the bar seemed not to exist. "Have you?"

"No, of course not," he said. "Who in the world would w—"

"Do you know anyone who has?" she interrupted him.

He shook his head.

"I wonder how I'd—how one would go about getting a listening device, anyway?" She idly started ripping up a soggy bar napkin. "I'm speaking theoretically, of course. Intellectual curiosity."

He shrugged. "Hell, *I* don't know. Why don't you ask Curtis Driscoll?"

Her jaw dropped. "Why on earth would I ask Curtis Driscoll?"

"He knows about that kind of thing."

"Are we talking about the same Curtis Driscoll?"

"I only know one."

"Black guy? Waiter at Ambria?"

Kirk nodded.

"I don't understand," she said. "How does some flighty waiter get to know about spy stuff?"

He shrugged. "All I know is, I heard him talking about it one night. He'd been to some kind of espionage movie and he was saying that the stuff the characters were using was pretty bogus. Said they should find out what people really use. Said he could be a technical adviser in Hollywood."

Natalie pursed her lips. "I confess myself amazed."

Kirk looked at his watch. "Listen, Natalie—"

She became aware that she'd fallen out of character and was now scaring him off. No matter; he'd served his purpose. "Oh, Kirk," she said, sliding off her stool, "look at me monopolizing you! The men of Chicago will never forgive me. Now I must run away." She blew him a kiss. "Promise you'll stay here and be as naughty as you can!"

He blushed bright red, but grinned in pleasure at her.

On her way home, she stopped at Curtis Driscoll's apartment and rang his bell; no answer. So she ran home, looked him up in the phone book, dialed his number, and left a message on his machine.

"Curtis, honey," she said, "it's Natalie Stathis. We've been living on the same block for almost two years now, can you forgive me for not being neighborly and inviting you up? Such a lot of settling in to do first! Call me when you get home, maybe we can split a bottle of wine tonight. I'll be waiting by the phone."

She hung up, thinking, That's going to intrigue the *shit* out of him.

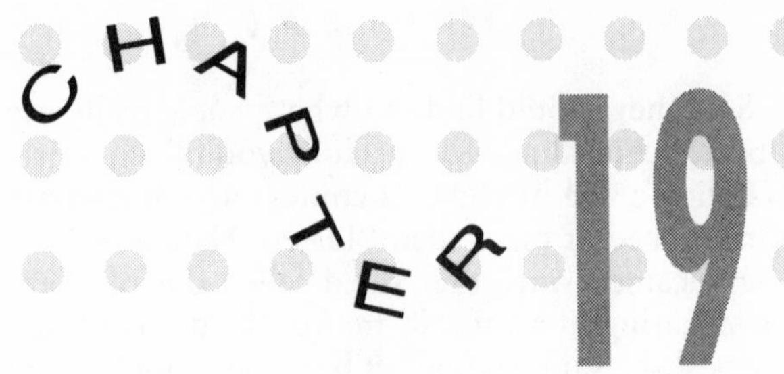

Chapter 19

Sure enough, Curtis called her at a little after nine. "Natalie, it's Curtis Driscoll," he said. No more outlandish jive talk; it was his statesman voice, with a touch of wariness in it.

"So kind of you to call back," she said with oozing charm. "Can you run up the block for a glass of Chardonnay with me?"

He paused. "You want something?"

"Curtis, of *course* I want something. I'm just trying to be civilized about it."

He chuckled. "What do you want?"

"Not on the phone."

A full eight seconds of silence. "Okay. You're at six twenty-two, right?"

Not a minute after she'd hung up with him, her doorbell rang. She buzzed the new arrival into the building, then realized that it couldn't possibly be Curtis—not so quickly. "Fuck, I should've asked who it was first!" she cursed aloud. "If it's Peter—"

It was Peter.

He bounded up to her landing, then faced her, looking ashen. "I need to talk," he said.

"Right now?" she squealed. Curtis would be here in minutes.

"Well, yeah, Natalie. I mean, I wouldn't come all this way to tell you I wanted to talk next week." He smiled wanly and sailed past her into her apartment.

She followed, frantically trying to think of a lie to get rid of him. "I'm on my way out"—but, no, she was in her kimono and slippers; "I'm not feeling well"—but then, he'd want to stay and nurse her; "I'm really busy right now"—but, busy doing what?

Too late. Peter was seated on the couch, his head in his hands. "Thank God you're finally home! I've been calling all day. I've got to talk this out with someone who understands, before I go nuts."

She sat across from him, on the edge of a cushion. "What now?" she asked in a fairly withering voice.

He was oblivious to it. "Last night," he began, "after you left, we got into another argument. In bed, yet! Lloyd's all pissed because I won. It was all over the socialization of medicine. He kept saying that the only incentive for progress in medicine was to keep it on the free market—y'know, keep the profit motive in it, and I said that's ridiculous. He said that the quality of care we'd get from a national health service would be lower because of the lack of the profit incentive, and that medical research would be slower, too. But he couldn't point to any specific examples where that was the case and I could point to specific examples where it wasn't, and for every detriment to a national health service he could think of, I could think of four in our system that were worse."

Natalie thought, I do not believe I am hearing this. She stole a glance at her wristwatch and began to panic.

"And I used the analogy of artists," Peter continued. "You know, profit has never been the sole incentive for artists; often it's not even an incentive at all, and if that's true, shouldn't it also be true for surgeons and physicians and researchers? And then I said that people who are sick aren't in the best position to choose from competitive medical suppliers, y'know, to determine any qualitative differences—because who has time to be that informed? And anyway, the whole nature of the medical profession is that they serve people who are physically impaired, and if you believe like I do that there is no mind-body dichotomy, then it follows that physical impairment means some kind of mental impairment, too, and to put mentally impaired people into a decision-making role when their health is at stake is to practically make sure they'll be victimized, or at least not choose well. Also, sick people don't often have choices. What's a guy with AIDS gonna say, 'Sorry, I don't want your AZT, it's too expensive'? He's got to have it, and that makes him a victim. He has to pay the price, and it's a steeper price every year. The free market is for free people, and sick people aren't free, they're slaves to their bodies. Lloyd always says that the role of government should be to serve the individual, and I say, well, isn't that what a national health service would do? But he goes all nuclear any time he hears the word 'nationalized.' So we ended up not fucking and I left before breakfast."

He stopped to take a breath. Natalie was sitting with her hands on her knees, unsure of what to say. She knew better than to let herself hope that this absurd disagreement meant a permanent break between Peter and Lloyd; it was probably only the latest of many ideological sparring matches they'd have, and she certainly couldn't allow Peter to come running to her after every one. In the first place, it was demeaning. In the second place, she had work to do now that he mustn't know about.

She regarded him coldly. "So?"

His eyes bulged. "What do you mean, 'so'?"

"So, what do you want me to do about it? You and Lloyd go scratching and hissing at each other like cats over some fine point of political theory that maybe three other people in the universe care about, and I'm supposed to tell you it's all his fault and you're wonderful? Peter, you say this is the relationship you've always wanted. Don't come running to me if it gets rough. I'm getting on with my life. I don't need it."

He sat back, abashed. "I can't come to you as a friend, is that it? To tell you how I feel?"

"As a friend, Peter? As a friend? A friend would say, 'How are you, Natalie?' A friend would say, 'Natalie, is this a bad time to talk?' A friend would notice the less-than-enthralled look on my face when he's in the middle of a seemingly endless story about a national health whatever. A friend would not come running up the stairs and immediately start a dreary monologue that's all 'me-me-me,' and that's exactly what you've just done."

His face was red now; there was a vein in his forehead, prominent and blue, that she knew from experience signaled anger. "Well, excuse me all to hell," he said through clenched teeth.

She got up. "Next time, call first."

"Maybe there won't be a next time," he said, leaping to his feet and storming toward the door.

She threw it open for him. "I'll take my chances on that."

As soon as he was out the door, she slammed it after him.

She stood quietly for a moment, then shut her eyes and breathed deeply. Well, she thought, at least I've gotten rid of him.

A few minutes later, Curtis Driscoll was on her couch sipping his wine as if it were laced with poison. His spine was absolutely rigid. "All right," he said. "What do you want?"

She slipped onto the couch next to him and twirled the wine in her own glass. She smiled. "You're all business tonight, aren't you, Curtis?" she said. "I wouldn't have guessed you had it in you."

He refused to banter with her. "You did say you wanted something. I recall you saying it."

She sighed. "Okay. Have it your way. I want to get a listening device. A bug. I've heard you might be able to help me."

He smiled at her. "Oh, for Christ's sake."

She flushed red. "Can you?"

"Natalie, what in the wor—"

"No questions asked," she said. "I forgot that part."

He sat back, daintily holding his wine. "It's not cheap, girl. You gotta pay me."

"How much?"

"How much you got?"

"Nothing. How much?"

He laughed wildly. "Girlfriend, what'choo wanna go play

games wif bugs fo'?" He was back to street talk. He obviously thought her hopelessly silly.

"I said no questions asked," she hissed.

"I never agreed to that." Back to the statesman.

She made a great show of refilling her glass. "I want revenge on someone," she said, saying the word aloud for the first time. It sounded strange—almost casual. "Okay, Curtis? You satisfied?" She put the bottle down, sat back again, and faced him.

"How's a bug gonna help you get revenge?"

She shrugged. "Knowledge is power."

He picked at his ear; a nervous gesture, she guessed. "A man, huh?"

"Maybe."

"Peter Leland."

She blanched; he must have seen it. "Certainly not," she said.

"Look, Natalie," he said, putting down his glass, "you could get into big trouble if you got caught, which you would, 'cause you're not smart enough not to."

"You don't know how smart I am."

"Sure I do. I know you through and through, girlfriend. Peter's got a new man, you're busted up about it, and you wanna make it rough for them. Give it up. You wanna sit around with a set of headphones listening to them eat and fuck and sleep and shit—all the time hoping they say something you can use against them, presuming that there even *is* something, which I doubt. Wouldn't you be better off getting some fresh air or something? Reading a good book? Going to a concert? Getting a man of your own?"

She got up. "If you're not going to help me, you can jus—"

"I didn't say I wouldn't help you." He rose to his full height and towered above her. "I just wanna make sure you got it in perspective first." He tilted his head. "A grand oughtta do it for now."

"A thousand dollars?"

"Uh-huh."

"It's that expensive?"

"From me it is. I got palms to grease."

"I don't have that kind of money. Can't you—"

He laughed, stilling her voice in midplea. "Girl, tomorrow

you'll wake up and you won't believe how silly you've been about this."

"If I get the money, can I still call you?"

"Sure, sure." He showed himself out. "But you won't," he said, as the door shut behind him.

She sat on the sofa and cried, thoroughly humiliated.

CHAPTER 20

The next morning she called the temp agency to say she was sick and couldn't work that day. The woman on the phone—an efficient, thoroughly despicable redhead named Monica—said, "Natalie, I have to tell you, we're a little concerned by your recent performance."

"What do you mean, 'concerned'?" Natalie snapped.

"Well, you've been a little haphazard in your work schedule. You turn down so many jobs, and miss days on the ones you do take, an—"

"So what?" she interrupted. "That's the benefit of temping. At least that's what your ads all say. 'Work when you want to.' "

"Yes, b—"

"I've been on your books for three years now and I've brought you a lot of money. And I'll bring you more. I type, I answer phones, I do all major word-processing functions, and last but not least, I bathe regularly. If you want to dump me, go ahead. I can always sign up with another agency. But I can't imagine *you'll* find someone to replace *me* as easily."

The grinding of Monica's teeth was almost audible. "All we ask, Natalie, is that you give us a little advance notice whenever possible."

"I'll do that. Since you asked so nicely."

Natalie spent the rest of the morning looking out a window, wondering if she should throw herself from it. She'd hurt Peter last night, and it made her wonder if she was really capable of taking revenge on him—especially now that that condescending prig Curtis Driscoll had demeaned her for even having the idea. Who did he think he was?

The trouble was, he had gotten to her. He'd made her feel childish and melodramatic. Revenge was something people on bad TV shows plotted for. This was real life.

The phone rang. If it was that bitch Monica again . . .

"Natalie, it's your mother."

She colored with anger, remembering her conversation with Calvin. "Oh," she said, as unwelcomingly as possible. "Hi."

Sandy didn't notice. "I had such a lovely weekend with Darnita," she said, her voice all chirpy with delight. "I took her to see a movie—a cartoon about a little dinosaur who'd lost his mother. I don't mind telling you, it upset me—that poor little creature, crying out for his mama! But Darnita enjoyed it thoroughly. Then we went to McDonald's, and I'd never been to one before. It was quite an experience! Did you know that almost all the food there is deep-fried? I'm not altogether sure people should eat there as often as they do."

Natalie was waiting for an opportunity to accuse her mother of lying about Calvin and Vera being offended by her at the wedding, but Sandy just kept barreling on.

"Anyway, I haven't been able to stop thinking about that wonderful child, ever since the social worker came to pick her up this morning. I watched the car drive away, taking her back to oblivion, and I kept thinking, that dear girl, I am her only hope! And then, do you know what? Her sister called me and thanked me for taking such good care of her! The idea of such polite people struggling to live civilized lives in the projects just overwhelmed me. If only I could do something more for them! I thought of setting up an educational fund for Darnita, but of course I don't have the money. If I did, though, I wouldn't hesitate. Would you?"

Natalie was taken aback by the question. "What?"

"If you had the money, wouldn't you donate some to Darnita's education?"

"I don't have any money."

"I know, but if you did, wouldn't you?"

"Mom—" She still wanted to get around to the subject of The Wedding Lie.

"If, for instance, you suddenly came into a lot of money, you'd put aside a thousand or two for Darnita's future, wouldn't you?"

Natalie felt something tingle at the base of her skull. "What is this about?"

"Just conjectural, dear. Idle chatter."

But she believed her mother capable of anything now. "No, you're up to something. What is it?"

"I'm just hoping for the best for poor Darnita, so th—"

"No, something about me coming into money. What's that about? I mean it."

Sandy sighed. "Well, I might as well tell you. You'll find out soon enough, anyway. Your father set up a trust fund for you; you get fifty thousand dollars when you turn thirty. I'm the trustee. Well, you turn thirty in two months, and it was going to be a surprise, but I wanted to touch you beforehand for Darnita's sake, not for mine. You'll remember your little 'sister,' won't you? You're the only ones who can help her, you and Calvin!"

Natalie wasn't seeing anything. There was a hazy white fog before her eyes. "You never mentioned this before," she said. She felt like vomiting.

"I had my reasons, dear, believe me. You see, I wanted you to have a career, and I thought if you knew you had fifty thousand dollars coming, you'd have no ambition. You'd just coast until you were thirty and never even try."

"But I didn't try anyway. I don't have a career anyway."

"I know, and that's my greatest disappointment. But at least I know it's not my fault. At least I know I didn't do this to you."

Natalie was so offended that it took her a moment to find her voice. "You—are such a bitch—" she garbled, tears collecting in her eyes.

"Natalie! How dare you speak to me that way!"

"I don't ever want to speak to you again," she said. "If I'm such a fucking disappointment, just give me my money and get the hell out of my life!"

"There's no cause for disgusting lang—"

"Just shut up and leave me alone!"

"Darling, I don't understand why you hate me all of a sudden, but that doesn't change what I've asked you about Darnita—"

"Sell your fucking house, Mom! Sell your fucking jewels and your fucking Landseer!" She hung up and immediately dialed Calvin at the bank.

"Hi, Tubs," he said brightly.

She didn't return his greeting, but said, "Did you know we get fifty thousand dollars when we turn thirty?"

"*You* get fifty," he said. "I get a hundred."

It was like two bolts of lightning had struck her at once. "How come you get more?" she shrieked.

"Our father's will. I wasn't born yet when he died, so he stipulated that if I was born a girl, we'd get an even fifty-fifty split, but if I was a boy I'd get more."

She almost levitated out of her seat with hatred. "You think that's fair?"

"Fair, schmair," he said. "It was all settled a long time before I came along."

"And you knew about this all along but never said a word to me."

"Mom asked me not to."

"Thanks so much, Calvin. My loving brother who almost regretted going on his honeymoon because I'd needed him. Christ, what a load of shit!" She turned off the phone and hurled it across the room. It hit a framed poster and shattered the glass.

There was nothing left of her life now, just a series of betrayals. She'd been betrayed by Peter, by her mother, by Calvin, by the father she couldn't even remember. The truest person in her life right now was that pig Monica at the temp agency.

She started to tremble and couldn't stop. She'd never felt such self-revulsion for having been stupid enough to care for these people.

Revenge was her consolation. She might have nothing left in her life, but soon she would have fifty thousand dollars, and what revenge that would buy she could only imagine!

She raced over to the phone, picked it from among the shards of glass, and turned it on. Fortunately, it still worked. She dialed.

"Hello," said her mother. She sounded as if she'd been crying.

"It's Natalie. I want to buy Carmen DeFleur."

A stunned pause. "You what?" Her voice was barely audible.

"You're always complaining about what a burden she is. Well, I'll buy her from you. You want money for Darnita? Sell me the dog. Five hundred dollars. Not a bad offer."

Sandy gasped. "I don't know you anymore," she said, her voice breaking. "You're not my daughter." She hung up.

Natalie cackled and dialed Curtis Driscoll.

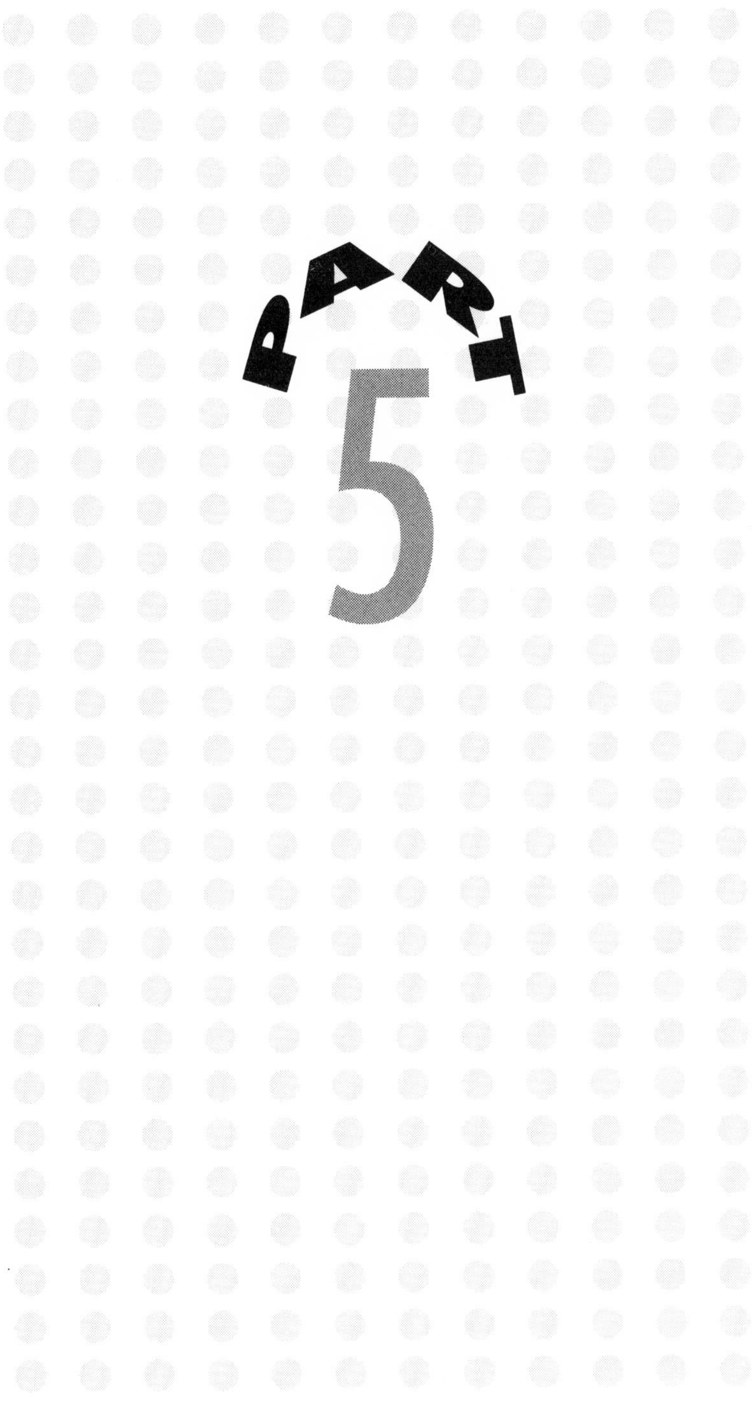

PART 5

Chapter 21

Natalie felt a peculiar elation looking at the squirrel she had just run over. It had darted into the street in front of her, and rather than swerve to avoid hitting it, some kind of fit had possessed her, whether of rage or of glee she couldn't determine, and she'd pressed her foot to the accelerator, sending her van careening into the helpless rodent. She heard a little pop, like a walnut being cracked, then stopped the van and peeked out the window at the creature she'd just nailed.

She'd run across its head, and its skull was smashed. There was something about the seeping carnage that thrilled her, even as she strove to figure out why on earth she'd done such a thing. A poor, defenseless squirrel—but, hah! That's the last time it would get in *her* way!

Both frightened by her loss of control and ashamed of herself for being frightened, she dismissed the incident from her mind, rolled her window back up, and drove another few blocks before parking along the side of a street.

She checked her wristwatch; thanks to the phosphorescent

glow of the Keith Haring "monkeys," she could see that it was 5:08 A.M. She reached up and turned the ignition key toward her, stilling the van's engine.

She sat for a while, enjoying the quiet, occasionally sipping from the thermos of hot coffee she'd brought with her. The little neighborhood was bathed in silvery winter tones; it was the kind of delicacy of color no camera could ever catch. Patches of snow caught the moonlight and held it, so that everything was illuminated, everything was visible. She sighed in contentment. These were her favorite moments, alone with the riches of a February dawn, sole witness to all this fragile beauty.

But within a few minutes the cold had invaded the van, and she started to shiver. She checked her wristwatch again: 5:17 A.M. "Time for the boys to get up," she said aloud. She crawled from the driver's seat to the back of the van, where she switched on a receiver and a reel-to-reel tape recorder she'd hooked up to a battery pack. She had a gas heater back here as well, but she was afraid of it and seldom used it.

She donned a pair of headphones. At five-twenty she heard the telltale bugling of Lloyd's alarm clock. He and Peter would be getting up momentarily.

But a full minute later, there was still no sound but the blaring of the alarm. She took off the headphones, returned to the front of the van, and peered out the window at Lloyd and Peter's house, which was right across the street. No lights in the bedroom window yet. "Come *on*," she hissed. "It's *cold* in here!" She went back and turned on the heater.

She refitted herself with the headphones. In another half minute the alarm was turned off and she could hear Lloyd's sleep-drugged voice. "I'll shower first," he said. She heard Peter's mumbled assent.

Then she heard Lloyd's footsteps as he left the bedroom, and the distant sound of the shower being started.

She'd chosen to bug the bedroom, over the other rooms in the house, because it witnessed the couple's most private moments. She'd placed the bug during her second and final visit to Lloyd and Peter, which had occurred after their friendship had soured and Peter had become wary of her. She'd dropped by just before the holidays with a combination Christmas present/housewarming gift/peace offering and had been received with cordiality. After excusing herself to "powder her nose," she'd dodged upstairs and affixed the bug to the back of the bed's headboard.

"What were you doing upstairs?" Peter asked suspiciously when she came back down.

"I told you, I needed to use the little girls' room," she said, smiling sweetly.

"We have a bathroom down here for guests."

She claimed to have forgotten, and apologized. Then she kissed them both good-bye and said she'd see them soon. But she hadn't called them since, and they never called her.

In fact, she was out of touch with nearly everyone now. It had been a lonely Christmas—she'd refused to go home and face her treacherous mother and brother, and had ended up drinking her Christmas dinner with poor, desperate Kirk Bergland at a Halsted Street bar with the other dregs of gay society. She'd ended up in tears, and that was the last she'd seen of Kirk, too.

So no one knew about her inheritance, and when Peter and Lloyd left the house and drove to work each day, they couldn't begin to suspect that the plain white Chevy van that always sat across the street from their driveway belonged to her; nor could they suspect that she herself was inside it, having monitored their private moments with an electronic bug she'd gotten illegally—and expensively—from Curtis Driscoll.

Actually, it had turned out that Curtis really *was* just a flighty waiter; but his boyfriend was a Chicago cop and had access to the tantalizing mounds of physical evidence taken into police custody on various criminal raids—evidence that included all manner of electronic gadgetry. While the case in which it played a part was awaiting trial, Natalie was free to use all this listening equipment (as long as she continued to supply Curtis with enough money to keep "greasing the right palms," as he put it).

While the faint sound of Lloyd's shower and of Peter's delicate snoring continued, she flipped though the notebook of transcriptions she'd been keeping since beginning her surveillance shortly after her thirtieth birthday. Her favorite pages were denoted by yellow Post-It stickers. She turned to one now.

Ah, yes. The morning of December 28.

LLOYD: Are you *sure* you don't want to invite Natalie?
PETER: We haven't been close in months.
LLOYD: Thought that might just be a tiff. (unidentifiable noise) Cut that out!
PETER: (laughing) You love it.
LLOYD: I'm trying to dress! Stop evading the issue.
PETER: What issue? (unidentifiable noise)
LLOYD: (laughing) God*damn* it, Peter.
PETER: There is no God, remember?
LLOYD: You said you've spent the last two New Year's Eves with her, and it was kind of a tradition with you two.
PETER: So? She ended it, not me. She was the bitch, not me.
LLOYD: She gave us that fruit-and-cheese basket.
PETER: But she didn't apologize. Honey, just drop it. It's going to be just couples anyway, right? Like we decided. Plus, you invited her brother and his wife, and they're feuding about God-knows-what.
LLOYD: There is no God, remember?

It was the most they had ever deigned to discuss her. That, in itself, hurt more than the dismissive tone Peter had taken when they did—or the knowledge that he was now keeping Calvin's company, not hers.

She flipped to another page. Another favorite of hers: January 12—a Saturday-night roll in the hay.

LLOYD: (moans) Oh—that's good, Peter . . . lower. . . . Listen, I've had some time to do some thinking . . . about the national health service issue, remember? We never got back to that. . . . Oh, *baby* . . . yes, just like that. . . . A national health service would just indicate to every citizen that he or she can drink and smoke and use drugs and not exercise, and if their bodies break down the government will bail them out. . . . You feel great, honey, now do the other one. . . . Now, you and I strive to stay healthy; we eat right, we work out, we g—oh, *baby!* . . . just keep that up for a while. . . . Anyway, why should we have to foot the bill for everybody else's bad health habits? Why should we have to pay to maintain a national health service for people who don't take care of themselves? That's what insurance is for. It's up to the individual to look after his health, and he does that by maintaining a nutritious diet and an exercise regimen and by taking out insurance to protect him in case of catastrophic . . . catastrophic . . . oh, God, honey, I'm close . . . ooh . . . I know medical costs are skyrocketing and insurers are turning down bad risks, but you don't throw out the baby with the bath—you don't solve a system's problems by getting a new system. And you don't teach people that the government will bail them out if they ruin their health, because then a lot of people will take that as *permission* to ruin their health. And we end up footing the bill. . . . I've said it before, private property is the great civilizer of the individual, and the body is the most private property of all, and if you hand over control of its care to the state, you become—you become—oh, God, honey, here I come . . . (untranscribable noises)

She chuckled again. The temptation to show that page to someone else was almost overpowering. The trouble is, she had no one left in her life she could show it to.

The shower sounds had ceased now; she knew from experience that it would be about five minutes more before Lloyd completed his grooming and reentered the bedroom to awaken Peter. She could still see her breath, so she turned up the gas heater. Then she flipped to another page—the page she'd marked with a red exclamation point on the Post-It sticker, because it was the most promising exchange she'd recorded thus far, in terms of setting the stage for her eventual revenge.

PETER: You think about what I said yesterday?
LLOYD: Not yet.
PETER: Why not? You've had plenty of time.
LLOYD: I know. Your tie's hooked on your collar in back.
PETER: Fix it for me, okay? (pause) It's such an unsavory business, honey.
LLOYD: What is?
PETER: Guns.
LLOYD: You don't know beans about guns.
PETER: By choice. Listen, I'd like to see you out of that store, out of that environment—

LLOYD: There. All fixed.
PETER: Honey, listen—I just—
LLOYD: Wipe your feet before you step on the Bill of Rights, Peter.
PETER: I'm not saying no one should sell guns, just not you.
LLOYD: Why not?
PETER: Because I don't like it. And I do have some say in it. If I'm your husband, I have some say.
LLOYD: (pause) What bothers you about it?
PETER: The kind of creeps who buy guns. Criminals, that kind of—
LLOYD: Peter, my not selling them guns doesn't mean they're not going t—
PETER: I know, I know, I'm not talking about cause and effect, I'm talking about *you*. I don't want you in that chain of events, even if it's okay in principle for you to be there. If you ever sold a gun to somebody who used it to murder someone, or something like that, I'd feel—I don't know.
LLOYD: (sighs) I'll take it under consideration. Seriously, I will.
PETER: I know you think I'm ridiculous.
LLOYD: Come here, you. (undecipherable noises)

Lloyd was back in the bedroom now. "Wake up, sleepyhead," he said. Natalie could hear the rustle of the sheets; he was obviously trying to jostle Peter awake.

She stole a glance at the tape to make sure it was still recording.

"Mmlgrph," said Peter. He yawned loudly. "What time?"

"Five forty-one," said Lloyd. His footsteps followed, then the ripping-paper sound of the venetian blinds being opened.

"Funny thing," he said. "That van across the street."

Natalie's heart stopped.

"What van?" Peter said in the middle of another yawn.

"White one across the street. It's there every morning and every night, but I know for a fact that no one on the street owns it. Last neighborhood meeting, I complimented the Wittkowskis on it, and they said it's not theirs, they thought it was ours. And I know it's not the Smiths', because they've been away for two weeks, and this van is in a slightly different spot every day."

So much for being as inconspicuous as possible, thought

Natalie. Goddamn Lloyd and his fucking nothing-escapes-me mentality.

"Might be someone casing the houses here," he said, his voice becoming more remote. He must be leaving the bedroom. "Think I'll just run across the street and have a peek inside it. Got to get the paper from the lawn, anyway."

Natalie ripped off the headphones, lunged to the front of the van, and twisted the key. The engine didn't ignite, and her hands, numbed by cold now, banged clumsily against the keys. She tried again and almost snapped her thumb off.

The engine roared; her foot was already pressed against the accelerator.

She removed her foot from the pedal and cautioned herself not to panic. Then she took a short breath, shifted into drive, and lurched into the street with a screech. She didn't even stop to see if Lloyd had come out of the house yet.

Her heart beating wildly, she continued down Wilson Avenue until she deemed herself safe, then started gasping for breath. Jesus Christ, that had been close!

She drove on a little farther, listening to her heartbeat as it thudded in her ears. She wouldn't rest until she got far, far away.

Then she noticed a thick, burning smell. She thought at first it must be coming from outside, but as she drove on it got more and more overpowering, until she remembered, to her horror, that she hadn't turned off the gas heater before nearly sending the van into orbit.

She swung the wheel to the right and parked at the side of the road. Then she peeked behind her and saw that the heater had tipped over and that a large section of the carpeting beneath it was now smoldering.

She screamed and jumped out of the van, ran to the back, and tried to open the doors, but they were locked. She ran back to the driver's side to get the keys from the ignition, but she'd slammed the door shut on getting out, and the door had automatically locked.

So there she was, on Wilson Avenue at a quarter to six in the morning, not half a mile from Lloyd and Peter's house, locked out of her new Chevy van, with its engine running and a fire started in the back.

She screamed. She screamed again.

Never mind the loss of the van—but if the borrowed equipment were somehow damaged, think of the trouble those corrupt cops could bring down on her head!

She ran around like a decapitated chicken, screaming, "Oh! Oh! Oh!" She was utterly at a loss. At this hour, few cars were likely to pass her, and none likely to stop and help.

She tripped and fell over a chunk of cement a few yards behind the van. That's it, she decided; I've crippled myself, and I'll have to lie here and watch my van explode. And with my luck, this is the route Peter and Lloyd take to work, so they'll be the ones to find me lying here unconscious, with pages of their private conversations scattered all around me.

But she wasn't seriously hurt, and after she got back to her feet she conceived the brilliant idea of using the cement block to break her rear door windows.

At first she was barely able to lift the block, but adrenaline gave her a rush of strength, and she charged the van wielding the cement block high above her head.

"Eeyaaargh!" she cried, barbarianlike.

Her first attempt at shattering the windows only resulted in a good four-inch dent in the door itself, about an inch below the glass. She shrieked, then stepped back a few steps and tried again.

This time the window cracked.

She went at it again, a guttural, animal roar accompanying her attack.

Soon the window gave way with a disappointing thud; the glass fell into the van, nearly whole—a latticework of cracks and splinters that had still managed to hold most of its shape.

Now what?

Smoke was billowing out from the window she'd just bashed in. Panicking, she ran around the grassy stretches on each side of the nearby sidewalk, gathering an armful of snow.

Then she clambered onto the van, stuck her torso through the shattered window, and started flinging clumps of snow down where she'd remembered the smoldering to have been.

Out of the corner of her eye—a miracle!—she saw a car drive by. She hopped down and rushed toward it; an elderly couple sat in its front seat, their mouths open. She waved to them frantically, but they sped away. At first she was astonished that they would abandon her—she, who was so clearly in distress—but then, on a moment's reflection, she figured she must look highly alarming, with her corduroys soiled by slush and snow, her manner spastic and deranged, and her wild hair sticking into her mouth because she didn't even have time to stop and yank it out. The old couple probably thought she was racing after them to murder them.

She dashed back to the van with a new armful of snow. The smoke stung her eyes and nearly choked her, but she frantically persisted in dumping more and more snow on the fire until she managed to douse it and kill the heater.

Now she hung off the back of the van—still running—listening to the hiss of the doused fire within, smelling the gas and the smoke and the damp carpet all at once, and wondering how she had ever come to this. Surely no revenge was worth such trouble.

She awkwardly reached through the window and opened the latch that released the back doors. Then she hopped down and flung them open.

The sooty mess was all on the left side of the van; the right side, with its precious cargo of electronic equipment, was untouched.

Peter and Lloyd are wrong, she thought; there *is* a God.

Chapter 22

On the morning following her near-disaster in the van, she awakened with a start at the sound of the telephone ringing. Scarcely anyone called her anymore.

She no longer bothered to keep the phone by her bed at night, so she had to get up, numb-faced, and track it down through the chaos of her apartment.

She followed its insistent ringing to the coffee table, beneath which she'd stuffed it a few days earlier while watching a bad movie on television. She retrieved it with a grunt of effort, and found its earpiece smeared with congealed tomato paste. She grunted in disgust, took a quick glance under the couch, and discovered a half-eaten pizza sitting there—of what vintage, she could only guess.

Well, she thought, that's what I get for not cleaning house for three months.

She took the still-ringing phone to the kitchen, gave it a quick swipe with a moist paper towel, then dropped the used towel onto a mound of Chinese take-out boxes that towered precariously above her wastepaper basket. When the paper towel hit, it sent the entire heap toppling over onto the tiled floor, spilling cold, gummy chop suey and greasy, greenish egg rolls in the process.

She turned away from the mess and, rubbing her eyes to get the sand out, answered the phone. "Hello?"

"Natalie, I beg of you." It was her mother.

"Mom, for Christ's sake."

"Don't hang up, please! This is important. It's Carmen DeFleur."

Natalie felt as though the entire apartment had just done a flip-flop, floor to ceiling and back again, and thrown her around the room with it. "No," she said softly.

"I know how much you hate us all, but you can't possibly hate that poor, dear thing. You offered to buy her from me once. Well, now it's time to come say good-bye."

"What's wrong?" She felt something funny in her face, as if it were puffing up and might explode. Tears were springing from her eyes like quills from a porcupine. This was awful, awful.

"She can't keep her food down. And her liver's not working. She's just an old dog, the vet says. Her system's shutting down. She—" And here Sandy Stathis started bawling. She whose hair had never been less than perfectly coiffed, she whose suits were always tailor-made, she who always presented to the world a face of such regal composure that no one could imagine her as anything but entirely self-possessed, was now heaving and sobbing with such Saturday-morning-cartoon hysteria that Natalie couldn't believe her ears.

And then Natalie started bawling herself.

"What—am—I going—to do—without—my dog?" Sandy gasped through her sobs.

Natalie gulped some air and tried to compose herself; she promised to come home at once.

Because of her grief, she was even less scrupulous than usual in putting herself together. She didn't even bother to check her closet, but went straight to her laundry hamper and grabbed a ratty sweatshirt and a pair of sweatpants in a color that didn't match. She sniffed them to make sure they were only borderline offensive, and yanked them past her still sleep-heavy limbs.

She was in a taxi on her way to Oak Park before she realized what her mother would say when she saw her. After all, it had been months since she'd been to the hair salon, months since she'd bothered to apply makeup, and months since she'd worn anything but sweats and a parka. She must look like a bum. Her mother would surely berate her.

But there were two shocks to be had on that score. First, Sandy Stathis herself looked like a bum; she was in her bathrobe, her face red and swollen from crying. Her hair was all ajumble, its gray roots showing. Natalie had never seen those gray roots before.

The second shock was that Sandy took one look at her daughter and said, "Oh, honey, I had no idea you'd lost so much weight!" And Natalie looked down at her body, noticing for the first time that she had. Then she realized she'd taken to wearing sweats because her finer clothes no longer really fit her.

She felt a momentary thrill of victory. "I guess I have," she said, examining her waistline as if for the first time. "Thanks for noticing."

"I didn't mean it in any congratulatory sense," Sandy said. "You look malnourished. Come and have a muffin while I get my clothes on."

Mother and daughter entered the house hand in hand. "She's at the vet's now," Sandy said. "They're waiting till we get there and say our good-byes before they give her the injection. Oh, God, this house just won't be the same withou—" She burst into a fresh hail of tears, then willed herself to stop and shook a little fist at herself, as if she might box her own ears if this sloppiness continued. "I couldn't go alone, and Calvin can't get away from the bank, and Vera—well, she doesn't *know* Carmen DeFleur, does she? Thank you for coming, in spite of how much you hate me."

"I don't hate you, Mom," said Natalie sadly. "I'm still really angry, that's all."

"Well, thank you for coming anyway. Let me just throw on a skirt and a blouse. I'm a mess. I love that dog like you don't know."

"I never realized."

"Oh, *God*, Natalie." She turned and hugged her tightly. "I'm more broken up over this than when Max died. What's wrong with me?"

In the car on the way to the vet, Sandy filled Natalie in on family business. "Well, Vera's pregnant, I imagine Calvin's told you. But, wait, no—you're not speaking to him, either, are you? Honey, it's not his fault. Never mind that—the point is, all of Vera's friends got pregnant, and she took one look at all the clothes they were getting at their baby showers and all her ideals went out the window. So apparently she now thinks it's okay if her baby is killed in a nuclear holocaust as long as it's wearing a Pierre Cardin sailor suit with matching booties. I don't like Vera very much, I have to tell you. She's done her best to cut me out of their lives."

Natalie felt a wave of pity sweep over her; she suddenly realized how achingly lonely her mother must be—and how much more so she would be once Carmen DeFleur was gone.

"The only comfort I've had is Darnita, who's been such a joy. I've even had her sister and her fiancé out to the house, which has raised some eyebrows in the neighborhood. I've not mentioned her sister before, have I?" She turned to look at Natalie and ran a stop sign.

"Mom, watch the road!" barked Natalie.

She snapped her head back. "I am. I saw that. Don't yell at me. Anyway, her sister's name is Lawanda, a dear girl. Only just eighteen, but a mother already. Her fiancé is named Quentin, isn't that funny? Last name you'd expect. He's twenty-one and unemployed; he's not the baby's father, and I don't know who is. Anyway, he lives in the same project. Used to be in a gang, don't ask me which one, but Lawanda helped him get out of it. But it's so hard, he can't find a job."

She pulled up in front of the animal hospital, parked the car, and turned off the engine. Then she just sat there and stared into her lap. "Oh, God, oh, God, I can't go through with this."

Natalie got out of the car and went around to the driver's side; she opened the door and took her mother gently by the arm. "Come on, Mom. We have to. Come on."

Later, back at the house, Sandy sat in her kitchen, still wearing her coat, while Natalie brewed some hot tea.

"If it's any help," she said, bringing the tea to the table and setting it before her mother, "I'll pay the vet bills. I can afford it."

She shook her head. "Thank you, dear, but it's not necessary. Calvin authorized me to take the money from his trust fund."

She felt a little sting of anger. "Very gracious of Mr. Hundred-Thou."

"He loved Carmen DeFleur, too, you know."

They sat for a while and drank their tea. Then Sandy looked up at Natalie, her face suddenly so old and careworn; Natalie felt a shiver of mortality seeing her this way.

"Darling," Sandy said, "you must know that in all the years I was trustee for you, I never once used a penny of that money for myself. I only used the money to pay for your education. Your clothes, your meals, everything else, that came from my own money. I did right by you."

Natalie grimaced. "I'm sure you did, Mom. We don't have to talk abou—"

"Don't interrupt. Now, my life is essentially over—"

"Mom, for Chri—"

"Shush! But Darnita's is only beginning. You should see that child respond to the slightest stimulus. She was born to be an elegant young lady. She appreciates the fine things in life. Yet through a horrible accident of nature, she was born into an environment that is hostile to everything fine. I want to give her an opportunity, Natalie, yet there's such a severe limit to what I can do. But you—"

"Mom—"

"Come out next weekend. I'm having a little party for Lawanda and Quentin, and Darnita is helping me. She's spent hours going through magazines, looking at table settings and picking out recipes—I've been guiding her as much as I can, but I'm letting all the final decisions be hers. She has such innate good taste, Natalie! Please come and see for yourself. It'll break your heart to watch her." She reached across the table and clasped her daughter's hand. "Calvin and Vera won't be here, so you don't have to worry about facing them. It'll just be the five of us. Oh, say you'll come!"

Looking at her mother's grief-ravaged face, she couldn't bring herself to say no.

CHAPTER 23

That night, just after midnight, Natalie drove down Wilson Avenue as quietly as she could, and cut her headlights a block from Lloyd and Peter's house. Their bedroom light was on. She parked across the street and prayed they wouldn't look out the window.

It was incredibly cold in the van. She'd put plastic sheeting over the broken window, but it couldn't prevent the heat from flying right outside. And she didn't dare fool with the gas heater anymore.

She crept to the back of the van, started the tape recorder, and put on the headphones.

". . . kind of attitude that has trouble written all over it." It was Lloyd's voice.

"What kind of attitude?" Peter's voice. They sounded so close; they must be in bed together.

"That cocky attitude," Lloyd said. "You know. Smartass. Unreliable."

"How reliable does he have to be?"

"To sell guns? Peter!"

A short pause. "Anyone else on the horizon?"

"No; I've run out of applicants. Maybe I'll place an ad. Too bad—I thought I could find someone here in the community. You know how I believe in that."

A longer pause. Then Peter said, "I appreciate you doing this for me, hon."

"I know you do. I just wish I understood why it's so important to you. It'll still be my store. Whoever I hire will still be selling my guns."

"I'd just feel better if it was an employee, and not you." The sound of shifting sheets suggested that they were snuggling up together. "I can't believe everyone you've interviewed has been such a loser."

"In my view, they are," said Lloyd. "I hold people to a very high standard, you know that. The person who works for me has to want the job for the right reasons. I sometimes wonder if that person even exists."

In the van, Natalie rubbed her hands together and muttered, "I sometimes wonder if *you* really exist." She readjusted the headphones, trying to cover her frigid ears.

"But *why* does he have to believe the same things as you?" said Peter.

"Because it's my store, because it's my statement. I don't want someone in there who's going to subvert it."

"You must be disappointed in people a lot," said Peter. "It surprises me you ever meet anyone who fills the bill for you."

A long silence now—so long that Natalie thought the headphones had gone dead. She took them off, banged them against the floor of the van, then put them back on it time to hear Lloyd say, "Disappointed? Yeah, I guess so. But it happens all the time. In fact, I look at it almost as a series of terrible epiphanies—of sudden realizations that people aren't capable of becoming what I want them to be. I always thought, if I just explain my political views rationally, I'll get a rational hearing and, probably, a rational agreement; but 'reason' is a dirty word to some people. And even people who claim to be rational aren't always. Like, I've met deeply religious people who call themselves rationalists.

"It's not just a matter of ideology, either," he continued. "It's everything. For instance, I never used to think that there were people in the world who can't be moved by art. But they exist. They can experience art—they can sit through, say, all four movements of a Beethoven symphony, they can stare as long as you ask them to at a painting by Titian, they can watch a play by O'Neill, they can listen to a poem by Yeats—and it means absolutely nothing to them, they come away completely unaffected. Even if they say they've enjoyed it, they look at you strangely if you ask them whether it's going to have any effect on their lives—as if the idea of being changed by art had never occurred to them. I'd always thought it was just a matter of getting people to art, just a matter of breaking down the barriers, but it's not. And I kept wondering about that, and wondering, and wondering—you know, why? Why is that? And later, when I saw that just about anything and everything is called 'art' today—you know, macramé, boxing, French cooking—I wondered about that, too.

"And you know what I decided was the reason for all that? I decided that we, as a civilization, are losing our capability to think in abstract terms. I love technology, you know that, I love what it's given us, but sometimes I have doubts, and you're the only one I've ever confessed this to; but I wonder if technology, in allowing us to increase the pace of our lives beyond anything we could've imagined a hundred and fifty years ago, and by giving us an endless stream of pop distractions in the form of television, computers, instant cures, processed foods—whether it's really robbed us of the time, and even the need, to think in the abstract. It's possible to go through your entire life without considering a moral issue, or an ideological or philosophical one, and never feel the lack—you know people like that. Your friend Natalie, for one."

Natalie's heart gallumphed at the mention of her name. Then a flash of anger seared through her body, like an electrical charge. She wished she could release that anger through her eyes, like a character in a Brian DePalma movie; she would have liked to set Lloyd's house on fire just by looking at it. And what made her angriest of all was that he was absolutely dead-on in his assessment of her.

"But when I first met you," he continued, "that was what struck me about you. You could consider things in the abstract—not just argue them from the knee-jerk position that every label has a platform and if you're 'liberal' or 'conservative' or 'religious,' then *this* is what you think and not *this*—your thinking was your own. You adapted to it. I don't think I could have loved you otherwise. Even if we disagree, it's not important to me as long as we're both thinkers. I suppose that makes me some kind of elitist; I believe only men and women who think in abstract terms, at least part of the time, are truly civilized."

Then began what Natalie knew by now to be the sounds of their lovemaking. She listened for a few moments more; then the cold gripped her in earnest, and it seemed like a cold beyond the mere realm of temperature. She removed the headphones, switched off the tape recorder, went back to the driver's seat, and drove quietly away.

She looked in the rearview mirror and saw the light in Lloyd and Peter's bedroom go out. Then she looked at her own reflection and saw that she was wearing a wild, bestial, baleful look; it was a look of desperate hatred—the look of a loser who's already been forgotten by the victor.

She felt like screaming; and so she screamed. She heard the sound, shrill and ragged, bouncing off the houses in the neighborhood, like a cue ball off the sides of a billiards table, ricocheting away from her until it was somewhere else, its strength reduced but its anguish undiminished.

A few blocks farther on, she turned on her headlights.

CHAPTER 24

Curtis called on Thursday. "You gotta return the equipment, girl," he said. "Trial's only two months away and Luigi's getting scared that the lawyers are gonna wanna check the evidence again."

"Okay," she said. She rolled off the couch and turned off the TV set; she'd fallen asleep while watching a movie whose title and plot she couldn't remember now. As she got to her feet, a half-eaten bag of potato chips fell from her lap and spilled onto the floor. The other half had been her dinner.

She let the chips lie and made her way through similar debris to her kitchen, which was piled high with dirty dishes and overfilled trash bags. At the sight of her, a cockroach fled into a drawer.

"It ain't gonna be a problem for you?" Curtis asked.

"Uh-uh," she mumbled, taking a Diet Coke from the refrigerator and popping it open. "Anytime you want, you can come get it." It had been days since she'd even bothered to tune in to Peter and Lloyd's bedroom conversations. Her spirit had withered; she'd just given up.

"Sometime this weekend?"

She took a quick swallow of soda and said, "Sure. Saturday night's okay."

"You're not doing anything Saturday night?" he asked incredulously. *"You?"*

"No." She went back to the living room and dropped onto the couch again. She picked a few potato chips off the floor and ate them.

Curtis whistled. "You feel okay, Natalie?"

"Uh-huh."

"You sure?"

"Uh-huh."

"All right, then." He sounded unconvinced. "See you Saturday."

"Uh-huh." She turned off the phone.

Well, that would work out fine. She had put the van in a garage because, with its back window broken, she couldn't very well leave it on the street anymore; she was taking a chance even leaving it in a garage, but she'd backed it into a stall until its bumper had touched the wall, so she was pretty sure no one was going to be getting through that window. And there she had left it, for days now. But she had to take it out on Saturday, to drive to her mother's party in Oak Park; so she'd get the receiver and tape deck out when she returned, and bring them up to her apartment for Curtis to retrieve.

She finished off the Diet Coke and all the potato chips she could rescue from the broadloom, then lay on the couch and wondered who had previously owned the bug and what he or she had done with it. A drug lord, perhaps, monitoring clients? A white-collar criminal, spying on a business rival? A mafioso, testing an underling's fealty? She felt a strange kinship with whoever it was. Maybe she'd even attend the trial. . . .

She slept for another eleven hours. When she got up, she felt weak. She didn't know what day it was. She went to the bathroom and threw up.

"I've got to get some decent food in me," she said aloud, looking at her chalky, emaciated reflection with alarm. But the thought of eating repelled her.

She sat on the toilet and tried to make her bowels move, but they wouldn't. So she rested her elbows on her knees and tried to figure out what she should do with her life. She'd memorized the notebook of transcriptions of Peter and Lloyd's private conversations, and she still couldn't conceive of a way of taking her revenge on them. Curtis had been right—there was virtually nothing in their lives she could use against them. Just that tension between them on the matter of the gun shop; Peter was so upset about the idea that someone might commit some terrible act with a gun that had been purchased from Lloyd. If that were to happen, there'd be trouble in paradise, for sure. But what could she do—stand outside Lloyd's store and beg each customer who came out to become a sniper or assassinate the mayor?

Eventually she gave up trying to shit, got up, and pulled up her panties. The toilet was empty, but she flushed anyway, out of force of habit. Then she got on her bathroom scale, held her hair away from her eyes, and checked her weight. A hundred and fifty-four. She was wasting away to nothing. Peter wouldn't even recognize her; he hadn't set eyes on her in months.

"I have *got* to get some decent food," she told herself again. She got off the scale and went back to the couch for another nap.

On Saturday she put on her favorite old Perry Ellis cocktail dress; it practically fell off her, but it was the only clean party frock she had. She tried to run a brush through her hair but gave up. She threw water on her face and took a cab to the Lincoln Park garage where she'd left the van. She'd left it there so long that she had to pay almost a hundred dollars to get it out again.

On the drive to Oak Park, she had a dizzy spell and ran into an ancient Cadillac Fleetwood, denting its passenger door. She had no proof of insurance with her, and the old Italian who owned the Fleetwood was rapidly becoming apoplectic. "Girls on drugs!" he cried, pulling at his hair. "Why does everywhere I go there have to be girls on drugs?" She couldn't imagine what he meant by that, but she gave him two hundred dollars in cash and he gave her a big smile and said she reminded him of his daughter.

When Natalie slipped her key into her mother's front door and entered the house, she was amazed at how clean the place was; it nearly sparkled. "Mom?" she called.

Sandy Stathis appeared from around the corner, looking

fine in a rose cocktail dress that Natalie knew to be at least twenty-five years old. "It's back in style again," she said, pointing to it.

But Sandy didn't even seem pleased that Natalie had remembered it; in fact, she came up to her with a look of grave concern and hugged her. "Honey, aren't you feeling well?"

"I'm fine," she said, pushing away. "Just tired, is all."

Sandy held her at arm's length, looked her over, and shook her head. "No, no, this isn't good." She felt Natalie's forehead and said, "No fever. Are you eating right?"

"Yes," Natalie lied.

"I'm sure you aren't. You look even thinner than last time I saw you, and you looked like an ad in a Catholic missionary magazine then. You come in right now and have a little sandwich." She pulled Natalie into the dining room, which was set up with a spectacular buffet. A whole side of beef sat at its center, with thin slices flopping off one end. There was a pewter champagne bucket holding a bottle of nonalcoholic cider, a pewter tray of poached mushrooms, a spread of shrimp, Carr's crackers, assorted cheeses, and more.

"Mom, Jesus," said Natalie, impressed.

"Isn't it wonderful?" Sandy said. "Some of these things have been in storage for *years*. Darnita dug them out. With my permission, of course. Darnita!" she called. "Natalie has arrived."

The tiny girl appeared from the other side of the table; she rearranged the silverware en route. She was wearing one of Natalie's old party dresses. It was a less-than-perfect fit.

"Hi, Darnita," Natalie said.

"Hi," said Darnita, her eyes wild with excitement. "Thank you for coming."

Natalie nearly laughed, but stopped herself; she could see that this was serious business for the girl.

"May I get you a drink?" Darnita asked.

"Yes, please, a glass of cider would be fine." When the girl turned and skipped back to the table, Natalie leaned over to her mother and whispered, "Why are we all talking like the queen of England?"

"Darnita insists on it," Sandy whispered back. "Everything has to be proper."

Sandy approached the table while Darnita struggled to get the cider from the champagne bucket.

"I'm going to fix Natalie a sandwich, honey," Sandy said, carving the beef and placing the slices on a thick wedge of French bread.

Darnita nearly exploded. "No! No! No! Gramma, the other guests aren't here!" She jumped up and down and stamped her feet.

"Manners, honey!" Sandy said, wagging a finger. "Natalie isn't feeling well, and the needs of our guests always come first, don't they?"

Darnita whipped her arms across her chest, threw a murderous glance at Natalie, and stormed to the other side of the table to sulk.

Sandy brought the sandwich to Natalie and said, "This was my wedding china. From when I married your father, not Max."

Natalie took a tiny bite of the sandwich; she didn't really want it. "That girl has ferocious ambition," she whispered, nodding her head in Darnita's direction.

Sandy grinned. "Yes, isn't it thrilling?"

A few minutes later they heard a terrible, congested roar from the street. They went to the window and saw a horribly rusted-out Olds Cutlass Supreme pull up in front of the house. The terrible noise died with the engine. Then a young black couple got out.

"It's Quentin and Lawanda," said Sandy, her hand cupped over her mouth in alarm. "That's not the car he usually borrows to come out here. Thank God they left the baby behind—that thing looks like a death trap! I hope the police don't tow it."

Lawanda was dressed in a skirt and sweater, but Quentin, who had more earrings than Natalie, wore a T-shirt that said FIGHT THE POWERS, a pair of Nike Air sneakers that were almost as big as breadboxes, and sunglasses that he declined to remove once he was inside the house.

Natalie was introduced, and although Lawanda was the picture of politeness, Quentin shook her hand without a word and then stood off by himself in a corner, gobbling slices of beef from his bare hands.

"Don't mind him, it's his way," said Sandy when Natalie

followed her into the kitchen to voice her concern. "He feels like an outsider, so he's trying to make it look like he doesn't care."

The party was something of a disaster; Quentin wouldn't speak, Lawanda was clearly intimidated by Natalie (even in Natalie's present wasted state), Sandy kept begging Natalie to eat, and Darnita kept laying down the law on etiquette as if she had invented it.

"Shrimp fork, *shrimp fork*," the child had shrieked when Natalie ventured to eat a shrimp with her fingers. The moral outrage Darnita managed to summon forth on this issue positively jolted Natalie, who reached over at once for a shrimp fork.

As for Natalie herself, her thoughts kept drifting from reality into morbid fantasy. In the middle of her mother's heartfelt tirade (totally lost on Quentin and Lawanda) on how catering was a lost art and had been for at least thirty years and probably longer, Natalie found herself picturing Peter and Lloyd in bed together, their arms and legs entwined, kissing each other with wide, wet mouths. During one of Lawanda's feeble attempts to get Quentin to join the conversation ("Tell Mrs. Stathis 'bout how you lifts weights, Quen." "I lifts weights." "Tell that joke you tol' me yesterday to Mrs. Stathis, Quen." "Forgot it."), Natalie found her mind wandering to the unlined, untroubled face of Lloyd Hood, its features set in a perpetual attitude of implacable calm, and she found herself wondering where the skin in his forehead and chin would fold if his face were suddenly to contort in excruciating agony.

And when Darnita, out of nowhere, turned to her and said, as would any hostess worth her salt, "May I get you anyfing else, Natalie?," Natalie started at the sound of her own name and said, "What? I'm sorry; I wasn't paying attention," and Darnita dashed into the kitchen and spent about ninety seconds weeping and shrieking in frustration. Sandy followed her to calm her down, during which time Natalie looked at Quentin and Lawanda and, smiling, shrugged her shoulders as if to say, Kids! But the young couple just stared at her as though she might bite them if they made any sudden moves.

An hour later, everyone was dying to leave. Darnita, however, was flushed with success; despite a few rocky patches, she had hosted a party for grown-ups, and now they were all professing how much they'd enjoyed it. (She hadn't yet learned about the useful adult art of social fibbing.)

Lawanda and Quentin said their good-byes and left, and now Natalie stood in the doorway. "Thanks so much, Mom. It was a trip. Oh, look, Darnita's cleaning up. Glad you taught her that part. More than I ever learned."

Sandy wouldn't banter back. She furrowed her brow and said, "I'm worried about you, young lady."

"Don't be."

"You can't tell a mother not to worry. You've lost too much weight in too short a time, and your eyes are dull. Something's wrong. It's not Peter, is it?"

"I haven't seen Peter in months."

"Then wh—" She was interrupted by the third, and loudest, dying groan from Quentin's borrowed Cutlass. "Oh, dear, I'm afraid he can't get that decrepit thing to start."

Quentin didn't want to give up; he sat in the street trying, and trying, and trying, and the car kept groaning, and groaning, and groaning, and Natalie could see that Lawanda was near tears. Some of Sandy's neighbors were out on their lawns now, watching.

Sandy bit her fingernail. "Oh, dear. What can I do?"

Natalie patted her arm, then went to the driver's side of the car and motioned Quentin to roll down the window.

"Yeah?" he said.

"I think I'd better give you a ride home," she said.

"I don't need no fuckin' charity, man."

"Quen!" Lawanda snapped.

"What you need is a ride home," Natalie insisted. "This car isn't going anywhere. You can come back for it later." She stood her ground, her eyes boring into him. "Come on. Get into my van."

The drive was, at first, uncomfortable. It was impossible to heat the van because of the broken window, and Lawanda's lips were turning blue; she hugged herself and shivered. Quentin kept eyeing the receiver and tape deck in the back as if he were considering stealing them.

But the closer they came to the city, the more animated the group became. "Fuckin' Bobby gon' try'n' make me pay for his piece-o'-shit car when it are him that have drive it down to nuthin'," he said. "I cain't pay shit. I ain't got no paper, man. What I s'posed to do? Roll somebody?"

"Oh, Quen, no," said Lawanda; she was almost hyperventilating.

"You don't have a job, right?" asked Natalie as they drove under the Pulaski exit sign. The city skyline was before them now, lit up against the night, majestic and faintly terrifying.

"Who gon' give a ex-Rama Z a job?" he said, naming a particularly virulent North Side gang. "Who are gon' give a paycheck to a nigger wif a record?"

Natalie suddenly got an idea that almost made her drive off the road.

"You know guns, Quentin?" she asked.

"Shit if I doesn't know gun."

"You own any?"

He shook his head. "Handled plenty."

"You want to work in a gun shop?"

He laughed. "Last place anyone ever hire *me*. I were Rama Z, man! I marked for life. You hear what I were just sayin'?"

She smiled. "You read much, Quentin?"

"I can read," he said defensively.

"But *do* you?"

"Ain't got time." He looked ahead of him.

She took the ramp from the Eisenhower onto the Dan Ryan expressway. "Do you know who Ayn Rand is?"

"No."

"Quentin, if I told you that reading a book by Ayn Rand could get you a job, would you read it?"

He looked at her. "I guess."

"It's a long book. A couple hundred pages."

He stared at her. "I just gots to read a book? Tha's all? Then I gets a job in a gun shop?"

She shrugged. "Well, you can't *just* read it. You have to believe in it. And you have to convince the owner of the shop that you believe in it. You have to make him think that that book changed your life."

He smirked. "Who are gon' b'lieve that?"

"This guy will. Trust me."

"Where I get this book?"

She swung off at the first exit. "We'll pick it up now. Start reading it tonight and don't stop until you're finished. And by next week, you'll have a job."

Quentin looked at Lawanda, then back at Natalie, then back at the road. "Shit if that happen," he said.

Lawanda and Quentin lived in a housing project on Clybourn Street, just north of Cabrini Green, the city's most notorious public-housing failure. Natalie was surprised to see how close Cabrini Green really was to the trendy River North shops and restaurants she once frequented. If she'd known then of this dreadful proximity, she'd have been a little less keen on wandering the neighborhood at night, drunk, with Peter.

Now, as she rounded the corner and sped away from Cabrini, she lowered her head a little, remembering the news stories she'd read of how bullets regularly fly across the playgrounds there and fell innocent bystanders. When nothing happened, she lifted her head again, feeling a little silly and embarrassed.

Lawanda and Quentin's building was about twelve stories high, but it looked as though Natalie could kick it down without much effort. It was slate-gray and streaked with grime, and its windows all stood open, giving it a burned-out, desolate look. Natalie thought it wouldn't be out of place in the worst sections of Beirut, or Belfast.

Quentin hopped out and held the door for Lawanda. "Thank you for the ride, Natalie," Lawanda said.

"Don't mention it."

She smoothed her skirt and said, "I hope you doesn't mind if I don't aks you up."

Natalie shook her head. "No, I understand. It's pretty late, and—"

"No, not that, it's just that the elevators is broke."

"Then how will you get to your apar—"

"Oh, we takes the stair. But it ain't a good idea for a white lady to do that. I only does it 'cause I gots Quentin wif me, and even then it sometime take some doin'."

Natalie shuddered and hoped they didn't see it. "Well—so long."

"So long," said Lawanda.

"You read that book, now," she admonished Quentin.

He held up the copy of *The Fountainhead* she had bought him. "It sure a *long* fucker," he said, tossing it up in his hand, as if weighing it.

"It'll get you the job," she said. "Just keep telling yourself that, if it gets tough."

As she pulled onto Clybourn again and drove away, she thought about Darnita growing up in that terrible environment. The child might be a little monster, but this place would squash her like a bug—it would kill the ambition in her, there was no doubt about that.

Better not to think about it. Instead, she tried to conjure up a way she might use Quentin to her advantage once he started working for Lloyd.

"Are you reading it, Quentin?" she asked him.

"Man, what you call me for? I say I read it, I will!"

"Are you reading it *now*, Quentin?"

"You never tell me this writer a woman. What I needs to read some woman for?"

"It's simple. If you want the job, you'll read it."

"I gots to get off the phone now."

"*Read* it, Quentin."

"Right." He hung up.

An hour later Natalie's doorbell rang. She knew it could only be Curtis, so she buzzed him in, then went to the door and held it open for him. She detected an odor of decaying banana somewhere in the door's vicinity and made a mental note to try to track it down later.

Half a minute later, Curtis entered her apartment and made a face. "What the hell happened here?"

She shut the door behind him. "What do you mean?"

"You look like hell, this place looks like hell." He kicked aside a greasy Wendy's bag. "Girlfriend, you are a *mess*."

She bristled. "I don't have a lot of time to clean." She went to the living room and motioned him to follow. "Come on in."

She'd stacked the receiver and the tape deck on her coffee table. "There they are. You can take them and leave."

He picked them up. "Where's the bug?"

She went white. "What?"

"The bug, Natalie. It's not here that I can see."

She sat down. "You need that back, too?"

He stared at her for a moment, then put the equipment back on the table. "You mean to tell me you don't have the bug?"

"I thought you just needed *this* stuff back."

He rubbed the bridge of his nose. "*This* stuff is nothing. That *bug* is the important thing. You mean to say you don't have it?"

"God, Curtis, it's still in Peter's house! What did you expect?"

"Well, you're gonna have to get it back, girl."

"I can't do that!" She put her hands on her face. "Oh, Christ, Curtis! I haven't even *spoken* to Peter in months!"

He sat down across from her and looked at her gravely. "You *better* get that bug back, Natalie. This ain't nursery school, you know. We bribed a cop to get you that equipment; it was being held as evidence for a courtroom trial. You don't get it back, the heat's on him, and if the heat's on him, the heat's on you, only worse. They'll come down on you hard, girl. The police force doesn't go easy on cops who take bribes; and no cop is gonna take a fall because you're afraid to talk to your old boyfriend. These guys play hardball. They don't fuck around."

She shot to her feet and started pacing the room. Cold sweat bathed her forehead. "But you've got a cop for a lover, right? That's how we could do this in the first place. Can't you work it out with him?"

"I *had* a cop as my lover. I'm through with that pig. I'm not even talking to him anymore. He had to send me a telegram to tell me he needs this stuff back, 'cause I kept hanging up on him."

"What's his name? I'll talk to him myself." Her breath was

coming hard now; she could taste blood on her tongue. This was real anxiety.

Curtis raised an eyebrow and sighed. "Okay. I'll leave it up to you two." He took a pen from his pocket and started writing on a partially soiled Burger King napkin he found lying on the coffee table. "His name's Luigi Gianelli. This is his home number. But don't think you can charm this guy with your big blue eyes, Natalie. He's no fool. And he's a real asshole, too. You don't get to be a gay man on the Chicago Police Force unless you're one tough-assed son of a bitch." He got up, leaving the receiver and the tape deck behind. "You deal with him from now on. Far as I'm concerned, that fucker's *history*." And with that, he left her apartment.

Natalie clutched her hand to her forehead. She thought she might faint. She picked up her phone and dialed Luigi Gianelli's number. It rang once—twice—three times. She paced the room, her heart pounding.

After four rings, an answering machine kicked in. "This is Gianelli," a gruff voice said. "I'm not in. Leave a message."

The electronic tone sounded, and Natalie panicked and hung up.

Jesus, she thought; that guy sounds like he could eat me *raw*.

CHAPTER 26

Two days passed before Natalie got up the nerve to call him again. This time he was home.

"Gianelli," he said. It sounded like an accusation.

"Officer Gianelli, this is Natalie Stathis."

"Who?"

"Curtis's friend." She paused. "The one who—uh—borrowed—well, you know . . ."

A long silence. Then, "Uh-huh."

"I thought perhaps we could meet."

An even longer silence. "Uh-huh."

"Friday night, the bar of your choice. That okay?"

He didn't respond; what was going on here?

"Say, Roscoe's?"

The longest silence yet. "Uh-huh."

"I'll be wearing a bright red sweatshirt, so you can't miss me. I'm sure we can work something out then. 'Bye!"

She didn't wait for him to answer, but hung up at once, and sat hugging herself. God, was *that* a creepy experience!

Suddenly her ceiling seemed higher, and the walls farther

away, and she felt dwarfed by the enormity of her difficulties and her danger. All she'd wanted was to ruin Peter and Lloyd's life; it had seemed so simple. She certainly hadn't counted on ruining her own. But she'd been abandoned by her only ally—abandoned to the mercy of a Chicago cop turned bad!—and there was no one to help her or even to console her; she was utterly alone, and frightened.

And the day of her judgment was swiftly approaching. How fitting that it should take place in a gay bar.

A day later, her spirits improved with a phone call from Quentin.

"I gets the job," he said.

Natalie leapt into the air. "Wonderful!"

"I didn't even has to meet him," the boy enthused. "He give me the job from just talking on the phone!"

"You didn't mention me, did you?" she asked, suddenly nervous.

"No, you tells me not to."

She was having dinner at the moment—peanut butter out of a spoon. She took another mouthful and said, "What did you say to him?"

"You eatin'?" the boy asked.

"Yes. What did you say to him?"

"Peanut butter?"

"Yes. What did you say to him?"

"Man, I be good at guessin' food."

"Quentin, *what did you say to him*?"

"Well, he aks me how I hear about the job and I tells him a friend have tell me, and he say how do your friend hear and I say I don't know. Then he aks me my background and I tells him, I gots to be honest wif you, I were Rama Z, but I have get out of it and now I wants to change my life. And I can tell he a little bit hesitation, but I go on and say, I knows gun, man, I knows 'em, but I isn't disresponsible wif 'em, so you can trust me. I think serious about gun, they important. Then I goes on a bit like you tells me about the Bill of Right, and how it are important to be a free individual who are free to choose, like Howard Roark in *The Fountainhead*. And right away Mr. Hood get all excited and say, oh, you likes that book?"

Natalie laughed out loud. "I knew it!"

"So I say, yeah, that book change my life. That book get me outta Rama Z and give me a real direction."

"Wonderful. This is wonderful."

"Thing is, I only read the first forty page so far. I just bullshit him from that. You think I gots to finish that book, Natalie? Tha's a awful long book."

"Absolutely. He's sure to bring it up again. Remember, I said read it and *believe* in it. What happened next?"

"Well, we talk about it for a while, then he tell me he need someone like me workin' at his shop, and he say he not even gonna talk to no one else till he meet me, and I say, oh, so I *do* gots to interview. And he say, no, you gots the job, but I just wants to meet you first to be sure. Man, he are okay, Natalie."

"Oh, he's one of a kind."

"He have earn my respeck, just—bam!—like that."

"Listen, Quentin," she said, lowering her voice, "I got you this job. I found it for you and told you how to get it. Isn't that right?"

"Yeah." He sounded suddenly suspicious.

"Now, where would you be without that job?"

"Up shit creek," he said.

"So you owe me a favor, now, don't you? A big one."

He paused. "Well, yeah, I guesses."

"Not 'I guess'—you do."

"Okay, okay. What you wants me to do?"

"I don't know yet. It might be something you have to hide from Mr. Hood."

A short pause. "Shit on that."

"Quentin—you owe me."

He sighed. "You tell me what you wants when you have figure it out, then we talk, okay?"

"Okay. And congratulations to you."

"Thanks."

She hung up, her mind whirling. She felt so alive that she ordered a pizza and ate the whole thing—more food than she'd managed to keep down all month.

CHAPTER 27

Natalie hadn't been to Roscoe's in ages, and now it seemed that all the faces there were new. What could have caused that? Surely AIDS couldn't have felled an entire bar's worth of men so quickly—although there had been times in the past when she'd thought that grisly disease unstoppable.

No, it was more likely that her crowd of familiars had found a newer, fresher, more exciting watering hole, and moved on—or simply paired off and become homebodies, like Peter and Lloyd; she felt ancient at the thought, a relic of another age. But in the end, she had to admit that it suited her. She couldn't bear the thought of even one of her old friends seeing her like this. She'd tried to pull herself together to resemble her old self, but she still looked like a shell of the woman she used to be. Her hair was dull, her eyes duller, and her clothes hung off her like the spare skin on a Shar-Pei. The mask of makeup she'd applied only made her look sorrier than ever—like a scrawny Christmas tree with too many ornaments.

Scarcely the ideal circumstances under which to face a corrupt Chicago cop who had a bone to pick with her. She hadn't fully figured out her strategy with Officer Gianelli; should she plead with him, try to bribe him, threaten to expose him? The last possibility made her shiver with fear; she didn't dare try to play hardball with an All-Star.

She moved through the crowd, looking at every face that passed in front of hers; none met her eyes for more than a second. She was the only woman in the bar; never mind her red sweatshirt, it would be impossible for Gianelli not to notice her.

She ordered herself a Bacardi on the rocks, then sat at the bar, toying nervously with a cocktail straw. The video monitors were showing old 1950s television commercials—women ecstatically using vaccuum cleaners, dishwashing liquid, hairspray. Could any of them have conceived that a member of their sex would one day develop problems as unorthodox as hers?

She felt a tap on her arm.

She put down her drink and turned. Standing there, wearing a scowl, was an enormous, hairy, barrel-chested man in a plain white T-shirt, black jeans, and a leather jacket. His eyebrows were big and frightening—they were as woolly and matted as roadkill—and his dark eyes narrowed in what Natalie presumed to be contempt.

"You Natalie?" he said.

She nodded, unable to speak. A cold, bad feeling had gripped the base of her spine and was traveling up her vertebrae, one by one, like a corrosive acid.

Officer Gianelli—for that's who this must be—motioned with his head that she should follow him. She slipped off her stool, forgetting her drink, and trailed behind him as he plowed his way through the bar, knocking less massive patrons to and fro. He didn't once turn to make sure she was still with him.

He led her to the darkest corner of the bar, where two empty stools sat waiting for them. He motioned her onto the one on the right, then swung his own beefy leg over the one on the left.

He sat staring at her while the music thoom-thoompa-thoomed in her ears. Why this torture? she thought. He hasn't even heard what I'm going to say!

She gulped. "Officer Gianelli—" she started.

He held up a finger, silencing her. Then in a low voice he said, "Luigi."

She blinked. "Pardon me?"

"Lu-i-gi. That's my name."

Thoroughly nonplussed, she stammered into an explanation. "I—I—I'm aware of how important it is that you get that bugging device back befo—"

He gasped loudly, seemingly inhaling half the air in the bar; heads turned at the sound.

Natalie stopped short. She stared at him, not knowing what to think.

His eyes squinted, and he burst into an explosive sob.

"Nothing matters except getting Curtis back!" he howled. "You've gotta help me, Natalie! I can't eat, I can't sleep—I—" He buried his head in his hands and just plain bawled.

Everyone in the bar was staring. She shifted on her stool and tried to look nonchalant. She diligently checked her cuticles and adjusted her watch very laboriously. Luigi gasped a few more times, then blasted forth with a fresh shriek of despair.

Someone in the bar chuckled. Surprising herself, Natalie began to feel protective of Luigi—this man who, mere moments before, had had her frightened half out of her wits. She sat up straight and coldly met the eyes of every man who dared to look in his direction; soon all had turned away and left him to sob and moan in private.

He pulled a handkerchief from his leather jacket and mopped his eyes. "Oh, mother Mary," he said, "I'm such a fuckin' wuss for crying like that. But I break down all the time now. I'm always on the fuckin' verge. If I say more than a couple words, my whole heart comes out my fuckin' mouth. On the job it's hell. Two nights ago I picked up this kid on crack; he looked just like Curtis. I cuffed him and read him his rights and put him in the backseat, and as soon I got behind the wheel I started fuckin' weeping and I couldn't stop. I had to fuckin' pull over for a couple minutes."

Natalie put a hand on his shoulder and clucked over his misery. "What happened?" she asked him. She was so relieved that he wasn't giving her any grief, that she felt positively maternal toward him.

He rolled his eyes heavenward and waved his handkerchief in dismissal. "Oh, what fuckin' always happens—he caught me with somebody else. Can I help it? I'm not made to be fuckin' monogamous, Natalie. I tried so fuckin' hard, and for months—" He wiped his nose and stuffed the soiled handkerchief back into his jacket pocket. "But nobody's ever meant fuck to me except Curtis. All I want out of life now is to be with him. He's fuckin' *got* to give me another chance. Natalie, you know him, you're his friend—"

"Not quite a friend," she said. "We're friendly, but I—"

"Whatever," he said testily. Natalie reminded herself that she should still treat this guy carefully; there was no telling what a bent Chicago cop was capable of doing. He sniffed and said, "I don't know where else to turn. He's already got all his friends giving me the fuckin' silent treatment. Makes me want to beat the fuck out of those little twinky sons of bitches, smash their fuckin' teeth in, the way they snub me. But then I know Curtis would never—I mean, I'd fuckin' *never* have a chance with him again if I did that."

What, Natalie wondered, could this brawny, macho cop with his rough-hewn, beer-commercial looks want with a slight, stylish gamin like Curtis? What could make for so powerful an attraction?

As if to answer her, Luigi pulled out his wallet. "Take a look at this," he said, and he opened it to a Polaroid snapshot of a black man's naked pelvis, with an enormous hard-on standing at forty-five degrees from the camera. In spite of herself, Natalie crossed her knees.

"Curtis?" she asked, trying to sound urbane and unaffected, but her voice was like a teapot coming to boil.

Luigi nodded, not taking his eyes from the snapshot. He reached into the wallet and produced a few more. "Here's another one," he said, handing it to her.

She took it from him and looked down at it with some apprehension, as if it were alive and might bite her. It was an extremely explicit shot; Curtis, still naked, was on his back, with his ankles wrapped behind his head, with all that might be revealed by such a pose revealed quite alarmingly. "Oh, my," she said.

"I know," Luigi said admiringly. "You wouldn't fuckin' believe what that guy can do. Sometimes I take these shots out at the station," he continued, handing her another one in which

Curtis was performing an act on himself that other men had told her was patently impossible, "and I get so fuckin' wired up I have to go into the can and just jerk off a load."

How poetic, thought Natalie as another photo of Curtis and his amazing appendage passed into her hands. She had to wonder at Curtis being so final in breaking up with someone who possessed such outrageous pictures of him; shouldn't he at least have waited till he could sneak them out of Luigi's wallet before telling him they were through? Well, maybe he didn't know the pictures were being taken. But no, here he was in this latest one, smiling at the camera while inserting into himself a dildo that looked distressingly like a Yule log.

She handed the photos back to Luigi. "I can see why you miss him so much."

"It's not just this," he said, apparently not wanting to seem excessively carnal. "I mean—this is a big reason why I love him, but there are others. He makes me laugh, he—uh—"

Natalie waited, but he appeared to be having trouble coming up with further examples. "Never mind, I understand," she said, patting his hand. "What I *don't* understand is why you carry those around in your wallet. What if you got shot or something, and were lying there unconscious? Your partners could go in your wallet and find those pictures, and they'd know you're gay."

"Ah, fuck it, everyone on the force knows I'm gay."

She raised an eyebrow. "That must make for interesting working conditions. Don't they hassle you about it?"

"They used to." He slipped the photos back into his wallet.

"Why'd they stop?"

"Simple. My uncle's a big-shot alderman. Anybody who gave me shit would suddenly get mysteriously transferred to some fuckin' war zone on the South Side, or way west. Pretty soon, the guys learned they'd better fuckin' treat me right." He tried to slip the wallet back into his jacket pocket, but it slipped out of his hand and fell. A dozen more Polaroids sprawled across the floor.

She slipped off her stool to help him scoop them up. Other patrons at the bar were stepping on them and he was shouting at them to move; he was on his hands and knees, clawing them up two and three at a time.

Natalie picked one up and was handing it to him when she noticed that it wasn't of Curtis. This was a white guy—a guy who looked very familiar. . . .

She placed him. It was Will Hammond! The man she'd stolen Peter from—the one who had called her a fag hag!

And even more astonishing: He was wearing a diaper!

Luigi snatched the photo from her hand. "Thanks," he said sheepishly.

"I know that guy!" she cried, pointing at the Polaroid as Luigi shoved it back into his wallet. "That's Will Hammond!"

He was blushing bright red. "Yeah."

"What's he doing in your wallet? Why is he wearing a diaper?"

He was sweating now. "Come on, Natalie. Mind your own fuckin' business."

"Listen, if I'm going to help you, you'd better tell me everything." She leaned forward and licked her lips; she was positively *desperate* to have some dirt on Will. That night at Bulldog Road had not been forgotten; she'd make him pay for calling her a fag hag.

Luigi stuffed the last Polaroid back in the wallet and slipped it carefully into his pocket. "All right, then," he said. "That's the guy Curtis caught me with, okay? That's the guy who fuckin' caused all my problems." He seemed on the verge of tears again.

"That sounds like Will," she said. "He loves ruining people's lives."

"I have this fetish, okay?" he said, stifling a sob. "I like to see guys in diapers. It's a tremendous fuckin' turn-on for me, okay? So fuckin' sue me. Trouble is, like, hardly anybody else is into it. I mean, if Curtis would do that for me, man, I'd never have to fuckin' play around anywhere else, ever. But sometimes I just get this urge. So I placed a fuckin' personal ad in one of the gay papers asking for someone to wear diapers for me. This guy, Will, answers, and he's a fuckin' *hunk*. So we get together, and what do you know, he's a wild man. I mean, not only will he wear diapers, he'll even crap in them, which, for me—I mean, I just fuckin' come in my *pants* over that."

This was so much more than Natalie wanted to know that she felt obliged to hold up her hand. "Okay, Luigi, I get the idea."

"All I really wanted was a couple snapshots," he said.

"Really, it's *okay*."

He rubbed the bridge of his nose, and she collected herself.

"Now," she said, "you're not seeing him anymore, are you?"

"No, no."

"Good. And you have no intention of seeing him again?"

"All I fuckin' wanted was a couple pictures. I barely fuckin' touched him."

"Yes or no, Luigi."

"No."

She folded her hands over her knees. "Okay. That helps."

"Just forget you ever saw those, okay?"

"That's not going to be easy."

"Just say you'll help me. Say you'll talk to Curtis."

She narrowed her eyes. "Tell you what. I'll consider it, if you let me have one of those pictures of Will."

"That's what it's gonna take?" he asked plaintively.

" 'Fraid so."

Glumly he removed the wallet again, thumbed through the Polaroids, and gave her a snapshot of Will parading around in cloth diapers with big blue safety pins. There was an awful, telltale bulge in the seat. She smiled evilly.

"So how 'bout it?" Luigi asked.

She slipped the Polaroid into her purse, snapped it shut, and turned to face him. She took a deep breath. "Well, as I said, we're not close friends, but yes, I'll talk to him. I'll try to convince him to give you another chance."

He took her hand. "Natalie, if you would, I'd do anything for you."

She raised an eyebrow. "Anything?"

"If you get Curtis back in my life, you just name the favor, and it's yours. I fuckin' mean it."

Her heart quickened, and her mind filled with new possibilities. She'd had to bribe a listening device out of this man, and now he was promising her everything at his disposal. And at his disposal was the full force and authority of the Chicago Police Department.

"Deal," she said.

He grinned in triumph. "I know he'll listen to you."

"I'm certainly going to try to *make* him listen."

He beamed a smile at her. "Buy you another drink?"

"Sure; Bacardi on the rocks, please."

He returned in a few minutes, having also gotten a beer for himself.

"Now," he said, handing her the Bacardi and climbing back onto his stool, "how 'bout toasting to our success?"

They did so, and Natalie took a sip of her drink, then crossed her legs and said, "Aren't we going to talk about that other issue?"

"What other issue?" He wiped his mouth on his bare wrist.

"The bug. The listening device."

He grimaced. "No. I don't care. I mean—yeah, I could lose my fuckin' job and it could be a big fuckin' scandal for the force—but Natalie, I mean it. Right now, nothing matters a fuck but Curtis. I'm in love with the guy. One thing at a time, you know? My first priority is my man."

Well, *that* was a relief. They finished their drinks, and, having nothing else to talk about, they decided to part. Natalie promised she'd call him as soon as she'd talked to Curtis.

"And I advise you to go straight home to bed, *alone*," she said. She'd caught him eyeing someone across the bar. "Don't make my job any harder than it is."

He grinned, kissed her on the cheek, and left. As soon as he had gone, she wiped away his kiss with her sleeve, her mouth twisted into a grimace of disgust.

She sat alone for a while, her mind working like mad. Plots and strategies flooded her mind; it was all she could do to sort them out.

Should she have Lloyd's store raided? She could have Quentin plant evidence that it was a front for the mob and have Luigi charge in and find it. But no, Peter would just stand behind Lloyd and help him fight the charge; it would only bring them closer together, and she wanted them ruined utterly.

Should she have Peter arrested for possession of cocaine and have Lloyd on the books as the informant? She could arrange that, with Luigi's help. But no, it was too complicated; it would involve seducing Peter into using cocaine again, and that was too daunting a task to consider; plus, if Lloyd denied having called the police, Peter would believe him.

Should she have Luigi help her frame *Lloyd* for possession? Something as ridiculous as that might strike Peter as being so absurd that it might actually be true—it might plant a seed of doubt in Peter, shattering his hero-worship of Lloyd. But no; Lloyd was just too straight-and-narrow to paint as a cokehead with any kind of conviction. Plus, he was so persuasive, he could talk his way out of anything. And, you never know, Peter might actually be *relieved* to hear that Lloyd had a failing.

She came up with scheme after scheme after scheme, and all of them fell short in some regard. But then, her concentration was less intense than it should have been, for she kept coming back to the big "if"—her ability to get Curtis back in Luigi's life.

She decided that waiting till morning would be too much agony. She polished off her drink, squeezed herself out of the bar, and trotted a few blocks over to Vortex, Curtis's favorite hangout.

He wasn't in the front bar, or the back bar, or on the dance floor, or in the video room; and she'd had just enough to drink, and enough dizzying emotion that night, to suddenly find herself disoriented by the lights and the crowd and the pounding music. And as she also hadn't eaten anything in about a day and a half, she found herself having to lean against a wall for a few minutes just to keep from fainting.

A steady stream of men passed her, laughing, singing, talking to each other, or just silently, sexually staring—eyes meeting eyes with the smoldering, unspoken, eternal question. But none of those eyes held hers for very long; they focused on her and rejected her in almost the same instant, as though she were nothing more than a mirage, a trick of the light.

But soon, someone did in fact notice her. "Oh, hi, Natalie."

It was Curtis! She willed herself to snap out of her funk. "Oh, Curtis, darling, hold on a sec." She pushed herself away from the wall.

He looked uncomfortable. He was clearly on the prowl tonight, and didn't want this wreck of a woman clinging to his arm. "What is it?" he asked curtly.

"I just had a chat with Luigi," she said, steering him out of the flow of traffic and into a corner where they could talk.

"Man, that's your problem. I told you, that guy is history, far as I'm concerned. I can't help you." He tried to pry himself away from her.

She tightened her grip on his arm. "No, that's the amazing thing," she said. "I don't need your help. He doesn't even care about the bug. All he could talk about was you."

Curtis pretended to be exasperated, but she could tell he would stand still for a little more. Who can resist hearing what a former lover has to say about him? "Well, that's too bad," he said, "but I—"

"I've never seen a six-foot-one Chicago cop cry," she continued, interrupting him. "I don't know what this guy meant to *you*, but you must've meant a lot to *him*."

He stuck his chin in the air. "Not enough to keep him from sleeping around."

"Everyone deserves a second chance, Curtis."

"He had his second, and his third, and his fourth."

Oh, thought Natalie; Luigi had conveniently forgotten to mention that.

She tweaked Curtis's chin. "Come on, you've punished him enough."

He looked down at her, furious. "I don't see that that's any of your b—"

She tightened her grip on his arm, silencing him. "Curtis, I'm *not* going to let you make a mistake like this! I'm not going to let you throw away something beautiful!" Her eyes bored into his with such insistency that she thought they might jump out of her head.

"Ow!" he yelped, yanking his arm away from her. "Jesus, girl! You outta your fucking mind? I'll haul off and slug you next time you dig your nails into me like that!"

She reached for him again, but he took a quick step back. She saw the look on his face—startled, frightened—and she knew she'd come on too strong. It was just that she was so close now—so maddeningly close! It was so unfair of him to resist—

so unfair of God, or fate, or whatever, to allow him to resist. Not after she'd been given a second chance, herself. She felt a little spasm of fury that made her want to simply club him into unconsciousness and drag him to Luigi's door.

But she had to calm down, had to try to look at this as rationally as possible. Here it was, her future, standing before her in the shape of a silly, slim, self-obsessed little waitperson. She must try to think like him, try to figure out what she might say to him that would make a difference.

He was smoothing out his sleeve. "You wrinkled me," he snarled. "Damn it, Natalie, this is *linen*. If it's gonna get wrinkled tonight, it's got to do its job first. Keep your cat's paws off me!" He started to inch away from her, but the bar was crowded, and it was slow going.

Christ, she wanted to rip his head off! Anger stung her face like a hive of killer bees. But she bit her lower lip, balled her fists, and shook off her anger. She called after him, "Curtis, please—you don't know how Luigi loves you! He spent half an hour talking about nothing else—and the things he said, my God! I only hope to live to see the day that someone loves me half as much!"

"Don't want to hear it," he said. "Don't even want to hear his name. Good-bye, Natalie." He was about three yards away from her now, trying to squeeze through a phalanx of nearly identical bleach blonds in white T-shirts and plaid blazers.

Natalie raised her eyebrow a little. Why didn't Curtis just try to edge around the blonds instead of insisting on pressing his way through them? The bar wasn't that crowded. She was certain he could be making greater progress than this. No, he must be deliberately holding back; despite himself, he did want to hear what Luigi had been saying about him.

But it might take all night to convince him to let her tell him; he'd make her grovel first, to exalt his ego, until he could gratify his desire to hear her out while at the same time seeming to do her a favor by listening. Transparent little flake, she thought; as if I've got all night. She made up her mind to call his bluff.

"Fine," she said, hiding her anger as best she could. He was still trying to make his way through the wall of blonds. "Fine, Curtis; I understand. And I respect your feelings, I really do. So long." And with that, she turned tail and headed up to the front bar.

As luck would have it, someone vacated a stool just as she arrived. She grabbed it, eliciting a murderous look from an aging lothario who'd been on his way to the same stool and who had apparently had his eye on it first. She gave him a phony smile in return, then swiveled around to the bar and ordered herself a Bacardi. She sipped it slowly; she had time to kill. Curtis would have to invent a reason to speak to her again, and he wasn't very bright. It might take him a good ten minutes. She checked her Keith Haring watch, intent on timing him.

She underestimated him. In a little under six minutes, he sidled up beside her. "Oh, hi again," he said, as if he hadn't noticed she was there until that very second. "Listen, I'm just here to order a drink. Don't start in on me about Luigi again."

"Wouldn't dream of it," she assured him, and she enjoyed the kind of panicked look that flickered across his face when she said this. She was thrilled by his discomfort.

He wasn't very assertive about ordering his drink. She noticed that he kept waiting to wave his five-dollar bill in the air until the exact moment the bartender had begun to turn away from him.

Natalie sipped her Bacardi quietly, feeling her blood race through her veins; it was an almost metaphysical experience—she'd never known silence could be so cruel a weapon, never known she could inflict such pain just by sitting still and silent. She liked the feeling.

Curtis was visibly shrinking beside her. His shoulders slumped. Now he dropped his head and looked down at his crumpled five-dollar bill.

"It's just that he hurt my feelings so much," he said, his voice small. She could barely hear him above the thump-thump-thump of the loudspeakers.

"Excuse me?" she said loudly, adding to his torture. "Did you say something?"

He looked at her with wide, vulnerable eyes. "No," he said hastily. "Nothing." He took a discreet glance to his left, then his right, and when he determined that no one else was listening, he said, in a stronger voice, "Just that he hurt me. My feelings, I mean."

She cocked her head, as if disappointed in him. "Lovers never do that, Curtis? They never hurt each other?"

"But, lots of times," he said, a little break in his voice. "He did it lots of times."

"I repeat: lovers never do that? Lovers are always perfect and considerate to each other and never cheat?"

He turned away from her, his jaw jutting out. She could tell he'd found a final reserve of pride, one last little bastion of no-no-no. She might lose him altogether now. She uncrossed her legs and spun around on her barstool.

"It's not so much a matter of how many times he cheats," she said, "but of how many times he comes back. Which is every time, isn't it? He's come back every time." And she thought of Peter, of whom this could no longer be said, and her determination fired up again. If Curtis didn't buy this line, she'd do something drastic—offer him money to go back to Luigi. Fifty bucks. A hundred. A thousand. And if he didn't take it—well, she just might lose her mind and kill him.

He pursed his lips. "Where's the fucking bartender, anyway?" he snarled, looking up. He waved his five-dollar bill pathetically, then dropped his hand and said, "So he loves me. That's supposed to solve everything?"

She put her hand on his arm. "I'm going to leave now. You look around this bar tonight and see what there is to see. Maybe you'll find someone you like; maybe you won't. But when you wake up tomorrow, it won't matter if you've got someone with you or not; you'll still miss him. Just like he misses you. He's in bed, alone, right now. I happen to know that."

Curtis looked at her as though she'd just told him she was from the planet Krypton. "Luigi, at home alone on a Friday night? Right, girlfriend. *That'll* happen."

"Call him if you don't believe me." She pecked his cheek, then slipped off her stool and started pushing through the crowd toward the door. Just as she stepped outside, she turned for a quick look back—and saw Curtis at the pay phone, dialing.

What she had pulled off tonight was a feat worthy of her

old self. Instead of trying to apologize for Luigi, instead of trying to absolve or explain his infidelities—none of which would have worked—she'd simply shown Curtis that apologies, absolutions, and explanations were beside the point; she'd shown him that he loved Luigi in a way that even he couldn't deny. And it had taken her only seconds to decide on that approach. Sometimes she wondered if anyone could withstand her manipulations.

Which, of course, reminded her of Lloyd Hood. Well, we'll see what we'll see about Lloyd the Wonderful, she thought. There was little doubt now that she could count on Luigi as an ally in her plan for revenge.

Out on the sidewalk now, she moved within an aura of cigarette smoke; it wafted from her clothes and clung to her hair like a halo. It had probably permeated her skin. For a moment, she thought of sitting on the curb and airing out, but without Peter it would be too poignant a thing to do. Instead, she flapped her arms and shook her head as she walked down Halsted Street, knowing she must look like a complete nut case, but not caring.

Because all that shaking seemed to knock some sense into her head. She seemed to shake something loose that rattled around between her ears and dredged up an idea.

A truly magnificent idea.

The walk up Aldine Street was quiet and restful; she could almost believe she was alone in the city. The old houses on either side of the street were mostly dark; a few upper-story windows were lit, but as Natalie passed them, these went out, one by one. The lights of Aldine went out as the lights in her head went on. She was delighted with the symmetry of it.

As she got closer to home, the plan took fuller form, and she marveled at its intricacy. She would need Luigi's help, and Quentin's, and both now owed her favors. It was a plan that would thoroughly discredit Lloyd in Peter's eyes, and provide Natalie with a glorious opportunity to take her revenge in person, without suffering any consequences whatsoever. And, as an added bonus, it would even enable her to get the bugging device out of Lloyd and Peter's bedroom.

She swept into her apartment, shut the door, and did a little pirouette into her living room; she was thrilled with what the future promised.

Then she noticed that her answering machine was blinking. She twirled over to it—kicking aside an empty corn chips bag—and played the message.

It was Luigi.

"I owe you *big*," is all he said.

CHAPTER 28

A few Fridays later, Natalie arrived at the New Town Armory just after four o'clock. She poked her head in the door and saw only Quentin behind the counter.

"He gone?" she asked *sotto voce*.

He waved her in. "Yeah, he leave just like he say he would. He tell me he can trusts me for a hour, so he have go home early to pack for his trip."

She crept into the shop. She'd never been here before; it was somewhat like a jewelry shop, full of glass cases, except that the glass cases all held lethal weapons. There was also a rack of gun magazines—she'd never have guessed there were so many—and lots of pamphlets and flyers urging patrons to take action to preserve and protect their right to bear arms. Natalie was slightly alarmed by it all.

There were also some T-shirts for sale. She picked one up and held it before her; emblazoned on the chest, in bright red letters, was THE ONLY WAY THEY'LL TAKE MY GUN AWAY IS TO PRY IT FROM MY COLD, DEAD FINGERS. She checked the label on the collar; 80 percent polyester. "Figures," she said. She folded it up and put it back on the counter.

Above the cash register was a poster that read, "THE RIGHT OF THE PEOPLE TO KEEP AND BEAR ARMS SHALL NOT BE INFRINGED"—THE SECOND AMENDMENT TO THE UNITED STATES CONSTITUTION. That was unmistakably the handiwork of Mr. Lloyd Hood, proprietor.

"This is pretty wild," she said, peering into the glass cabinets. At first the guns all looked evil and frightening, but after a slow stroll around the shop she found herself viewing them almost as abstractions—just shapes and colors and textures. She was surprised at their variety; some were squat and shiny, some long and sleek, some bulky and cannonlike. Some had wooden handles, some leather, some mother-of-pearl. Some were silver, some black, and some a kind of platinum blue. Some were almost pretty; some were carbuncular and ugly.

"You know what all these are?" she asked Quentin.

"Some I does, some I doesn't," he said. He was whirling around in the swivel chair by the cash register.

She went over to him. "Let's see what you've picked out for me."

He stopped the chair from spinning, then took an enormous pistol from behind the counter and set it before her. She jumped at the sight of it.

"Tha's a Colt forty-five ACP," he said, laughing at her reaction. "Go on, pick it up."

She lifted it with her right hand; its weight surprised her. "Heavy," she said. "Don't you have something smaller?"

"Yeah, but you tells me you wanna scare somebody. Ain't much scarier than that, 'cept maybe a assault rifle. We gets you a twenty-two if you wants. Or a AK-forty-seven."

"No, no, I don't want a rifle, for God's sake," she said. She turned the Colt over in her hand a few times. "No, I guess this is fine."

"It's a automatic pistol," he explained. "You holds down the trigger, the whole clip discharge, bam-bam-bam. You are need some lesson 'fore you can shoots it."

"No, I don't want any lessons," she said. "I just want you to load it and hand it over."

He leaned across the counter. "First, woman, there are a

seventy-two-hour wait while the police checks out your registration. And I gots to be careful 'bout the police. My job depend on it."

"Never mind the police," she said. "I can handle them."

"Still, you doesn't learn how to shoots that thing, you gonna blow somebody's head off and maybe it be your own."

"I have no intention of shooting it, I assure you," she said. "I just want to scare someone. That's all."

"Then you doesn't needs it loaded."

"Yes, I do," she said. "Trust me, Quentin. I know what I'm doing. I'm not going to shoot this gun, ever, but it *must* have bullets in it." She put it down and slid it across the counter to him. "Load it for me, please."

He sighed. "Man, you gonna lose me this job, ain't you?"

"What do you mean?"

"You up to somethin', woman. First you tells me you wants a gun, but I can't tell Mr. Hood nothin' about it; then you tells me to tell you when he have go out so you can come in and buy it; *then* you tells me you wants it to scare somebody. And *now* you says you don't wanna take no lesson 'cause you ain't gonna shoot it, but put a clip in it anyway. What else you gonna aks me?"

"Well, there *is* one more thing," she said, batting her eyelashes.

He rolled his eyes. "What?"

"I want you to fake the registration. Put any name on it but mine. Fake all the information. Make it seem like some young guy bought the gun. Look, I've already got a fake permit." She slipped the document from her purse and presented it to him. "Don't ask how." Thank you, Luigi, she said to herself. "And don't worry about the police. They're not going to come after you on this, trust me. And if Mr. Hood asks you later, just tell him that the guy who bought this gun showed you all the right forms and you copied his information down just like he had it. He'll believe you."

"You still gots to wait seventy-two hour," he insisted. "Mr. Hood fire me if I doesn't make you wait."

"He won't fire you, Quentin. I'm taking the gun today."

"Aw, shit!" He got up from the chair and stalked the length of the counter and back. "You usin' me, bitch! You sets me up in this job just so you can gets a gun to do some bad business, and now you gonna go off and leave me to take the shit! Man, I lose my job for sure over this shit, and you gots your gun so you ain't gonna care! I can't do it. You knows I can't!"

"You will not lose your job, Quentin," she said firmly. "*If* Mr. Hood threatens to fire you, just throw a couple of quotations from *The Fountainhead* at him; he'll change his mind."

"Fuckin' *bitch*," he said; his breath was coming hard, and he leaned against the counter menacingly. "First job I ever has that matter shit. Mr. Hood treat me like I got my goddamn shit together. Now you says I gots to go screw him."

"You owe me," she said in a low voice. "You wouldn't have this job at all if it weren't for me. Now I'm telling you, you *won't* lose your job, and if, by some bizarre chance, you do, I'll get you another one. Okay?"

He turned his head and wouldn't answer.

"Go and load the gun, now," she said. "And bring a registration form, too. I'll help you fill it out. Look, I've already got a name made up." She pointed to the form. "Bernard Davidson. Doesn't that sound authentic?"

He glared at her. But even though his jaw jutted out and his lips pursed in anger, she could see the submission in his eyes.

On Saturday morning, Lloyd Hood left town for a weekend seminar on economic freedom at the Cato Institute in Washington, D.C. The subject was "How to reform U.S. farm policy," and he was positively giddy about it. The date of the seminar had been indelibly etched into Natalie's mind; she'd heard Lloyd mention it about a thousand times during the months she'd eavesdropped on his bedtime conversations with Peter.

She'd also heard him mention the back door's spare key, which he kept taped to the rainspout next to the kitchen window in case he or Peter got locked out of the house.

It was all she needed to know.

She was ready.

CHAPTER 29

On Saturday night, Peter drove up the driveway at 9:58 P.M., parked, and entered the house through the front door. He threw his gym bag on the floor, kicked off his shoes, and hung his jacket in the hall closet.

Then, stripping off his sweatshirt, he went into the kitchen, where he opened the refrigerator and took out a peach. He bit deeply into it, and a rivulet of juice ran down his chin; he wiped it away with his wrist.

He jerked upright, as though he had heard something. He looked around. "Hello?" he called out.

No answer.

He took another bite of the peach and shut the refrigerator door.

He walked out of the kitchen and into the living room. Holding the peach between his teeth, he pulled off his polo shirt; he was now bare-chested. He dropped the shirt to the floor, turned on the television, and left the room. He took the peach from his mouth with his left hand, then lifted his right arm and smelled his armpit.

"Phew!" he said.

He bounded up the stairs and into the bathroom. He turned on the shower, then bounded back downstairs and into the living room. He sat down, bit into the peach again, then pulled off his sweatsocks and let them lie beside the chair.

He watched about five minutes of *The Golden Girls* without laughing, during which time he finished off the peach. Occasionally he dried a dribble of juice from his chin.

Once, in the split second of silence between commercials, he sat up and twisted his head to look behind him.

"Who's there?" he said.

There was no answer, but he sat for a long time as if one might yet come. The television set continued to blare its tinny hyperbole, as if trying to win back his attention.

Eventually he turned back to the set, just in time for the show's closing credits. He got up, switched off the set with his bare foot, and sauntered into the kitchen, where he flipped open the lid of the wastebasket and dropped the peach pit into the plastic sack that had been fitted around the basket's rim. He let the lid drop back into place, then unzipped his pants, slipped his hand beneath the elastic of his undershorts, and scratched at his pubic hair.

He left the kitchen and trotted back up the stairs.

At the top of the stairs he turned left and reentered the bathroom, where he slid open the shower door and put his hand beneath the shower nozzle. The stream of water hit his hand.

"Yipes!" he cried, shaking his whole arm. He bent over and adjusted the Hot and Cold knobs above the faucet.

Then he dropped his blue jeans and let them lie on the mat in front of the shower. Now he was wearing only his undershorts.

He went to the linen closet in the hall and opened it. From the third shelf, he took a powder-blue terrycloth bath towel.

Then he turned his head to his right and saw somebody in the corridor with a gun. A gun that was pointing at him.

Downstairs, the television was blaring again.

Behind him, the shower was still steaming.

He dropped the towel and backed up a few steps.

The intruder was dressed in blue jeans, high-top sneakers, and a parka. The intruder wore a Teenage Mutant Ninja Turtle latex face mask that covered the entire head. The intruder carried an enormous handgun.

The intruder waved the gun to the right.

Peter bumped into a wall and kept backing up. He backed into the room at the intruder's right, which was the bedroom.

The intruder motioned him to get down on his knees.

Peter got down on his knees.

The intruder went behind him and held the gun to the back of his neck. Peter closed his eyes and gasped. "Oh, Christ," he said, and his voice was hoarse.

The intruder produced a length of acrylic rope from the pocket of the parka. Then the intruder forced Peter to the floor, and Peter lay down with his left cheek pressed to the carpeting; he was facing a wall only a few inches away.

The intruder sat on Peter's shoulders, facing Peter's feet, and pulled Peter's wrists toward the small of his back. With the acrylic rope, the intruder tied Peter's wrists together. The gun rested on Peter's back, between the intruder's knees.

A sharp, acrid stench filled the room. The intruder looked at Peter's undershorts, which were now filled with what Peter was too frightened to keep stored in his bowels.

The intruder turned and looked at Peter's face for almost fourteen full seconds, then turned back and finished tying the rope.

Then the intruder tied Peter's ankles together.

Peter was now completely immobilized, by his bonds if not by his fear. The intruder got up and took a pillowcase from one of the pillows by the bed and started ransacking the dresser drawers. Socks, ties, and underwear were soon strewn all about. The intruder found a wristwatch and a ring and put them in the pillowcase.

At the side of the bed, the intruder opened the drawer of a nightstand. It was filled with books with titles such as *The Politics of Plunder* and *The Economics of Time and Ignorance*. The intruder's eyes rolled.

Then the intruder reached behind the headboard and pulled something away that had been affixed there. This was deposited into a tiny manila envelope, which the intruder then deposited in the right-hand pocket of the parka.

The intruder looked at the alarm clock on top of the dresser. It read 10:17 P.M. The intruder then unplugged the alarm clock and put that in the pillowcase, too.

Then the intruder went to the door of the bedroom and looked back at Peter. Peter was still on the floor, his head turned; he was white as a ghost. He looked up at the intruder. His breathing sounded like gasping.

The intruder blew him a kiss from the mouth of the Teenage Mutant Ninja Turtle mask.

Then the intruder passed the bathroom, where the shower was still running, went downstairs and into the dining room, and took some silverware and dumped it into the pillowcase. From there the intruder went to the living room, where the television was still happily carping away about nothing. The intruder started to unplug the VCR.

Before this could be completed, the intruder got up and looked out the window.

A police car could be seen just three blocks distant.

The intruder picked up the gun and the pillowcase and started to leave the room but bumped into a bookcase on the way. The bump made the intruder depress the trigger of the gun, which exploded four bullets in succession before it knocked the intruder into the next room and flew out of the intruder's hand.

The intruder whispered, "Shit!"

The pillowcase was lying in a heap by the bookcase.

The gun had skittered across the floor and was lying at the bottom of the staircase.

The intruder got up a little dazedly and unlocked and opened the front door. And waited.

Seconds later, the police car pulled up. A police officer got out and approached the house. When he came to the front door, he swung it open.

"Why, how very fuckin' careless," he said in a low voice. "Guy who lives here must've left his door unlocked when he came in tonight. Just fuckin' asking for a thief to come in, wasn't he?" He smiled. "Good thing I just happened to be in the neighborhood."

The intruder stepped out of the shadows and removed the Teenage Mutant Ninja Turtle mask. "Here's your bug," she whispered as she retrieved the tiny manila envelope from the parka and tossed it to him. He caught it and slipped it into his breast pocket. "Gun's over there," she continued, pointing, "and some things I was stealing are over there."

"Great," he replied. He took his gun from his holster. "Well, you better get the fuck out of here, right?"

"Right."

"Victim upstairs?"

"Yes. And you're in for a treat. He's shit in his shorts."

The police officer grinned. "All *riiight!*"

He raced up the stairs, and the intruder slipped out the back. She locked the door behind her, taped the spare key to the rainspout, and disappeared into the night.

Chapter 30

Flushed with excitement and success, Natalie almost skipped the three blocks to where she'd left the van. She kept replaying the events of the night in her head: Peter's almost palpable fear; the wild, desperate look in his eyes; the ease with which he had been immobilized.

Suddenly she stopped short. Wasn't this the street?

It looked like it; but her van wasn't here.

She ran to the corner and examined the street sign. Yes, this was Sunnyside; this was where she'd left the van.

Had she perhaps left it farther west than this? No, there was the house with the funny awning she'd noticed when she was parking.

She looked up and down the street; there were no Tow Zone signs. This was, as far as she could tell, a perfectly legal place to have left the van.

Shit.

Shit on a stick.

It had been stolen.

Her fault, really. She'd never gotten around to getting that back window replaced. All a thief had to do was slice open the plastic and climb in.

Shit on a shit sandwich!

She checked her watch. Almost ten-thirty. If Luigi were doing his job, he'd have called in his report by now. There was probably already an APB out on someone of her height and weight wearing an olive-drab parka, lurking around this neighborhood.

This neighborhood where you never, ever saw taxicabs.

She thought her brain was going to explode.

A car pulled around the corner and she ducked behind some bushes. Of course it turned out not to be a police car, but she wasn't taking any chances.

She had no idea what to do. Brazen it out? Walk up Wilson and act innocent? Or sneak her way home through the backyards and practically convict herself if she were caught?

She could hear a dog baying somewhere, and she thought, That might be tied up behind someone's house. With big teeth and lots of saliva.

She decided to risk brazening it out on Wilson.

It seemed like a year had passed by the time she reached the little bridge over the branch of the Chicago River that bordered Ravenswood Manor. There was no one around, so she reached into her parka, withdrew the latex Ninja Turtle mask, and flung it into the water. Then she trotted away, panting in relief.

She was still in danger; cars approached her, going west on Wilson, and their headlights were so bright she couldn't tell if they were patrol cars or not. And the cars that came from behind were just as bad; she could hear them coming, but didn't dare turn around to see what they were. They, on the other hand, would have plenty of time to get a good look at her as she walked so boldly in the field of their headlamps.

Then, what she was dreading would happen, happened.

A car drove up behind her, and she could hear it slowing down until it was beside her, keeping pace with her. Was it a squad car? She didn't dare look.

Time slowed to a crawl. The hum of the car's motor was still in her ears, the white blur of its body still large at the corner of her eye.

"Hey," said a voice.

She furrowed her brow. Didn't sound like a cop. She kept walking.

"Hey. Sexy."

Definitely not a cop. She turned her head a few inches and saw that her admirer was one of four Hispanic boys in a Ford Econoline van. One of them was hanging out the window, a bottle of Southern Comfort in his hands. He was almost blind drunk.

"You wan' come for us with a li'l ride?" he slurred. His voice was breaking; he couldn't be past puberty.

The other three boys—including the driver of the van—were staring out at her now. Her instinct was to tell them to go fuck themselves, but at any moment a police car might come down the street, looking for her in her parka.

"Sure, guys," she said. "That'd be great!"

The driver slammed on the brake, and she scooted over to the van and hopped in the front seat. The boys were hooting and hollering.

"Man, you're sexy," said the boy who had called out to her. "You wan' me to show you how sexy you are?"

"He can show you," said the driver, while one of the boys in the back shrieked with hilarity. "Heraclio can show you good and hard, man!"

"That's sweet of you," said Natalie. She couldn't believe she was actually prepared to go through with this, just to get out of the neighborhood.

"I show you good and hard, is right," said Heraclio. He tossed his head back, took a good, long swig of Southern Comfort, then tossed his head forward again. It didn't stop till it hit the dashboard.

He was out cold.

The boys howled with laughter. "Heraclio can't hold his hootch for shit!" they screamed. "Heraclio is a wuss!"

The boy behind Natalie nudged the boy next to him, who sat behind the driver. "I guess that means she's yours, man. Hey, Juan, she goes to 'Fredo, right? It's 'Fredo's turn."

"That's right, 'Fredo," said the driver, who had taken the Southern Comfort from Heraclio's limp hand and was now chugging it himself. "You show this lady how sexy she is. Show her so she don't forget! Okay?" he added to Natalie.

The alternation between crudity and courtliness baffled her, but they weren't yet far enough from Ravenswood for her to decline and get out. "Okay," she said with a forced smile.

She looked back at 'Fredo—she guessed that was short for Alfredo—and met his eyes for the first time. And then the shock of recognition practically knocked her out the window. She hadn't spent most of her adult life in the company of gay men without learning to pick them out on sight, even in a crowd. Of course, there was the occasional freak who proved invisible to her radar—Lloyd Hood, for one; but looking at 'Fredo now—at his posture, the set of his mouth, the indefinable *something* in his eyes—she knew beyond a shadow of a doubt that he was gay. He probably didn't fully know it himself, yet; but he must suspect. The look of panic on his face was a giveaway; there was no way he wanted anything to do with Natalie.

"Come *on*, 'Fredo," said Juan, the driver. "We don't got all night. We still got to get me a girl next. I ain't had my turn, man."

"You can go now," said 'Fredo. "I'll drive."

The third boy cackled. "You a faggot, 'Fredo? You afraid of her?"

Natalie's anger flared. She got up, squeezed behind the driver's seat, and grabbed Fredo's hand. "Come on, big guy," she said. He resisted ever so slightly, but he had to give in to her. His honor was at stake.

She took him to the back of the van; it was filthy, with old towels and magazines and boots and bottles piled up everywhere. She winced, but forced herself to endure it.

Then she put her hands on 'Fredo's shoulders and forced him down. The other two boys were watching—Juan by way of the rearview mirror.

She leaned over and whispered in his ear, "Don't worry, we don't have to. We'll pretend. We'll make them think it's real."

A look of uncomprehending gratitude stole across his face; he started to smile, then stopped himself.

She unbuckled his belt and unzipped his zipper, and pulled his jeans and his underwear down. His penis hung like a wet noodle from his abdomen, but the boys up front couldn't see that.

"Oh, my *God*," Natalie shrieked. "You better go easy on me with that thing!"

The boys bayed at the moon, like wolves.

Natalie loosened her own jeans and slid them down, and then her panties. She took 'Fredo by the arms and pulled him down on top of her. Her head was resting in something that smelled like an old sandwich. The van went over a bump, and 'Fredo clung to her.

"Just rub against me and pretend," she whispered.

But he was stiff as a board, terrified; he couldn't move. And so as the van headed eastward, farther away from Ravenswood and closer to the lake, Natalie bucked her hips up and down and gave easily the most overblown, exaggerated, utterly theatrical performance of her career. She screamed, she moaned, she panted outrageously; she cried, "Stop! Stop!"

And eventually she faked an orgasm that, had it been real, would have registered on the Richter scale.

"Go, *'Fredo!*" the boys yelled. "All *right!*"

He was lying on top of her still, as afraid as he'd been all along. She stroked his hair and whispered in his ear. "Listen," she said, "these guys are clowns. You don't need them. You're perfect the way you are, and when you figure out what that is, don't be afraid to be it. Okay?"

"You are a very nice lady," he said.

They were at Irving Park and the lake now. She got to her knees, zipped herself, and said, "You can let me out here, guys. I'll walk home. That is, if I *can* walk."

They pulled up in front of an old apartment building. Natalie climbed over the still-unconscious Heraclio and stumbled out into the night. A piece of bologna fell out of her hair and onto the grass.

As the van sped away, weaving left and right on Sheridan, she could still hear the boys, yelping and yelling at the top of their lungs.

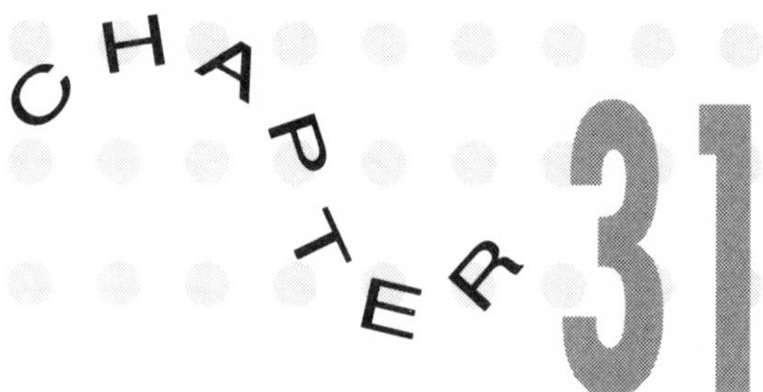

CHAPTER 31

Natalie slept more soundly than she had in months. When she awakened, she called Luigi Gianelli.

"Well?" she asked.

"Can I call you back?" he said. "I'm on my way to church."

The corrupt homosexual cop who hocked confiscated property and had a feces fetish didn't want to miss Mass. Life in the nineties was getting more complicated every day. "No, it can't wait," she said.

"Okay, I'll fill you in and then we're square, right?"

"Then we're square."

"Okay. I go upstairs, I untie your boyfriend, I help him clean himself up—"

"Very Christian of you."

He laughed. "Fuckin' *hot* number he is, too."

"Never mind that. You're married, remember?"

"Hey, this was the line of duty!"

"I don't want to hear about it. Go on."

"Anyway, he's pretty shook up. He can't remember much

except he keeps tellin' me it was a guy in a fuckin' Donatello mask who held him up."

Natalie rolled her eyes. Trust Peter to know exactly which Teenage Mutant Ninja Turtle it was. "Uh-huh," she said, carrying the phone into her kitchen.

"Well, I give him the whole story that I was just drivin' by and saw the door hangin' open, and that I surprised you—I mean, surprised the thief—in midact. And he says, 'Is that when he shot at you?' Which kind of threw me. You didn't fuckin' tell me you were gonna fuckin' shoot up the place!"

She was flinging open cabinet after cabinet, looking in vain for coffee. "It was a last-minute addition. Go on."

"So I says, Yeah, that's when he fuckin' shot at me, but I managed to chase him away. So your boyfriend believes it, right? And when he sees that you—that the thief—dropped the gun, man, he does exactly what you fuckin' said he would. He says, 'I wanna know where that gun came from. I wanna know where that gun was bought.' "

Natalie squealed with delight. She couldn't find any coffee, so she dug yesterday's filter out of the trash and put it back in the coffee maker.

"So I say we'll find out," Luigi continued. "He keeps sayin', 'I wanna know where that gun was bought.' Like I didn't fuckin' hear him the first time. So I make a full report, nothing stolen, nothing damaged except the floor and a wall and a bookcase which've got bullet holes in 'em. End of story. He even buys the whole idea that he must have left the front door unlocked."

Of course he does, thought Natalie. Peter was always the first to blame himself for everything. She got a dirty cup and saucer from the sink and rinsed them.

"So you want your gun back?" he asked her.

"No! *God*, no. Keep it."

"You sure? Pretty fuckin' expensive item to just throw away like that."

"I don't *want* it, Luigi. It served its purpose."

"Okay. Well. Then, I guess we're square."

She rinsed the film from her coffee pot and slipped it back into the coffee maker. "We sure are. You owed me big, you paid me big. You wanted your bug back, you got your bug back. We're square as they come."

"Great. Well—listen, I hate to just fuckin' hang up, but Mass starts in ten minutes, and I—"

"Go ahead, go. Say a novena for me."

"See ya, Natalie."

" 'Bye, Luigi."

She hung up and shivered. She didn't mind having *that* scary creep out of her life forever.

But how successful had she been? Peter would certainly find out that the gun had been bought at Lloyd's store. But would he blame Lloyd? At first she was certain he would. Now, however, as days passed, she thought he might blame Quentin instead, for letting the gun go before the seventy-two-hour waiting period—or blame the police, for failing to notice and act on an obviously falsified registration (thank you once again, Luigi). Or maybe he *would* blame Lloyd, but Lloyd would talk him into forgiving him.

She had no way of knowing, and that was what ate at her. She called Quentin, who told her that yes, Lloyd had questioned him on Monday about the registration; he'd assured him that there was nothing suspicious about the buyer or his I.D. He'd also told Lloyd that the buyer had said he was a close friend and big customer of Lloyd's and threatened to have him fired if he didn't give him the gun right away, and if Howard Roark were in that situation he wouldn't go running around trying to find his boss for an okay, he'd just make a decision, even if it was the wrong one. So Lloyd had dropped the matter. And then Quentin told Natalie he didn't owe her anything anymore, and if she called one more time he'd tell Mr. Hood everything.

She could no longer eavesdrop on Peter and Lloyd's bedtime conversations; and she couldn't just call them up to chat, not after all this time. Plus, she was actually afraid of seeing Peter again. He remembered her as being about twenty pounds heavier than she was today. What if he saw her, and connected her new, emaciated build with that of the Ninja Turtle/robber? She got dizzy worrying about it; but she still couldn't bring herself to regain those lost pounds—the thought of food disgusted her.

Calvin would probably know all about the fallout from the robbery attempt, since he and Vera had apparently gotten so cozy with Peter and Lloyd, but Natalie was still furious with him and wouldn't demean herself by calling him.

On Friday night she pulled herself together, put on some makeup, and went out to the Halsted Street bars, but the few old acquaintances she met said they hadn't seen or heard from Peter and Lloyd in ages, and had Natalie lost weight, and didn't she look terrific? And Natalie, fearing that she might become the object of gossip herself, and that such gossip might get back to Peter ("I saw Natalie this week, she's lost a ton of weight, and she was asking what's new with you"), decided that she'd better just slink back home and avoid the glare of the spotlight.

Not knowing how her revenge had worked was driving her increasingly crazy. On Tuesday she had a temper tantrum and a fit of tears over a snapped shoelace, and on Wednesday and Thursday she found her day interrupted by long, narcoleptic seizures—and not once during all this time did she leave her apartment, or speak to another living soul.

On the second Sunday following the "robbery," Natalie woke up in a panic, unable to catch her breath. She was still lying on the couch, a jar of peanut butter with a spoon in it by her side. The TV was still on, and it was giving off that lonely, phosphorescent blue it gives off only in the wee small hours of the morning, when it's the only light anyone dares use.

Natalie lay there gasping for what seemed a small aeon, and when she had regained her breath, she sat up and put her hand on her heart, waiting for her fear to subside. A man dressed as some kind of animal was on television, inciting viewers to buy new carpeting *immediately*. If they waited even a second, it would all be too late, and their lives would be ruined utterly. He had one of the most grating Chicago accents Natalie had ever heard. "Carpits, carpits, *carpits!*" he shouted at the viewers, waving his paws. A big subtitle flashed on the screen as he said this, and Natalie supposed that this was for the benefit of out-of-towners who had never heard a native Chicagoan speak before.

Eventually she took a deep breath, and relaxed. She wasn't dying; her throat had closed up, that's all.

The spate of commercials ended and the TV was suddenly illuminated by a superimposed logo spinning madly; it made

Natalie want to retch. When it came to a halt, it could be seen to read THIS IS CHICAGO, and a bunch of horns were playing a dissonant, atonal jazz riff that was particularly jarring at this hour of the morning.

The riff was cut short by the appearance of a blond, stiff-haired, wide-smiling show-biz type in a suit and tie. He was seated behind a desk on a low-budget soundstage. "Welcome back to *This is Chicago*," he said, grinning insincerely and revealing rows of impossibly white teeth. "We're talking to Alice Bremner, author of *Women Who Love Men Who Love Men*. Alice, the book is based on personal history, isn't it?"

The cameras cut to a close-up of a hefty young woman who had three enormous ponytails emerging from her head at various points and who was wearing what looked like a large purple seat cushion. She smiled and said, "Well, Frank, the book is based on a lot of research and analysis, but it has its *origins* in my personal history."

"So you yourself were one of these women who, uh—who—"

"Love men who love men," she finished for him. "Yes. The term on the street, by the way, is 'fag hag.' "

The audience tittered, and Natalie rolled her eyes. "I need this. This I need," she said, and she started sifting through the debris on her coffee table, looking for the remote.

"Well, okay," said Frank the host, nodding at the camera to show that he was going to be cool about this. "We've talked about how these women attach themselves to, uh, gay men and, uh, sort of become obsessed with them in spite of, in spite of . . ." He ground to a halt. He wasn't being as cool as he'd have liked.

"In spite of the humiliation," Alice Bremner finished for him.

He nodded. "But let's talk now—and you should know this, having been there—what *makes* a woman a—a fag hag, is it?"

Alice nodded her head. "Fag hag. Yes. Right."

Natalie shrieked. "Shut up! Who let you in here?" She knocked over last month's *People* magazine, a pair of soiled chopsticks, and the paper bag her last order of chow mein had come in. Where the fuck was the channel changer?

Alice Bremner paused and looked contemplative for a moment, then said, "Well, Frank, there are a number of reasons. I think, first of all, most women who put themselves in this position aren't very attractive to men."

Natalie shrieked again. She dropped to the floor, stuck her hand under the couch, and felt around the floor beneath the springs.

"Oh, now, hey," said Frank, "you're a perfectly lovely wo—"

"Thank you," Alice Bremner interrupted him, "but a woman's perceptions of *herself* are the only important thing. And most 'fag hags' have very low self-esteem." She tossed her hair behind her head. "They aren't, or don't consider themselves attractive to heterosexual men, so they cultivate friendships with gay men, because gay men aren't threatening to them. If there's no possibility of romance, there's no possibility of *rejection*, either. Which is comforting to someone who is very afraid of rejection."

Natalie pulled her hand out from under the couch and got up on her knees. "You stupid cunt," she sneered at the television.

"But," said Frank, "if they don't see any possibility of romance, then how—I mean, uh—how does th—"

"*At first* they don't see any," she cautioned him, raising her forefinger. "But later, after the woman has made friends with this dazzling, handsome, funny man who shares all his intimate thoughts with her and who seems to like her for who she is, it's only natural that she find herself falling in love with him. And, as you probably know, when you're in love, all things seem possible. Even though she knows for a fact that her dear friend is attracted only to other men, she begins to see in his kindnesses and intimate gestures toward her, increasing evidence of romantic feelings. And it becomes her obsession to help him realize that that's what they are."

Natalie dipped her hand into the peanut-butter jar, scooped out a goopy fistful of it, and flung it at the screen. To her delight, it hit Alice Bremner square in the eye. "Hah!" she barked.

But Alice Bremner, oblivious to this blow to her dignity, just kept right on talking. "She sees his friendship as the basis for reforming him," she said. "And it doesn't matter how many times he denies that he has any sexual feeling for her, she'll just keep plugging away at him, convinced that he's just blocking it. And the more he rejects her, the more insecure about herself she becomes; the more he rejects her, the lower her self-esteem gets. But, paradoxically, this only convinces her that her gay friend is her only chance at love; it only makes her more determined to have him. I mean, at least *he* talks to her, which, she now knows for certain, no heterosexual man ever would."

Frank had his hand on his chin, the better to pretend rapt attention. "Don't her friends tell her she's on the wrong track? Doesn't her family set her straight? I mean, it seems pretty obvious—"

"Most fag hags don't have a lot of friends, Frank—except for homosexual men, who aren't likely to realize what's going on inside her head."

The peanut butter fell from the screen, leaving a shiny smudge on the glass.

Frank leaned back in his host's chair. "Well, how did *you* break out of this—this behavior, Alice?"

She crossed her legs, which, the camera now revealed, were adorned with neon-orange tiger-stripe lycra tights. "It wasn't easy. Every woman who loves a man who loves men will one day face the ultimate rejection from him—the one final 'No' that makes her realize she's been fooling herself all along. It usually happens after he's found a lover. For the woman involved, it can be a very dangerous epiphany. I'm *still* in therapy. But I was lucky; my gay friend, Greg, was very supportive of me, and felt bad that he'd been the cause of so much of my craziness, and he went out of his way to help me heal. A woman whose gay friend just dumps her and walks is in for a very hard time."

Natalie got to her feet, somewhat woozily, and went over to the TV itself. She placed her finger on the POWER button. But she didn't immediately switch off the set. What was she waiting for?

"So now you've written this book," said Frank, holding up a copy of *Women Who Love Men Who Love Men*. "Is this part of the, uh—the healing process?"

She nodded enthusiastically. "Oh, yes! It's been very cathartic. But I also wrote it to help other women who fall into the trap I fell into—women who find themselves believing the impossible. There are a lot of them. Ask any gay man; I think every homosexual alive can tell you about one insecure, desperately lonely woman who attached herself to him like a barnacle, whom he at first considered a dear friend—maybe for years—only to realize much later that she was emotionally unbalanced. It's for those women that I wr—"

Natalie punched the POWER button.

"*Stupid*," she said, seething, standing tall and speaking to no one but herself. "Another goddamn expert on everybody else's life. Just because *she* was a fag hag. Just because *she*—"

Tears were begging to be released; but crying would be an admission of some kind, and she had, as she reminded herself again, no admission to make. She was furious with herself for even having to remind herself. It was too silly and humiliating, letting a cheap TV show bother her even that much.

She had a bowl of Ben & Jerry's cookie-dough ice cream and went to bed.

The next day, out of a vague sense of desperation, she called her old agency and asked for another temp job. Fortunately, it wasn't the bitch Monica who answered the phone; it was Agnes, the rather matronly rep who'd originally hired her.

"Sure, Natalie," she said. "Glad to have you back. Little hiatus do you good?"

"I guess."

"Fine. I'm just checking the books now. Ever worked at a talent agency?"

"What do I have to do?"

"Answer phones, light typing, clerical. It's a small shop. Some computer work; and specialized stuff, like processing talent payments. They'll train you."

"How long?"

"Hard to say. Right now there's a movie being filmed in town, so lots of locals are being used. They've got enough work for about three days to a week, depending on how fast you are."

"I'll take it."

Three weeks passed and she still hadn't heard anything about Peter and Lloyd. Since the minutiae of their daily lives had been her sole obsession for months before the robbery, this continued deprivation was almost beyond endurance.

She tried to bury herself in her work. The job at the talent agency had taken her two days, not three to five, and the head of the firm, an old battle-ax named Jennifer Jerrold, was so impressed that she hired her full-time. The agency mainly represented voice talents for TV and radio commercials, and its office was on Michigan Avenue, near the major advertising agencies. Natalie was learning a lot, but in a kind of frenzied way; she was just trying to fill her head with distractions.

Soon a paranoia gripped her, and grew larger every day. What if Peter knew it was me all along? she wondered. During the entire ugly scene, he never once indicated that he *didn't* know who it was. He had only said those two words, "Oh, Christ." He hadn't said, Who are you? What do you want? What are you doing here? Only, "Oh, Christ." Did that mean he already *knew* who it was, *knew* she was there for revenge?

No, no; if he'd known who it was, he would've told Luigi. But as days passed and her paranoia increased, she thought, Maybe he didn't tell Luigi because he was embarrassed that he'd been tied up by a woman. Maybe he was afraid to tell a police officer that he'd been attacked by a woman he'd slighted in favor of a man. (After all, he was undoubtedly too upset to realize that Luigi was gay, too.) Or maybe Peter was just trying to protect her. Maybe he and Lloyd were right now planning some way to get her committed to an institution for the criminally insane.

But no; he couldn't have known it was she, because he wouldn't have been able to recognize her. She'd lost too much weight. But, she reminded herself later, other people had seen her. Other people might have reported to Peter how thin she'd become.

Or maybe Peter *didn't* recognize her during the robbery but had been putting the pieces together over the past few weeks and was just now figuring it out!

Finally, she psyched herself out to the point where she would cross four lanes of traffic rather than pass a policeman. And every time her telephone rang at home, she sat gripped by fear until her machine took it.

Jennifer Jerrold came over to her desk one morning and sat

on top of it. "How are you, Natalie?" she asked, her voice both intimate and affected at the same time. (It was her usual manner of speaking; she'd had a career on the stage.)

"Fine, I'm fine." What does she know? Natalie wondered.

"You sure? Because we're all a little worried about you."

"Why?" That had been too defensive. Keep calm! Maybe she knows nothing!

"Well, your work is tops—I mean, you know that. But you seem a little—well, a *lot*—nervous."

"I'm fine, really." She took a breath and tried to stop herself from picking at the skin around her thumb; in the past few weeks, she'd almost flayed it. "Just a little trouble sleeping. Thanks for asking." She smiled; it was an atrocious, unconvincing sight.

Jennifer nodded, returned a weak smile of her own, and got up. "If you need to talk," she said, and she let her hand rest on Natalie's shoulder for a moment. Natalie wondered how many times she'd done that for effect in a play. It was so phony, so rehearsed—such an obvious *gesture*.

On her lunch hour, she grabbed a bag of Fritos and a Coke at the cigar store in the lobby, then trotted down the stairs to the little park next to the dock on the river. There was a dark corner down there where she could eat without being seen.

But it was unseasonably warm, a breath of spring before its time, and there were many others who had come here to enjoy eating outside after having been confined to cafeterias and fast-food joints all winter.

Natalie tried to make her way to the corner, but she noticed two women from her office sitting on one of the benches she'd have to pass, and she didn't want to walk by them for fear that they might talk to her or, even worse, invite her to join them.

She turned and started to dash back up the stairs, but she didn't watch where she was going and ran straight into another woman, who was coming down. Natalie lost her footing, and fell backward, and landed hard, knocking the wind out of her.

Suddenly people were swarming all around her, staring down at her. "You okay?" they kept repeating in small voices. "Miss? You all right?"

Then someone crouched over her; she tried to focus on him.

"Natalie?" he said. "Natalie Stathis?"

Her eyes cleared. It was Peter.

"It is you!" He reached behind her head and lifted it, then pulled his hand away. There was blood on it. "My God!"

She saw him turn and scan the crowd, then look up; a uniformed policeman was standing on the bridge overhead. "Officer!" he cried. "Down here! Quick!"

Dizzy and confused, Natalie could only comprehend that Peter was clutching her arm and calling a policeman. "*Noooo!*" she shrieked, and she fainted dead away.

CHAPTER 32

Something was sticking her, and it wouldn't go away. The discomfort drew her out of the depths of her unconsciousness, and she awakened to find a needle taped to her arm.

She looked up and saw that the needle was connected to a tube, and the tube was connected to an I.V. bottle. Something was dripping from the bottle into the tubing, and from the tubing into her.

She looked around, a little dazedly. It was a hospital room, of course. And there was Peter, sitting by the bed, his elbows on his knees and his chin in his hands.

"Leave you alone for a few months and look what happens," he said.

For a hazy, mind-jumbling moment, it seemed almost natural that he should be there. Everything was so strange—the muted pastel of the walls, the bulky monitoring device that held her I.V., and high above her bed the television set that was tuned in to an image of a big, industrial clock. And the eerie quiet—that most of all. It all pointed to some vague, barely perceived realignment in her life—some sense of a rubber band having snapped, sending her flying into the air until gravity pulled her down again, and down hard. There was a little whirlpool of fear and excitement in her stomach, but calm pervaded; this was something new, some fresh beginning. Of *course* Peter would be here for that.

She looked at him, at his face, so angular and aristocratic, his eyes so piercing and ethereal, like the eyes of wolves. His short haircut was still strange to her; she hadn't been this close to him in months—except for the robbery, when she'd had her vision partially obscured by the latex Ninja Turtle mask, and at which time she had, besides, been preoccupied with things other than Peter's beauty.

With him at her bedside, she felt a flush of confidence and reassurance she'd almost forgotten; her descent into petty revenge and dangerous self-disgust did not exist. His presence was cleansing; it had washed away all the guilt and shame and anger that went before it—washed away even the memory of it. Looking at him now, the room eddying around his head like a halo, Natalie couldn't even recall why they'd been apart so long—only that the separation had grieved her.

She tried to lift her head, but felt woozy and let it drop into the pillow again. "What's wrong with me?" she asked.

"Concussion, malnutrition, dehydration," he said. "I say you're out of your mind, too, but the doctor is reserving judgment."

With each gulp of air, she was feeding her consciousness a little more of her present until her memory was again gorged with all the details of her predicament; it was a literal rude awakening. She remembered the times when, as a child, she'd dreamed of being given a perfect, perfect doll that winked and spoke and clapped its hands and even danced, only to wake up and find her arms empty and the doll a vanished wisp of fancy. It was just like that now, except Peter hadn't vanished; he was still here, right at her side but across a chasm as insurmountable as any dream.

She rubbed her forehead with her free hand. "I thought you were having me arrested."

"Why?"

"You were calling that policeman over."

"No, I mean—what would I have you arrested *for?*"

She tried to shift her arm to lessen the discomfort, but the needle stuck to her like a leech. "I don't know," she said. "Guess I wasn't thinking too clearly."

"Natalie, what's wrong?" He leaned forward. "You look like hell, you were acting like some kind of nut down by the river—it's like you've gotten all weird and seedy since I last saw you. And, I mean, it hasn't even been that long."

"Oh, I don't know, Peter," she said, emotion welling up in her. "I don't know. I guess it's just—I guess—well, Carmen DeFleur died."

He sat back and sighed. "Oh. I'm sorry."

Even now, she had to smile at his ingenuousness. Only Peter would immediately accept that a dog's death was capable of bringing her to this low ebb.

"How's your mom taking it?" he asked.

"Pretty bad. I don't know. I haven't seen her in a while."

He smiled, and they sat and stared at each other.

Finally the silence compelled her to ask what she knew she must ask and dreaded asking: "How's Lloyd?" Even speaking his name was painful to her. She blamed him for this, for the hospital, for all of it.

"He's fine," Peter said, no trace of feeling in his voice. "I called and told him where I was. He'll be coming down, by himself, a little later. I called your mom, too. She should be here any minute."

Oh, great. The two people she most wanted to see. Thank you so much, Peter.

"Well, what's new?" she said, trying not to fall back asleep. There must be some kind of drug in that I.V. bottle.

"Nothing much," he said.

"Oh, come on." She was pretty sure now that he didn't suspect her of being the Ninja Turtle, so she felt free to investigate further.

"Well, we had kind of an upset a couple of weeks ago. Lloyd was out of town, and I came home and stupidly left the front door unlocked. And a thief came in and held me at gunpoint."

"*No,*" she said. "Oh, my God, are you all right?"

"Oh, yeah. But it was about a day before I realized that. It was pretty heart-stopping at the time, I'll tell you that for nothing. This guy forced me down to the floor, sat on my back, and tied my hands and feet together."

In spite of herself, she was shocked to hear his version of the event—as if his descriptions were worse than anything she thought she'd done. "Did he get away with much?" she asked, trying not to let Peter see her lip tremble.

"Not a thing. This cop happened to be driving by, and he saw the front door hanging open and someone in the window walking around with a Teenage Mutant Ninja Turtle mask on, so he stopped to check. The thief actually fired a couple of shots at him—there are bullet holes in the house to prove it! But then the thief ran away without taking anything. Even dropped his gun. And the cop found me upstairs and untied me."

"Honey, this is unbelievable!" she said. "I feel so bad, sitting here feeling sorry for myself when you've been through so much!" Her heart was doing flip-flops. Tell me about the gun, she commanded him telepathically.

But he wasn't receiving. "It wasn't so bad," he said. "The worst thing is, I was so afraid, I actually crapped in my pants. The police officer was really weird about that. He wanted to take my dirty shorts as evidence."

Natalie burst into almost convulsive laughter.

"God, I don't think it's funny, I think it's *gross*. That was one skanky cop, let me tell you."

She was laughing so hard, she got a fit of coughing. She motioned him to wait a moment, then calmed herself and said, "So what does Lloyd think?"

Peter's face darkened. "Lloyd is pretty upset about it."

She waited; surely he had more to say.

But no. He crossed his legs and said, "Oh, and guess what—I think the thief was gay!"

She was floored. "What? What makes you think that?"

"He blew me a big kiss as he walked out the door." Then he started laughing, and Natalie joined in.

While they were sharing this moment of hilarity, Sandy Stathis dove into the room, her hair in her face and the sash of her coat trailing behind her. "Oh, Natalie, thank God you're all right!" She raced over to the bed and clutched her daughter's free hand. "I couldn't bear to lose you so soon after Carmen DeFleur!"

"Gee, *thanks*, Mom," said Natalie, giving Peter a Do-you-believe-her? look on the sly.

"Oh, you know what I mean." She sat on the bed, still holding tight to Natalie's hand. "What do the doctors say?"

"I'm afraid I'm going to have to be spayed," said Natalie, and Peter choked down a laugh; Natalie turned and winked at him.

In that moment, it almost seemed that nothing had changed; they were still Natalie and Peter, poking fun at the world in general and at Sandy Stathis in particular. Nothing mattered, nothing was to be taken seriously, and the whole of creation existed only to give them pleasure and fun.

But then he got up and said, "Now that your mom's here, kid, I've got to get back to work." He bent over and kissed her forehead. "Take care, okay? And eat something!" He nodded at Sandy. " 'Bye, Mrs. Stathis."

"Good-bye, Peter dear, and thank you for calling me."

Then he was gone, and everything that was good was gone with him. Natalie's face fell into a scowl.

"Oh, honey, what's wrong?" Sandy asked, going around the bed to the chair Peter had just vacated. She removed her coat and threw it across Natalie's feet.

"Nothing, Mom. I'm going to be fine."

"But you were laughing so gaily just a few minutes ago, and now you look so glum."

"Peter told me a joke, and now it's over, that's all."

She sighed. "My poor, poor baby. This is all about him, isn't it? The not eating, the not sleeping—"

"What if it is?"

"Honey, if only I could tell you how much you n—"

"Excuse me?" It was a voice at the door. Natalie looked up and saw Hank Bixby standing there, looking large and ineffectual. A murderous rage swept through her. She shot a glance of undiluted hatred at her mother.

"Oh, Hank," said Sandy, turning to see him; "sorry to dash up here and leave you, but I just couldn't wait to see if Natalie was—"

"I understand," he said. "Hi, Natalie. Lost some weight, I see."

She didn't answer him.

He looked uncomfortable, then pointed down the hall with his thumb. "There's a place a few doors down where you can read magazines. I'll wait till you're finished."

"Thank you, Hank."

When he had gone, Natalie growled, "Mom, how *dare* you?"

"How dare I what?"

"Bring that man up here to see me!"

"I didn't bring him up here to see you, honey; I asked him to drive me. I was too upset to drive myself."

"You treat him like he's family. He has no business knowing that I'm in the hospital. I have no privacy. You tell my private affairs to everyone."

"Don't be silly, dear. I don't even know your private affairs. And if I ask Hank to drive all the way to Oak Park and then chauffeur me to the city, I certainly owe him an explanation of why I can't drive myself."

Natalie shook her head. "You'll never change," she snarled.

"No," said Sandy; "and I'm beginning to think you never will, either." She rose from the chair and picked up her coat.

"Where are you going?" Natalie asked.

"Home, dear. Now that I've seen you're well, my mind is at ease, and I can go home." She slipped the coat over her arms.

"You came all the way out here just to sit with me for ninety seconds?"

"Just to see that you're well, dear," she said, readjusting the sash so it wouldn't drag on the floor again. "To tell you the truth, you're not the kind of company I care to keep anymore. I've given you every opportunity to return my love and respect, but for the past six months—no, the past six *years*—you've spurned me, every time. And your attitude just now—well, it's the last straw." She walked out the door with her hands in her pockets and said, "You're on your own, Natalie. I'm not going to bother you anymore."

Natalie heard her call Hank in the corridor, then Hank's heavy feet clomping down the hall to meet her. And then, a few seconds later, she heard the dinging of the elevator.

And then there were no more sounds beyond the efficient hum of the hospital.

Natalie felt like a trapdoor had opened in her stomach;

something had fallen through and revealed a great emptiness in her. Never in a million years would she have expected her mother to walk out on her like that—especially in a hospital! She'd honestly thought Sandy might embarrass her by requesting that a cot be set up by her bed so that she could stay the night with her. But to have this happen instead!

She sat absolutely still for another forty minutes, feeling, first, a wave of guilt, then a wave of rage, then guilt, then rage—and so on. A doctor came in and felt her forehead and checked the I.V. and lectured her on how to take care of herself, and she registered maybe one word in ten. He left her, and she sat staring at nothing until the sun set and she was sitting alone in the dark.

Someone knocked on the door. "Hello? Natalie? You awake?" he whispered.

She turned on the overhead lamp. The sudden incandescence made her shut her eyes. "Who is it?"

"It's Lloyd Hood. Can I come in?"

She felt a jolt of alarm; how long had it been since she'd faced her enemy? Christmas, perhaps. She began to perspire in anxiety, and thought for a moment about pretending to have been asleep, so that he would apologize and slink away—but no, at this point she would've welcomed the devil himself. Anything to get her mind off her mother. "Yes, sure," she said, waving him in.

Her eyes adjusted now. She watched him as he entered; he had a red rose in his hands. "I bought this from a Korean kid who was selling them at an intersection," he said. He gave it to her and she sniffed it.

He sat down. He was wearing a leather jacket and khaki pants—Peter's old uniform. As a matter of fact, she noticed now that they were Peter's old clothes. Apparently he'd just adopted his lover's wardrobe, lacking any significant style of his own.

"How are you?" he asked.

She was in a mood to be abusive. "I've been better, Lloyd. What did you expect?"

He seemed chastened. "Sorry. Stupid thing to say. I guess I don't know *what* to say."

"Then why did you come?" She was merciless.

He raised an eyebrow. "Good question. I guess I've been

at a loose end for a while. Peter says you're good to talk to."

Me? she wanted to say. Me, the subhuman who can't think in abstract terms? But she merely said, "Oh?"

"I don't know if Peter told you about the robbery attempt."

She raised an eyebrow. "Yes, he did."

"We've been having some difficulties since then."

Her heart almost stopped. "Difficulties?"

"Apparently, the gun the thief used—the gun he was holding on Peter—was bought at my store."

She pretended to have to let that sink in. "*Oh*," she said.

"I have a young kid working for me now, an ex-gang member—not too bright, but his head's in the right place. I left him alone for an hour and he sold a gun to someone who came in and pretended to be a friend of mine. Someone with a lot of phony I.D., so that we ended up with a faked registration. There's a seventy-two-hour wait to buy a firearm, to allow the police to check your registration, but this guy played high-and-mighty and scared my kid into giving him the gun right away. Besides which, the police never caught on that the registration was a sham, anyway. It's a bad business all around."

"And this turned out to be the same guy who broke into your house and threatened Peter?"

"Seems to be. Same gun, anyway."

"Well, don't beat yourself up about it," she said. "It's not your fault."

"Isn't it?" he asked. "Peter thinks it is."

She lowered her head. "I see."

"Peter says that for me to sell a gun to someone who uses it against someone else practically amounts to being an accessory to the crime. He says that when so many deaths occur each year because of shootings, even *advocating* selling guns is wrong. He says you can't weigh a principle against a human life. And, of course, I disagree with him, and I give him the same rational arguments I've been using all my life—but every time I do, he comes back with the same response."

"Which is?"

He looked away from her, at the I.V. monitor, and ran his fingers up the side of it, as though measuring it. "That I've never looked down the barrel of a loaded gun, and he has. That I've never had to face the possibility that at any second a bullet could shatter my skull, and he has. That I've never been threatened by a lethal weapon in the confines of my own home, and he has. And I don't know how to answer that."

"I guess not."

"And even worse—Natalie—I don't know—if I want to." His voice was thickening with emotion now. He turned back to her and met her eyes. "This has really rocked me. When I think of how close I came to losing him! He's the center of my world, do you understand? I've always said that free trade in guns helped make America great, and I still believe that, but you know what? I don't care about America anymore. Not compared to Peter. *He's* my country now, *he's* my ideology. He's my ethics and my politics and my economics. He's always said that love is totality. My God, I realize that now." A tear escaped his left eye. "Do you understand the enormity of it when I say that I'm willing to be wrong for him?"

With her free hand, Natalie clutched her throat. This wasn't what she had expected.

"So he's asked me to sell the store, and I'm going to. I'm keeping my arsenal in the basement of the house, but I'm getting out of the actual gun business. I can't stay in it, not now. Peter's given me doubt. I can't function with doubt. I need certainty." He ran his hand over his scalp. "Besides, I'm tired of fighting, anyway. There are a couple of aldermen who've built entire careers around trying to get me rezoned out of their wards' vicinity. I'm tired of having to take them on." He suddenly looked up and said, "This is more than I intended to say. I'm sorry for bending your ear on this, Natalie. It's unfair of me, isn't it?"

"Not at all," she said. "I just can't believe you're really selling the store."

He shrugged. "I am. Peter asked me to, and I can't say no. I've never looked down the barrel of a loaded gun, and he has. And it was a gun I sold. It just goes round and round, Natalie, until I think I may go nuts. I've got to stop it, and selling the shop will stop it."

"But what will you do?"

He lowered his head and started examining his thumbs. "I'm not sure. I'll think of something. As a matter of fact, you yourself gave me an idea I may l—"

"Knock, knock," said a female voice at the door. They looked up and saw a nurse leaning in. "Visiting hours are over. I'm afraid you'll have to leave, sir."

"Sure," he said, smiling wanly at her. He got up and pecked Natalie on the cheek. "Thanks for listening, Natalie. You shouldn't be such a stranger. Peter misses you terribly. Will you come out to the house if we ask you?"

Only to blow it up, she thought, but she said, "If I'm free," and then watched him go.

As he was leaving, it occurred to her that he was the only person she'd seen in the past few weeks who hadn't commented on her loss of weight. Maybe he was too pie-in-the-sky to notice.

Yet the more she replayed his visit in her head, the more something else bothered her about what he'd said—something beyond the obvious fact that he'd told her, in effect, that she'd failed; she hadn't ruined Peter and Lloyd's life together, she'd merely soured it a little. But there was something beyond that, something that made her uneasy, something that upset her. . . .

She finally put her finger on it. The entire time he'd been here, Lloyd had kept repeating "Peter says, Peter says, Peter says," in the same way that Peter once incessantly spouted "Lloyd says, Lloyd says, Lloyd says."

That was why they'd survived. They deferred to one another. They made room. They listened to each other, allowed each other to be strong, protected each other.

They really were married, weren't they? They complemented each other, like pieces of a jigsaw puzzle that interlocked exactly.

She realized now, for the first time, that she could never ruin their life together. She could raze their house, destroy their careers, and cut off their limbs, but they'd manage to find a way to grow old together.

She put her fingers around the bud of the rose Lloyd had given her, then crushed its petals to pulp and flung them across the room.

She wasn't giving up. There was one thing she had left to try. The thing she hadn't let herself consider seriously, before now. The thing that, if she did it, could never be undone. The step that, once taken, could never be retracted.

But it would take a lot of planning and a lot of money. And

she needed to be physically strong, too. How had she let herself get so weak?

An orderly brought in her dinner tray. "Here we are," he said, setting it before her. "Try to eat as much as you c—"

Natalie started gobbling the food before the orderly could even finish speaking.

CHAPTER 33

The next day Natalie had only one visitor, and an unexpected one at that: her employer.

Jennifer Jerrold came through the door like a queen into a throne room. She acted as though she'd been in that exact hospital room a thousand times before. She took off her black slouch hat and tossed it onto the counter by the sink, without even looking to see that the counter was there.

Her long, salt-and-pepper hair was tied in a braid that fell down her back, and she wore a black jumpsuit and black boots. She was also holding the ugliest potted plant that Natalie had ever seen. It looked as though acid rain had got to it and mutated it.

"Well, you might have called," she said. She put the plant on the stand next to Natalie's bed. "Here. This is for you."

Natalie arched away from it, as though she feared it might reach over and suck her blood.

Jennifer sat down, crossed her legs, and immediately lit up

a cigarette, in blatant violation of the notice on the wall that forbade her to.

"Sorry," said Natalie. "I just forgot. How'd you know I was here?"

"Bettina and Sally said they saw you fall down the stairs yesterday at lunch," she said, exhaling a puff of smoke that expanded in the air and obscured her face. "So I didn't expect you back that afternoon. But when I still hadn't heard from you this morning, I started calling hospitals."

Natalie unobtrusively tried to move the stand with the plant away from her. "I'm really sorry, Jennifer. For what it's worth, I think this is the turning point for me."

"Meaning what?"

"No more craziness. I'm coming back to work a whole person. If you'll have me back, that is."

"Course I'll have you back. You're the only girl I've ever found who doesn't bitch about having to wade through all those AFTRA forms. When may we expect your return?"

"Oh, gee. Not tomorrow. Day after, I guess. They're releasing me today, but the doctor says to take it easy for a day, just hang out at home."

"What happened, Natalie?"

"I got a concussion when I fell down those stairs. But also, they say I'm malnourished. And dehydrated."

"Sounds like you've just spent a year in the Peace Corps." She took another drag off her cigarette, moved her mouth as if she were chewing on the smoke, then all at once coughed it out. "Natalie, Natalie, whatever is the matter with you?"

"I could tell you, but you'd think I was nuts."

"Bet I wouldn't," she said. "Got to be a man. What, you think you're the first to go through this?"

She turned beet red. "You think you know everything."

"You mean you think I don't?" They both laughed at this, then fell silent for a moment.

"Is that okay?" Natalie said at last. "I mean, if I come back to work in two days?"

"Yes. Fine. I don't care. We're slow right now, anyway." She looked around the room for the first time. "Lucky you. No roommate."

"I'm just in for twenty-four hours of observation, really, so they stuck me in one of the private rooms."

Jennifer espied an unopened can of Coca-Cola on Natalie's stand. "You going to drink that?"

"Not really—all that sugar."

"Mind if I have it?"

"Not at all." She passed it to her boss, who popped the top and sipped at it noisily.

They stared at each other for another moment until Natalie said, "It's funny, seeing you like this. Out of the office, I mean."

"It's funnier seeing you in bed." She put the can on the chair's wooden armrest.

"No, I mean—I haven't had a real job before, I used to just temp, so all my bosses before you were just these faces. Here today, gone tomorrow. It's kind of weird to have a boss who shows up in my life like a real human being."

"Oh, I'm *often* mistaken for a real human being."

Natalie laughed again and said, "You know what I mean. It's just nice to know someone cares. Someone who doesn't have to, I mean."

"Natalie, I want you to stop it right this instant. You are trying to flatter and embarrass me and I won't have it." She stubbed out her cigarette in a plastic drinking cup. "I am not Mary Poppins. I am not Florence Nightingale, and I am not Barbara Bush."

"Well, no, b—"

"I'm also smart enough to know what you're up to, even if you don't know it yourself. You talk about me so we can't talk about you. Fine, if that's how you want it. But I'll give you a piece of advice, anyway: Forget about him."

"Forget about who?"

"Whoever he is. Forget about him. If he drove you to this and still doesn't care, he never will."

She colored again, but this time with anger. "You don't know that."

"I know everything, remember?" She was looking around for a box of tissues; she found it, reached over, and yanked one out. "You need some perspective, that's all. You can't see anything but this man right now. You should take a trip, go someplace where the whole world doesn't revolve around anything you even recognize. Oman, or Honduras, or mainland China." She blew her nose, and it sounded like a fanfare of trumpets.

"I can't afford to get away," Natalie lied.

"I'll lend you the money." She balled up the tissue and dropped it on the floor.

"Why? Why are you taking such an interest in me?"

She shrugged. "It's my hobby. Some people collect stamps, I collect lives. I have a whole network of them. Yours could be one. Not your whole life, of course; just the crises. Those are the interesting parts. I like the crises. They make me feel alive; that's why I try to be part of them. Then, when life gets dull, I relive them. I sit and remember Alice's divorce, or Barry's throat cancer, or Cassandra's trouble with her son, and how I helped them through all that. It's kind of like being involved in a soap opera, only it's my soap opera. I'm too ambitious for the regular kind; I want to jump into the TV and tell all the characters what to do."

Natalie felt warm and relaxed, as if having Jennifer take care of her were the most natural and desirable thing in the world. But she still had her agenda; she still had her last-ditch attempt at snaring Peter.

"That's so sweet," she said, "and I do appreciate it; but I think the thing for me, right now, is to get back to normal. I want to work at my job and get my health back. Maybe I'll take a trip someday, but not right now. I hope you understand."

Jennifer shook her head. "Why does everyone I try to help have to be so goddamn sensible about it?" She uncrossed her legs. "Of course I understand, dear. What time is it, do you know?"

Natalie checked her watch. "Ten after two."

"Kyle's meeting me here any second," she said. "We're going to a friend's opening in Milwaukee tonight. You mind if I wait here for him? He has your name, he'll find me."

"I don't mind. Who's Kyle?"

"My husband. Didn't you know that?"

"I didn't even know you were married."

She raised both eyebrows. "I thought that gossipy little kaffeeklatsch would've given you my whole life story by now."

"You mean Bettina and Sally?" She shook her head. "They haven't really accepted me yet."

"Your fault, dear. But at least, now, you have them intrigued. They couldn't stop chattering about your accident on the stairs—you'd have thought it was a major new twist in Middle East policy or something."

Natalie dropped her head back in her pillow. "I *hate* that. I *hate* being gossiped about."

"Then move to the Faeroe Islands or a cave in Tibet, sweetheart. It's your only hope."

"What were they saying?"

Jennifer sighed and lit another cigarette. "Just speculation. They have you down as either a paranoid schizophrenic, a heroin junkie, or a sufferer of anorexia nervosa. And they were positively giddy about the young man."

"What young man?"

"The one who seemed to know you—who carried you up the stairs after you passed out and got your blood all over his sweatshirt. Apparently he was gorgeous. You know how to bring my little office of snoops to the boiling point, honey."

She grimaced. "Oh, God, I just *hate* this."

"Who was he, anyway? Don't tell me that was actually *him*."

"Okay, I won't tell you that."

Jennifer's jaw dropped; she hit her forehead with her hand, and in so doing, knocked over the can of Coke; it clattered to the floor and started gushing its syrupy contents. "Natalie, you're something," she said as she leaned over and picked up the can. "Did you deliberately have that accident, for his benefit? God, I can't believe I asked that—of course you didn't." She yanked some more tissues from the box and started to mop the spill. "You don't watch out, you're going to have *me* sitting around whispering about you with Bettina and Sally."

"You do, and I quit."

A nurse came in to investigate the noise and threw a very efficient fit at the sight of Jennifer's lit cigarette, which was now dangling precariously from her lower lip. The nurse spat and hissed and waved her hands in the air, then threw open a window with the exact gesture Natalie had seen Moses use to part the Red Sea in a movie once. Jennifer got up and put out her cigarette in the sink.

Just then a shockingly handsome, fortyish man in a blazer

and black T-shirt knocked on the door and peeked in. "Hello?" he said.

"Hel-*lo!*" said Natalie.

"Oh, Kyle," said Jennifer from the sink. She picked up her hat and waved it at Natalie. "This is Natalie." She waved it at the newcomer. "This is Kyle."

"Hi," said Kyle.

"Hi, yourself," said Natalie, who was looking at him and thinking, Gay as a goose.

"No respect for orders," the nurse said, still fuming. "Have to watch you people like you're children." She took the potted plant from Natalie's stand and put it on the windowsill, for which Natalie was grateful.

"Well, we're off," Jennifer said, fixing her hat on her head at a fashionably daring angle. "I'll see you—well, whenever we agreed."

"Have a good time in Wisconsin."

"Honey, that's impossible." She took Kyle's arm and dragged him out the door, and Natalie thought, She probably has to drag him past all the orderlies, too.

The nurse was tucking in the corners of Natalie's sheets now. "You should tell your mother to obey the rules," she said sharply. "NO SMOKING means no smoking!"

Natalie half-smiled to herself. She was willing to bet that the nurse didn't think Kyle was her father.

The scene had given her newfound resolve. If Jennifer Jerrold can do it, she thought, then so can I.

Although Jennifer Jerrold had almost certainly never had to do what Natalie was planning to.

PART 6

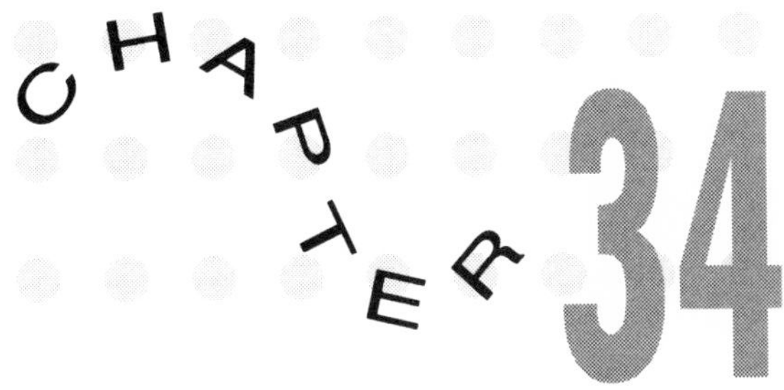

Jennifer erupted into the office and stormed toward Natalie's desk. Natalie looked up, alarmed.

"Morning, Jennifer," she said.

"I could kill you," the talent agent snarled. She lobbed a copy of the new *Illinois Entertainer* at her.

Natalie caught it and looked at it. Quentin was on the cover; he was practically fellating a microphone and had his arm outstretched, finger pointed accusingly at the camera. He was drenched in sweat and illuminated by spotlights. His two backup singers were behind him. All were in their sunglasses and big, knotty sneakers.

It was a picture from his recent performance at Cabaret Metro. The cover headline was, AYN RAP 2000: FORMER GANG MEMBERS TURN LIBERTARIAN POP STARS.

"Didn't you tell me you knew him?" Jennifer demanded.

"I used to, but I—"

"No buts. I asked you months ago to arrange a meeting with him for me. He's getting bigger and bigger, Natalie, and I *want* him. I'm tired of handling just a bunch of voice talents and movie extras. I want a big act in my roster."

Natalie was flipping through the magazine, trying to locate the article. "But I told you, Jennifer—he insists on black management."

"I never wear anything *but* black," she said proudly.

Natalie smiled at her and shook her head, then found the article. She only skimmed it, as she had read the same story many times over the past few months. It told how former Rama Z member Quentin Butler left the gang at the urging of his fiancée, then discovered the novels of Ayn Rand. Unable to find lasting employment, he founded a rap group, Ayn Rap 2000, and translated the late novelist's polemical writings into the cadences of the masses. One lyric went, "They take the best of us and steal our power to be free/The sanction of the victim is the only tool they need." Music critics didn't know what to make of the group, but audiences were going nuts for them.

Well, good for Quentin, was all she had to say. He'd started making money, bought himself a new IROC-Z, and moved Lawanda and Darnita out of the project. He was looking for a house, but in the meantime was living in a high-rise apartment at Chestnut and Michigan, at the southern tip of the Gold Coast.

She closed the magazine and looked up. Jennifer was still looming over her. "Get me a meeting with that boy, and if I sign him, I'll make you a partner in this place," she said, leaning closer so that Bettina and Sally wouldn't hear. "And that would mean money, honey. Lots of dreamy, delicious greenbacks."

Natalie shrugged. "I'll see what I can do, but I honestly d—"

"That's all I wanted to hear," Jennifer said, standing upright. "Just let me know when and where." She went into her office and shut the door.

Natalie sighed. It was hopeless. Quentin hated her guts, and besides, the only way she could possibly get to him was through her mother, as apparently he and Lawanda were still close to Sandy and trusted her judgment. But the last time Natalie had called home, Sandy had been in the middle of an Accessorizers Anonymous meeting and couldn't talk—"It's a crisis situation here," she'd said; "Carolyn says Nathan found her cache of shoes and told her it makes Imelda Marcos look like a sensible shopper. All we can do now is damage control." But she'd never called Natalie back. It was almost as if she could sense that her daughter was calling only because she wanted something, and wasn't fooled for a second.

She put it out of her mind. There was something else she had to think about. It was Calvin and Vera's first anniversary today, and although she still wasn't speaking to them, she considered the event noteworthy for another reason: It marked a full year since Peter and Lloyd's first meeting.

She'd spent months preparing for the next, and ultimate, step in her campaign to set right the great wrong that had been done to her when Lloyd had come into Peter's life. She'd been ready, now, for the past few weeks, but hadn't had the resolve to actually put the plan into action. But this seemed like the ideal day to begin; there was something almost poetic about laying the groundwork for Peter's separation from Lloyd exactly one year after the day they first came together.

She knew where to start, too. She opened her desk drawer and pulled out a pink WHILE YOU WERE OUT slip, dated a month earlier. It informed Natalie that a Mr. Lloyd Hood had called her, and requested that she call him back. His number was scrawled at the top.

It was about time she found out what that was all about.

"What a surprise," said Lloyd. "When you didn't return my call, I thought you were angry with us, or something."

"Oh, don't be silly. I've just been busy the past few weeks."

"You're doing well, there, then?"

"Oh, yeah. I've brought a couple of new voices on board who are pretty much in demand. I'm making good money."

"Great! How'd you find them?"

"Gay bars, of course. Where else would you go to recruit a bunch of unknown actors?"

He laughed. "Listen, the reason I called was to thank you."

She knitted her brow. "Thank *me*? For what?"

"Well, after I sold the shop, I was kind of at a loose end, but in the back of my mind I had this idea that you put there. Remember that dinner, a long time ago, when you said I should do something for the homeless in my neighborhood, since I didn't feel it was the government's job? And I started thinking about a survivalism center for homeless people?"

Oh, brother, she thought. "Sure, I remember."

"Well, it's been up and running for about three months, now, and I figure, it was your idea, maybe you'd like to come and see it."

"I would absolutely love to."

"Now, I don't want you to get your hopes up," Lloyd said as he escorted her down the ruins of the Uptown neighborhood's seediest stretch. "This may not be what you expect. It's turned out to be completely different from anything *I'd* expected."

"How so?" she asked as a bum with vomit on his shirt watched them pass, his eyes dull.

"Well, I learned pretty quickly that training homeless people to anticipate a breakdown of civilization is pointless, because, for them, civilization doesn't work anyway. Most of them are incapable of looking beyond the next three or four hours; they're fixated on their next meal, or where they'll spend the night. A lot of them are mentally ill, too, and that poses its own problems. Sometimes I wonder—if I'd known what I was getting into, would I have started this? But it's too late; I'm committed now."

They passed a corner grocery that was boarded over with plywood and cardboard but apparently open for business all the same. Natalie looked through the door as they passed, and saw a group of sweat-stained, ratty-bearded men standing in the aisles, not buying anything. Their eyes met hers, and she felt herself shrink without knowing why.

She and Lloyd continued down the broken, sun-bleached street, and Lloyd kept up his patter. "The whole city is watching me, now," he said, shaking his head. "If I give up, it's going to be called a failure for survivalism. But what kills me is, if I succeed, it may end up being called a triumph for liberalism. The press has got hold of me, did you know that?"

"I hadn't heard," she lied. She'd seen the front-page article in *The Chicago Reader* two months back, with the headline, REDEMPTION OF A RIGHT-WINGER.

"I nearly keeled over when I saw what they'd done to me,"

he said as they passed a vacant lot that looked like pictures Natalie had seen of the surface of Mars, only littered with old bottles, shoes, and newspapers. "This free-lance writer comes to see me, bats her eyes a lot, and makes me think she's impressed by me, then goes and writes this article that totally distorts everything I said. I told her, explicitly, that owning a gun shop and establishing a survivalist project for the homeless are two sides of the same ideological coin, but she ended up painting me as a reformed right-wing nut who's now embraced good, liberal values like 'helping people.' I *told* her this isn't altruism, I *told* her that it's a calculated investment in my community and that I expect a significant return—and what does she do? She makes me out to be the biggest altruist this side of Mother Teresa. I nearly popped a blood vessel. Peter had to physically calm me down. Now I get all sorts of chummy phone calls and visits from the kind of liberal whiners and do-gooders I used to hate the sight of. And of *course* she mentions I'm in a gay relationship as if that happened *after* I sold the shop—as if I'd been somehow massively blocking my homosexuality by playing with explosive phallic symbols, then one day woke up, dumped the guns, and found my inner self and true love all at once. If I ever see that reporter again, I'll—I'll—" He searched for an appropriate punishment. "I'll give her a chiding she'll never forget," he concluded savagely.

Natalie almost laughed. Lloyd was as dizzily unreal as ever. "I'm sorry to hear about that," she said.

He waved his hand to dismiss it. "It's over now. And at least I've gotten a couple of speaking engagements out of it; they pay pretty well."

They had come to an abandoned commercial building that looked like no one had rented space there for a hundred years. "In here," he said, opening the door to the empty retail store in front. "We've had to move around a lot, but the owner of this building has let me use it for next to nothing for a couple of months now. I guess he figures even a little rent is better than none."

The air inside was thick with dust; there were about twenty folding chairs ranged around the room, with a card table set before them. Five of the chairs were filled with bedraggled, pockmarked, absolutely filthy people. Natalie wanted to run from them.

"Five?" Lloyd said. "Only *five?*"

A few of them turned to look at him; only one actually greeted him. "Hiya, there, Lloyd," he said. "Hi. It's me, Daniel. Remember me? Daniel." He waved and smiled; he was missing about seven teeth.

Lloyd grimaced and shook his head. "I should've figured. Weather's getting cooler. Not as much incentive to come and sit someplace air-conditioned." He pulled out a chair for Natalie. "Care to watch for a while?"

She shrugged. "Okay, I guess."

"Hiya, Lloyd," said Daniel. "I'm back again, just like I said. It's me, Daniel, remember?" He was waving his entire arm now.

"Yes, I remember you, Daniel, hello."

"I brought my wife, Barbara, again," he said, pointing to the woman next to him.

"I'm not your wife, you pervert!" the woman said; she drooled as she shouted. "Get your disgusting hands off me or I'll call the police!"

Daniel sat and turned away; he looked as if he might cry.

Lloyd rolled his eyes. "It's not as bad as it looks," he said under his voice. "They *do* learn. We did a unit on dehydration and heat strokes in July, and I'm convinced that that saved a couple of lives. And I taught them all about safe sex, too; you'd be surprised how many of them were interested in that."

Natalie just wanted to run home and take a bath. "What's today's topic?" she asked, wanting to get on with it.

"Nutrition," he said. "I talk about nutrition every other week. It's that important to them. They have no idea what they should be eating; all their money goes to junk food."

Suddenly Daniel bolted up and made his way toward the door.

"Daniel, wait," said Lloyd, blocking the old man with his arm. "The lesson hasn't started yet. Where are you going?"

"I don't have to stay here, you can't make me stay," he said.

Lloyd beamed with pride and whispered to Natalie, "He learned that from me!" Then he turned back and said, "Of course not, Daniel, and I'd never try to make you stay against your will. But if I ask you to, *will* you stay? We're going to talk about food again today."

He sighed and looked straight at Lloyd. A small universe seemed to fill up the space between their eyes. "I'm pretty hungry, Lloyd," he said.

Natalie felt the room spin. She'd never heard such despair in a human voice before; she'd never heard such casually expressed hopelessness. It seemed beyond endurance; she couldn't imagine it. Was that what Lloyd was fighting? Her estimation of him began to rise—but she just as quickly put it down. Don't think about it, don't think about anything, she admonished herself. She looked at her shoes and emptied her mind.

Lloyd led Daniel back to his chair. "After the lesson I'll lend you a little money, and you can spend it on some dinner, okay?"

"Okay," said Daniel, brightening a little.

"But I'm going to tell you the kinds of food I think you *should* spend it on. You make the final decision, but first I'm going to tell you what's best for you to eat." He looked back at Natalie and said, "It's important to cultivate their sense of responsibility, especially for their own welfare. That wouldn't be possible if I bought the food *for* them, like a soup kitchen. I'm not feeding pets, I'm breeding intelligences."

Daniel sat huddled in his seat, and the woman he had introduced as his wife turned and looked at Natalie. "Who's *she*?" the woman asked.

"That's Natalie, a friend of mine," Lloyd explained. "A visitor, just for today."

"Is *she* gonna give us money, too?"

"No one's going to *give* you money, Barbara. I'm *lending* it to you, remember? Someday, when you're on your feet, you'll pay me back."

"What if we *never* get on our feet?" asked a thin, thirtyish young man who sat with his mouth agape. He was wearing mismatched shoes and a dirty woolen cap.

"Never say never," said Lloyd. "If you think you're going to fail, you will."

"Can we have our money yet?" asked Barbara.

"Not yet." He went behind the card table. "We're going to have a little talk first."

"I was amazed by your patience," Natalie said later as Lloyd drove her home in his and Peter's Celica. "I'd have lost my mind. You're very good with them."

"I treat them with respect," he said. "I'm proud of that. In every one of them, I see a potential hero. I keep thinking, if I get them to see this as adversity, not as the constant condition of life, maybe they'll find the courage to fight it."

"I don't know. They seem pretty hopeless."

He looked hurt. "You just wait. They've come a long way already."

"But so many have dropped out, you said. There are only five left!"

"I expect the rest will be back, sooner or later, if only for the handout. And we're bound to get some new people when winter comes. They kind of wander in and wander out. I mean, I'm not advertising or anything—it wouldn't do any good. The whole thing's been handled by word of mouth since the beginning." He chuckled. "Boy, what I didn't know then."

It was getting dark, and she was feeling strangely cozy with Lloyd. "Tell me about that," she said.

"Well, I started out pretty grandly, with a room at the Uptown Community Center, but no one even came to the first meeting. So I offered food at the second and got a capacity crowd. Then I started talking about my plans to teach the homeless how to defend themselves—not with guns, or anything, but with makeshift weapons—and the yuppies in the area practically had one big collective seizure when they heard about that. So I got kicked out of the community center. Then some of the residents banded together and hired a lawyer, and they convinced a court to slap a restraining order on me; so I can't teach anything about self-defense. I'm still pretty angry about that.

"Anyway, after that I decided that maybe what they needed was a place to keep provisions for survival in case of an emergency. So I bought some cheap lockers and rented space in another building for them, then taught the class what they should keep in them—bottled water, dried foods, medical kits, and so on. But anytime someone actually put something in his locker, it was burglarized right away by someone else. You see, I'd had to give them a lesson on memorizing their combinations, which resulted in about half the class walking around reciting theirs out loud—and that was that, as far as security went. But anyway, by that time most of the class was using the lockers for the most inexplicable junk I'd ever seen—old newspapers, bags of empty cans, you name it.

"And then I realized that the basic principles of survivalism are pretty much what these people need every day of their lives, so I started treating them like the emergency was already here —which, for them, it is. There's no established order in their lives, no central authority they can call on; they have no means of obtaining food outside of scrounging and begging, no access to the fruits of our culture—it's like they're living in an impenetrable jungle, even though they walk down the streets right next to people like you and me.

"So I started teaching them basic nutrition and health care, and I taught them their legal rights—including the right to privacy, the whole concept of which just blew their minds; I told them what a shelter could demand, legally and ethically, from a sheltered person; in short, I tried to get each of them to think of his life as a business, as a going concern. I wanted them to realize that even within the most limiting circumstances, they can make choices that can better their condition. And my hope is that they someday become productive members of the community and help better the quality of *my* life. Because I firmly believe that you only get out of society what you put into it. You were the one who taught me that, at that dinner a year ago."

She felt a little thrill when he said this; he really *was* enthralling when he got going—he was passionate and driven and wouldn't even consider defeat. She hugged herself in pleasure.

Then she looked at her reflection in the rearview mirror and saw a dopey smile sprawled across her face, and she was shocked; shocked, because she'd almost let herself be seduced by this man, the way Peter had been seduced—charmed, like a snake, by the music of his words.

She almost threw up.

She forced herself to remember why she'd contacted him in the first place. Her driving purpose mustn't be allowed to wither away due to weakness.

He had turned onto Grace Street now. "Hold on," she said; "it's up just a few more doors—that one, there, with the porch."

"It's beautiful," he said as he pulled up in front of the house. "When did you buy it?"

"Couple of months ago," she said, pulling herself together and opening the door. "I'm making good money now, and interest rates were low, so I thought, *hell*."

"Well, congratulations. Peter and I would love to see it sometime."

"As a matter of fact," she said, standing on the street now and bending at the waist to speak to him, "I'm having a housewarming party next weekend. A lot of the old crowd will be there—they're all so curious to see Peter and the four-star lover who took him out of circulation."

He blushed. "Well—I'm sure we'd love to come."

"Invitations went out today," she said. "But I wanted to give you yours in person. You know, for old times' sake. I haven't seen much of you guys, and I—well, you know . . ."

He smiled. "Yeah, I know."

She slammed the door and waved good-bye. He waved back, pulled into the street, and drove away.

She stood looking after him, still waving, and thought, You're not so bad, Lloyd Hood. I actually hope you enjoy your last few days with Peter.

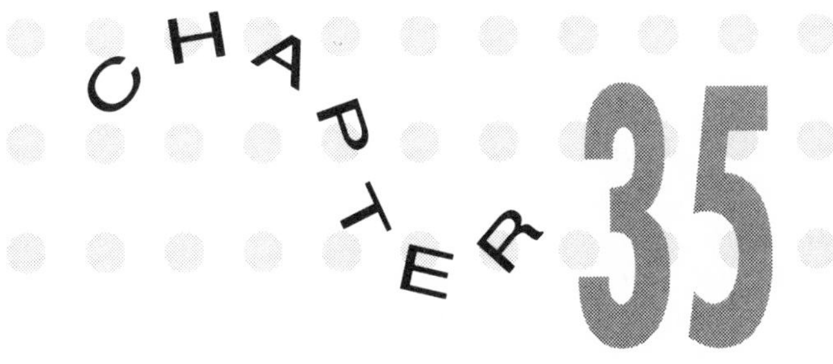

"Natalie, you look absolutely *sensational!*"

"Thank you, Joel, darling. Come in, come in."

"Last time I saw you, you looked so *ill.*"

"Take your jacket?"

"Thanks. I was worried about you, I mean it."

"Beautiful leather! Love the studs."

"Thank you. But now, you look *great.* Love your hair."

"How sweet! I had a bad spell. It's over now."

"I should say so. You're just *glowing* with health."

"Follow me. The party's already started."

"Great house! You must be doing *super.*"

"Fairly super, thanks."

"That the kitchen?"

"Yes."

"It's huge!"

"I'll give you the tour later. Here we are. Does everyone know Joel? Joel, Kevin. Kevin, Joel. Joel, Thomas. Thomas, Joel. Joel, Brandon. Brandon, Joel."

"Hi, Joel."

"Hi, Joel."

"Hey, Joel, long time, no see."

"There's the door again. Would someone get Joel a drink, please?"

"Natalie, can I change the music?"

"Sure, Brandon. The compact discs are all on the shelf. Now excuse me, won't you?—Well, hello, boys!"

"Hi, Natalie."

"Hi, Natalie—you look *great.*"

"Why, thank you! Come on in."

"Thanks. Great place!"

"I'm so glad you think so."

"How long you had it?"

"Bought it in June. Take your jackets?"

"Thanks. It's gorgeous. How many rooms?"

"Ten."

"*Ten!* That's incredible."

"Yes, it's very spacious. Beautiful jacket! Linen, isn't it?"

"Uh-huh; a gift from my boy, here."

"Oh, how sweet! Follow me. So you two are still in love?"

"Very."

"*Very* very."

"So glad for you both! Well, here we are. Do you know everyone? Michael, David, this is Joel. Joel, this is Michael and David. Michael, David, this is Thomas. Thomas, Michael and David. Kevin, Brandon, this is Michael and David. Michael, David, Kevin, Brandon. Brandon, I don't remember owning any Lena Horne CDs."

"I brought this one with me."

"Well, if you *must* play it, at least turn it down a notch. Oh, there's the door again. Someone be an angel and get drinks for Michael and David. I'll be right back.—Kelly, darling! so glad you could come!"

"Hi, Natalie. You look *ravishing.*"

"You old flirt! Come on in. Take your jacket?"

"Sure. Terrific place. You own it?"

"Me and the bank. *Fabulous* jacket! Tweed?"

"Uh-huh. Got it at a flea market, if you can believe that."

"It's a classic! Hang it up for you?"

"Thanks. I can't get over how good you look! Last time I saw you, I thought you were sick."

"I was, but that's over. Follow me."

"Love the couch. New?"

"That it is. Give you the grand tour later."

"What's behind that door there?"

"Oh, just a closet."

"A closet with a padlock?"

"The old owner had some strange habits. Anyway, here we are. Well, do you know everyone? Kelly, this is Michael, David, Thomas, Joel, Brandon, and of course you know Kevin. Brandon, I mean it, turn it *down!*"

"But this is my favorite! 'Fish gotta swim, birds gotta fly, I gotta love one man till I die . . .' "

"Someone be a dear and get Kelly a drink."

"Natalie, do you have any grenadine?"

"I don't think so. Will lime juice do? I've got plenty of that."

"Hey, Natalie, who's the print on the wall by?"

"Frida Kahlo, a very great artist. Isn't it beautiful?"

"It's wild! Can't take my eyes off it."

"Natalie, did you hear about George and Bobby? You'll *die.*"

"Oh, you *must* give me all the dirt, but can it wait a second? There's the door again. Excuse me.—Kirk, darling! thank you so much for coming!"

"God, Natalie, you look so *beautiful!* I haven't seen you since Christmas, when you were *way* too thin."

"Thank you, doll! Come in. Why—hello, Will."

"Oh, you know Will? We're together."

"Yes, Kirk, Natalie knows me. We're old friends, aren't we, Natalie? Matter of fact, I'm surprised I didn't get an invitation to this little soiree. I'll save us all a deal of embarrassment and blame the mail delivery. Lucky thing Mr. Bergland here was good enough to ask me, or I'd have missed this little do entirely. So wonderful to *see* you, Natalie dear. Kiss, kiss."

"May I—uh—take your jackets?"

"Yes, but do be careful with mine. It's silk."

"Of course, Will. Yours, Kirk?"

"Thanks, Natalie."

"So, Natalie, how much did this dump set you back? If it was more than eighty, you were robbed."

"Uh—why don't you both follow me? You can meet everyone."

"Oh, Christ, Natalie, *why* are you playing Lena Horne? Did she die today or something?"

"Here we are. Kirk, Will, this is Joel, Brandon, Kelly, Thomas, David, Michael, and Kevin."

"This is it? For heaven's sake, Natalie. When do the *real* guests show up?"

"Will, I'm warning you—"

"Where's the bar? Excuse me, sweetheart. Ooh, nice chest on you! David, wasn't it? You ready to leave yet? Just let me knock back a drink or two first."

"Will—"

"Don't get any ideas about me and Kirk here. We're not a couple. God forbid! We just came together. In the mundane sense of the word, I hasten to add. Hey, what'd I say? Fine, sweetheart. Your loss. You don't look so good from behind, anyway."

"Natalie, who *is* that guy?"

"Believe me, David, he wasn't invited."

"But you *know* him?"

"Come on, we *all* know someone like that."

"He's a jerk!"

"That's what I mean."

"He's treating his date like dogshit."

"I know. Poor Kirk. Maybe I should—excuse me a moment, I just had an idea.—Kirk, darling, don't look so glum!"

"I'm really sorry about this, Natalie. I just met Will a few days ago. When he heard I was coming here, he really played up to me. Guess I'm just a sucker for a pretty face. I thought he really liked me. He was so sweet, right up to the moment we walked in the door."

"Darling, *I'm* the one who's sorry. He was just using you to worm his way in here."

"I know. Maybe I should go."

"No, no! I have a better idea. Come with me.—That's right, this way. Up the stairs."

"Where are we going?"

"My bedroom. But don't get any ideas, you naughty boy!"

"Natalie, you make me blush."

"Just through here. Now, it's here in my desk somewhere . . . shit, I wish I'd learn to put things in some kind of order. I remember I put it—Ah! Here it is. I *knew* this would come in handy someday. Have a look."

"A photo? Is it of—oh, my God. That's Will."

"Yes, it is, isn't it?"

"Why—why is he wearing a dirty diaper?"

"Well, from the look on his face, I'd say for enjoyment, wouldn't you?"

"I'm—stunned."

"I thought you'd laugh."

"Is it funny?"

"Darling Kirk—it's a *scream*. Don't ask me how I got it. Just take it downstairs to the bathroom, and I'll send in the rest of my guests, one at a time. Now that they've spent a few moments alone with Will, I'll bet each and every one of them will consider this snapshot the highlight of the evening."

"Oh, yeah! Natalie, you're so terrifically *wicked*."

"And after everyone has seen it, we'll make a group presentation of it to Will. We'll see how sophisticated and superior he acts *then*."

"You're incredible. I was ready to go home and cry my eyes out."

"Revenge is so much more *fun* than that, Kirk, doll. Now let's sneak back downstairs again.—Oh, put that in your shirt pocket, we don't want anyone to see it before we're ready!—There, the bathroom's over there. Yes, go on in.—Well, darlings, how's everything going?"

"No one told me there'd be no champagne here. Natalie, don't you have *any* champagne? Even bad domestic labels?"

"I'm sorry, Will, I don't."

"That's what I get for going to a party outside the reaches of civilization. Well, I guess a glass of this sewer brew you call gin will have to do."

"Whatever you like.—Oh, Brandon, could you come here for a moment, please?"

"Natalie, I turned it down, I *swear*."

"I know you did, darling, I just want a word with you."

"Okay. What?"

"A little closer. That's it. Listen, Brandon, I want you to go and meet Kirk in the bathroom for a moment. Nothing kinky or sexual involved; he just has a surprise he wants to share with all the guests tonight, one at a time."

"You promise it's nothing kinky? I mean, I'm not really attracted to him."

"Well, actually, it *is* rather kinky, but it doesn't involve you or him."

"I see. Okay, I'm intrigued. Where's the bathroom?"

"Right over there, to your left. There you go.—So, Joel, how about a drink for your hostess before the doorbell takes me away again?"

"Sure, Natalie, what's your pleasure?"

"Bacardi on the rocks, please. Thanks so much for bartending while I've been busy with my guests."

"No problem, I enj—oh, my God! Did you hear that scream?"

"Yes, dear. Sounded like it came from the bathroom. Why don't you go and see what it's all about? And send Brandon back when you get there."

"What?"

"Just go, Joel. Trust me. Door on the left. Go on.—Oh, hello again, Will."

"Natalie, what was that scream I just heard?"

"A scream? I didn't hear anything."

"I could swear I heard a scr—"

"Oh, Will, just try to relax and enjoy yourself."

"Well, honestly, Natalie, how *can* I with that awful *thing* on the wall staring at me? I mean, really—a Frida Kahlo print! Aspiring to upper-middle-classdom, are we? Don't tell me: You subscribe to public television, too."

"Whatever you say, Will. Oh, excuse me.—So, Brandon, did you enjoy yourself?"

"Christ, Natalie! I couldn't believe my eyes! What an absolute fucking *riot!* Where on earth did you—oh, did you hear that? Joel must have just seen it."

"And there's the doorbell, as well! Brandon, be a dear and

send Kelly in to see our little surprise. I've got to go welcome our new arrivals."

"So, more guests, Natalie?"

"Yes, Will, more guests. Excuse me."

"Of a better caliber, I hope."

"As a matter of fact, it's probably Peter and his lover, Lloyd."

"Oh, joy! So I finally get to meet her!"

"Better watch out, Will. 'She' can eat you for breakfast."

"That would be lovely, but then who'd be left to eat Peter?—Did you hear that? Now, Natalie, you can't deny it; that was the *third* scream tonight! What in the *world* is going on in that bathroom?"

"Just a little sadomasochism. I try to see to all my guests' needs. Now I really *must* get that door."

CHAPTER 36

Natalie lurched into the kitchen for more beer. Peter followed her.

"I've been trying to get you alone all night," he said. "For God's sake, Natalie. You didn't tell me Will Hammond was going to be here!"

"I didn't know myself, till he showed up," she said, shoving bottles of Amstel Light into the freezer to get them cold more quickly. "Kirk brought him."

"Kirk? Kirk *Bergland* is here with him?"

"Yes." She wiped her hands on a dish towel.

"Hardly Will's type."

"I know. I think he just used the poor boy to get into my house. He's been trying to ruin the party from the moment he got here."

"Tell me about it! Last I saw, he was doing his level best to get a rise out of Lloyd."

She raised an eyebrow. "And is it working?"

He smiled. "What do you think?"

"I can't even guess."

He put a finger to his lips, then led her over to the kitchen doorway. "They're just around the corner," he whispered; "listen carefully."

She craned her neck and could hear Will saying, "I'm *so* glad you're not offended that I got to dear Peter before you did, Lloyd, love."

"Why would that offend me?" Lloyd asked. "I hadn't even met him yet."

"Well," said Will, "*some* terrible people would say that you were getting my leftovers."

"That's a matter of perspective," Lloyd said matter-of-factly. "And if I allowed myself to think in those terms, my natural perspective would be to look on *you* as *Peter's* leftovers."

Natalie almost spit out a laugh. Will must be steaming.

"But," Lloyd continued, "I really can't accept such a cheap view of human relationships."

"How very commendable," said Will. "After all, we're all sisters, aren't we?"

"We are?" Lloyd asked.

"Well—yes, we are."

"I've never understood that. Calling gay men 'sisters.' What does it mean?"

Will hemmed and hawed for a few seconds. "Why—that we're all *soulmates*, you daffy thing."

"*Are* we? *I* don't really think I'm *your* soulmate. No offense—I just don't feel that way about anyone but Peter. But even if we *were* all soulmates, why wouldn't we call each other 'brothers,' instead? I mean, we're all men."

Will laughed. "Well, dear, some of us have a little *woman* in us."

"Tell me about that," Lloyd said with keen interest. "Because I've never felt that way, myself. Even when it comes to sex, I've always felt my love to be that of one man for another; which, if anything, would be *farther* removed from any feminine reality, not closer. What exactly is it about yourself that you consider womanly? Is it a certain something that you objectively know all women to share—some trait that Margaret Thatcher and Madonna and Mother Teresa all possess? Because I can't imagine what that would be—beyond similar biological equipment, which I'm sure you don't have in common with them."

There was a long pause; then Will said, "Will you excuse me for a moment?"

Natalie ducked back into the kitchen, and she and Peter huddled together and giggled. "Poor Will," said Peter. "His bitchiness is no match for Lloyd and the Socratic method."

Natalie opened the freezer and felt the beer. "Come on, get *cold*," she ordered it. She turned to Peter. "So, you having fun?"

"So far, yeah. There must be a dozen guys here I haven't seen in *ages*."

"They've missed you." She met his eyes. "*I've* missed you."

"Well—you know how it is when you're married."

"Still happy with Lloyd?" she asked in a low voice.

"Oh, God, yes. Very," he said. "He's just so incredibly good for me, Natalie. He's actually gotten me to *paint*, believe it or not. Which I've never done seriously before—you know, I was like everyone else, I dabbled." He shrugged his shoulders in dismissal. "But Lloyd just kept hammering away at me about honing my craft, refining my vision, creating works of art that have the capacity to, you know, *change* things. To point the way to a better world. So, anyway, I've done a couple of canvases, but nothing I'd show to anyone yet. Lloyd is a pretty good critic—he right away can tell me where I went wrong, where I pulled back when I was just about to, you know, *say* something. Because I didn't want people to laugh at me. Because, you know, it's so easy to adopt a cynical attitude out of fear—because no one ever laughs at cynicism. Ever notice that? People seem to respect it, why, I don't know. Lloyd can't figure it out either, and he's been working on it longer than I have. But he says what takes real courage isn't cynicism, it's enthusiasm, it's saying, Here's what I believe, and I don't care if you think it's unsophisticated and silly. I guess I always believed in that, too, you know, believed in celebrating the best in me, but never did because it seems like no one wants to see the best in anyone anymore. They want to see the grungy side. But I've got this integrity, you know? This streak that I'm kind of proud of, and I want to do something with it, that mayb—" He caught Natalie's eye for the first time and suddenly stopped short and flushed, as if embarrassed at having caught himself boring her. "Anyway, yeah, I'm very happy with Lloyd, to answer your original question." He took a swig of beer, his face still beet red.

Far from bored, Natalie had felt a brief stab of anger. She'd often tried to get Peter to paint her portrait, but he'd always had an excuse. She gritted her teeth and said, "I only asked, because a few months ago you were having difficulties."

"Well, sure—every marriage has difficulties. I mean, you don't stay starry-eyed with each other forever. So, no, it's not really paradise anymore, if that's what you mean. But it's definitely a suburb."

She smiled at him. "*I* still feel I'm in paradise when I'm with you."

He lowered his eyes. "So, anyway—um—when do we get the grand tour?"

She sighed. "Soon as this fucking beer gets cold." She opened the freezer and felt the bottles again. "Everybody's waiting for it."

"It'll never get cold if you keep opening the freezer every thirty seconds."

At that moment, Lloyd walked into the kitchen with a bewildered, somewhat sour look on his face. "Natalie, I just went to use your bathroom, but there was someone else in there, and he showed me something very disturbing."

"*Oh*," cried Natalie, her hands flying to her face; "oh, God, don't tell me Kirk's still *in* there!"

"What did he show you?" asked Peter.

"It was a picture of that Will fellow," he said. "The one you used to date. It was such a degrading picture. I can't believe he was actually *showing* it to anyone."

"What was so degrading about it?" Peter asked, his eyes twinkling.

"I don't even want to say. Just be glad you didn't see it, honey."

Peter immediately bolted from the kitchen and made a beeline for the bathroom.

Natalie let out a delighted shriek, then collapsed into the most convulsive laughter she'd known in more than a year.

Lloyd stared at her, waiting for her to calm down, and then

said, "Natalie, I'm not having a *bad* time by any means; but I really don't understand the first thing about this party."

Before she could answer, they heard Peter scream.

Ten minutes later, Natalie was giving Peter and Lloyd the tour they'd requested. By now, the entire house was filled with gay men; they were leaning against the walls of every room, or sitting on the stairway, or reclining on the furniture; they were chatting, networking, gossiping, flirting, and drinking. The smell of marijuana drifted through the house. Someone was dishing out cocaine in the kitchen pantry. Natalie was ecstatically happy.

"And this is the bedroom," she said, flinging open the door to her inner sanctum.

Two men sat up from her bed, caught in the act.

"Ruin those sheets and I'll kill you," she scolded them. Then she shut the door again. "Now," she said, leading Peter and Lloyd down the hall, "over here is the master bath . . ."

A few minutes later, the tour concluded downstairs again. "That's it," she said, standing in the crowded hallway. "That's *ma maison.*"

Lloyd pointed down a connecting corridor to the door with the padlock on it. "What's behind that?" he asked.

"Just a closet," she said. "The previous owner left a lock on it; I have to have it sawed off."

"Maybe there's something valuable stored in there," Peter said, rubbing his hands together greedily. "Like an old coin collection, or unknown Picassos."

"He didn't *die*, Peter—he moved out. He would've taken his valuables with him. I'm sure it's just an oversight."

Michael and David came into the hallway and passed by Natalie, pausing long enough to tell her, "If you don't want this party to be remembered as a disaster, you have to do two things: First, stop Brandon from playing Peggy Lee records, and second, get rid of that repulsive Will character."

"Okay," she said. "I guess it's time to make the presentation to Will. Let's get Kirk."

A few of her guests overheard her, and they started trilling with excitement. They trotted alongside her to the bathroom, where Kirk was still displaying the infamous Polaroid to all those who wanted a second and even a third look at it.

"I've never seen anything so disgusting in my entire life," said a tall redhead as he grinned in complete pleasure.

"Kirk, darling," said Natalie, sticking her head in the door, "maybe it's time to show Will our little treasure before somebody breaks down and shoots him and you lose the opportunity forever."

Kirk, now roaring drunk, smiled a toothy smile. "Oh, I don't know if I can . . ."

"Come on," said a musclebound blond next to him; "I'll help you. I want to see the look on that fucker's face." He lifted Kirk by the armpits and virtually carried him out the door.

In this way was Kirk borne all the way to the living room, where Will was still dispensing his barbs and insults. Word had spread about the presentation, and by the time Kirk was suspended by his arms in front of Will, Polaroid in hand, virtually the entire party had assembled to watch the fireworks.

All except Natalie and Peter, that is. She'd grabbed his arm when Kirk's little journey began, and led him away from Lloyd, saying, "Hang back with me, honey, I have something to show you."

She took him to the padlocked door, produced a key, and unlocked it. "I lied," she whispered; "there's something special down here I was saving till now." She swung open the door; it revealed a staircase.

From the living room, they could hear Kirk say, "Listen, Will, we've all enjoyed this so much tonight, it's only fair you get to see it, too."

And as Natalie and Peter started down the staircase, the house was filled with Will's piercing, eardrum-shattering scream.

"Natalie? Why'd you shut the door? I can't see where I'm going. What's down here, anyway? Natalie? Are you still there?—Goddamn it, this isn't funny. Turn a fucking light on.—I can hear you breathing. Where are y—*ouch!* Goddamn it! What the fuck was that?—I'm bleeding! What did you stick me with? What's gotten into you?—Natalie, I'm not kidding.—HEY, HELP! SOMEBODY UP THERE, OPEN THE DOOR! *HELP!* SOMEBODY UP TH—uh . . . uh . . . oh, shit. I don't feel . . . oh, you didn't . . . ohhhh shhhii . . ."

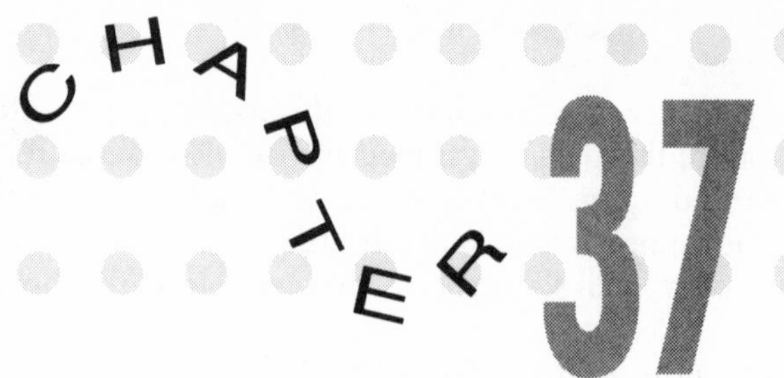

Chapter 37

Saturday became Sunday. Darkness became dawn. Clamor became quiet.

Natalie couldn't believe how long it was taking everyone to leave.

"Don't forget your compact discs, Brandon," she said, dumping them into his arms as she shoved him out the front door.

"Thanks," he said, counting them.

"So wonderful to have you, but I must get my beauty sleep now."

"Wait—where's my Rosemary Clooney? I'm missing my Rosemary Clooney!"

"I'm sure it'll turn up, and I'll bring it to you in person."

"Promise?"

"Scout's honor." Actually, she knew full well that Franklin Hernandez, who hated show tunes, had grown so annoyed with Brandon that he'd taken the Rosemary Clooney disc and shoved it down the waste disposal unit in Natalie's kitchen sink. The act had met with delighted laughter all around.

Just two more to go, she thought, including the most difficult one. There he was now, his eyes hollow and his cheeks sunken. "Lloyd, darling, I'm *sure* he'll turn up." She kept the front door open, as if to entice him through it.

But he came up to her and stopped there, his hands open as if in supplication. "I just don't understand it, Natalie. He wouldn't have left without telling me. He just *wouldn't* have."

"Of course not. I'm sure there's a logical explanation." She almost felt sorry for him. Poor, pathetic Lloyd.

"You're sure you didn't see him leave?" It was about the ten-thousandth time he'd asked her that.

"Honey, one moment he was here, the next he was gone." *How* do I get him to *go*? she wondered.

"Did anyone else disappear at the same time?"

"Not that I noticed. What are you thinking?" She gave up and shut the door.

"You know what I'm thinking. It wouldn't be so awful. It wouldn't be the end of the world. He was drunk last night. There were a lot of desirable men here. It wouldn't be the end of the world. I'd understand. I'd be disappointed in him, but I'd forgive him."

Kirk Bergland stumbled downstairs, his eyes beet red. "Oh, my *God*," he said, his voice hoarse as sandpaper on a sidewalk. "Somebody stop all those oxygen molecules from colliding into each other and making so much noise."

Natalie opened the door again. "So much fun, Kirk. Let's do it again, soon."

"Kirk," said Lloyd, "did you see Peter leave?"

"Only person I saw leave was Will. Natalie, thank you for that moment. As usual, you're my heroine." He kissed her on the forehead and stumbled out onto the porch. "If you find my shoes, give a call, okay?"

"Of course, sweetheart." She shut the door again. "Lloyd, what can I say? If I see or hear from Peter, I'll let you know at once."

"I've searched the house high and low. I couldn't find him anywhere."

"I know, I helped you. Remember?" She stifled a yawn.

"The only place I haven't looked is that closet." He stared at the padlocked door.

"Well, he could hardly have gotten himself in there, now, could he?" Goddamn you, *go home!*

"I guess not." He met her eyes again; he looked as though he hadn't slept in months. "It's just not like him. It's *not.*"

There was a knock on the door. Jesus *Christ*, what *now?* She opened it, and Kirk was standing there. "Forget something, hon?"

He was holding the Sunday edition of *The Chicago Tribune.* "No, no—I just happened to look at your paper on the lawn, and I saw this picture. Isn't this a friend of yours?"

On the front page was a full-color photo of Luigi Gianelli beneath the headline, SIX COPS INDICTED FOR BRIBERY, THEFT. Oh, my God, she thought. She felt faint.

"Good heavens, Kirk," she said; "what makes you think I know any cops?"

"I could've sworn I saw you talking to him one night at Roscoe's."

"A gay cop? Oh, come on. You must be mistaken."

He looked at the photo again. "Hard to mistake a face like that."

Lloyd leaned into the doorway and looked at the newspaper. "I don't believe it. That's the cop who rescued Peter!"

She whirled. "How did you know that? I mean—it is?"

"Yes. We met him on Halsted Street one night. Peter stopped and thanked him again. We saw him go into Little Jim's, so we knew he must be gay, and that kind of surprised us."

"See, Natalie?" said Kirk, excitedly. "It *was* him you were talking to."

Lloyd turned to her. "You know him?"

"I—vaguely remember—talking to someone who looked like that," she said. Her forehead was perspiring now, and her upper lip was growing moist. "I had no idea he was a cop, though. This is silly—you're both looking at me as though I'd done something wrong!" *That* was a stupid thing to say! she scolded herself at once.

Lloyd shook his head. "Sorry. Right now, everything seems like it's part of one big conspiracy to take Peter away from me."

"Peter's missing?" said Kirk.

"Both of you go home and get some sleep," she urged them. "You'll feel better."

She walked them down the driveway. Suddenly Lloyd stopped and pointed behind her. "That your van?" he asked.

She turned, and saw that, during the night, one of her guests had opened her garage. Who the *fuck* had done that? And there was her van—the same one she'd used to spy on Peter and Lloyd, the same one Lloyd had become suspicious of, the same one she'd gone to all the trouble of restoring after it had been stolen and stripped. What a curse that thing was turning out to be!

"Yes," she said brightly; "I just got it last month."

"Looks familiar for some reason."

"There are lots like it around," she said desperately.

"Jesus," said Kirk, reading the paper; "you wouldn't *believe* all the bad shit your friend Gianelli's being accused of."

"He's *not* my *friend*, Kirk." She'd practically snapped his head off.

The two men looked at her in alarm.

"I'm sorry, I'm overtired. We should all get some sleep. I'm sure Peter will turn up, Lloyd. I'm *sure* of it."

"You're right, I know." He sighed and turned to Kirk. "Need a lift home?"

"That'd be great. Thanks." He gave Natalie the newspaper and followed Lloyd to the Celica, his stockinged feet getting soaked by the dew on Natalie's lawn.

Suddenly Lloyd stopped, and tears filled his eyes. He shook his head slowly. "I forgot. Peter has the keys."

This was just getting worse and worse. Natalie thought she'd pull her hair out from frustration.

"Let's share a cab," said Kirk, obviously taking pity on him. "We can straighten all this out later if we don't die from our hangovers."

"You're right," she called after them as they started down the sidewalk to Broadway, where cabs were more frequent. "I'm sure everything will turn out fine. I'm sure Peter is even closer than you know."

CHAPTER 38

She checked the intercom half a dozen times that morning and heard nothing. She ran out to the supermarket, picked up Brynocki from the kennel, and got home around one; still nothing. Finally just after two, she listened in again, and she heard him. "OPEN UP! GODDAMN IT, OPEN UP!"

She put Brynocki on his leash, got the key chain from under a potted plant, and went down to face him.

At the bottom of the stairs, she unlocked the door to the secret room and swung it open. Brynocki strained on the leash to get in.

Peter backed away from the door. "Christ," he said. "A German shepherd, too. You've seen *way* too fucking much TV, Natalie."

She patted the dog's head. "Brynocki's here to make sure you don't try anything stupid, like escaping."

"Now, why would I try that?" he asked. "You've separated me from my lover, locked me in a prison, and now put a guard dog on me who looks like my ass is all he wants for dinner. Escape? This is my idea of heaven!"

"Sarcasm is the lowest of the arts," she said. Immediately it occurred to her that she was parroting her mother, and she shuddered a little. She entered the room and shut the door behind her. "Brynocki, sit," she said, and the dog obediently sat at the door. She turned to Peter. "If you lay a hand on me, Brynocki will tear it off."

He backed away from her.

She looked around the room. "I don't think this is so bad," she said, coiling the leash in her hands as she surveyed the setup. "There's a big bed and lots of comfy furniture, some Nautilus equipment so you can stay in shape, a TV, and a VCR with all your favorite movies. A bookshelf with all those books you've been meaning to read ever since I've known you—*Moll Flanders, Lolita, Remembrance of Things Past.* Some artist's equipment so you can paint the big-shot paintings you're so hot on." She turned and pointed to the other side of the room. "Plus, your own refrigerator, a private bathroom—*God*, Peter. What *else* could you want out of life?"

"Freedom," he said. "Self-determination. The ability to choose."

She shook her head, as if he'd said something terribly childish. "Accept the fact that your life has changed."

He went to the bed and sat on it. "What did you drug me with?"

"Never you mind. Something that would keep you out for a few hours, that's all. Not that it was even necessary. This whole place is soundproof. You could've screamed bloody murder, and no one at the party would've heard you."

He sighed. "Where'd you get the money for all this?"

"My father left it to me. Well, I've had to borrow some beyond that, but it's weird—once you've got a couple of thousand in the bank, it's easy to get a loan. The more you have, the more they'll lend you. I think that's kind of funny."

He grimaced. "My sense of humor is a little dull at the moment."

She sat in the easy chair next to the TV. "When did you wake up?"

"Couple of hours ago."

"Really? I've been listening on the intercom and I didn't hear you. What've you been doing?"

"Just sitting here, trying not to hate your guts."

"Oh, good," she said with a smile.

"I said 'trying.' I didn't say 'succeeding.' "

She scowled. "Look, it's no good fighting this. I've got you. You're mine. *Accept* it, Peter."

"Is this how you want me?" he said. "Like some kind of fucking pet?"

"It's not permanent," she said, her face growing red.

"Oh? When am I allowed out?"

"When you accept that you belong with me. When you accept that we were meant to be together."

"In other words, never."

Her face felt puffy; she thought she might cry. "I don't know why you're being so horrible about this."

He laughed and shook his head. "You really don't, do you?"

"No."

He looked away from her. "I'm just going to sit tight and wait this out. It's ridiculous. It can't last forever. Lloyd won't rest till he finds me, and how difficult can it be to figure out that you're behind it?"

"I've got news for you," she said, smiling in triumph. "Lloyd isn't even looking. He thinks you snuck off with someone else last night, and says he's through with you and never wants to see you again."

Peter grinned at her. "You're lying."

"You wish!"

"No, I *know*." He rubbed his forehead. "I suppose you're at a disadvantage here. You've never had a lover. You don't know what it's like to know someone better than you know yourself. You've never had that kind of total intimacy. I *know* Lloyd Hood. And, to a lesser extent, I know you. I know he'd never give me up. And I know that you're a cheap little liar."

Her anger flared. "Better watch what you say, Peter. I can starve you to death down here if I want."

"As if I'd eat anything you put in front of me!"

She blanched. "You can't refuse food."

" 'Can't,' Natalie? You may have made it impossible for me to do a lot of things, but even now, even though I'm nothing but a fucking prisoner, I still have the power to make personal decisions. If I don't want to eat your food, I won't."

She got up and started to leave. "You'll change your mind."

"Lloyd always said you were an animal," he said. "A completely amoral being, all ego. But no, I had to go and convince him otherwise. I had to make him think you had some ethical sense."

She whirled and shook the coiled leash at him. Brynocki got to his feet. "This is the whole trouble," she said, her voice breaking. "You talk just like him now! You're not even close to the man you used to be!"

"I don't deny that." He stood.

"You're brainwashed, is what it amounts to," she cried. "And I'm going to deprogram you! You were happy with me before, you're going to be happy with me again!"

He raised one eyebrow. "When was I happy with you, Natalie?"

"Before Lloyd. You know you were!"

"You mean, when I used to cry on your shoulder because I was so lonely and lost? When we used to go out and I'd dull my senses with alcohol and cocaine virtually every night because I was so miserable? When I couldn't get up before noon, and couldn't sleep without drugging myself? *That* happy, carefree period of my life? Is *that* the time you mean?"

She reeled, as if he had struck her. She'd never expected this—never known that this was how he felt, that this was how he regarded their years together. To her, those years had been precious, a sort of personal Golden Age, but Peter spoke of them as though they had been trash.

The disparity between their perceptions frightened her; she couldn't suppress the urge to flee. It was as if her entire sense of reality had been called into question. Caught by Peter's cold, baleful gaze, she backed up all the way to the door; then, her hands trembling, she hooked Brynocki to his leash and left without another word, locking the door behind her.

She ran all the way up the stairs, a mystified Brynocki at her heels.

Lloyd called her at a little after four. "Have you heard anything?" he asked.

Still shaken by her confrontation with Peter, she had to

command herself to sound innocent and sympathetic. "Not a word," she said in hushed tones. "Oh, poor Lloyd!"

"Don't pity me, Natalie. I'm not drunk anymore; I've had six hours of sleep. I've got a clear head now, and I know something's wrong. Peter hasn't left me."

"I only hope that's true."

"What you hope is scarcely the issue here," he said. Why was he being so brutal to her? "I'd appreciate it if you'd let me know the moment you see or hear from him."

"Of course, Lloyd. You don't even have to ask."

"Somehow," he said, "I have a feeling that I do."

As if that weren't disturbing enough, Curtis Driscoll, of all people, called her about an hour later. "Did you see the paper today?" he asked.

She'd almost forgotten. "Oh, yes. Poor Curtis! I'm so sorry. Is it horrible for you?" She was fixing Peter's dinner. She cradled the phone between her chin and shoulder as she stirred her spaghetti sauce.

"Not really. Luigi's bad news. I loved him, but I knew that all along. Listen, I'm going away for a couple of months; I don't want to be around when he starts talking."

She stopped stirring and took the phone in her hand. "What do you mean?"

"Well, you must know that he doesn't have the highest moral profile around," he said. "Wouldn't surprise me if he started naming all the names he can, just to take a bunch of us down with him."

Natalie had to sit for this. "Surely he wouldn't!"

"Listen, I'm his lover, and *I'm* scared of that happening, so *you'd* better be goddamn *terrified*."

And she was.

She found it difficult to carry the tray of spaghetti down the stairs with Brynocki's leash around her wrist as well. The dog raced ahead and she nearly dropped the entire dinner; as it was, a glass of mineral water crashed to the ground, and she had to be careful not to cut her feet. Need to think of a better way to do this in the future, she told herself.

"Brynocki, *heel*," she snapped. The dog stopped, panting heavily and excitedly, and waited for her to catch up.

She reached the door and took a deep breath, to summon up her confidence. Then, propping the tray atop her bosom, she unlocked the door to Peter's room and opened it.

It was completely dark.

She reached in and turned on the light. Peter was sitting on the bed, wide awake.

Her anxiety gave way to anger. "For God's sake," she said, taking the tray back into her hands. "You might as well make the best of this. Read, paint, do *something*."

Brynocki tugged her in. She entered, put the tray on the butcher-block table by the TV, and unhooked his leash. "Sit," she said, pointing to the door. The dog trotted over to the doorway and sat, drooling patiently.

"I thought we might watch a movie with dinner," she said brightly. "I have all your favorites here." She scanned the rack of videotapes. "*Star Wars, Monty Python and the Holy Grail, Young Frankenstein*—the choice is yours."

He cocked his head and stared at her. "I'm giving this one last chance," he said. "Do you deny that, by keeping me here and threatening my safety if I try to leave, you're violating every principle of civil and human rights, as recognized and exalted by this and vitually every other country in the world?"

She waved a hand at him in disgust. "More Lloyd talk," she said. "I don't have to listen to this."

"Do you deny it?" he asked her again.

"*Who Framed Roger Rabbit?*" she said definitively, taking the videocassette from the shelf. "We both liked that a lot when we saw it."

He sighed. "Okay, I tried." He swung his legs over the side of the bed. "I told you that I still have some power to choose," he said, "and I choose not to acknowledge your presence. From now on, you are invisible to me."

"You can't keep that up," she said, smiling at the preposterousness of it. "It's not possible." She put the tape into the VCR. "Now get over here and eat your dinner. You must be *starving*."

She sat at the table and tucked a napkin into her collar.

The movie started, and, recognizing that in so small a room it would be difficult for Peter not to watch it, she turned up the volume to a level where it couldn't possibly be ignored.

He got up from the bed and locked himself in the bathroom, thwarting her.

She put her hands on her hips as the raucous din of the cartoon filled the room. He'll have to come out sooner or later, she told herself, and she patiently ate her spaghetti.

But he didn't come out, and forty minutes into the movie, she realized he wasn't going to. She put her head in her hands and started crying. The movie continued at its riotous pace until she couldn't stand the sound of it any longer. She turned off the VCR, put Brynocki on his leash, and locked the secret room for the night. Then she went up to bed and sobbed into her pillow until she fell asleep.

The next morning was Monday. She got up early and made Peter a breakfast of oatmeal and wheat toast. She took it down to him, and found him sleeping on top of his bed, fully clothed.

She left Brynocki by the door and tried to shake Peter awake. "Peter. Peter, honey. Breakfast."

But he wouldn't rouse; either that, or he was pretending to remain asleep. Eventually she had to give up, or be late for work. She left the oatmeal on his table.

"Call for you," said Bettina the moment Natalie walked into the office. "Guy's been on hold for ten minutes waiting for you to get here."

Natalie furrowed her brow, threw her purse into her chair, and slipped off her coat, then picked up the phone. "Natalie Stathis," she said.

"Natalie, it's Lloyd."

"Oh, Lloyd! Tell me you have good news."

He laughed. "I almost have to admire you," he said.

"What do you mean?"

"I mean you're good, that's all."

"I don't underst—"

"Peter didn't show up for work today," he blurted.

She checked her watch. "It's only a little after nine," she said. "He may still—"

"He won't be there."

"Lloyd, I hope you're not beginning to crack. That wouldn't solve anything."

"I really owe you a lot, Natalie," he said. "You've taught me so much in the year that I've known you. Want to know what the latest lesson is?"

Her heart was beating wildly. There was positive menace in his voice. "What?"

"All my life I've believed in reason, and in rational thought, as the highest calling of an intelligent mind. I've never given credit to any other means of charting or determining behavior. But now I'm learning the value of intuition. Now I find myself believing that it's possible to obtain objective knowledge in the absence of any empirical evidence."

"I don't follow you." He was frightening her, and frightening her good.

"Then I'll put it into words even you can understand," he said; "I'm saying that it's possible to have a valid hunch. Like the one I've got."

Her eyelids dropped shut. "*Oh*," she said, trying to sound excited; "do tell!"

"Not yet," he said. "Even though I'm sure I'm right about this, I'm going to try to get proof, first."

"Anything I can do to help?"

"No," he said; "no thank you, Natalie. You've already done more than enough."

He hung up without saying good-bye, and Jennifer Jerrold, on her way to the soda machine, caught sight of Natalie's face and said, "What a look of horror! If it's related to business, I may have to fire you. If it's related to your personal life, I insist you fill me in."

She shook her head. "I think I left the curling iron on, that's all."

"Oh. What a disappointment. Run off and check, then. I'm

not an ogre, Natalie. I don't demand that your beautiful new house burn down in the line of duty."

"Thanks. I think I will."

She picked up her purse and raced home.

Fifty minutes later, she pulled up to her house and saw that Lloyd and Peter's Celica was gone. She rushed inside and found, to her relief, that the padlock was still in place; Lloyd hadn't broken in and toyed with it, after all. Still, she wanted to see Peter for herself, to make sure he was still there, still hers. She summoned Brynocki and went down to the secret room.

She unlocked the door and opened it, but mere seconds after she did so, she heard the bathroom door click shut. Peter had hidden himself away from her again.

The lights were off, and the room was cloaked in darkness. Why did he insist on that? Well, at least she knew he was still here.

She turned on the lights and looked around. Nothing seemed amiss. Except . . .

She smiled.

He had eaten the oatmeal.

Victory number one.

CHAPTER 40

That night, she made a delicious pot roast and sweet potatoes and opened a bottle of Cabernet Sauvignon. She'd decided that Brynocki was well-behaved enough not to require the leash, so she simply whistled for him, and he jumped to his feet and followed her.

In fact, he seemed so happy and oafish that she began to wonder if he were really the same dog she'd seen in action at the breeder's kennel.

She opened the door to the cellar, looked at him, and said, "Brynocki, sic 'em."

The dog snarled and barked savagely at nothing, his fangs bared beneath his quivering snout.

Yes, he was the same dog.

"Good boy, Brynocki. It's okay."

His tongue lolled out of his mouth contentedly.

She went down to the secret room, unlocked it, and opened the door. Darkness, as usual.

Immediately, she could smell Peter's body odor. Then she noticed the thickness of the air.

She turned on the light. He was sitting on the bed, wide awake. He had a two-day growth of beard and was wearing the same clothes he'd had on since the party.

She put the tray on the butcher-block table, then went and checked the air-conditioning unit. It had been turned off. She switched it back on.

"Why'd you do that?" she asked, turning to face Peter. "I can barely *breathe* in here." She tugged at her collar.

He refused to even look at her.

"I made pot roast for dinner," she said, nodding toward the tray. "Let's not let it get cold."

He examined his cuticles. His face looked haggard and gray.

"This is absurd," she said, growing angry. "You sit here in the dark all day, now you make it so that you're practically suffocating—what on earth is the matter with you?"

He got up and headed for the bathroom.

She raced ahead of him and barred his way. "You know," she said, "with all the time you spend in the john, you might at least take a shower. I've given you shampoo, a hair dryer, an electric razor, new clothes—but you sit here stinking like a—"

He tried to get past her. Brynocki got to his feet.

"Give it *up*," Natalie said, maneuvering to stay in his way. "You can't keep this up forever. You already broke down and ate the oatmeal!"

He stopped and looked at her with such an expression of loathing that she got goose pimples; she knew at once she'd made a mistake.

His nostrils flared; he reached out and grabbed her, and threw her to the floor. Brynocki careened forward, snapping and snarling—but before the dog could reach him, he was safe behind the bathroom door.

Lying in bed that night, Natalie couldn't seem to unclench her fists. She had to concentrate, force her fingers to relax, and rest her hands on the blanket. But her concentration would inevitably wane, and she'd find herself digging her fingernails into her palms until the pain shocked her into awareness of it. Once, she came out of a deep reverie to find herself muttering something, something to Peter, and the last words she caught were, "forced me, God, I never meant for you to pay like this," and she couldn't remember anything she'd said before that. She shook her head to clear it, suddenly frightened of herself.

She had the feeling that she had come to the end of a long rope but had never given a thought to what to do when the rope ran out. She'd been too busy hanging on. She hadn't anticipated Peter's behavior, or Lloyd's suspicion—not because they couldn't have been anticipated; she could see that, quite the contrary, they might almost have been expected. But she simply couldn't face the idea of failing, because nothing came after it. She'd thought long and hard about how to get Peter locked away in her basement; she'd spent hours planning it, weeks having the escape-free room constructed, and thousands paying for it. Yet she'd never given a thought to what she'd do once she had him in there. She'd known better than to allow herself to consider that.

What had she done to herself? What had she allowed herself to do? Ruin everything? Well, it was ruined anyway. Now it would all fall down around her ears; but at least she'd have the satisfaction of knowing she'd fought for her man.

Her fists had balled up again; this time she did indeed draw blood. She watched it run down her wrist, a rivulet of ooze black as hate, and she thought of Peter. She couldn't rid her mind of the way he had looked at her tonight—so full of loathing and rage. She couldn't forget that he had thrown her to the floor.

She peered into her future and tried to see herself in a week, a month, a year; but there was nothing but darkness, no matter how far she projected.

She licked and swallowed the blood from her hand. Fuck the future; darkness was just fine with her.

The next morning, she felt more hopeful. She dressed for work, then went down to the kitchen and made Peter oatmeal again; after all, he'd been unable to resist it the day before.

She unfastened the padlock to the stairs and whistled for Brynocki, then picked up the breakfast tray and carried it down to the secret room. The dog loped down the stairs after her.

She unlocked the door and kicked it open with her foot. As expected, the room was dark. "Good morning," she trilled, and, resting the tray on her breasts, she extended one hand and turned on the lights.

She gasped.

Peter had taken something—a chair, presumably—and smashed the TV and the VCR to pieces; the same with the stereo. He had ripped the cord from the refrigerator, torn its door from the hinges, and toppled the entire unit. Food was spilled everywhere. He'd taken the paints she'd bought for him and splashed them over the walls. He'd ripped the bed to shreds, too; there were feathers flying everywhere.

He was nowhere to be seen, but the door to the bathroom was shut.

She set down the breakfast tray, stormed over to the bathroom, and pounded on the door. "This is so *fucking* childish," she screamed. "I could *kill* you for this. You're going to regret it, Peter. You're going to fucking regret this like you've never regr—"

She happened to look down, and her voice died; water was seeping under the door. She listened; she could hear him running the faucets and the tub. He was trying to flood the place.

She raced out of the secret room, Brynocki loping at her heels. She locked it behind her, then dashed across the cellar to the plumbing closet. Wildly, she turned the knobs controlling the pipes to Peter's bathroom until they could turn no more.

Then she leaned against the wall, panting. Brynocki stood in front of her, his head cocked.

Fine, she thought. He doesn't have any water now. If that's the way he wants it, that's just fucking *fine*.

She was so angry, the entire basement seemed to whirl around her head. Her panting turned into grunting. What she'd known before had been Rage 101—she'd just now gotten her Ph.D. She took a step forward, the room still spinning wildly, like in a Van Gogh painting, a swirl of colors around her head, all scarlet hues and black. And she started to laugh. The sound of that laugh frightened her; she didn't recognize it as her own. It was the laugh of a film-serial dragon lady.

As she made her way up the stairs, her nylon stockings

caught on a rail and ran, and, with a roar of fury, she ripped them right off her body, clawing them to ribbons in the process.

Then, barelegged, she went to work.

"Free for lunch?" Jennifer Jerrold asked as she donned her black slouch hat.

Natalie's head snapped to attention. "What?"

"I asked you if you're free for lunch." She buttoned her trench coat.

"Oh. I guess. Sure."

"Let's go. It's a goddamn monsoon outside. Hope you brought an umbrella, 'cause I didn't."

"I didn't, either." She grabbed her coat.

"You didn't?" Jennifer stopped by the door.

Natalie almost bumped into her. "No."

"I thought for sure you would've brought an umbrella."

She shrugged.

Jennifer sighed and started unbuttoning her coat. "Let's just go to the coffee shop downstairs, then. I'd rather not face the monsoon unarmed."

They ordered tuna salads glumly, knowing the salads would be rubbery and salty when they arrived.

Natalie stared into space.

Jennifer put a hand on her arm. "Natalie, I didn't ask you to lunch just because I thought you had an umbrella."

She looked at her and tried to pull her arm away. "I know that."

"You okay?"

She shook her head, and then something came over her; her face clenched, and she began crying uncontrollably.

Jennifer moved her chair to the other side of the table and put her arm around her. "There, there," she said. "Tell Jennifer what the big, bad world's done now."

"It's Peter," she sobbed. "It doesn't—no matter what I—he won't see—"

She put a finger to Natalie's lips. "Now, honey," she said, "isn't this the one I told you to forget, months ago?"

Natalie nodded, wiping her nose with a paper napkin from the table.

"You see there, what happens when you don't listen to Jennifer?"

She had recovered now; she put her hand on her head and said, "It's awful. He treats me so badly."

"Well, then he's a cad, and he's not worth all this crying." She began fishing through her purse for something.

"That's not true. He's—I mean, he does have some cause to resent me, but not as much as—he pushed me, Jennifer!"

She stopped her searching. "He *what?*"

"He threw me to the floor."

She shook her head and resumed digging through her purse. "Well, then, he's—ah!" She withdrew her cigarettes and clipped the purse shut. "Then he's not only a cad, he's a bully. Next time you see him, you slap his face, Natalie. Just like in the movies."

She grimaced. "I can't do that."

"Why not?" She tapped a cigarette out of the box and lit it.

"I—I—"

Just then the waitress arrived with their tuna salads and placed them on the table. "Will that be all for now?" she asked.

"Fine, thanks," said Jennifer, scooting her chair back to the other side of the table.

Natalie took a quick gulp of her Diet Coke and collected herself. I almost told her! she thought, alarmed. I've got to get a grip! I almost told Jennifer Jerrold, the Mouth with Legs, that I'm holding Peter prisoner!

She ate her salad quietly for a few minutes, then, to change the subject, said, "Jennifer—how did *you* do it?" It was, after all, a question she'd been dying to ask.

"Do what?" She had a fleck of mayonnaise on her lower lip, which she wiped off on her sleeve. She was alternating her cigarette with her salad, to Natalie's disgust.

"Win your man," said Natalie, trying not to look at her.

She lifted her cigarette to her lips. "I don't think our situations are analogous, Natalie." She took a puff, then picked up her salad fork again.

"But they are. Kyle's gay, isn't he?"

Jennifer dropped her fork. "Did Bettina and Sally tell you that?"

"Bettina and Sally didn't have to."

She shoved her plate away. "All right, he's gay. So?" She started puffing faster.

"So, our situations *are* analogous."

Jennifer raised an eyebrow, looked at Natalie for what seemed a *very* long time, and then leaned forward. "Natalie, do you have any friends?"

"Of course I have fr—"

"I mean friends you can confide in. Reason I'm asking is, as long as I've known you, you've dropped little hints about yourself here and there, like pellets for lab rats to nibble on. But I don't feel I know you. And what disturbs me is that all these little bits and pieces that come out are kind of shocking. Like you've got a lot of stress and heartache in your life, but it's all churning up inside you—you never let it out. Unless—I mean, *do* you have a best girlfriend you can call and cry to and yell at and share secrets with, and just gab on the phone with about nothing?"

Natalie looked at her plate. "It has to be a girl?"

"Yes, it has to be a girl."

She picked up her fork and toyed with her salad.

"Natalie," Jennifer continued, "you need friends. You need a context. You need some perspective. Even family would do; a mother is the next best thing to a girlfriend, but I never hear you mention yours."

"We don't speak."

She stubbed out her cigarette. "So I'm it?"

Natalie cocked her head.

She folded her arms. "Okay, then. Here goes. My story, by Jennifer Jerrold. I was never pretty in the conventional sense. Hell—I was never pretty in *any* sense. But I smoked and cursed and made a lot of wisecracks, and for some reason that seemed to attract lots of gay men. Maybe they saw me as the kind of clownish sidekick who'd never try to get down their pants. I certainly saw them as the only kind of men who'd pay attention to me. They were the only ones who liked me for *me* and didn't judge me by my face or my boobs. When I got older, I got tired of going to dinner parties alone, so I proposed to one of my gay friends. He turned me down, so I proposed to the next and the next until—well, Kyle took his time getting here."

"Do you love him?"

"That's none of your business." She fetched another cigarette. "Any more questions?"

"About a million."

"Save your breath." She stuck the cigarette in her mouth and lit it. "Don't settle for this kind of life, Natalie. Find a man who wants you. I mean, who wants you so much it *hurts* him. I had one, once. I was stupid enough to let him get away. I remember the look in his eyes—haven't seen it since, but it marked me. Find some man to look at you that way."

"But Peter—"

"Will never look at you that way." She blew a little ring of smoke. "Forget him." She tapped the cigarette into an ashtray. "And find some friends."

When Natalie and Jennifer returned to the office, Bettina said, "Mr. Hood called *twice* for you, Natalie. He says to call him back." Natalie thanked her and continued walking.

"That *him?*" Jennifer whispered.

Natalie shook her head. "Someone else."

"Good," she said before disappearing behind her door.

Five minutes later, Natalie's extension rang. She lifted the receiver and said, "Natalie Stathis."

"It's Lloyd."

"Oh, hi," she said, her voice high-pitched and reedy. "What news?"

"I'm so glad you asked that, Natalie," he said. "I'm so glad you asked me what news. Let me tell you what news."

Lloyd Hood being sarcastic? She had a bad feeling about this.

"The news is," he continued, "I managed to get a call through to your old friend Luigi Gianelli this morning."

Dear God, she thought. I'm sunk.

"And do you know what I did?" he asked.

"No, what?"

"I lied to him. I told him I was your attorney."

"You *what?*"

"I told him I was your lawyer, Natalie."

Her face turned scarlet. "I can sue you for that."

"Somehow, I don't think you will. Anyway, I told him that my client, Ms. Natalie Stathis, didn't want to compromise herself by calling him personally, but that she naturally wanted some kind of assurance from him that she needn't worry about her reputation in the coming months."

Natalie was silent; her heart was stone cold. She was staring at the blotter on her desk, at the little ink blotches and coffee-cup stains that smudged its surface. She put her hand on the blotter and felt the weave of the paper.

"Nothing to say?" Lloyd asked. "Well, anyway, you'll be pleased to know that Officer Gianelli says he has no intention of implicating anyone else during the investigations into his misconduct. Especially not a lady who's done as much for him as Natalie Stathis."

She shut her eyes and ran her hand across the length of the blotter. At the very tips of her fingers, she could feel where the weave of the paper had been distorted by saturation with water or ink or coffee.

"I was encouraged by that, Natalie, so I ventured a little bit farther. I said I particularly wanted Officer Gianelli's assurance that my client's name would not in any way be connected to any incident involving Peter Leland. And do you know what Officer Gianelli said to that?"

She reached over and felt the smooth, fake-leather borders of the blotter. They were cool to the touch.

"He said, and I quote: 'What other incident is there?' "

She slammed down the phone.

Not a minute later, it rang again. She refused to pick it up until Bettina looked over her shoulder and said, "Natalie, your *phone*," as though Natalie might have temporarily lost her hearing.

She picked up the receiver. "Natalie Stathis."

"You didn't let me finish."

"I don't have to listen to vicious allegations an—"

"I also called Art Weymouth. Do you recall the name, Natalie?"

"Art—Weymouth . . ." It did sound familiar. Where had she heard it before? . . . Oh, God. She remembered.

"He was the previous owner of your house, Natalie. I called him, and guess what I did?"

"You lied to him," she said, her voice low.

"Very good! You're catching on. I told him I was your

fiancé. I said I wanted to saw off the padlock on the closet by the laundry room, but if he had a key I'd be glad to pick it up from him, open the lock, and return the lock to him. And do you know what he said?"

"Lloyd, I don't have time for this nonsense. I have work to do."

"He said he didn't know what I was talking about, that there *was* no closet near the laundry room, and that he never owned a padlock in his life."

There was a long silence. Natalie looked around the office and could tell that Bettina and Sally were pretending to be busy while actually hanging on every word she said. Jennifer's door was still closed.

"I think it's time we talked, Natalie," said Lloyd.

"We're talking now."

"You know what I mean."

"I haven't known what you meant since I met you." She hung up the phone quietly, then grabbed her coat. "Bettina, I feel sick. I'm taking the afternoon off."

Bettina and Sally looked at her as though they were ice cream junkies and she was the Flavor of the Month. She knew she'd no sooner be out the door than they'd be gossiping about her. Well, it couldn't be helped.

She had to leave. It was her first duty. She had to go and board the sinking ship.

She was almost out the door when her extension rang again. "I'm not in," she called out, slipping on her coat and sailing out into the hall.

But forty seconds later, Bettina came running out to catch her as she stood by the elevators. "I know you're not in," she said, "but I thought you'd want to know—it's not the same guy calling as before." She wore an ear-to-ear grin, clearly thrilled with all this intrigue.

Natalie decided it would look too melodramatic to refuse the call; she wanted to preserve at least the fiction of normalcy. So, her heart pounding, she went back into the office and picked up her phone. "Natalie Stathis," she said, standing at her desk as if she would dismiss this annoying call in a moment. But she sounded like a parody of her former cool, unflappable self.

"Natalie, it's Luigi Gianelli."

She shut her eyes in fury. "Well, well—old loose-lips! How are you?" Her voice was dripping with venom.

"Fine, thanks," he said, oblivious to her tone. "Actually, better than ever. Natalie, I'm sure you've seen the papers lately."

"Oh, I never miss *Doonesbury*," she sneered.

He had the audacity to laugh. "Don't try to cheer me up," he said. Natalie held the phone a few inches from her face and stared at it in disbelief.

She put the phone back to her ear in time to hear him say, "Listen, Natalie, I've done a lot of terrible things, and I'm going to pay for them—but what's more important is, I *want* to pay for them. My parish priest, Father Alcotta, is helping me turn my life around and atone for my sins. He's told me to ask forgiveness of all the people I've wronged in the past few ye—"

"I forgive you, I forgive you," she whispered savagely, not wanting Bettina and Sally to hear. Anything to get him off the phone. All she wanted to do now was get home as soon as possible.

"Well, thank you, but there's more to it than just that, Natalie." A brief silence. "You see, I've been embezzling money from you. And I intend to pay every penny of it back, with God's help. But with the legal fees I'll have to pay now, that may not be possible for a while."

She shook her head impatiently. "What are you talking about?"

"What can I say? That bugging equipment I supposedly 'borrowed' for you? That you had to keep paying me to keep? I bought it. On the open market. *Anyone* can buy that stuff there. Even you."

She thought she might explode. It was even difficult to speak. "You mean—it wasn't evidence—it never—"

"I bought it, Natalie. For a couple of hundred bucks. It was perfectly legal. I mean, there *is* a law that is supposed to make it a crime to own any electronic device that's primarily used for eavesdropping; but the key word there is *primarily*. This is America, Natalie. Land of ingenuity. Manufacturers of bugs just came up with other *primary* uses for them. And so anyone can buy one for a lot less than you ended up paying me over that couple of months. I can't believe you never looked into getting one that way yourself."

"But Curtis said—"

"What does Curtis know? He's a fuckin' wai—excuse me; I mean, he's just a waiter. He likes to pretend he's involved in all this cloak-and-dagger stuff. I think that's what attracted him to me in the first place. So when he told me what you wanted, I almost told him to call you back and say, 'Get it yourself'; but then I thought, Hey, I can maybe get a couple of grand out of this if I play my cards right."

She sat down and swiveled her chair so that her back was to Bettina and Sally. "You son of a bitch," she hissed.

"Worse than that, Natalie—I deserve worse than that." There was a small break in his voice; he seemed truly ashamed of himself.

She put her hand to her forehead and shut her eyes. "Wait—I don't understand. If you really owned that equipment, why did you suddenly want it back? Curtis said the trial was coming up and you needed it back for that." She massaged her temple in an attempt to prevent the headache she knew was coming.

"Well," he said in the enthusiastic cadences of someone baring a long-shrouded soul, "by that time Curtis had left me, and I was grasping at any excuse to get to see him again. I told him I needed the bugging equipment back for the trial, because I thought he'd bring it to me himself, and then, once I got him alone, I could get him to take me back."

She shook her head in astonished despair. "*That's* why you were so weird on the phone when *I* called you about returning it instead. *That's* why, when we met at Roscoe's, you didn't give a damn about the bug, just about getting me to help you get Curtis back."

"Yes." His voice was almost inaudible. "I'm so sorry, Natalie. I've been cruel, manipulative—I mean it, I'll pay back every dol—"

"So in other words," she blurted, suddenly not caring if the whole office heard her, "I never had to get involved with you in the first place. But because I did, now my worst enemy has a good idea what I've been up to, just because he called you and pretended to be my lawyer."

"What?—Who pretended? I—That guy wasn't—Natalie, how could I have kn—"

She hung up on him.

It was all crumbling down; chunks of it, plummeting down everywhere. The structure of her life, and of her lie—falling, crumbling, collapsing under its own monstrous weight.

She grabbed her purse again and raced from the office, her eyes out of focus. She hit her shoulder on the doorjamb on the way out. Behind her, Bettina and Sally's silence was more mocking than the most derisive laughter.

The elevator opened as soon as she pressed the DOWN button. She got in and began her descent.

While driving home, the road ahead of her barely visible in the pouring rain, she thought, Maybe I can drug Peter again. Maybe I can haul him to the van, and then just drive somewhere, away from Lloyd. Take him somewhere far away where he doesn't know anybody or have any bearings, and just keep him tied up until he comes to his senses. . . .

But no, no. He'd escape. He'd get away and run, run, run, run. . . .

This was it. It was over.

Suddenly a pair of nuns huddled beneath a single black umbrella tried to cross the street in front of her. With her windshield wipers working so furiously, she almost didn't see them until it was too late; as it was, she swerved to avoid hitting them, and in the process sent a sheet of water over them, unquestionably drenching them.

The whole incident was so laden with ridiculous symbolism that Natalie found herself cackling.

Well, maybe it's not *completely* over, she thought, her spirits restored. She wasn't just going to open her doors and say, Come in, Lloyd, let me show you where he's been.

He was going to have a fight on his hands. He'd have to scrape her flesh and blood off that basement door before he opened it. And God help him if she got him *first*.

It was petty, it was demeaning, it was evil. It was what she wanted more than anything.

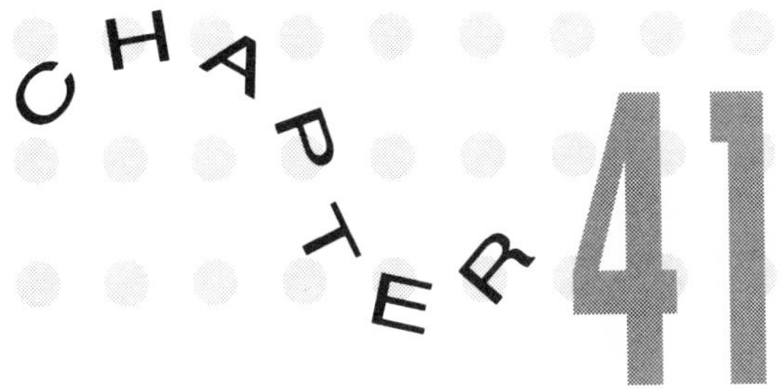

CHAPTER 41

By the time Natalie got home, the sky was dark; the rain was still steady. She dashed from the garage to the house and got soaked in the process.

In the kitchen, she slipped out of her wet skirt and jacket and shook her hair. "Brynocki," she called, "here, boy!"

The dog didn't appear.

Suddenly she envisioned a horrible scenario in which Peter had escaped the basement, confronted Brynocki, and been eaten alive. In her blouse and slip, she rushed to the corridor and saw that the basement door was still padlocked.

She heaved a sigh of relief. "Bry-*nock*-i," she called.

The dog slithered down the stairs, his tail between his legs and his head hung low. He practically crawled over to Natalie, then lay with his snout between her feet. "What's wrong with you?" she said, stepping away from him. "Did you poop on the carpet again, or wh—"

A clap of thunder shook the house, and Brynocki scurried over to the couch and hid his head beneath it.

Natalie was astonished. Her guard dog—her vicious killer—was afraid of thunder.

She thought of calling the breeder and complaining, but it was too late now. Lloyd would undoubtedly be here soon. She went over to Brynocki and kicked him.

He yelped in fright, and tried to cram himself all the way beneath the couch.

"Oh, for *God's* sake," she said. "I don't *fucking* believe this."

She checked her watch; it was two-thirty. What might Peter be doing? She was afraid to face him—and she dreaded looking again at the mess he had made of the secret room.

She went to the intercom and pressed the LISTEN button; she could hear nothing. Not even the sound of his breathing.

I should go and check on him, she thought; he's been without water all day.

But instead she went up to her bedroom, sat on her bed, and didn't move. She was absolutely terrified, unable to take any action at all. She simply couldn't face Peter; yet she also couldn't decide *not* to face Peter. So she put her head on her pillow and let her mind swing back and forth, back and forth.

Eventually she fell asleep. She had a dream that she was driving down an unfamiliar expressway, with Peter in the passenger seat doing lines of cocaine. Where are we going? he asked her, and she said, I don't know. She looked out her window and saw Lloyd running beside the van, keeping pace with it. He said, Bet I can beat you there! and he ran even faster. Where? Where? she cried. She floored the van, but it only seemed to be slowing down. Peter said, Bet I can beat you there, too, and he opened the passenger door and got out while the van was still moving. In a split second he was gone from sight. She couldn't see what happened to him and she screamed for him, then decided to turn around and look for him. But as she turned the van around, she hit something. What was it? She was afraid to look. She got out of the van and walked slowly to the front; blood was running across the highway, staining her shoes. When she reached the front of the van she looked and saw—

She awakened with a start, sweat streaming from her forehead. She was still in her slip.

The doorbell was ringing. She checked her watch. Seven o'clock.

She rushed to the bedroom window and peeked out through the curtains. The Celica was parked in the driveway.

No, no, no, she thought; I'm not answering that.

It rang again, and again, and again. He can't know I'm in here, she thought. He can't possibly know that.

It was still raining relentlessly, and the first sight she had of Lloyd himself was of his big, burgundy umbrella as he walked back to the car.

That's it? she thought. He's giving up, just like that? Could I be so lucky?

He opened the car door and stuck one leg in, then folded up his umbrella and tossed it on the back seat. And just as he was bending to duck inside the car, he happened to look up at the house—and he stopped.

She immediately stepped back and held the curtains shut. Had he seen her?

He was still standing there, staring, rain matting down what little hair he had. He must have seen her! He'd be back at the front door in no time!

But no; he got into the car, turned on its headlights, backed into the street, and drove away.

She let her breath out all at once, and was suddenly aware that she'd been holding it for almost a full minute.

Relieved beyond belief, she went downstairs to the intercom and listened again. Still nothing.

At the very least, she had to give him something to eat.

Feeling strangely lighthearted, as if no action had any reaction, as if all events were disconnected, and as if she were perfectly immune to consequence, she whipped up a quick dinner of fried eggs and bacon and took a bottle of mineral water from the refrigerator. Peter would need that. Dear Peter. Loyal Peter. She whistled a Disney tune as she bustled out of the kitchen.

She got the key chain from beneath the potted plant and went to the basement door.

And then she balked, and the roller coaster took another plunge. The basement was the lowest pit of hell; dear, loving Peter would overcome her and lock her down there in his place, and who would help her?

She called Brynocki. "I mean it," she said; "get over here, you piece-of-shit coward!" The dog backed into a corner and refused to budge.

A flash of lightning splashed the house with momentary incandescence; it was followed by a low, rumbling roll of thunder that sounded like God himself was moaning. She shook her head and unfastened the padlock.

"Whistle while you work," she sang merrily.

She put her hand on the doorknob and turned it.

"Hitler is a jerk," she trilled.

She swung open the door.

"Mussolini bit his weenie, now it doesn't work." She shrieked with glee.

Humming a reprise, she walked down the stairs alone, the dim light bulb over her head barely illuminating her way. It threw shadows of monstrous Natalies in her path. They seemed to be trying to frighten her back upstairs.

Five steps, six, seven eight; she'd never counted them before. How many were there?

Twenty-one.

An odd number. It disturbed her.

She tried to sing again. "Jingle bells, Batman smells, Robin laid an egg." Her voice was weak and tremulous; she gave it up.

She took her key and extended it toward the lock. Her hand was trembling.

She inserted it in the lock; she turned it. The tumbler fell.

And then the door swung open and Peter was right there, his eyes like firecrackers. She screamed and threw the tray at him. It hit him square in the face and he yelled in pain, and his arms flew out at her.

She tried to slam the door, but his torso was in the way; he moved, and she caught his shoulder between the door and the frame, and he yelled. She let up for a minute to allow him to free himself, and immediately he was back at her, shoving harder than she could, gaining ground, gaining ground.

She propped herself against the opposite wall and put her full weight against the door, and pushed like her life depended on it—which perhaps it did. His face appeared from behind the door; it was smeared with fried egg, and his teeth were bared. He roared.

"Brynocki!" she screamed. "Oh, God! *Brynocki!*"

Finally, she was able to call on some reserve of strength she didn't even know she had; she knocked him back and pinned his neck in the door. He started to choke horribly, but she held him there a little longer. When she finally released the pressure, he ducked inside, and she locked him in, her fingers barely working.

Then she fell to the floor and wept.

Her phone was ringing. She rushed upstairs and answered it. "Hello, Natalie. So sorry I haven't been returning your calls."

"Mom?" she said, her voice like a child's. "Is that you?"

"Oh, don't be so melodramatic. I said I was sorry about not calling. Don't act like I've just come back from the dead."

She started bawling.

"Honey—what's wrong? Is this a bad time?"

"Everything's gone wrong, Mom."

"Stop that blubbering and tell me. What's happened?"

"Peter—Peter—"

"Heavens, not Peter again! You told me a year ago—"

"Mom, I want Darnita to have all my money. What's left of it."

"What do y—I'm not following this conversation, Natalie."

"I'm sorry about saying no before. The things I've done—"

"Are you in some kind of trouble?"

She coiled the telephone cord around her neck. "I wish I could write you a big check right now."

"Stop it!" Sandy cried. "Stop it right now, and tell me what's wrong!"

From the back of the house she heard a volley of gunshots and a tremendous shattering of glass.

"Oh, my goodness!" said Sandy. "Natalie, Natalie, what was that?"

"I have to go now, Mom. I love you." She lifted the receiver to the cradle.

"Natalie, don't you dare han—" Click.

She reached into the silverware drawer and removed a carving knife.

The house was dark. There were corners that were darker than others. Here in the kitchen, for instance. Right by the oven.

She stood there, motionless, and waited.

The rain was pummeling the earth, as if trying to beat it senseless.

The lightning was like a burst of brilliant hatred.

The thunder was the sound of a death rattle.

"Brynocki," Natalie whispered hopefully. "Oh, God, Brynocki, come *on*."

The dog did not appear.

Lloyd did.

He was dressed all in black: a sleeveless black T-shirt, black shorts, black hiking boots, a black bandana. His face was smeared with black.

And he was carrying a rifle.

Goddamn Rambo queen, she thought.

He stepped into the kitchen, and she tightened her grip on the knife.

"I thought that was you there," he said.

She passed the knife from one hand to the other, as if it were hot to the touch.

"You know the high regard I have for private property," he said. "I hope you realize what a violation of my moral code it is to destroy your window like that, and to enter your house without permission; I hope you realize I would never have done these things if I didn't think a much higher value was at stake."

So much for the resemblance to Rambo.

"This has really gone far enough," he said. "Maybe I've been too hard on you, I don't know. I think, now, that maybe you're ill and need counseling and treatment."

Oh, you *fucker*. She flashed the knife at him.

He stood still and silent for a moment. "Natalie," he said slowly, "that may seem to you like a very big knife, but this is a very, *very* big gun."

"Too big," she said; "I get close enough, you can't even aim." She lunged at him.

Flash of lightning. Peal of thunder.

He darted away from her and into the house. She'd missed him.

Quiet, now.

Where was he?

She crept out of the kitchen and into the dining room. "I'm out in the open, now," she called out. "Go ahead and shoot me, Lloyd." She stood, in her blouse and slip, and spread her arms, still wielding the knife in one hand.

Nothing.

She smiled. She knew he couldn't bring himself to harm her.

She padded down the corridor to the basement door. This is it, she thought; the last stand. The beginning of the end.

He appeared at the end of the corridor, a silhouette. "That's where he is, isn't it?" he asked.

"You think you know everything," she snarled. A stupid remark, but she wasn't feeling her wittiest.

"What could make you do this to him?" he asked. "Lock him up like this, take away his freedom, cut him off from everything he—"

"You wouldn't understand!" she bellowed.

"Try me. I'm an intelligent man. I'm a good listener."

"A good listener with a gun."

He rested the rifle against the wall and stepped forward. "Okay. Now I'm just a good listener."

"Then listen to this: One more step, and I gouge my own throat out." She held the blade below her chin.

He stopped. "You do need help, Natalie. If you really mean what you just said, then you desperately need help."

"Of course I mean it. I don't say things I don't mean."

"Yes, you do. All the time, you do."

Well, she had to admit he had her there.

He started down the corridor. "I'm coming, anyway."

Was he *crazy*? "Fine. Hope you can live with my blood on your hands."

"I'm a gambler, Natalie. If you value your life so little, then you'd probably throw it away sooner or later, whether I prompted you to or not. But I'm betting you *do* value your life. I'm betting you won't jeopardize it."

She watched his silhouette get bigger and bigger, blocking out more and more light. "Then I'll jeopardize yours," she said, turning the knife in his direction.

"If that was your intention, you wouldn't announce it," he said. "You'd just wait till I reached you and then *do* it."

He was right in front of her now. She could smell his sweat, hear his breathing.

He grabbed her wrist.

The knife clattered to the floor.

"I'll ask it again: Why, Natalie? Why'd you do this to Peter?"

A howl of pain rose up in her—something primal and primeval, ancient and awful; it came up from the earth and charged through her like electricity, and took half of her with it when it left her. "*Be-cause*," she wailed, haltingly, wretchedly, "*I—love—him—so—much!*" She gasped for breath.

He was looking at her; she wished she could see his face. "You couldn't have done this if you loved him, Natalie. You couldn't have locked him up like an animal. It isn't love you feel for him. It may be almost as strong, but it isn't love. It's something else. Something bad."

"Some—thing . . . bad?" she whimpered.

He nodded.

She collapsed into his arms and unleashed everything she'd held inside for so long; she wrung herself out and lay limp in his arms, at his mercy.

She knew she could trust in that—his mercy.

A few moments later, she was descending the stairs, Lloyd directly behind her.

She was shaking like a leaf; it felt like her teeth would vibrate right out of her gums.

She unlocked the door to the secret room.

It ripped open from the inside, and Peter leapt out, a cry of rage on his lips; he sailed past her and into Lloyd's arms. The two of them careened into the opposite wall.

"Hold on! Hold on!" cried Lloyd.

Peter stood back. His face was streaked with egg yolk, and he had horrible, deep purple bruises on his neck and arms. "Lloyd?" he said in disbelief. "Oh, my God—it's finally you!" He paused. "What on earth is that all over your face?"

"Burnt cork," he said. "What on earth is that all over *yours?*"

"Egg, I think." He cocked his head. "We're both going to end up with megazits, you know."

They fell into a lover's embrace and kissed.

Natalie stole up the stairs and took a seat in the kitchen. She would wait until they came back up, wait until someone decided what to do with her.

A thunderclap rocked the house, and Brynocki slithered into the kitchen and cowered under Natalie's chair. She looked down at him. "I'm going to feed you cat food till the day you die," she said.

Then she glanced up and saw the intercom unit. She reached over and pressed LISTEN.

"—have her arrested?" It was Peter's voice.

"She's got problems, Peter. Emotional ones. Jail's not the answer."

"You're really asking me not to press charges."

"Yes, I'm really asking you that." A pause. "Come on. She was your friend."

"Seems like a million years ago."

"Do this for me, okay? No police. No charges. No anything. Just ask her to get some professional help."

"She won't listen."

"She will now. It could make all the difference to her."

She took her finger off the button. Lloyd Hood, protecting her from Peter? She had to sit and think about that for a while. What a funny, funny world it could be.

What a goddamn fucking hilarious world.

She started to laugh.

Then she heard the sirens. They were getting louder every second; she had no doubt that they were coming for her. Who had called the police? Who had even had time?

She sighed. Her mother, of course.

Good old Sandy. The fucking bomb could drop, and she'd find some way to make the nuclear winter worse for her daughter than for everybody else.

It was a small comfort to Natalie that, in this chaotic new world, there was at least that one constant.

Sandy Stathis was unsentimental by nature. She didn't coo over babies, cry at weddings, or comment on how peaceful the deceased looked at funerals. She didn't like public shows of affection, parades, or people who prayed at the dinner table. She preferred *Pride and Prejudice* to *Wuthering Heights*, and looked objectively at proposed solutions to Third World hunger. It wasn't that she was an unfeeling woman; merely that her feelings were more refined, and thus less likely to be triggered by the obvious or the overwrought.

She had her blind spots, however. Her late husband Max was one of them; she got positively drippy at the thought of him.

And then there was Christmas.

Every year, on December 2, she would begin signing her Christmas cards (purchased the previous January for one-third off), including in each a personal greeting of three or four lines. This would invariably render her nostalgic, which would ruin her for days.

Then she would undertake her shopping, and, although

normally oblivious to such vulgar blandishments, she would become hypnotized by the treacly encouragements to buy, buy, buy that screamed from every Yuletide window. She'd fall under the sway of the music and the merriment and the mercenary glee with which the shopkeepers lured her into their clutches.

Around December 14 she would have a tree delivered to the house, and bring out her box of holiday ornaments, wreaths, and garlands, some of which had been in the family for generations, and which she cherished. And while, during the year, a visitor would find nothing more recent or more syncopated than Tchaikovsky on her turntable, during high December they would be greeted by syrupy, embarrassing carols sung by Perry Como and Johnny Mathis and Burl Ives. She would sing along with these, in a high and merry voice that was uncannily like the shriek of an arctic seal being clubbed to death.

This year, she was worse than ever. After all, she'd spent the previous Christmas alone, since Natalie had refused to see her, and Calvin and Vera had gone skiing with Vera's parents in Aspen. But this year Sandy would have a full table, and the sheer, Dickensian magnitude of the holiday feast ahead of her had rendered her incapable of resisting even the hokiest seasonal cliché.

". . . seven, eight, nine, *ten*," she said aloud, counting the place settings at the dining-room table. "Good, good." It had been almost twenty years since she'd used so much of her Wedgwood china. She rubbed her hands together and danced back to the kitchen. In the background, John Gary was singing "The Little Drummer Boy," and she accompanied him: "The ox and lamb kept time, pa-rum-pum-pum-pum." When Natalie was a little girl, her mother's duet with John Gary on this song could tempt her frighteningly close to second-degree murder.

In the kitchen, Darnita was sprinkling nutmeg across a punch bowl filled with plain eggnog. (Sandy would stand a bottle of Myers's next to it on the serving table, for those who wanted to spike their own mugs.) "Not too much, dear," Sandy cautioned her.

"I'm makin' a picture of Santa," said Darnita. When Sandy went over to examine the girl's artistry, she saw only an amorphous blob of nutmeg shavings drifting around the bowl.

"Beautiful, dear," she said, putting her hand on Darnita's shoulder. "Let's put it out for our guests to admire, now, shall we?"

"I'm not finish wif his beard yet!" the girl cried.

"Don't be silly, it's a perfect beard." She picked up the bowl and carried it into the dining room while Darnita howled in protest behind her.

Twenty minutes later, Calvin and Vera arrived. Sandy submitted to being pecked on the cheek by each of them, then took their coats and ushered them in for some drinks and fresh-baked Christmas cookies.

"Natalie here yet?" Calvin asked.

Sandy shook her head. "Expecting her soon."

Vera, now several months pregnant, lowered herself into the most comfortable chair in the house and immediately started issuing commands. "Get me some eggnog," she ordered Calvin. "No rum in it because of the baby. Get me a plate of cookies and whatever else is ready. Change the goddamn record before I lose my mind."

Shortly thereafter, Quentin pulled up with Lawanda and the baby in a shiny new car that Sandy could only presume was designed to resemble a ballistic weapon. It was so red it hurt her eyes.

Lawanda had dressed prettily for the occasion, and had wrapped her baby in beautiful Christmas lace; but Quentin had on leopard-print Lycra tights, gargantuan black Nike Air sneakers, and a T-shirt that said WHO IS JOHN GALT? in glitter letters. As usual, he would not remove his sunglasses.

"How very festive," said Sandy, eyeing the outfit.

"Natalie here?" he asked.

"Not yet. May I get you an eggnog?"

"A *what?*"

"An eggnog, dear."

"What the hell are *that?*"

A few minutes later, Hank Bixby rang the doorbell. He was carrying a large gift box with a sheet over one side, and before Sandy could invite him in, he bolted past her, then turned and said, "Would you shut the door, please?"

"Why—I—yes, yes I will," she said, a bit stunned.

After she'd done so, he said, "Sorry, don't mean to be rude, but your present's in this box, and it can't be in the cold too long or it'll get—uh—ruined."

"How mysterious!" she said, delighted. "I can't *wait* to see what it is!"

He put the box down and slipped off his coat. "Natalie get here?"

"No, but any moment."

A half hour passed before the bell rang again. Sandy opened the door and welcomed in Jennifer Jerrold and her handsome young husband, Kyle.

"Mrs. Stathis, it's uncommonly kind of you to have us," said Jennifer, letting her silver fox drop from her shoulders as if counting on Kyle to catch it—which he did.

"Natalie insisted," said Sandy, showing them in. "You'll have to thank her." She kept sneaking disbelieving glances at Jennifer's astonishingly gaudy makeup.

"Has the dear girl made her entrance?" Jennifer asked, placing her purse on a chair she passed in the hall. ("Kyle, remember where I left that," she ordered.)

"Not yet," said Sandy. They'd reached the living room, where the rest of the party had gathered.

"Unforgivable of her," said Jennifer. "She knows I always like to be the last to arrive."

Sandy smiled weakly, and made the round of complicated introductions. Jennifer shook hands with Vera and, looking at the girl's protruding stomach, said, "Bad case of sperm poisoning you've got there." Vera turned white.

Then Kyle shook hands with Calvin, and Calvin cried, "*Hey*," yanked his hand away, and held it as if it had been stung.

Jennifer turned and hit her husband on the shoulder. "Kyle, you leave that young man alone!" she scolded him. "He's not here for you!" Then she turned and strode toward Quentin, her hand outstretched. "Mr. Butler," she said; "I can truly say I've *long* been looking forward to meeting *you*."

Sandy, sensing impending disaster, rushed over to the stereo and turned up the volume.

After ten excruciating minutes of the Jim Nabors Christmas album, played at a decibel level that not only prevented conversation but also seemed likely to have a detrimental effect on the delicate bones of everyone's inner ear, Natalie entered the room.

"I let myself in!" she shouted, dangling her key from her fingers to aid her explanation. "Can we turn that down, please, Mom?"

Sandy gave the VOLUME knob a twist to the left and then rushed to join her guests, who were all assembled around Natalie, greeting her.

"How are you?" "You feeling okay?" "So glad to see you!" "Thanks so much for inviting us." "You look sensational!" "Sit by me at the dinner table." The barrage of affection seemed to stun Natalie; she took a step back and smiled luminously.

Dinner began a few minutes later. The tone for the meal was set by Hank, who, when Calvin pulled his sister's chair from the table for her, leapt and grabbed it out of his hands with a surprisingly fierce, "Let *me*." It was the beginning of a seemingly endless stream of embarrassing attentions to Natalie, attentions that caused her to redden perceptibly, like an apple ripening in a time-lapse film sequence.

"Everything okay?" Hank asked her.

"Mm-hmm," she said, nodding. She'd just filled her mouth with wine.

"I mean, *really* okay?"

"*Chill*, fool," snarled Quentin. "She say i's okay once, then i's okay."

"We're naming the baby Dolores if it's a girl," Calvin told Natalie. "Maxwell if it's a boy. After Dad. Nice, huh?"

"Nice," said Natalie, wiping her mouth with a napkin. "He'd've liked that."

"I mean," Calvin continued, "it's not a hundred percent settled, if you can think of any other sugges—"

"Cal, for *Christ's* sake," said Vera.

Darnita, her eyes wide, looked straight at Natalie and said, "Did you really was in jail, Natalie?"

An appalled silence followed; all at the table busied themselves by moving their knives and forks either closer together or farther apart.

"Not jail exactly, honey," Natalie said, feeling the aversion of everyone's eyes as keenly as she'd felt their stares a moment earlier. "A different kind of place—a place to get better."

"That's enough, dear," said a badly upset Sandy. "Have some mashed potatoes." She started scooping these onto Darnita's plate in quantities far beyond the girl's capacity to consume, even if she kept eating till New Year's. Her little eyes widened in increasing horror, but Sandy just kept on scooping. "Natalie's just *fine*, now, Darnita," she said, her voice as brittle as hardtack. "So we don't need to know anything more, do we? Of course we don't!"

"*Gramma*," Darnita shrieked at last, "stop putting potatoes on me!"

The tension, tight as a violin string, broke, and was followed by much more laughter than the girl's admonition deserved. Jennifer took the opportunity to rescue Natalie from any further scrutiny by stepping into the spotlight; she began a running narrative, lasting almost to the dessert course, about her experiences in Chicago theater, filled with anecdotes both hilarious and star-studded. It was also unrelievedly bawdy. Sandy found herself having to continually reach over to cover Darnita's ears.

"So I told him," Jennifer said of an ex-leading man, jabbing a drumstick in the air like an extension of her finger, "it's *your* fault you got it, not mine, and the only thing I'll say is, don't pick at it or it'll bleed."

Vera said, "*Eww*," and everyone at the table laughed except Sandy, who kept saying, "Oh, my word! Oh, good heavens!"

After dinner they all gathered in the living room to pass out the presents that had been piled under the tree. Everyone had a gift for Natalie. Sandy gave her a silver bracelet from Tiffany; Calvin and Vera gave her a world atlas (Natalie had no idea what they'd been thinking of); Quentin and Lawanda gave her a Public Enemy compact disc; and Jennifer and Kyle gave her a black bra and panties. ("You'll be amazed how confident you'll feel in them," Jennifer said, "even if no one else knows you have them on. I'm wearing mine right now, and I feel *terrific*.")

Hank Bixby handed his gift to Natalie. "This is from me," he said rather redundantly.

She opened it. "*The Complete Poetry of William Butler Yeats*," she said. "Oh, thank you, Hank."

"I've marked some of the ones I think you'll like best," he said, clearly nervous.

She opened the book to a Post-It–marked page and read a

few lines aloud: "Earth in beauty dressed/Awaits returning spring./All true love must die,/Alter at the best/Into some lesser thing./*Prove that I lie.*" She closed the book and said, "That's lovely!"

"I like to think it's possible to prove that he's lying," said Hank. "I like to think it's possible to spend a lifetime proving it."

She looked into his eyes and saw something unrecognizable—something that made her feel like the only other person in the room. In spite of herself, she caught her breath. Was this what Jennifer had meant?

"Hank, I'm sorry, I didn't get you anything," she said, embarrassed.

"That's all right," he said with a shrug.

"To be honest, I didn't even know you'd be here."

"Well, it was a last-minute thing. My parents are divorcing, you know, and they were kind of using me as a weapon to get at each other—you know, who gets Hank for Christmas? My mom's in San Francisco visiting my sister, Josie, my dad's at his cabin in Wisconsin, and rather than choose, I decided maybe I'll just stay neutral and celebrate Christmas at home, alone. That's when your mom invited me here and it seemed like a nice alternative. She's a great lady."

As if on cue, Sandy stuck her head in from the hallway and said, "Natalie, phone for you."

"I'll read these, I mean it," Natalie said, putting down the book and getting up from the floor.

When she reached the phone, her mother mouthed the words, It's Peter, then handed the phone to her.

She took off an earring and put the phone to her ear. "Merry Christmas," she said.

"Merry Christmas to you."

There was an uncomfortable silence.

"It's sweet of you to call," she said. "Where are you?"

"Lloyd's parents' house. It's the first time I've met them."

"Are they fun?"

"Are they ever! They're socialists! Lloyd is so embarrassed by them, he's just dying. I'm having a great time."

"Well, give him my best."

"I will. How are you doing?"

"Better. Still in therapy, but I think I'm pretty much like everyone else now. You know, not a disaster, just a contained mess."

"You'll do fine."

"I'm *doing* fine. Everyone's been so supportive. Tonight has been good for my ego."

"I'm glad."

"Hank Bixby is treating me like I'm some kind of fashion model."

"Hank Bixby? The geek from Calvin's wedding?"

She felt a flash of anger, surprising herself. "He's not a geek, Peter. He's very sweet and sensitive. He gave me a book of poetry."

Another awkward pause. "I'm glad it's all working out."

"Peter, you know how sorry I am."

"I know—we don't need to go through that now."

"You're right, you're right."

"Just get yourself back on track. That's all I want to see."

"I wish things could be back the way they were."

"You and about four billion other people in the world."

She paused. "But not you."

"Well, no, not me."

She sighed. "Friends?"

He didn't answer for a moment, as if he were giving the idea some thought. "Well—okay. Friends."

"Merry Christmas to you and Lloyd. I love you both. And I owe you so much. I mean it."

"We both love you. Merry Christmas to everybody there."

She put down the phone gently and fought a little cyclone that was whipping around in her breast until it had stilled into a manageable wisp. Then she put her earring back on and rejoined her family and friends. Just as she rounded the corner to the living room, she heard her mother shriek.

"Oh, Natalie! Come and see what Hank's given me!" She raised her arm, and perched on her index finger was a dazed-looking parrot, a little bigger than her hand. It had brilliant green feathers.

Natalie approached and said, "Can I pet him?"

"Sure," said Hank; "he's been hand-raised, so he loves people. I have a cage for him in the car, too," he added to Sandy.

"And some food. He's a conure. He won't grow much bigger than that."

"Hank, he's gorgeous!" Sandy said, pursing her lips and making smacking noises at the bird—who, it must be said, seemed somewhat dismayed by this.

"I knew you could never have another dog after Carmen DeFleur, but I thought this house needed a pet, and this little guy should keep you company."

"You're an angel! I'll name him Victor Galworthy. That sounds appropriately noble."

"Oh, Mom," Natalie groaned in exasperation. "Why can't you just name him Speedy, or Gus, or Tootsie, or some normal pet name?"

"Animals have their dignity, too," she said insistently. "I keep telling you."

A few hours later, mother and daughter hugged good-bye. "Thank you for everything," said Natalie. "I love you, Mom."

"I wish I could convince you to stay the night," Sandy said.

She shook her head. "Can't. I have to feed Brynocki in the morning."

"You should've just brought him."

"Just as well I didn't. He'd have eaten Victor Galworthy." She paused. "Anyway, I'll be back tomorrow to help clean up."

"All right, then. Merry Christmas, darling."

"Merry Christmas, Mom."

Natalie was nearly home when an odd compulsion came over her. She passed her house and kept driving, down to Halsted Street, where she took a left and motored up through the gay ghetto.

There was a surprising number of men in the streets, some of them in Santa Claus drag, some dressed in unidentifiable costumes, most just bundled up in black leather against the cold.

At the stoplight by Cornelia Street, a stream of people crossed in front of her. There was an overweight, overdressed girl—she couldn't have been more than twenty-two—on the arm of a strikingly handsome man with gales of blow-dried hair and a thick mustache. She was chirping away at him drunkenly, while he looked all around him, his eyes searching, searching. . . .

The girl slipped on a patch of ice and fell in front of Natalie's van. The man helped her up; she was laughing wildly—she couldn't know how ridiculous she must look to him. She rested her hand on Natalie's van for a moment, until she righted herself. Then she patted her hair into place, turned to Natalie, and waved. "It's okay!" she cried, continuing across the street. "You can move on now!"

She and her handsome friend slipped into The Men's Room, which was fairly crowded, considering that it was Christmas night. Natalie craned her neck to try to follow the girl's progress through the bar, but the windows were dark and filled with men, and it was difficult to see. She thought she could make out her blond curls above the sea of male hairlines. . . .

The driver of the car behind her honked. She looked up and saw that the light had turned green. She pressed her foot on the accelerator and moved on.